THE BEAUTIFUL BONES

A Deputy Ricos Tale

by

ELIZABETH A. GARCIA

Praise for One Bloody Shirt at a Time,

Elizabeth A. Garcia's first novel

"I finished your book last night, and it's FANTASTIC! Seriously, one of the best reads ever; I couldn't put it down once I started (and today I am sleep-deprived!) I've loved your short stories, and I love your novel! I can't wait to find out what Deputy Ricos is up to next. I'm hooked! You seriously rock!"

~Cheryl Zinsmeyer

"That book mesmerized me!"

~Voni Glaves

"Beth your book is a hit! I have known you for 21 years and wish you had started writing years ago! Now, JoD & I look forward to your next Deputy Ricos story!"

~Chuck Mundy

"Oh No! Beth, I made the mistake of starting your novel "One Bloody Shirt" a bit before my normal "lights out" last night , but I was enjoying it soooo much I kept pushing myself to stay awake. So to anyone that hasn't started the novel yet- make sure you give yourself some "reading time" when you begin - it is hard to put down!"

~Keith Godwin

"OMG by the time I was halfway done I was looking for another one. Could not find one, then at the end of the book it says this is your first. WOW! I CANT WAIT FOR THE NEXT ONE!!!!! Thank you so much."

~ Deb Bennight

"It flowed so smoothly; there was not one part that "dragged" (as some novels do). It made me laugh and it made me get a tear in my eye. I loved the characters. The geographical description of the area made me feel like I was immersed in it. I have never been to Terlingua, but after I read the novel, I felt like I knew the area. I cannot wait until the next one comes out! You are officially my favorite author. Your book was awesome!!"

~Sharon Oates

"Can hardly wait for everyone to get as hooked as I am reading the Deputy Ricos Tales!"

~Elvira Arnberger

"I absolutely adored it! I couldn't put it down, and read it far too quickly because the writing is so good that I'm sure I missed some of the nuances. Add me to your fan club, please!!"

~Priscilla Maulsby

A few words about

The Beautiful Bones

Deputy Margarita Ricos is a smart, young Chicana with attitude, who grew up on the last piece of the United States before the land surrenders to the Rio Grande and Mexico begins. Her home sits in the southern part of Brewster County, the biggest county in the largest state in the lower forty-eight. The county has more spectacular square miles and mountains than it does inhabitants.

The first day of December is a crisp, blue-sky, sunshine-on-the-mountains kind of day in the border community of Terlingua, Texas. For the Sheriff's Office, it's a predictably slow time of year. That is until Sheriff Ben Duncan hands his youngest deputy a thirty-year-old mystery to solve. Five years before Margarita was born, a twenty-two year-old woman vanished from an arroyo near the Christmas Mountains of the Terlingua Ranch Resort. No trace of her has ever been found.

On the second day of December, a tourist is reported missing. The deputies find his abandoned car and camp in an uninhabited area of Gate Two of the same resort, and not far from the same mountains. He, also, is twenty-two years old.

Margarita and her partner, Deputy Barney George, set out to find two missing persons. One has been gone thirty years, the other about thirty days. Could there possibly be a connection to disappearances separated by so many years?

Their search for answers takes them to Gate Two and several other places on the Terlingua Ranch, to the resort town of Lajitas, TX, to Ojinaga, Mexico and even as far away as Wyoming.

v

Several local characters populate the story, including a pair of wild hawks, and a disgruntled man who believes Margarita is wrong for law enforcement; the job should have gone to a man. If you've met the deputy, you know that doesn't set well.

Acknowledgements/Forward

With gratitude to my multi-talented daughter, Margarita Garcia, who designed the cover of my novel based on her own photograph. I'm indebted to Margarita and Amber for the many hours of reading, proofreading, and most of all, for their constant encouragement. I refer to them as "my girls" but they're grown women who live their lives in a way that inspires and uplifts me. The best attributes of Deputy Ricos belong to my girls.

I also want to thank my first readers, who suffered through clunky writing and over-used adverbs and verbosity in general and still encouraged me to keep on. Besides my girls, they are: my sisters Martha and Mary Lou, my friends Rob, Elvira, Skip, Judy P, Lynda, and Priscilla. Thank you for your helpful feedback and, in some cases, for enduring the same stories, rewritten more than once. I couldn't do it without you.

A confession about the plot: I used a true, more-than-thirty-year-old Terlingua mystery as the basis for this novel, but *everything else* about it came from my imagination. No one knows what happened to the woman who disappeared so long ago, including me. One person must know, but he/she has never come forward. Please hear this! Any resemblance to anyone living or dead is purely coincidental. And for the record, I never knew the sheriff thirty-plus years ago, or the other players in this story. I haven't tried to glorify or demonize anyone. *I made all of it up!* It's fiction, written solely for enjoyment. So please enjoy, and thank you for your abiding faith in me.

Peace and love,

Beth Garcia
February, 2013

*In memory of the real "Serena Bustamante," and for all women
everywhere who have "disappeared."*

CHAPTER 1

"When I despair, I remember that all through history, the ways of truth and love have always won. There have been tyrants and murderers and, for a time, they can seem invincible, but in the end they always fall. Think of it. Always." ~ Mahatma Gandhi

I unhooked my gun belt and dropped it onto the desk. The thud was so loud it woke the phone.

"Sheriff's Office, Deputy Ricos speaking." I moved to the window to check the distant view of the Chisos Mountains in Big Bend National Park. They are always there, but I like to be sure.

"Sorry Margarita," said Brewster County Sheriff Ben Duncan. "Emergency—I'll have to call you back." He hung up.

My boss's office is in Alpine, Texas, eighty miles from the small border community of Terlingua where I work with my partner, Deputy Barney George. Our office is the south county extension of the sheriff's.

I sank into an overstuffed chair and propped my boots on the desk. From that perspective, the view is different, closer. Details can be seen on Cactus Hill that the faraway view of the Chisos lacks. For instance, earlier that morning a thin, sparkling sheet of ice had encased the branches of the mesquite, desert willow, and other small trees, as well as the prickly pear, ocotillo, and other stabbing growth on my hill. The reddish-brown boulders and

1

pebbly rockslides gleamed as if scrubbed. It had been a glitter-ing fairyland when the sun began its climb over the mountains in the east. Three hours later, the ice had become big, wet droplets, unable to maintain its grip in a faceoff with the sun.

I was about to doze off by the time the phone rang again.

"Are you busy?" Sheriff Ben asked when I answered. "I have a special assignment for you."

"You have a special assignment for me?"

Home planet to Margarita.

"Yes, for you. You're not busy, are you?"

"No sir, I'm not," I admitted; he already knew I wasn't.

It was the first day of December and things were quiet, so quiet Barney was at home enjoying time with his family. We were taking turns keeping the office open.

There had been an influx of visitors for the Thanksgiving holiday, but the majority of them had gone. Winter tourists were mostly families during the holiday periods and retirees escaping the cold north. Neither group caused much trouble for Brewster County law enforcement.

"It's a cold case," the sheriff said.

"Cold as in—?"

"Cold as in unsolved, Margarita. It's thirty years cold."

"Thirty years?" I swung my boots off the desk and sat up straight. "Did you say *thirty?*"

"Yes. About thirty years ago a young woman disappeared from Terlingua. I mean to say that she vanished." He paused a moment while someone in his office spoke to him. Then he returned his attention to me. "Get up here and I'll tell you about it."

I grabbed my jacket, stuck the 'Call 9-1-1 for emergencies' sign on the door, and sprinted to my Sheriff's Office Ford Explorer. I had to go back for the gun belt.

* * *

Our sheriff has a manner that says *cut the crap,* but he's a gentleman and is mostly revered by the people he serves. He's on the still-working side of sixty-five, but stands tall and seems younger than his age, even though his hair is completely white. He says it has been for years. Law enforcement work took an early toll on our sheriff.

"According to the records," he began to explain, "on a warm spring day a young woman named Serena Bustamante disappeared on the Terlingua Ranch Resort, not far from the Christmas Mountains. She was twenty-two years old at the time. No trace of her has ever been found."

He paused to drain the coffee from his mug. "After she was reported missing by her family, the sheriff went to investigate and found her Chevy Camaro abandoned in an arroyo. On the backseat was an overnight bag that held several changes of casual clothes, toiletries, and various pieces of lingerie. Riding boots had been tossed onto the floor in back. The car wasn't stuck in the sand or broken down. In fact, it started without a problem and was driven out by Serena's brother, Joey Bustamante."

"Did her brother know what she was doing there?"

"No, but he said Serena was involved with a married man named William Hampton who lived on the ranch. You'll see him referred to as 'Curly' in the reports, a nickname you'll understand when you see his photo. Her family disapproved of the affair, but Serena was headstrong and insisted they were in love and planning to marry. According to her, Curly was divorcing his wife."

I groaned at the slim-to-none likelihood of that. "So Serena's family suspected she was there to meet her lover?"

"Yes. The arroyo is a mile or two from Hampton's house," explained Sheriff Ben, "so that was the assumption they made."

"Who was the sheriff then?"

"It was Houston Blanton. Do you know him?"

"No sir. Do you?"

"I've seen him but can't say I know him. Back when he was a sheriff in Brewster County, I was a policeman in San Antonio."

I had questions about that, but he continued. "Hampton was a real estate developer and investor and still is, as far as I know.

He had inherited a large estate from his parents, including bank accounts worth several million dollars."

"What luck some people have."

The Sheriff laughed and agreed. "Even before that, he was involved in real estate deals with his father up in Montana and Wyoming. He was a wealthy man before his father died."

"How did he end up living in Terlingua?"

"The way I understand it, the senior Hampton acquired a full section of land on Terlingua Ranch Resort in a poker game. After he died, his son came to check it out and fell in love with the area. He brought his wife to see it. She must have agreed because, after a few years, they moved there. They had a unique home built that they designed themselves."

"Is that the octagonal house with a hand built stone fence?"

"Yes, that's the one."

"It's been abandoned for years, hasn't it?"

"Well yes, for thirty. Even though he was never arrested, Curly was tried and convicted by the local folks. There was so much hassle he moved his family back to Wyoming several months after Serena vanished. The investigation stalled for lack of evidence, and the sheriff had no legal means of keeping him. And Serena's family was relentless, calling and demanding to know where he had disposed of her body. In fact, her family is the reason we're re-investigating this case now."

"What do they hope to accomplish? I mean I know they want us to find her, but what can we do now that wasn't done thirty years ago?"

"They claim the Sheriff's Office didn't care about Serena's demise because she was Mexican-American, with Mexican being the key word. Her brother says local law enforcement believed she was a 'Mexican tramp,' and that she got what she had coming."

"Do you think it's true that law enforcement didn't care?"

"I can't say that. I have the old paperwork, and it seems they did the best they could. Huge searches were organized involving many people, and more than once. The law enforcement guys at Big Bend National Park helped, too, checking along the park's border with the ranch. A concerted effort was made to find either the woman or her body. The Hampton property was also investigated for a sign of disturbed earth or anything else that looked suspicious."

"And nothing was found?"

"That's right. I did find one fault with the original investigation, involving a dam that was being built on an arroyo which came through the Hampton property."

The Sheriff rose to refill his mug. He offered me coffee which I declined, having made that mistake before. I'm pretty sure it was his coffee that got the Walking Dead moving in the first place.

He continued, oblivious to how entertaining he was. "You see, that wet concrete would've been an obvious way to get rid of a dead body. When Sheriff Blanton arrived at the house, the cement was still curing. Instead of busting that thing apart, he interviewed the undocumented Mexican workers. They assured him there was not a body there, and he moved on."

"That seems like a glaring oversight."

"I think so, too, but about ten years later the investigation was re-opened at the insistence of the missing woman's family, and an ultrasound was taken of the dam. The sheriff didn't bother with any serious examination of it before that. They checked out every last inch of that dam, and it showed nothing but cement."

"Could there have been a mistake or an equipment malfunction?"

"Not likely, although it's possible. Sheriff Blanton felt it was working properly."

"Yeah, but he's the same guy who took the word of some undocumented workers that the boss hadn't stashed a dead woman in the new dam," I pointed out, causing the sheriff to laugh.

"Right," he agreed, "but he wasn't an idiot. He made a judgment error regarding the dam, but everything else about the investigation seems competent."

"So what do you have in mind for me?"

"Please take this file back to your office and read through it. You need to get a feel for everything, the way things happened, who said what and when. Then I suggest you meet with Joey Bustamante and Sylvia Bustamante Miller, Serena's brother and sister. They live here in Alpine. See what you think about what they have to say. Then you and I will meet again and make a plan."

I took the thick file, shook his hand, and left for home. On Highway 118 from Alpine to Terlingua, I had plenty of time to think. It's a scenic drive that cuts through mountainous, high desert grassland as you leave Alpine, and then drops down to a long, flat stretch of Chihuahuan desert. The road passes cattle ranches, stands of juniper and cottonwood, buttes, stony outcroppings, and curious rock formations. The rugged mountains sticking up in the southern part of the county are the most captivating, but our whole county is a case of Nature showing off.

The dying sun was working its late-afternoon magic on our landscape, but I barely noticed. How would I find a woman who had most likely been dead for thirty years? Where to start? There are so many places to dispose of a body: scores of still-open mine shafts and thousands of acres of unpopulated desert. And then there are the caves, and the Rio Grande. Take your pick.

Even if a body was dumped in the open, out there among the cacti and creosote bush, it would not be found. Bones would be scattered by scavengers. If anything was left after thirty years, it would have already been reduced to powdery shards by the relentless, moisture-sucking sun.

The thought of a blazing sun made me crave a cold beer, followed by a shot of smooth gold tequila with lime and salt. Beer. Tequila. Lime. Salt. Repeat as needed.

I reminded myself that I no longer drank.

CHAPTER 2

Joey Bustamante greeted me warmly, and with so much enthusiasm I thought he was going to start hugging me.

"Yes, yes," he exclaimed when he answered the door and I introduced myself, "so pleased to meet you, Deputy Ricos." His dark eyes shone. "Sheriff Duncan said he had assigned a young Hispanic woman to our case. You can't imagine how grateful we feel. Come in, come in." He practically lifted me into his home, which was fragrant with something just-baked.

"Sylvie!" He shouted over his shoulder and ushered me towards a cozy living room. "Of course you'll want something to drink. I've made lemonade, but if you prefer something different—"

"Lemonade would be fine, thank you."

"Come in and sit wherever you'll be most comfortable, and I'll be right back." He disappeared into the hall, still calling for Sylvie.

Joey is not much taller than I. He has thick, dark hair with only a bit of gray around the temples and golden-brown skin that is not wrinkled. Between his hair and skin, and the way he practically bounces, he seems younger than sixty-two.

Soon he was back carrying a tray of glasses, a pitcher of fresh lemonade, and cookies. A woman accompanied him. He introduced her as Sylvia Miller, his sister.

She took my hand and was friendly, but more reserved than Joey. Sylvia is older than her brother, with dark, almost-black hair where it isn't gray.

They sat in easy chairs that were side-by-side and across from me. I explained that I wished to record the conversation for my reference, and asked each of them to give the requisite permission. I started the recorder early so they'd be comfortable with it, or forget about it, by the time we got to the important details.

Joey poured tall glasses of lemonade and garnished each with a thick slice of lemon. He handed one to me, along with a sugar cookie, and then served Sylvia.

"Are you the baker?" I asked.

"Oh no," Joey said with a chuckle, "my wife Claudia made them. She'll be along in a while. She went to take our grandchildren home."

"Thank you for coming, Deputy Ricos," said Sylvia. "We've never felt that Serena's disappearance was given the attention it deserved."

"Sheriff Duncan explained that." I smiled and invited her to call me Margarita.

She returned the smile and told me in Spanish that my name is lovely, old-fashioned. I volunteered that I was named after my father's abuela, grandmother, a woman he cherished. After that exchange, we returned to English.

"Are you married, Margarita?" Sylvia asked. She had spied my ring.

"I'm a widow."

She looked surprised and then sad. "A widow at your young age?"

"My husband was killed in an accident." He was riding a bull in a rodeo, but I don't tell everyone that and hoped she wouldn't ask.

Joey headed off his curious sister. "Do you want me to start?"

"Yes, please. First, tell me about Serena."

"I picture her as if no time has passed since she disappeared. Sylvie and I loved her so much. She was born ten years after me, and fifteen after Sylvie, so everyone spoiled her. Serena was a sweet child and grew into a lovely woman. You wouldn't believe the number of men who chased her and even asked her to marry."

Sylvia stepped over to a bookshelf in the corner of the room and brought me a framed 8 x 10 photograph of Serena. The same one was in the file, but it was wallet-sized. The young woman was beautiful. Her radiant smile made me want to smile back.

"How old was she in this photo?" I asked.

"She was twenty-two. This was taken a short time before she vanished."

I was twenty-five, close to Serena's age, and already felt a kinship with her.

"She was happy and kind-hearted," continued Joey. "She dated different men and was always going to dances and parties, but nobody turned her head until she met Curly Hampton." Joey's fists clenched at the mention of the name.

"How did she meet him? Wasn't he older than Serena?"

"He's my age, so yes, he was ten years older. He rented office space here in Alpine and advertised for a secretary/bookkeeper. Serena was working as a clerk for an insurance agent but wasn't making much. She answered the ad and was hired on the spot, even though she had no bookkeeping experience to speak of."

Joey paused to take a sip of lemonade. "He said he would teach her, that the bookkeeping wouldn't be complicated."

"I remember when she came by after the interview," added Sylvia. "She was so happy and excited. Her pay had almost doubled. She said Mr. Hampton would be in Alpine one or two days a week to leave dictated letters or contracts for her to type and give her instructions for the week ahead. The rest of the time she answered the phone and took messages. He said he would be in touch daily by telephone. It did sound like a perfect job."

"At first we didn't notice when she and Hampton started dating," said Joey. "She had her own apartment by then, but we saw her often. She began to speak of a man in a way that made us think she was falling in love. All of us wanted to meet him. We knew he was someone special because Serena had never been in love before. She avoided having us meet him for months. None of us cared as long as she was happy, and she was."

"How long did she date him before you discovered it was her boss?"

"Almost a year before we knew it formally, but we figured it out before then. Serena would be out late or not come home at all on the days her Mr. Hampton was in town," Joey said. "I spied on her once. I'm ashamed to admit it, but I was worried about her. I borrowed a friend's truck and sat in it across the street from Hampton's office. I had just gotten off work, so it must have been about five-thirty. His truck was in the lot, along with Serena's Camaro. I can't tell you what I was looking for, but I was looking."

"What did you see?"

"Well, nothing. It was winter, and it began to get dark. I kept thinking they would come out to eat, so I stayed put even though it got cold. After a while, the lights went off. What would they be doing in the dark? I doubt if it was dictation."

He shrugged his shoulders and tried to laugh it off, but it wasn't convincing. "Later we found out Hampton had a bedroom in his three-room office suite. There were other times when one of us would go by her apartment and his truck would be there late. In the morning, it would still be there."

"We were upset by that," said Sylvia, "but didn't have time to worry about it. By then Joey and I were married and busy with our children. Our family was close, and we got together at least once a week and on holidays. If Curly was in town, Serena begged off with some lame excuse or other. If he wasn't in town, she came alone."

"Our parents began to question her about why she wouldn't bring her young man to meet the family," Joey said. "Our mom said, 'He's a married man, isn't he?' Serena burst into tears, and the truth came out.

"Mom insisted she break it off. Serena cried and explained that she was in love with him, and he loved her, too, and was leaving leave his wife. She said they hadn't meant to fall in love, but it happened. After similar conversations, Mom said she wouldn't hassle her about it anymore, but warned her that she was headed down a path that would lead to hurt."

Joey and Sylvia looked near tears. "Mom never got over the loss of Serena," said Joey. "Of course it would've been the same if any of us had vanished. But I think the fact that she had repeatedly warned her youngest child made it worse. She never expected to be right in her dire prediction."

"Did either of you meet Mr. Hampton?" I asked.

"We met him the Christmas before Serena disappeared," answered Joey. "He invited her to go to Europe after the holidays and I insisted on meeting him. He came to my house for dinner, along with Serena, Sylvia, and her husband. The thing that rankles most is that we liked him."

"He was funny, intelligent, well-educated, and quite handsome," said Sylvia. "He seemed to genuinely love Serena."

"Regarding his wife," Joey said, "Curly claimed they had 'an understanding.' He said he would ask for a divorce after their return from Europe so he could marry Serena and give her the whole-hearted love and attention she deserved."

"We were spellbound," said Sylvia. "He seemed to be everything a woman would want in a husband, and wealthy besides. His money meant nothing to Serena, but we thought it was an added plus. We knew she would be well taken care of."

"After that meeting," continued Joey, "there were a few others from time to time. Our parents were angry at being left out and consented to meet Curly. They swore they'd keep their opinions to themselves."

"What did they think of him?"

"They liked him, but Mom continued to say that a man should first divorce his wife and then pursue other women and not in any other order. Dad finally agreed that sometimes things happen, out of order though they may be, and it's nobody's fault. Serena knew she had done wrong. We all knew it, but it's the way life is."

"Please tell me about the time of the disappearance," I said.

"Serena left town without saying anything to any of us, which wasn't unusual," Joey said. "Mom called her on Saturday morning to invite her to a cookout on Sunday afternoon. The message on Serena's machine said she would be away for the weekend, and back on Sunday night late. All of us assumed she was with Curly since his visits to Alpine had become more frequent. We relaxed after he said he was getting a divorce. How stupid we were." Joey's small frame sagged, and he stared glumly at his fists.

"We weren't stupid, Joey," said Sylvia softly, "but we were trusting and naïve." She reached over to squeeze her brother's hands.

"We didn't have a reason to doubt what he said because Serena was so full of joy."

Joey sighed. "We didn't see it coming, that's all, and it was such a shock. When Serena didn't return on Monday morning and didn't call, that seemed odd, but we still didn't worry. Then Curly called me about dinnertime, and asked if Serena was okay. He said she hadn't come into the office and wasn't answering her phone. She was expecting by then, and he was afraid she was sick or having problems related to the pregnancy. It wasn't like Serena not to show up for work or to call if she couldn't make it. She hadn't contacted any of us."

"Did Hampton sound normal to you?"

"Yes, he did, but he was worried. I told him I would check with some of her friends and call him back. I did that, and nobody knew where she was. After that, I called the sheriff, Houston Blanton. He said we should give it until morning and call him if she failed to report for work again. I didn't like that, but agreed to wait. My mind wouldn't let me think anything awful had happened to her."

Joey paused so long I had to encourage him to continue. "So you waited until Tuesday morning, and then what happened?"

"I went to Serena's apartment first thing and then to her work and found no sign of her at either place. After that, I went to the sheriff's office and was told he was at a local coffee shop. He was drinking coffee and gossiping with a bunch of good ol' boys. It took all my determination to drag him away from them and back to his office where we could talk privately.

"I've never seen anyone so slow to act. I was frantic and furious with him. I had to tell him the whole story about Serena and how we'd thought she was with Hampton. 'Curly Hampton?' the sheriff asked in that ridiculous accent he had. 'Why would she be meetin' ol' Curly?'" Joey mimicked a south Texas drawl perfectly. Under other circumstances, it would've been funny.

"I told him they were in love and were planning to marry soon," he continued. "The sheriff laughed in my face. He had the audacity to say that Curly Hampton was a married white man and, 'he wouldn't take up with no Mexican girl no matter how charmin' she is.' It took everything in me to keep from killing the sonofa-bitch right there."

"Sheriff Duncan told me that you felt Blanton hadn't done a professional job because of his prejudice against Hispanics," I said.

"That's the way we saw it. He assured us he'll do everything he can to resolve this case. We were glad he put you on it because we thought you might understand how it felt to be treated the way he treated us."

"So how did you get Blanton off his dead redneck butt?"

Joey grinned and lightened up. "I persevered. He had no choice but to get moving or say outright that he wasn't going to help me. I made it clear I would find the help we needed. I was ready to call the Texas Rangers, my senators, or even the President. By God, I was not going to sit around while my baby sister might be in trouble."

"What did the sheriff do first?"

"He agreed to go south and talk to Curly since I had exhausted every other source of information I could think of. He made note of all the friends I had spoken to, and then wrote down the make and model of her car. He wouldn't let me go with him in case Serena tried to contact me or came home. Several hours later, he radioed his office to say he had found her car in an arroyo. They called me with the message that I might want to join him."

"And of course you went."

"Oh yes, I went. There was Serena's car, like he said. By then a deputy had joined him and he was busy taking fingerprints and looking for clues. I asked about a set of tire tracks near the aban-doned car, and the sheriff said they would make a plaster impres-sion of them. 'Might tell us somethin', might not,' he drawled. They had already taken casts of some muddled footprints, but they never got anything conclusive from them as far as I ever knew.

"Sheriff Blanton said Hampton had admitted to seeing Serena, but his wife didn't know yet, and he wanted to spare her public embarrassment if possible. That disturbed me greatly. For one thing, he said he was getting a divorce. How could he do that with-out notifying his wife? For another, I thought it was arrogant for him to be worried about her, and more likely his own self, when it looked like something bad had happened to Serena. Her car was near his home, and yet he swore they didn't have anything planned that weekend and he had no idea she was coming south."

"What did the sheriff think?"

"He feared it was foul play. He might not have suspected Curly until they opened the overnight case and saw that red thing. It was the type of garment a woman uses to tease a man and well, you know." He smiled and turned bright red.

"When he saw it," Joey continued, "and the way the suitcase was packed for a few days, he turned to face Curly with murderous rage on his face. He didn't say a word, but Curly began to stammer and fidget. I wanted to kill him."

Joey studied his hands. "Curly said the overnight case didn't mean she was visiting him; she could've been planning to meet someone else. Can you imagine? He was talking about Serena, not some slut. She had never made love before, which he knew better than anyone. And she was pregnant with his child."

Joey and Sylvia exchanged a sad look. "That did it," he continued. "I started to run at Curly, but the sheriff grabbed me by the arm. He said, 'Now don't do somethin' you'll regret' in his maddeningly slow way. I swear it took him twice as long to say a thing as a normal person. To this day, I regret not beating the living shit out of him."

Sylvia laughed. "Did you mean Curly or the sheriff?"

"I meant Curly, but I should've laid into that sheriff, too. I missed my chance."

"Reports indicate the tire tracks were not from any of Curly's vehicles," I said.

"That didn't prove anything. He could've borrowed a friend's truck—they did think it was a truck or other heavy vehicle. Or he could've stolen one. Or maybe he had someone else dispose of her. He's a rich bastard and could buy anything." Joey clenched his fists and placed them on his knees.

"What happened next?"

"The sheriff wasted no time in organizing a search. He mobilized one heck of a number of people in a short time. He got most of his deputies on it and even a few deputies from other counties.

Some volunteers from the national park came, too. Many locals helped, as well as Serena's friends and most of our family except the old folks. The search was organized and well-planned, showing that Blanton knew the territory. The one time I thought he was competent was during the searches."

"Was anything useful discovered?"

"No, nothing, except one of the deputies talked to an elderly man who swore he saw a woman driving a full-sized pick-up truck away from that arroyo. On further questioning, though, it seemed he was confused and wasn't even sure what day it had been. So that went nowhere. Subsequent searches went the same way. Serena had disappeared from the face of the earth."

I knew that from reading the reports Sheriff Duncan had given me. One set of footprints was thought to be Serena's, but that was not definite. The others were not conclusively Curly's either, or anybody else's for that matter. There was confusion about the length of time the footprints had been there.

I asked Joey about the dam, which got him heated again. "What kind of idiot asks a guy's illegal employees if the boss has been up to something criminal? Those poor guys would have thought they'd be implicated if he'd hidden a corpse in there with or without their help."

"In going over this case," I said, "the thing that struck me was the dam. But other than that blatant error, it seems Blanton did a more-or-less decent job of investigating Serena's disappearance, his prejudice aside."

"Yes, I know, but if you could've seen the dam. The cement was still wet the day I went, which was Tuesday. To me that screamed of an easy burial place, but the sheriff asked the workers about it and moved on. I almost went back to take it apart myself, but I figured I'd already caused enough problems to land me in jail. I had a family to support, so I let it go."

Again, Joey stared at his hands. "The sheriff thought I had a violent nature. If I do, it never came out before that bastard did away with my baby sister."

"Besides Curly Hampton, can you think of any other person who might have wanted to harm Serena?"

"No! It was Curly."

"I know you think it was, and it sounds that way to me, but will you consider something different? Relax a moment and think back. Were people jealous of her? She was a beautiful woman with a good job. Could that have angered one of her friends? Could she have met someone in the Terlingua area that was jealous or angered by her for some other reason? Maybe there was a confrontation that got out of hand. Let's take Curly from the equation and see who else comes up."

Sylvia's response was heated. "You think we haven't done that? We've spent countless sleepless nights thinking of other scenarios, but there is no other way to explain it, nothing."

"The other person with a reason to kill Serena would've been Curly's wife, Christina," said Joey. "But she was so shocked to find out about her husband's affair that it was impossible to consider her a serious suspect. The sheriff told me that when the news of Curly's affair came out, she cried and wondered out loud if she was crazy for not realizing her husband was being unfaithful to her."

"Still," I said, "that doesn't rule her out. I read all this in the reports, and if she was acting, she's good. But people lie and go to extravagant lengths to hide guilt."

They nodded in agreement.

"What else can I do," I wondered out loud, "so much time has passed."

"Please try," begged Sylvia. "Joey and I feel that Blanton overlooked something important because of his prejudice. He thought Serena was after Curly Hampton's money and that she got pregnant to ensnare him. He was so wrong about her. She loved Curly. Getting pregnant was not something she planned. Besides, as far as she knew, Curly was planning to marry her anyway."

"He seemed happy Serena was carrying his child," added Joey. "He bought baby things and left them hidden around the office and her apartment. She was delighted by that." Joey sighed and rubbed his head with both hands. "It's so hard to think he killed her. They were in love; I know it. What could've made him do it?"

"Strange things happen when you throw in wives and children and vast fortunes," I said, sounding more experienced than I felt.

"It would mean everything to us if Serena is found so we can bury her," Joey said. "She deserves that, at least." His voice broke. "I feel as if I failed her."

"You're not to blame, Joey," I said. "It sounds to me like you were the best of older brothers."

After thirty years, his love for his sister was as intense as ever. Perhaps it couldn't rest in peace until he was sure that she did.

CHAPTER 3

By the time we said good-bye, I felt as if I was leaving old friends. When I told Joey and Sylvia I appreciated their help, they thanked me with tears in their eyes.

"If you have any questions, please contact us."

"I will, Joey."

"You'll keep us informed of your progress?"

"I promise." It was tempting to tell him not to hold his breath, but he and Sylvia said they felt hopeful for the first time in years. Their belief in me was touching, but I walked away with well-meaning promises weighing me down.

I called Sheriff Duncan at home since it was after six o'clock. He knew I was meeting with Joey and Sylvia, and instructed me to call him after, no matter when.

"Come for supper," he insisted, "there's plenty."

Marianne Duncan met me at the door, gave me a hug, and made me feel welcome. She is a slender woman in her early sixties, a retired attorney. She once told me she never got to practice much law between having babies and raising them. Sheriff Ben has been married to her more than forty years. I've worked closely with him, so I know he still courts her as if he hadn't won her hand and heart long ago. Once when I was still training with him, we stopped to buy her fresh flowers, and he mentioned that he intended to make her fall in love with him every day.

"Come in," boomed the sheriff, taking over hospitality duty from his wife. He shook my hand and, with his other hand, affectionately gripped my shoulder. He indicated his study with a nod. When I entered, he shut the door behind us.

"Please sit and tell me everything," he said.

I sat in an easy chair across from the sheriff's desk and sank into the heady smell of leather. A cheery fire blazed in a rock fireplace close by.

"I like them," I said. "I want to help them find out what happened to their sister, but I don't see what I can do that hasn't already been done."

"I know," he said, "but I couldn't turn them down. I don't want you to think I'm an overly-emotional old man, but they got to me. And there may be truth to what they say about prejudice because the sheriff overlooked two important things."

"The dam," I said. *That damned dam.*

"And the wife," added Sheriff Ben. "Because she cried at the news, he passed her by like he was sure she didn't do it. Perhaps his prejudice and stereotyping did make him blind to certain things. At times, he seemed focused on the investigation and at other times he was hasty to write something off, being sloppy. You've read it all, so you know what I mean, right?"

"Right, I agree. It's almost as if he was two different lawmen."

"And he wasn't old enough to be losing his mind yet." Sheriff Ben laughed and got up to tend the fire. He made it glow brightly.

"So," he said when he sat again, "what are your thoughts?"

"I think we should do another ultrasound on the dam in case Sheriff Blanton messed that up. I'd like to re-interview as many of the Mexican workers as I can find. I'm willing to speak with everyone who was questioned before, but I would pay special attention to Mrs. Hampton. That might lead to something that didn't come out when Blanton worked the case."

"Excuse me for interrupting, but you need to know the Hamptons are divorced. She moved back to Cody, Wyoming, where they were from originally, and he lives on a ranch near the Grand Teton Mountains National Park outside of Jackson Hole."

20

"Ten minutes 'til supper," said Marianne's disembodied voice from the other side of the door. "I'll call you."

"Thanks, darlin'." He grinned at her through the door and then turned back to me. "What else?"

"I should talk to both of the Hamptons after I redo the ultrasound, and then we can decide where to go from there. Will I need a search warrant for the property?"

"No. When Hampton left, he gave the Sheriff's Office written permission to do whatever needed to be done on his property. I have the keys to the gate, house, and all the outbuildings." The sheriff removed a padded envelope from a drawer and set it on the desk.

"Well then, I'll take a horse and ride their property to satisfy myself there is nothing suspicious-looking. I'll investigate all the buildings, including the house. It might take a few days."

"Would you like to take a horse from here?"

"No, I'll use my dad's. He won't complain if I stop and start and he never tries to run away." I watched him finger the envelope. "Are you coming with me, Sheriff?"

"I was getting to that. I know I told you we were going to work together on this. The truth is that's changed. You'll be a special task force of one."

"Is that like an Army of one?"

He laughed. "Yes, like that. I can't spare anyone to work with you because we're so short-handed in Alpine right now."

"That's okay," I assured him. "I have Barney."

"He can help, but he's working his own case."

That was a surprise, and I wondered why he had separated our cases. Was it the two of us he was separating?

"I'd like to take him with me when I go to the Hampton property," I said, "for moral support. I think it'll be spooky to go there alone."

"By all means take him." He handed me the packet of keys. "Do you think you can find a horse large enough for your partner?"

I laughed. "I'll try."

Marianne knocked on the door and entered. "Dinner is served. Crime fighting can wait an hour or so while you heroes eat, don't you think?"

"You bet," I said. "I'll just lay my mask and cape aside."

"Not too close to the fire," quipped the sheriff.

* * *

On the eighty-mile drive home, I thought about Serena, whose picture was on the seat beside me. Aye Dios, que triste. Whatever happened to her, she was almost certainly dead. It's not like Chicanas from close-knit families to run away and never be heard from again. Why would she run away when she had everything she wanted? And what possessed Sheriff Ben to hand me such an old case?

It was cold and wind gusted from the north hard enough to sway the heavy Explorer. It made me miss Kevin, my crazy bull riding husband. I turned up the heater and tuned the XM radio to a hip-hop station, then to an oldies station playing The Big Bopper. *Ah baby, you know what I like.* I clicked it off.

The satellite phone began bleeping to signal an incoming call.

"I tried your cell phone," Barney said without saying hello. "Are you just now coming back from Alpine?"

"Yep. I'm still in the cell phone dead zone. I had dinner at the sheriff's house."

"For real?"

"Would I lie?"

"Of course you would."

"I'm serious. I enjoyed a delicious meal with Mr. and Mrs. Sheriff Ben."

"I guess you rate."

"I do, but it wasn't about that. The sheriff needed a favor. He's given me an impossible case." I told him about Joey and Sylvia, and a condensed version of the long, sad story of their sister, Serena. I hadn't seen Barney in two days because he was temporarily serving as bailiff in the circuit court in Alpine.

"I guess you need me to help you," he fussed, as if he didn't want to. He and I are the only full-time deputies in south Brewster County, and we stick together. We normally work as a team which brought me to a question.

"Sheriff Ben said you had your own case. Since when does he assign us separate cases? Did somebody tell him we have fun working together?"

He laughed. "It's not that. He called me while you were interviewing those folks. He said he wants you on the Serena case because you're a young Latina. He's trying to keep her family happy. He gave me a case of another missing person, but this one is a man, and recent. The sheriff doesn't care if we help each other."

"Good. Will you go with me to the old Hampton place? I think it would be scary and sad to be there alone. I plan to investigate on horseback because horses can cover more ground and go where vehicles can't."

"Okay, that sounds good."

"Will I be able to find a horse in the state of Texas big enough to carry you?"

"You're hilarious, Ricos."

The locals call Barney 'Roadblock.' He is six-and-a-half feet tall and has shoulders that could block a lane of traffic. He's not drop dead gorgeous or anything, but he has blue eyes that are extraordinarily blue.

"You'd better find me something to ride or I can't go," he grumbled.

"I'll ask Neal," I said. "I think he has a mare that would be perfect."

Neal is a friend who tried to start a horse outfitting business to take tourists into the remote and scenic Christmas Mountains. Kevin and I helped him get it going and sometimes guided for him. When Kevin died, both of us abandoned Neal. For a while, I had given up everything I ever did with Kevin. After a year and a half, I was slowly returning to life.

"I'll find out tomorrow," I said. "How did your court duty go?"

"It was easy, more boring than challenging. I brought a few guys from jail and took them back, maintained order, kept the judge and the rest of the court safe. It was all in a day's work, Ricos. Of course, I was stellar."

"That's according to you."

* * *

When I pulled up to my dark house, I sat in the vehicle a moment, thinking about Kevin. He always kept the lights blazing if I wasn't home. The place seemed to radiate warmth, perhaps because I knew he was waiting for me.

My home has a front porch, my favorite place. It faces Cimarron Mountain and has room enough for two wicker rocking chairs and a few planters. The plants had been moved inside. I leave them out until freezing weather threatens and then put them back in the house.

In my mind, I see Kevin come to the window. He pulls back the curtains we made from colorful Mexican blankets and peers into the dark, his handsome face pressed against the pane. I turn on the Explorer's inside light and blow him a kiss. He blows one back, laughs, and motions for me to come on inside.

Oh, Kevin, I miss you.

I jumped down from the Explorer and sat in a rocker. In spite of the frigid air, I was drawn to spend a moment watching 'my' mountain. On that moonless night, Cimarron was a bumpy black hulk standing against an even blacker sky full of stars. The night was so clear they looked bigger and brighter than usual.

"What happened to Serena Bustamante?" I asked my mountain.

The only answer was the soft sigh of a cold wind.

CHAPTER 4

Barney sat at his desk drinking coffee, or at least looking at it. He seemed half asleep and stared blindly into the mug.

I plopped into his visitor chair. "Tell me about your missing person."

"I don't see how you can be so wide awake at this hour."

"I run. It wakes me up. And it's not that early."

"You can say that because you don't have babies at your house." He handed me a paper bag still warm from its aromatic contents. "Here, Julia made you some egg burritos with potatoes, onions, and jalapeños."

"You have the most amazing wife."

"Don't I know it? There's a sports bottle with orange juice in the fridge."

I removed the juice and sat down to eat. I'd had breakfast, but it was fruit. My health regimen flies out the door in the face of homemade burritos, no matter what. A person has to have some kind of vice.

Barney watched me, grinning. "Pretty good, huh?"

"Past good," I said with a full mouth. "Way past. How does she cook like this with two babies?" Barney and Julia have a daughter two and a son three months.

"I did my part by rocking them while she cooked. I'm an outstanding dad."

"I don't doubt it."

"What's this? No smart comment?"

"I'm busy."

"You eat, and I'll talk," he said.

"That's funny. It's normally the other way around."

"Do you want to hear about my missing guy or not?"

"Sí, tell me."

"His name is James Taggert. He was reported missing by his aunt, who lives in Houston and calls him Jimmy. He's from Houston, too. He told her he was heading to Big Bend to clear his head and to camp and hike. She reported his failure to return home to the National Park Service, and they called the sheriff when it was determined he had left the park." Terlingua sits on the western side of Big Bend National Park.

"Taggert planned to be gone two weeks," said Barney. "It has now been four."

"And she's just now calling?"

"She said she thought he might be off with a girlfriend, but Monday night she was watching TV and realized he doesn't have a girlfriend."

"She sounds a tad mental."

"Right-O. The sheriff said he had the impression she was drinking, so it could be that. Anyway, she wanted to make somebody aware that he's missing. She faxed the sheriff his photo, and he faxed it to us."

Barney handed me a grainy photograph of a frowning, brown-eyed, bearded man wearing thick glasses. His light brown hair came past his shoulders and was unkept-looking and frizzy.

"She says he's twenty-two," continued Barney. "He puts his hair into a pony tail. He always wears glasses because he can't see without them. He's five-ten and weighs approximately one hundred and sixty-five pounds.

"According to her, he worked two jobs but has now been fired from both of them due to unauthorized vacation. He worked at a Wendy's as the assistant manager and moonlighted as a waiter at Chili's. His apartment is as he left it, and the rent is paid until the end of next month. She's paid his electric bill so the power won't be cut off. She does seem to care about him, spacey as she is."

"So you've spoken with her?"

"Yes, the sheriff asked me to call her."

"Is she sure he was visiting this park?"

"Yes. Unless there's another national park next to a place called Terlingua. I don't think so, do you?"

"I'm sure there's only one Terlingua."

"He called her after he'd been here a week. He loved the park but was headed to Terlingua for the music scene, to go rafting, and to check out a place called Gate Two, which I assume means Gate Two of the Terlingua Ranch Resort. He had met someone in the park who told him it's accessible by car and yet is remote, scenic, and private."

"That's Gate Two all right." I got up and went into the bathroom to clean my face and hands. "That was delicious. Please thank Julia for me."

"I see you didn't leave me anything," grumbled Barney.

"You said they were for me."

He laughed. "Yeah, I ate plenty at home."

"So are we supposed to investigate?"

"She wants us to take a look and see if we spot his car. It's an old beat-up Honda Civic, 80's vintage, green. I thought we could ask around and see if anyone has seen him. If he was into the music scene, he'll have been spotted someplace."

"Maybe he found a girlfriend here and doesn't want to go home," I suggested.

"Possibly, but have you seen him?"

"No. I think I'd remember him. He's—different looking."

"I'll give him that."

"Now we have something else we have to do," I complained.

"Aren't you the deputy who whines when there's nothing to do?" Barney didn't let me answer. "It's a good excuse to ride around together and talk to people."

"We don't need an excuse for that, and besides, I already have plenty to do."

The phone rang, and I grabbed it. A shaky, old lady's voice asked, "May I speak with Deputy George, please? This is Ms. Harding calling."

Barney put the phone on speaker function so I could hear, too.

"Ms. Harding, this is Deputy George."

"Oh, Deputy," she said with a quivery voice, "I am so worried about Jimmy. I came over to his apartment this morning to be sure I'd turned off everything. I also wanted to get his mail." She sniffed. "The place has been ransacked."

"Ms. Harding, are you there now?"

"Yes."

"Are you sure no one else is there?"

"I'm waiting for the police to come."

"Ms. Harding, are you sure you're alone in the apartment?" Barney persisted.

"Well, yes, I think so. I went all through it." She began to cry. "I think something bad has happened to my poor Jimmy."

"Do you know what someone would be looking for?"

"No idea and I can't tell if anything is missing." She paused to blow her nose. "I know he doesn't leave money or credit cards around, and he doesn't own anything of value. I think someone was looking for records or something." Her voice got higher and shakier as she spoke. "His desk is a mess. All the drawers have been pulled out and dumped on the floor. Everywhere is a mess. What am I going to do?"

"Try not to touch anything until the police get there. They'll tell you what to do."

"I'm so frightened for Jimmy."

"We're going to look for him now. I'll call you later." There was a sudden commotion in the background. "Are the police there?"

"Yes, they've just arrived."

"Please tell the investigating officer I'd like to speak with him after he checks out the apartment, okay? Will you give him my name and number?"

"Of course I will. Please find my Jimmy. And thank you, Deputy George. You are the sweetest man."

Barney reddened. "Glad to be of help, ma'am."

"Shut up, Ricos," he said when he hung up. "I don't need any of your smart-ass comments today."

"I'm sure I don't know what you mean, you sweet man."

"Feel like taking a ride?"

"Do I have a choice?"

"Hell, no, you don't," he said. "Let's go."

"Well, at least let me go to the bathroom and get my jacket. It's chilly today."

"Women," the 'sweet' man mumbled loud enough for me to hear, "always slowing a man down."

"Well, excuse me if I don't have the bladder of a camel like you do," I yelled from the bathroom, "or the face."

* * *

Terlingua Ranch Resort was once a working cattle ranch of many thousands of acres. In the sixties, it was sold off in sections and even in pieces as small as five acres. The gates are numbered one through nine. They are not true gates that open and close, but are numbered entryways into different parts of the ranch, flanked by native stone columns. Gate Two is a short distance from our office on the right-hand side of Highway 118 as you go north towards Alpine.

Although the day was cold, it was crystal clear with a bright blue sky that I associate with winter in the Big Bend country. Everything seems clearer and closer against that sky.

"Just another day in paradise," observed Barney.

"Somebody has to live here," I said. "I'm glad it's us."

"You'd have a better chance of meeting Mr. Right in a place with more people."

"Do *not* start."

"I was just stating the obvious."

"So you're saying you want me to move away?"

"Well, no. You know that's not what I meant. I was lamenting the fact that there are not many eligible men here."

"There are plenty of men. Now drop the subject. Please."

He laughed and gave it a rest.

We headed down an unpaved road with stunning Willow Mountain on one side. Like many peaks in Big Bend, it has a volcanic origin but is especially notable for its columnar jointing, what I call 'washboarded effect.' No matter what you call it, it's among the grandest of mountains.

After about a mile, the road goes up a rise onto a mesa covered by thick stands of ocotillos, a forest of them. The ocotillo's long, spiny, whip-like branches are bare until rain. Then leaves burst out, practically overnight. They produce delicate red blossoms that resemble miniature orchids and hold sweet nectar, like honeysuckle.

Kevin liked bull riding, but besides me his first love was science, so we explored on our ATV when time allowed. I knew Gate Two. There were hundreds of good places to set up camp, starting with Ocotillo Mesa. It has a terrific view of Indian Head and the Chisos Mountains.

Indian Head is a unique place, hard to describe. You have to see it to appreciate what I mean. It's a jumble of rocky hills and giant boulders, brownish-red in color—or burgundy, brown, red, or gray—even purple, depending on the location of the sun, whether there are clouds or not, and the time of year. Indian Head is full of caves, shallow indentions, and peculiar rock formations. On some of the boulders are pictographs left by earlier, primitive peoples that once inhabited this land. There's a hidden spring which has attracted humans for as long as there have been humans in the area. The dirt road that weaves its way to Indian Head is one of my favorite places to run.

We passed few houses, and those were spaced far apart across the mesa. For a while the road seemed to bring us closer to the Chisos Mountains, then it veered away, down into a small ravine.

The Chisos are the only mountain range in the U.S. that is located entirely within a national park. They, too, defy an easy description. 'Rugged and wild' comes to mind, but that's barely a start. In places, there are sharp spires of rock sticking straight up, jagged afterthought formations, and bald rock faces. Like everything else, the Chisos change subtly in the sunlight and shadows. Native peoples called them the 'ghostly mountains' because they are sometimes shrouded in mist or clouds. Indian lore states that at night they run off to play with other mountains.

After many turns and dips we saw the green Honda Civic. It was sitting off the road in a flat area that makes a perfect pull-out. Barney parked us next to it. There was no one in it; that would've been too easy. We sat still a moment to observe the surroundings. In a valley, next to a towering rock face, we saw a tent. Maybe we had found our man, maybe only his trail.

"Let's treat this as a crime scene," said Barney, indicating the car. "It looks abandoned. One tire is flat, and there're no tracks so it couldn't have been moved recently. Look at the windshield."

We got out of our vehicle and moved around Taggert's.

"There's dust inside and out," Barney observed. "See that national park entrance fee receipt on the windshield? Look how faded it is. You can't see the dates or amount paid anymore."

I peered at it and agreed.

"I'll print the car," he announced. "What do we have to lose? We don't know what we'll find at that tent down there."

That comment gave me a chill. I have an aversion to dead bodies.

I stared at the campsite through binoculars without seeing movement or anything of note. The camp looked as abandoned as the car. The tent leaned to one side and appeared to be halfway collapsed.

When Barney finished lifting prints from one side of the vehicle, I moved to that side, pulled on gloves, and opened the door. I was surprised it wasn't locked. There were a few fast food containers littering the floor, but mostly cups. The ashtray was overflowing with butts. The glove compartment held a travel-size packet of tissues, a Texas map, batteries of two different sizes, and a few condoms. In the back seat was a brown and tan striped suitcase.

"Want to print this suitcase before I look inside it?" I asked.

"Yeah, hold on."

While Barney lifted fingerprints from the suitcase, I placed a few cigarette butts into an evidence bag. In a different bag, I placed the discarded drink cups. It could be a waste of time, but you never know when a DNA sample might be needed.

The suitcase contained what you'd expect: clothing, toiletries, and more condoms. Under the back seat, stuck way up under it, were two magazines. One was entitled 'Man Mania,' and the other one, 'Studs.' Yes indeed. They were full of photos of men undressing or, in most cases, nude.

"Whoa!" It popped out before I could stop myself. Barney snickered and kept lifting prints. I flipped through pages of men stripping, kissing, men doing various things to other men. You get the picture.

"Enjoying some on-the-job pornography, Ricos?"

"I'm amazed," I said without looking up. "Some of these guys are scary. Do you think these photos have been manipulated?"

"No doubt," he said without seeing them.

I showed him one. "Scary is right! I think our missing Jimmy might be gay," was Barney's take on it.

"Really, Pard?" I thought about it. "Maybe he's questioning."

"He's twenty-two and looking at magazines of naked men. I say he's gay."

"Okay, Mr. Know-It-All, but twenty-two is young. It takes some people a while to figure out who they are."

"Are you speaking from experience?"

"No, I'm just sayin'. Maybe he had a woman with him, for all you know. I'd like to point out that I enjoy looking at naked men, and I'm not a gay male."

He gave me an exasperated "Huh," and then, "Leave those gay-boy 'zines right where you found them and shut that suitcase."

"I'm not finished with my investigation."

"Well, I can't wait to see the report you write for the sheriff."

After a few more minutes, I closed the magazines. "You sure don't see men like those every day."

"So now you're interested in men loving men?"

"I don't care who people love, and two naked men are better than one."

"Be sure to notate that in your report to the sheriff."

"Our sheriff doesn't have to know everything."

"True," Barney said, "you might give the old guy a stroke."

"Gay or not, I do like looking at those big sexy men."

He stood up on the other side of the car, towering above it. "I'm starting to get to you, aren't I?"

"Don't we have a campsite to check out?"

We headed across the desert towards the tent. We carried water and a first-aid kit, not knowing what we would find. It took us fifteen minutes to get there. It had seemed farther away; distances are deceiving in the desert.

What we found was a deserted campsite. The tent was full of dust and sand. A road map of Mexico was spread out inside, held down by rocks. Some dirty clothes were balled up in a corner. A portable radio, a two-gallon container of water, and a few tins of food were also left behind. A sleeping bag was laid out and covered by a blanket that was full of dirt. Next to the bag was a paperback mystery, the bookmark a credit card receipt imprinted with James Taggert's name. I took photos, and then put the receipt in an evidence bag, but left everything else.

Ants marched in and out, carrying away their plunder. A package of peanut butter crackers had been gnawed into at both ends and was providing a tasty feast for looters.

Outside was a fire ring of rocks with a night's supply of firewood stacked beside it. Whatever ash it held had been blown away by the wind, leaving only charred rocks and dirt. There were no longer any discernible footprints except ours.

"What does this mean?" I wondered. "Did he get hurt hiking and not return? Did someone take him away? Did he throw himself off a cliff or shoot himself in a cave? His things tell us he was here and nothing else."

Barney dropped onto a boulder near the fire ring. "I never thought this would be so difficult. I guess I thought we'd find him."

"What now?" I did a slow 360-degree turn with the binoculars, squinting in the brightness. All I saw was acres of tranquil desert, hills, mountains, and about a thousand cliffs. A human could be lying at the bottom of any of them.

"I don't know," Barney said. "Did someone kill him?"

"Maybe, but I don't think so. His aunt found his apartment ransacked today. Wouldn't that come first, then killing? It seems like the bad guys would've found out what they needed to know before they killed him."

"Maybe they tried, and he wouldn't talk," Barney suggested.

"Possibly, but how would Houston bad guys find him here? Maybe he ran away from Houston, but if he was running, why would he leave his car and stuff here? It doesn't make sense."

"What about that map of Mexico? Was his plan to go there or has he already gone? Again, why not take the car at least as far as the border?"

"Maybe it's broken down," I said.

"Or someone picked him up."

"Let's try to hotwire it," I suggested. "You're good at that, aren't you?"

"I wouldn't say I'm good at it," said Barney, offended. "But I do know how."

He tried, but the battery appeared to be dead. We decided to have the car towed to a mechanic to determine if anything else was wrong with it. We checked the spare, and it seemed fine so the flat tire was not what caused him to abandon the car if he had abandoned it. The more questions we asked, the more we had.

"We'll have to do a search, you know," Barney said on the hike back to our vehicle.

"I know. I was thinking that, too."

"He could be anywhere."

"Yeah, he could be sprawled at the bottom of a cliff or lying on a beach in Mexico, drinking tequila with a shapely woman on each arm."

"You mean a shapely man on each arm," Barney corrected. He hip-butted me and nearly knocked me down.

"Yeah," I sighed, "I wish I was with him."

CHAPTER 5

At the office, the red message light on the phone was blinking. The first call was from the sheriff, asking us to return his call. The second was from the police detective in Houston who had been in Jimmy Taggert's apartment.

While Barney called the Houston officer, I went into my office to call the sheriff.

"Is Barney going with you to search the Hampton place?" he asked. "I didn't mean to insinuate to either of you that you had to work alone. But I do want you as primary on the Serena Bustamante case and Barney as primary on Jimmy Taggert."

"Yes sir, we understand. We looked for Taggert this morning and found his car and campsite, but nothing else."

"We need to organize a search."

"I agree."

"Looking for Taggert will have to take priority."

"That's what we think." Serena had already been missing thirty years. Jimmy had been gone from his home about thirty days. There was still hope for him, not much for poor Serena.

As I spoke with the sheriff, I studied the photo of the missing woman. She had a flawless complexion, shoulder-length hair the color of dark chocolate, and eyes that matched her hair. Her smile came from her heart and sparkled in her eyes. I could see why Curly had fallen for her but not how he could have brought himself to kill her, if he had.

She wore a crisp red sundress with wide straps, had a gold locket at her throat, and a red ribbon in her shiny hair. The dress showed off her curves and the golden color of her skin.

The sheriff said he would make arrangements for a Department of Public Safety helicopter to help us search the area. They make their equipment and personnel available to rural law enforcement agencies when they're needed. The Texas Rangers are a division of the Texas Department of Public Safety. The sheriff also said he could spare two deputies from Alpine for one day to help with the search.

"I'll call you back," Sheriff Ben said. "If the chopper is available tomorrow, we should go ahead with it so in case Taggert is injured or lost we find him alive. And you'll be free to get on with your investigation of the Serena Bustamante case."

Finding Serena would be just as impossible in a week as it was at that moment, but I kept my mouth shut. I knew if I found out what happened to her, it would be sad, and I didn't need any more reasons to be sad.

I went back to Barney's desk and sat in my usual place in front of him.

He looked up from notes he was making. "Lieutenant Walker says the apartment was so ransacked it was hard to tell if the motive was revenge or if the perps were looking for something in particular. They lifted some good prints and are checking the databases now."

"How did they get in?"

"They picked the lock and damaged the door in the process."

"What about his aunt?"

"He said she was a basket case. They encouraged her to go home and rest. They asked her to leave the apartment like it is for now, and they padlocked it and left crime scene tape over the door."

The fax machine rang once and whirred to life. We watched it as if we expected it to do something besides spit out a fax.

"He's sending a 'Missing Person' notice for us to post," Barney continued. "That's it coming in now. Maybe when we show it around somebody will know something."

It was the same photograph Jimmy's aunt had faxed, but with details added such as "tattoo on the left buttock."

"A tattoo of what?" I wondered. "It doesn't say."

"I'd be afraid to ask," Barney said. "Besides, it's not as if we're going to see his left butt cheek—I hope."

"When do you think we'll hear back from the Houston Police? I guess not until after the database search?"

"Right. What did the sheriff have to say? Let me guess. He wants to search tomorrow."

I nodded. "He's calling the DPS to see if we can coordinate a search with their helicopter. He'll call back in a while."

"What say we grab some lunch and go talk to people?"

"Sounds good." I'm always ready to eat. It seemed like a long time since the breakfast burritos.

* * *

After a quick meal, during which we made a sort of plan, we headed out to see who knew what about the missing Jimmy Taggert. We left a flyer with the cashier at the café when we paid. She said she'd never seen the man before but would check with the other employees. We put a notice in the window.

Our next stop was the Cottonwood General Store, where the clerk said she had seen our missing man about two weeks ago. He had come out of the national park and stopped to buy supplies. The store is about a mile from the park boundary and is the first business you come to after exiting the park.

"Oh, yeah, I remember him," she said. "He asked about Gate Two and about the music scene. He was friendly and talkative. I told him that I didn't know much about Gate Two, but I did tell him where music would be played and how to get to the different places. That was the first and last time I saw him."

While we tacked a poster on the store's bulletin board, another clerk stopped to say she had seen Taggert eating at the

Starlight Theatre, a restaurant and bar in the Terlingua Ghost Town.

"He stayed until closing, listening to music and drinking beer," she said. "I know that because I was there, too. He danced with me, but he didn't try to pick me up like many single tourists do."

Barney gave me a knowing look and arched one eyebrow. I was ready to stomp his foot, but he didn't say anything stomp worthy.

Jimmy was remembered at the Chili Pepper Café since he had eaten there a few times, and at La Kiva, where he'd been twice to hear live music. They recalled seeing him at the Starlight Theatre since he had been there several times, too. Most people mentioned that he was notable because of his straggly hair and bushy beard. He looked like a tough biker-gang type but was gentle and soft-spoken.

When we left the Starlight Theatre, our last stop for the day the bartender, Darcy, followed us out. She had just come on duty and overheard what we were saying to the owner and wait staff.

"I had no reason to say this in front of everyone," she said in a low voice, "but this fellow asked me about gay bars. The way he asked, I assumed he didn't want the whole world to know. He'd been in here twice by then, and I guess he trusted me. We got along well, but it'd be hard not to get along with him. He was a heavy tipper and was friendly and laid back."

"Thank you, Darcy," I said, "Anything else about him?"

"Yes, he seemed lonely. Oh—after I said there were no gay places here, I told him about the gay bars in Ojinaga."

Barney watched her with his mouth open.

"Well? I've been here several years, and I'm a top-notch bartender," Darcy said defensively. "We should know these things as a customer service, you know?"

"Right," agreed Barney. "You amaze me, Darcy. I mean I knew you were a good bartender, but I didn't realize just how good you are, I guess."

"You never asked me any tough questions," she said and winked at him.

"Did he seem interested in Ojinaga?" I asked, seeing that Barney had been thrown off-track by the wink.

"Yes he did. He lightened up and left me a huge tip that night. I didn't get to thank him because he didn't come in again."

Ojinaga, pronounced Oh-hee-náh-gah, is a Mexican town of about twenty thousand people located sixty-seven miles from Terlingua, across the border from Presidio, Texas.

We thanked Darcy for her help and walked to the other end of the porch. The Starlight Theatre is at one end, the Terlingua Trading Company at the other. Between the two businesses is a long, handmade wooden bench used for beer drinking, news passing, gossiping, scenery gazing, and weather watching. It is known as The Porch. If someone tells you to meet them at The Porch, that's where they will be.

Because the Terlingua Ghost Town sits on the side of a mountain, The Porch is high enough to have a brag-worthy vista. Desert expanses, hills of various sizes, and mountains unfold in layers, with the Chisos Mountains providing the backdrop to all of it. The Porch is a popular place to watch the sunset play out its impressive range of colors against equally impressive scenery.

A large crowd had already gathered, primarily locals, and all drinking, telling jokes, and sharing opinions while waiting on sunset. Barney and I grabbed a place on the floor to the front of the bench and sat with our backs against a column.

"You can sit on my lap, baby," invited an already-drunk river guide I barely know. He is six feet tall and has thick blond hair he wears in a short ponytail. His eyes are large and green, and if you didn't know him, he could take your breath. He's called Sage, either after the plant or—it had to be the plant.

"I hope you're not talking to me, pal," said Barney, which defused the situation for the moment.

I shot my partner a grateful look, and everyone laughed except Sage.

"We're wondering," I said, jumping in fast so we didn't have to stick around long, "if any of you have seen this man?" I passed the flyer.

"Is he wanted?"

"He's missing. He came here to camp and to enjoy the sights, but he has never returned home."

39

"Why are you looking for that ugly loser when you could have me any day or night of the week?" wondered Sage. "I'm much better looking."

"According to whom?" asked another local, and everyone laughed.

Barney turned towards the mouthy guide with a steely glare. Sage took the hint and didn't speak again. Instead, he sucked on his beer and gave me dark looks.

One man admitted he had seen Jimmy Taggert when he and some other locals were playing music at La Kiva. He didn't remember anything special about him but had noticed him. There weren't many listeners that night, and Taggert was the sole person who put a tip in their jar.

"I have a joke," declared another local character.

It might have been a good one, or not, but Gilly Tucker saved us from hearing it. He came on the scene noisily, greeted everyone, and accepted a beer from a buddy.

"What's up?" he asked, and looked straight at me.

"Have you seen this man?"

He took the flyer from me and studied it. "I've seen him twice. Once he was at the Starlight when I was eating there. He asked about river trips, and they suggested he talk to me." Gilly is late-forties, a former river guide. A bit of gray in his hair hints of his age, but he still has the sturdy, in-shape body of an athlete. His hazel eyes are bright and full of good humor.

"The other time," Gilly continued, "I saw him in Ojinaga. He was walking with his arm around another man, a flamboyant type of man. I don't care about that, but I remember thinking it was odd. He seemed like such a manly man. But that doesn't have anything to do with being gay, does it?"

Nobody seemed to want to touch that.

"No, it doesn't," I agreed.

* * *

Back at the office the message light was blinking again. Barney returned the sheriff's call and put the telephone on speaker function.

"We're searching tomorrow," Sheriff Ben said. "The DPS will loan us their helicopter and one of their officers. He'll ride down with the pilot. Deputies White and Gomez will meet you at your office at eight o'clock."

We exchanged a raised eyebrow over having to work with Alpine deputies. My partner is fond of saying, "They're about as helpful as a head injury." To them, we're the South County Losers. If any of those guys ever get a clue how great it is to live and work in Terlingua, there will be a deputy uprising.

"Sounds good, Sheriff. Jimmy Taggert was seen in Ojinaga recently with a gay man," Barney blurted. Sometimes his mouth won't stay shut.

"Well now, this makes things interesting," commented the sheriff. "If he isn't found here, when do you plan on going to Ojinaga?"

I know my partner wasn't expecting that. He looked stricken. "We haven't decided yet, sir. I'll get back with you on that."

I started to laugh but stifled it.

"Barney," I said when the sheriff signed off, "it'll be okay. We can wear our uniforms. Nobody will think you're looking for sex with a gay man."

"Oh shit," growled Barney, "It's not that, or it's not just that. It's dangerous. I mean at night in those places."

"Get a grip. Who said we had to go at night? It's not as if this is an undercover sting. And we don't need to know about anyone's secret life or anything."

"Hell no, we don't."

"Stop biting your nails. I know some people in Ojinaga."

"Oh, that makes me feel so much better."

"I can go alone."

"No. I'll go with you. I'm not a coward."

"Maybe Taggert didn't take his car because he made a friend who took him to Ojinaga and that's who Gilly saw him with," I said with exaggerated enthusiasm.

"That could be, but wouldn't a flamboyant man be noticed in Terlingua?"

* * *

Lieutenant Walker from Houston called to tell us one set of prints they lifted belonged to a small-time criminal named David 'Little Davie' Davison. He had a criminal record including burglary, assault, drugs, and running a prostitution ring.

"Busy little guy," commented the lieutenant dryly. "We're looking for him now. He hasn't been out of prison six months, and I doubt he'll want to go back so soon. If we can find him, he'll talk."

Barney thanked him and told him we were searching tomorrow and would keep him informed. The lieutenant promised to do the same.

Barney hung up and sat staring at me.

"What?" I asked.

"Don't get mad, but about this gay thing."

"What about it?"

"Well I, uh, was wondering how you meet gay people in a foreign country without being gay."

"You don't have to be gay to know someone gay."

"For God's sake, I know that, Ricos."

"I met some lesbians in Ojinaga through a lesbian cousin of my dad's when I was a teenager. She and I have remained friends through the years. I've met some of the gay crowd through her. You'd be amazed."

"Undoubtedly."

"That's how I plan to find the flamboyant man. I know an attorney, Franco Orozco, who'll help us. He has a huge circle of gay friends and clients, males and females. He's an equal opportunity lawyer."

Barney laughed. "You're an education, Ricos."

"Stick with me and you'll learn a few things."

"Yeah, but will it be anything useful?"

"Who knows, but I guarantee it will be interesting," was my retort.

CHAPTER 6

Most of the time, when I go somewhere out of uniform, I am 'one of the gang' and I get hugged. Often I get hugs in spite of being in uniform. In Terlingua, we greet each other like we mean it. Because I was born and raised here, everyone knows me or thinks they do. So when I pushed through the door of the grocery store and heard, "Well, well, well. Lookie here at this!" my heart sank. I knew the voice, the scornful tone, and most of his whiny complaints.

It was would-be redneck Wynne Raymore. I say 'would-be' because I think he is educated and hides it. He is deeply bitter, granted, but I don't buy the redneck act.

He stumbled all over himself with fake excitement. "It's our *girl* deputy!"

Since backing down is not in my nature, I didn't, although later I wished I had. The nice-enough-looking, late-thirties ne'er-do-well aims to do as little as possible with his life, but he does enjoy grandstanding.

"Our girl deputy in a *dress*," he continued overly loudly.

Kill 'em with kindness, my mom says, so I tried that. "Good evening, Wynne."

"Well heck, where's your uniform, girlie-girl?" He sounded like an imbecile, but an innocent, good-humored one. Some of his buddies laughed, but Wynne looked me up and down in a way I didn't like. "Guess you're just a plain ol' girl now, huh?"

"I guess so, Wynne."

"I like this look on you. What's the occasion?"

I ignored him and started putting what I wanted in a shopping basket, but he came after me. "I heard you won the Sheriff's Office marksmanship contest again this year."

"Yup, I did."

"I guess we should call you Little Miss Annie Oakley, huh?"

"Not really, Wynne."

"That would make you LMAO."

"Good one."

"Well, it does suit your so-called career choice, Margarita."

"You know what she used to say about men, don't you?"

He looked confused. "Who?"

"Annie Oakley."

"No, guess I don't."

"She said, 'I ain't afraid to love a man. I ain't afraid to shoot him, either.' I feel pretty much the same way right now."

"Is that supposed to make me laugh?"

I shrugged and moved on. If I got angry, it would encourage him. If I refused to get angry, that would also encourage him. There was no way to win with Wynne.

He followed and kept jabbing at me. "You wouldna won if I'd been there."

"You've made that claim before, but you weren't there."

"Well, we should have a shootin' contest sometime, you and me, pistols. We could have a duel, like the real old west, you know?"

"Sure. Catch me later, Wild Bill."

I gathered the items I needed and tried to ignore him. If Wynne and I had a duel, he would die. Annoying as he was, I didn't want to be the one to kill him.

"Girls shouldn't be in law enforcement anyhow," he bleated from one aisle over. That was an old rant, too.

"They don't allow girls to do it," I explained with false patience. "You have to be grown up."

"You know what I mean. *Women* shouldn't be allowed to do it."

"Women can do anything men can do."

That brought him around the corner into my aisle. "That's feminazi bullshit!"

"It's a fact, Rush Limbaugh. Now back off."

Wynne was red with anger. "You waste the taxpayers' money pretending like you know what you're doing, and drivin' around like you own the damn county."

"I'm sorry you feel that way."

"You don't like white men much, do ya?"

"What? I was married to one. My mother is a 'white' woman." I stopped speaking because what was the point? Wynne is a man you can't confuse with facts. Again, I moved away from him.

He followed. "Whatcha gonna do now?"

"Pay for these groceries."

"You know what I mean—you gonna party? I'll go with you."

"The sad thing about you, Wynne, is that you're a good-looking man. Sure, you could use a bath and a haircut, and a change of clothes, but you'd clean up nice."

He tugged at the filthy, faded, red-white-blue "Love it or Leave it" bandana tied hippie-style around his scruffy head. "What are you gettin' at?"

"You rag on other people about what they're doing, but all you do is hang out and drink beer all day and see how loud you can belch. You're a tool, Wynne."

"A tool? You mean like a pile driver?"

"I mean an inanimate object without feelings or thinking capacity."

Wynne stroked his chin in contemplation. "I'm thinkin' what you need is some serious time with my tool."

"That's enough Wynne. Don't talk to me anymore."

"Or?"

"Or you might regret messing with me."

He made a face. "Ooh—I'm so scared."

"You ought to be."

Wynne sneered. "You're way smaller than me."

That was true, and he was built to withstand a hurricane. Still.

"Size isn't everything," I said. "Please don't make me prove it."

Wynne was silent for a few minutes. His buddies had abandoned him, and I thought without an audience he might leave me alone, but I should have known better. I turned, and he was so close I almost bumped into him.

"Get away from me!"

"Don't be like that." His voice had turned soft and sweet, and he put his hand on my arm.

I jerked away. "What is it you really want?"

"What I *really* want is to put my hand up your skirt." Fire flashed in his brown eyes, but not the sexy kind.

"You should leave her alone," warned Margie, the store's clerk on duty. Better late than never, I guess.

"Mind your own business, Margie," Wynne shot back.

"Take your problems out of this store!"

Wynne moved closer.

"Are you sure you want your ass kicked by a woman wearing sexy high heels?" some other customer asked.

"Listen Wynne," I said. "It's okay not to like me. I don't like you, either. Can't you just ignore me?"

"Naw, I'm not gonna."

"So again I ask, what is eating you?"

"That stupid sheriff still won't give me a job."

Ah-hah.

"Did you go to the law enforcement academy since the last time we spoke?"

"I shouldn't have to. I was in the military, which you never were."

"Unless you were an M.P., being in the military doesn't exempt you from the academy. You need to have hands-on police experience or else school. I know the sheriff has explained that a half-dozen times."

"Would it count as hands-on police experience if I put my hands all over you?"

I tried to walk away, but he started touching me and things got serious. First he grabbed my arm to turn me around, and not gently. It hurt.

"Wynne, I know self-defense," I warned, "and I work out."

When he did it again, I performed a basic self-defense move, which was to kick him hard in the knee. He yowled and lunged at me like an injured bear, so I shoved my palm as hard as I could against his nose. His scream seemed to come more from fury than pain, but his hands went to his face and blood sprayed over both of us.

"I warned him," I said to the small crowd that had gathered.

With an apology to the clerk, I abandoned the items at the counter and hurried outside. There, the air was crisp and clean, and Wynne wasn't breathing it. Part of me wanted to march back in and kick his ass for real. My clothes were bloodied, and my heart pounded in my ears. Still fuming, I headed home to dress again for my dinner date with Barney and his wife, Julia. Our plan was to meet at the Ocotillo Restaurant in Lajitas, seventeen miles away.

* * *

When I arrived in the resort town a short time later, I didn't stop. I flew past it to a rock wall that overlooks the Rio Grande, got out of my car, and rested a while to calm myself. The extra-irritating thing was that as long as Kevin had been alive, I never got overt harassment from the Stone Age thinkers. Behind my back, sure, but not in my face, and nobody touched me.

Kevin was not a trouble-maker, nor was he a huge man, or a fierce one, but his presence had protected me like an invisible shield, irritating as that was. He was known as a tough bull rider, so maybe that was it. Whatever it was, he was gone, and I was fair game, or so the Flintstones thought.

The few lights from Lajitas were obscured by a small clay hill so the stars could not be ignored. The plaintive cry of a night bird broke the silence, and then all was quiet again except for the soft whisper of the river.

"Wynne Raymore is an ass," I alerted the night sky.

No comment from above, but watching the glittering canopy gave me perspective. In any community, there are bound to be a few Wynnes. What he thought was of no more importance to me than my problems were to the stars. I took some deep breaths of the fragrant evening and went to meet Barney and Julia.

The Ocotillo sits on a bluff above the Rio Grande. It's an attractive place, but in the daylight hours it can't compete with the river, the birds-eye view of Mexico, or the mountains that go on and on, farther than the human eye can see.

Barney and Julia were seated at the bar. He greeted me this way: "Man, you look terrific. What have you done, Ricos?"

"I'm innocent."

"Like hell."

"I want a lawyer!"

I had my heart set on a potent Ocotillo Bloody Mary, but my mouth ordered a Coke with lime. Barney had beer, his drink of choice in all situations. Julia was nursing their baby, so she joined me on the nothing-stronger-than-a-soda team.

I greeted Julia and then addressed Barney. "What is it you think I've done?"

"Did you really break Wynne Raymore's nose?"

"I doubt if it's broken."

"Oh, it's broken."

"News sure travels fast."

"You better know it, Pard."

The hostess seated us at a table near a window that looked out onto the Rio Grande and beyond that, to Mexico. Since it was dark, the only view was a lighted agave and a few lovely desert willows.

"The medics were called," Barney continued, "but your mother will have to set the nose. They were going to take him to her clinic when the dispatcher called me." My mom is the local doctor.

When I didn't say anything, he added, "The sheriff is concerned."

"Concerned like he wants to give me the boot, or concerned as 'did the big, mean man touch his female deputy inappropriately?'"

"Is that what happened?"

"Yes and verbal abuse. He begged for it, Barney."

"Well, we are talking Wynne."

Our waiter came up and introduced himself as Billy. I had noticed him bending over a table when I walked in. Besides that asset, he was tall and slender, with white-blond hair cut short and spiky, and bright blue eyes with dark lashes. I could almost hear women's hearts breaking in his wake. Aye Dios, for a second there I thought I heard mine hit the floor.

"Aren't you new here?" Barney asked the hunk.

"I started yesterday, so bear with me, okay? I see you have drinks already."

"We went to the bar when we came in," Barney said. "He fixed us up."

Billy wore dark blue tux pants that were a tight fit and had a satiny black stripe down the side, and a long-sleeved shirt of a lighter shade of blue with a bow tie and vest that matched the pants. The other waiters were dressed identically, so it wasn't the clothes.

"Can I get you an appetizer, or are you ready to order?"

"I think we'll wait a few minutes," said Barney.

He left with a promise to return, and my partner went back to bludgeoning me for details.

"So you were saying Wynne touched you inappropriately."

"Do we have to talk about it? Can't you just take my word that he deserved a swift kick in the crotch?"

"My God, Ricos, did you kick him there, too?"

"No, but he deserved it is what I'm saying. I kicked him in the knee, and when he kept on grabbing me, I shoved the heel of my hand against his nose, like this." I showed him using my face because there was no way he'd let me demonstrate on his.

"The sheriff is going to call you."

"Fine. He'll back me up when he hears the whole story."

"What is the whole story?"

"Wynne started on me the first second I was there, exclaiming the arrival of the 'girl deputy.' Then he wouldn't let up."

"But you are a girl deputy."

"Don't you start," warned Julia. We smiled at each other in feminine solidarity.

"I'm a grown woman. I don't mind being a girl deputy, but when it's said in a demeaning way, it gets to me."

"I would've smacked him, too, Margarita," Julia said.

"He said he wanted to put his hand up my skirt and other uncalled-for things. He wants us to have a duel as if he would live through that."

Barney laughed. "No kidding."

"I should be able to wear a skirt like anybody else."

"Definitely," agreed Julia.

"Maybe he'll leave me alone now."

"Well, if he has half a brain he will," Barney said. "But again, it's Wynne."

"I'm sorry, Julia," I said. "This dinner isn't much fun so far. Why don't you tell us about your day?"

After some encouragement, she told us about it with such humor that her day seemed more interesting than ours.

Julia is a small Latina with bright brown eyes and dark shoulder-length hair. She and Barney would seem mismatched, at least in size, but they adore each other. He watched her, enthralled. When she saw the look in his eyes, she smiled an I-love-you smile at him and stopped talking.

"Go on, honey," he encouraged.

"Nurse the baby, burp the baby, change the baby, nurse the baby, and repeat. Keep the toddler from killing herself. No, no, don't put the fork in the electrical outlet. Don't bite the doggie's tail. It's never-ending. I guess my life seems dull next to what you guys are doing."

"Nothing about you is dull," Barney assured her with a sweetness I rarely saw in him. He turned to me. "Right, Ricos?"

"Right, I was thinking your day sounds more challenging than ours."

"Would you like to have children, Margarita?" she asked.

"I can't say. I'd like to have a husband first."

"You'll never have one if you don't start going out," my partner reminded me.

"She'll go out when she's ready, Barney," said his wife softly.

"What about that waiter, Ricos? I see your eyes following him around."

"He's cute." I couldn't believe I was noticing men. I had barely realized they existed for eighteen months.

"Would you go out with him?"

"Maybe."

"Is that anything like a yes?"

"It's not a 'no.' Now leave me alone."

Soon Billy was back, offering to refill our drinks, which he did with flair.

"I can tell you've done this before," I said.

"Done what before?"

"Served drinks, worked as a waiter? Does any of that seem familiar?"

He laughed. "You got me. Yes, I'm a perpetual waiter. I try to do other things, but I keep coming back to this. Maybe it's an addiction, like strong drink or loose women." He thought a moment. "Nah," shaking his head, "it's nothing that exciting. I deceive myself. Another habit we won't discuss."

"Do you recommend anything in particular tonight?" Barney asked.

He didn't, but he and Barney got into a hilarious discussion about steak being the choice of 'real men' until Julia and I wished we could slap them. Billy was more than eye candy; he had personality and wasn't afraid to use it.

I perused the menu, looking for something new to try. Billy watched me, then said with a French accent, "Ahhh, zee young lady, she does not read. Pleeze, I help zee bee-u-tee-ful mademoiselle with zee reading." He wiggled his eyebrows at me.

"She's single," Barney said.

I kicked him hard under the table.

I ordered the vegetable pasta dish. Barney ordered the Jack Daniels steak rare, his favorite thing on the menu. It is also the largest. Julia ordered a Caesar's salad with the comment that she was trying to get back to her pre-baby size.

I thought Barney would make a wisecrack, but he surprised me. "You're the most beautiful woman I ever saw, Julia," he said and took her hand.

We told Julia about the Jimmy Taggert case and the smooth way Darcy had headed him to Ojinaga after he asked about gay bars. Billy walked up to our table as I mentioned looking for Taggert in gay bars.

"Excuse me, miss." He set a plate down at my place. "I couldn't help but hear you say I might be a sex worker at a gay bar."

"Oh, no, I didn't," I started to protest, but he stopped me.

"I'm not offended. I hear it all the time because of my overwhelming sexiness, but I'm not a sex worker." Billy eyed Barney lecherously. "But for you, Baby, I could be anything." With that, he strutted off.

"Huh," said Barney.

Billy came back with hot rolls. "Was that hussy bothering you?" he asked in a different persona. "I can have him thrown outta here."

"It's okay," I said, "we liked him."

"Is that so? Well, I happen to know where he lives."

A more serious Billy checked back to be sure everything was okay. The food was delicious, and we said so. He went off to wait on other people saying, with a dismissive wave of his hand, "Oh, I see I have others to annoy this evening."

Later, when he came to see if we wanted dessert, he asked if he could sit down a moment. We welcomed him to join us.

He sat in the empty chair next to me. "You know my name, but I don't yours," he said and seemed shy for the first time.

"I'm Barney George, and this is Julia, my wife," Barney said. He shook Billy's hand. "This is Margarita Ricos."

Julia shook Billy's hand, but when I reached to shake he took my hand in both of his and kissed it tenderly. "I'm charmed. No, I'm captivated." He studied me with a serious expression. "I bet people ask if you were named after the drink."

"You wouldn't believe how many."

"And that offends you?"

"It gets old. What kind of idiots would name their daughter after a drink?"

"Drunks might I suppose, but I see your point. So what do you do, Margarita Not-Named-For the-Drink?"

"You mean for a living?" Small talk was not my strong point.

"Yes, that's what I mean. You know I'm a waiter, albeit not a good one. I want to know what you are besides lovely."

"I'm a deputy sheriff."

Billy's eyes widened. "Do tell."

"I'm a deputy too," said Barney.

"I'm raising children," said Julia. "It has its moments."

"Well," Billy said, awe-struck. "What we have here are two super-heroes and a mama superhero raising more of them."

"We're just regular people," laughed Julia.

Billy turned to me. "You're no regular person but are you really a deputy sheriff?"

I nodded.

"Here?"

I nodded again.

He gave me a dreamy look. "You could write me tickets all day long. Seriously."

The bartender yelled, "Billy!" and he jumped up. "I'm not sup-posed to be sitting with you, I know. I hope you don't think I'm a complete loser. Come back again and I'll wait on you properly."

"Oh—don't do that," I blurted.

"Okay then. Come back and I'll ignore you. When I'm not too stuck up to wait on you, I'll spill food all over you, and bring your meal late from the kitchen so it gets cold. Okay?"

"Okay," we agreed.

He shook his head and walked away mumbling.

After a while, he was back with the check. "I hope to see you again soon. I'm new here, and it's hard to meet fun people."

"How long have you lived here?" I asked.

"Oh, a few months, more or less. I've been looking around, getting to know the place. I started going broke, so I had to get a job."

My cell phone rang. I had meant to turn it off. Busted! It was Sheriff Ben.

"I have to take this," I said. "I'll step outside." I turned away from them and answered the call. "Hello, Sheriff."

"Was breaking his nose necessary?" He lectures us about keeping our cool and not hurting the people we serve, even when they deserve it and even if we're not in uniform. We respect that, but our sheriff's rules don't cover every situation.

"I didn't mean to break his nose, but in uniform or out of it, nobody can grab and touch me like he did. I reacted fast because he wouldn't keep his hands off me. I warned him several times, Sheriff."

"I know. I already spoke with the clerk, and she filled me in. I want to hear your side before I return Wynne's call."

I told him what had happened from my point of view. He was already familiar with Wynne's repetitive rant that women shouldn't be allowed in law enforcement and that he should have my job instead of me. The sheriff didn't like that idea any more than I did. His only scolding was for leaving the scene.

"I'm sorry, Sheriff, but I got out of there so things wouldn't get worse."

"Wynne plans to press charges, but my advice to him will be not to press his luck. The next time he treats you so disrespectfully, I'm coming down there and will bring him up here. Time spent with me will cool him down."

"Thank you, Sheriff."

"Carry on."

My mother called the second I flipped my phone shut. She has special radar or something. "What is going on with you?" she demanded to know. "Are you all right?"

"I'm fine."

"Wynne Raymore has a swollen, bruised knee. He has to use crutches. And you broke his nose. I assume you wouldn't have hurt him without good reason."

"I was defending myself. He kept touching me and saying inappropriate things. I can't talk right now, Mom. I'm eating dinner with Barney and Julia."

"You're not hurt?"

"No, Mom."

"Come see me tomorrow."

I agreed to do that because that's how it is with my mom. Agree, or stay on the phone the rest of your life.

"Well?" asked Barney when I returned to the table.

"The sheriff already knows Wynne, so everything's okay."

My partner was incredulous. "I couldn't have gotten away with breaking somebody's nose."

"Maybe not, but Wynne would never pick on you. Nobody in their right mind is going to harass a big ol' lug like you."

"When I see him, I'm gonna tell him to stop messin' with you or he'll have me to deal with."

"Don't do that. It's a sweet thought, but it'll make things worse. I think I made my point and—" Billy was back, so my attention was diverted instantly.

"So," Billy said, "we waited on you."

"You did?"

"I was saying I haven't been in any trouble with the law yet."

"Are you a troublemaker?"

"Not as a general rule, but I could make an exception in your case." Then he made a sad face. "I don't have a car, though."

"I can't write you a ticket if you don't have a car," I pointed out.

"We'll think of something," Billy consoled, patting me on the shoulder.

"How'd you get here if you don't have a car?" Barney asked.

"Well, I had a car, but it broke down near El Paso and would've cost more to fix than it was worth. So I sold it for junk and took the bus to Alpine and hitch-hiked down here from there."

"Do you have to work this weekend?" I asked, surprising myself and everyone else. I ignored the incredulous looks coming from Barney.

"No, I only work Tuesdays, Wednesdays and Thursdays right now. Why do you ask?"

"I plan to attend a friend's daughter's quinceañera here in Lajitas. Would you like to go with me? There'll be locals there. It's a good way to meet people."

"I already met you," he said softly, flirting with his amazing eyes. "What's a quince—whatever you said?"

"It's a traditional Mexican fifteenth birthday party for girls."

"Yes, I'd love to go. Thank you for inviting me." He was so pleased I felt embarrassed.

"I'll pick you up about six for the dinner. There's a dance after that. Do you like to dance, Billy?"

"I love to dance."

"Good."

"Will I need a gift?"

"I'll bring one. You don't know the girl and won't be expected to take her anything."

"I live in employee housing, number fifteen," Billy said. "I can hardly wait to go anywhere with you, Margarita." His sincerity made me blush hot.

That is how I came to meet Billy Warren, a man full of surprises.

CHAPTER 7

I jumped out of bed when the alarm rang, eager to get on with the day. Maybe we would find Jimmy Taggert. That seemed a lot more probable than finding Serena. If a body hadn't turned up in thirty years, what were the chances I would happen to run across it now?

I was seated at the kitchen table eating a bagel with butter and drinking a glass of apple-cherry juice, when Barney pounded once on the front door and came in yelling my name.

"I'm in the kitchen."

"Good morning, sunshine," he practically sang. "What's for breakfast?"

"Bagels and juice, want some?"

"Nah, I ate."

"Have a seat. What brings you here so early?"

He pulled out a chair and sat next to me. "Listen, I don't need a broken nose or anything, but I think your new boyfriend is gay."

"I don't have a boyfriend, Barney."

"I'm talking about Billy Warren, you know damn well."

"I invited him to a quinceañera, not to sleep with me." To be honest, I thought Billy could be gay, but I was willing to do the research.

"Hey, it's none of my business," my partner conceded.

"That's right. So why are you here?"

"I am afraid you'll get hurt."

"So you're making up a lame story?"

"I think he is that's all. He's funny and has that stylish haircut and smells nice. He moves like a ballet dancer. That has 'gay' written all over it."

"Isn't that a gross generalization?"

"Maybe, but I still say he is. Want to bet me?"

I thought about it while I munched a banana. "What's the bet?"

"I say he plays for the other team, and if I'm right, you cover weekends for a month. You're betting he's straight, and if you're right, I'll cover them."

"You're on."

We shook on it.

"You're slipping," he claimed. Then he grabbed a banana and shook it at me. "He's going to disappoint you."

"All you think about is what you're going to eat next and sex."

"True, my pard, true, but you've got it out of order."

* * *

I pulled up to the office at the same time as Barney. We heard the unmistakable whomp-whomp-whomp of big blades and hurried into the building to avoid the dust-and-dirt storm as the helicopter landed.

I listened to a brief message from Billy on the answering machine: "Margarita? I hope you're a deputy and not pulling my leg. I didn't ask you how I'm supposed to dress so could you call me at work tonight and leave a message?"

"That man is definitely gay," Barney asserted from my office doorway.

"Shut up. He isn't."

"Straight men never ask a woman how to dress."

"Only bubbas like you don't care about their clothes."

"Are you kidding? I'm a trendsetter when I dress up."

"Yeah, right," I said with as much sarcasm as I can manage in the morning.

"How would you know?"

I let the matter drop in the interest of more important things to do.

Once the copter was idle, we went out and introduced ourselves to the two DPS officers, Chet Martin and Joaquin Amarillo. The pilot, Captain Martin, suggested that one of us ride with him for a first glimpse from above so he could get a feel for the size of the search area.

"What about you?" he asked, and looked right at me.

"You know it!"

"Sure," groused Barney, "go ahead and pick the woman."

Sergeant Martin grinned at him. "You'll have your turn."

"You can't go," I said to my partner from the passenger seat. "You'll break it."

"Drop her off somewhere," Barney instructed Chet, who laughed.

I strapped myself in and put on the earphones Chet handed me.

"It'll be noisy," he advised, "but we'll be able to communicate through these. They have a special microphone attachment."

I nodded to indicate I understood.

"We're gone," said Chet, and slowly we rose above the parking lot. I couldn't stop grinning. For a moment, we were at the same height as Cactus Hill then over it and headed towards Indian Head. Everything glittered in the early morning light.

"Do you like our scenery, Sergeant Martin?"

He smiled. "Please call me Chet. Your scenery is breathtaking.""

We passed over the thick stands of ocotillo on the mesa I named for them and before long we were over the Honda and then the campsite. Chet began making slow circles, moving out more each time until we were getting farther and farther away from the collapsed tent.

I peered through binoculars that featured self-adjusting focus, but it took a while to get the hang of it because of the constant movement. At first it made me feel cross-eyed and nauseated.

We were not far off the ground and were causing a dust storm below. When we reached mountains or any other obstruction, Chet skillfully maneuvered us higher. I continued to search with the binoculars, but saw nothing moving except desert plants being knocked around by the chopper-induced windstorm.

At the base of a sharp incline, I spotted something red. We passed over it several times but couldn't get close enough to determine if it was a body. The steep wall of rock presented a danger for the rotating blades. Chet pulled back and landed about thirty yards away on a flat spot.

When I started to jump down, he touched my arm. "Keep your head low. Watch those blades."

I nodded. "Okay, be right back." I ducked and ran in a semi-crouch.

The red was an old, torn quilted jacket. It could have been left by anyone at any time and by itself meant nothing. I shook it vigorously to remove sand and any critters it might harbor and then took it as litter to discard.

"If I came here with some time off," said Chet, "would you take me hiking?"

"Sure."

Then he noticed my ring. "Are you married, Margarita?"

"No. I was. I'm a widow."

"Oh, I'm sorry. You're so young."

"Are you married, Chet?"

"No. I've never been married. Women don't like men who fly all over and are never home." He frowned, but it turned into a smile. "I'd like to look at this scenery up close. I've seen most of Texas from the air, but I never get to see much from the ground."

"Have you ever flown over the Chisos Mountains?"

"Yes, we made it a point to come that way this morning. They're amazing, so stark and rugged, and yet they have forests. This place has to be the best-kept secret in Texas."

"Haven't you been here before?"

"No, there's another pilot, Ernie Sanchez. He has more seniority and bumps me if Big Bend is the destination. This time we drew straws, and I won."

We took off and looked around a few minutes more before heading back.

"It's tempting to keep flying," I hinted, even though Chet wore the silver star of the Texas Rangers and I didn't think he would agree to play hooky.

"Yes, it's tempting," he admitted, but he returned us to the office.

Our team had gathered and was studying a map of the area, making red marks around the perimeter of a circle. They informed us the circle represented a two-mile radius from the location of the campsite. They marked known caves large enough to conceal a man, of which there are few, and cliffs from which a man could fall, of which there are many.

We were two deputies from Alpine, two DPS officers, one volunteer from Terlingua Fire & Emergency Medical Services, a national park ranger, Barney, and me. The medic wore a white vest with a red cross over his jacket so he could be spotted by the air crew and brought to the scene if an injured Jimmy Taggert was found alive. An extensive first aid kit was loaded into the helicopter and secured behind the seats.

The plan was to start from the campsite and each searcher hike an approximate two-mile route so that we each formed one of six spokes on a wheel. Chet and Barney would search from the air. All of us had radios so we could communicate.

The six hikers crowded into my Explorer, and I drove us to the campsite while we talked about our destinations. One route ended at the national park boundary, one at the entrance gate on the highway, another to the right and behind Taggert's former camp, one to the left and behind it, one on Wild Horse Mountain, and one at the base of the Christmas Mountains. I had been assigned the Christmas Mountains route. The terrain is rough but well-known to me from hiking and ATV-riding.

We met Chet and Barney at the abandoned tent.

"Deputy George and I will check in from time to time to see how you're doing," Chet said while my partner wordlessly gloated. "We'll fly out past the search area, but if you need us, use your radio."

I momentarily envied the trip Barney would make in the air.

As I headed towards my destination, I watched for tracks, for debris that might tell a story, or for any other sign of a human, dead or alive. Along my route, there was one known cave large enough to hold a man, but many places from which to fall.

I tried to pace myself so that I kept moving but still had time to see what I was looking at. It was aggravating to have made that stupid bet with Barney. Normally I don't wager with him unless I'm sure, but in some unfathomable allegiance to a man I barely knew, I was willing to gamble with my weekends.

More than anything, I wondered about Jimmy Taggert and what had happened to him. His demise had probably been at the hands of criminals.

I stopped to pick a shredded plastic grocery bag from cactus thorns and added it to the other litter I had collected. For a while, I worked my way around boulders and thick clumps of prickly pear cactus below a steep ridge. The going was hard, but it was necessary to get close in order to see a body if there was one.

After a while, I sat on a boulder to drink water and remove the heavy jacket. I jumped at the squawk of my radio.

"Chopper to Deputy Ricos," said Barney.

"Come in Chopper."

"Whatcha got, Ricos?"

"Nada."

When I began walking again, my thoughts turned to Serena. I was half-looking for her, too. Yet for all I knew her body had been hauled away from the area. And there was still the possibility she could have run away, but why? More likely her lover had panicked and killed her because of the predicament he was in. That was the most obvious answer, but since it had never been proven, perhaps it wasn't provable because it didn't happen that way.

A lone coyote ran across the path and startled me from my rambling thoughts. We stared at each other a second and he bolted. I was filled with longing to follow, to run wild and free across the desert, listening only to my heart.

* * *

First to radio for a ride back to the camp was the medic, who ended up at the entrance to Gate Two. He had the most direct route to follow with the least stops to make. He was assigned that route to keep him accessible, should anything arise that required his skill. I heard Barney tell him they'd pick him up in five minutes or less.

After thirty more minutes, one of the Alpine deputies called in to say he had reached his destination at a fence and posted private property. Chet and Barney would bring him back to base. After that, the other DPS officer called in, ready to come back, too.

Ahead, close now, were the Christmas Mountains. My route had been up and down, over boulders and down into washes. I had many cliff-bottoms to check and hills to climb. My muscles had begun to complain.

I saw something to my right that looked like an arm bone sticking out of a jumble of boulders. I did not want to find a dead body. *Please let it be something else.*

"You have to look," I said, and my voice echoed, sounding hollow and eerie.

I forced my thudding heart and trembling legs over to the white bone and stared down at a whole bunch of bones. At first I was unsure what I was seeing and thought it was Serena. It couldn't be Jimmy Taggert. Was there another missing person? When I got my mind to calm down, I realized it was the carcass of a mountain lion, dried out and bleached white by time in the sun. I let out a long, relieved breath.

After twenty more minutes of investigating along the base of the mountains, I radioed Chet and Barney to come for me.

* * *

Our team met at a long table in the Chili Pepper Café for a late lunch. Sheriff Ben was waiting when we arrived. We each told our story, but not one of us had seen anything useful. I found a dead lion and someone else thought they spotted a live one. Several of us saw coyotes and hawks. Two reported seeing fox. One saw a golden eagle and another, a peregrine falcon. It had been a field day for wildlife viewing but nothing else.

"Well," said the sheriff, "we've done what we can as far as the air and ground search go. Our trail is at least two weeks old, which puts us at a disadvantage. Deputies George and Ricos have a few leads to follow." He smiled at us. "We'll see what they turn up."

"Any word from the Houston P.D.?" asked Barney. Lt. Walker had instructions to call the sheriff in our absence.

"Yes, they picked up Little Davie Davison. He admitted that he was hired by two guys to toss the apartment. It's his belief they were trying to intimidate Mr. Taggert. Davison was paid to make it appear that he was looking for something."

"So then Taggert's in trouble with some small-time criminals," I said.

"Maybe not so small-time, but definitely criminals," said the sheriff. "They may have found him, or he may have run from them. If he's running, he won't be back."

After we had eaten, everyone left but Barney, Sheriff Ben, and me.

"What's your plan now?" asked the sheriff.

Barney looked glum. "Ojinaga here we come."

I gave the sheriff an abbreviated version of our plan, and he nodded. "Sounds like you know what you're doing. I'll to leave it up to the two of you. Call me if I can help." With that, the sheriff paid the bill and left.

"When are we going to the Hampton land?" Barney asked.

"Let's put the Jimmy Taggert case to rest first."

"Ojinaga tomorrow, then?"

"Yes, but first, let's visit with Darcy. She seems to know a lot about the gay scene of Ojinaga."

* * *

Darcy arrived at the Starlight Theatre at the same time we did. They were not yet open for customers.

Barney took a stool at the bar. "Darcy, could we talk while you set up?"

"Sure." She winked at him.

Barney turned red and said nothing more.

"You were very helpful yesterday," I began. "We hope you can tell us more about the gay bars in Ojinaga."

Darcy stood with her hands on her slim hips. "You want me to give up my trade secrets, huh?"

"Taggert was seen in Ojinaga with a 'flamboyant' man. We need to find him, or anyone who knows where Taggert went. If we can determine that his trail leads away from Terlingua, we can put this case to bed."

"Of course I'll help you. The bar I like is El Tecolote Nocturno." The Night Owl. "It's behind a motel of the same name, and not everybody knows about it. It's fun, and straight people are welcome there, too."

"I know where that is," I said, "but I've never been in it."

"Since Jimmy was so friendly, I sent him to see a friend named Rudy Ramón. Rudy speaks some English, and I trusted him to help Jimmy find his way around if you know what I mean."

"Do you mean find him a date?"

"Yes—or a prostitute."

Barney's head swiveled around like an owl's, but he said nothing.

"You know there are male prostitutes, right?" Darcy addressed Barney, but he had returned to his intense study of the bottles behind the bar.

She winked at me and continued. "Rudy was a well-known drag queen in Chihuahua, and he might have worked as a pro at one time, but he met a man from Ojinaga that swept him off his feet."

"Wait a minute," I said. "That story sounds familiar. Is his love an attorney?"

"I think so, but I'm not acquainted with him."

"Does Rudy look like a young version of Brad Pitt?"

"Yes, somewhat, you know him?"

"No, but I know the attorney who lives with him. He's been a friend of mine for years. He told me that he'd met somebody who changed his life for the better."

I expected a snide comment from Barney, but he was still memorizing the order of the liquor bottles, or whatever he was doing.

"Can I contact Rudy by phone?" I asked.

"He has a cell phone, but the number has changed, and I don't have it. I can tell you how to get to his house. If he's not there, the maid will know where he is."

She gave me the address and detailed directions.

"Thank you for your help."

"Thanks, Darcy," Barney managed to say.

"You come back sometime when you're not on duty, Big Boy," she said in a Mae West voice.

Barney flushed red and nearly ran me over in his rush to the door.

CHAPTER 8

At home, I showered and sat on the porch to watch my mountain guard my desert. Hiking and climbing had made me sore, but a hot shower and cold beer always work wonders. That was then. Instead of beer, I drank blueberry tea while contemplating the various humps and ridges on Cimarron. It has sheer drop-offs and deep canyons that appear one way one moment and different the next. It's sorcery, courtesy of the ever-moving sun and clouds.

A couple of red-tailed hawks flew into my line of sight. One performed extreme acrobatics while the other played the straight hawk. Perhaps she had already feasted and was bored with screeching and diving. Songbirds are colorful, animated, and I love to hear them sing, but a hawk—a hawk makes me want to soar. They have a majesty about them that sets them apart from other flying creatures.

My thoughts went from what Darcy told us to my Ojinaga attorney friend, Franco, and then by a long and circuitous route, to my new friend, Billy. Wondering about him gave me the idea to go to the Ocotillo and drink something so I could spy on him. Billy was a man built for watching.

So it wasn't the greatest idea, but I was bored sitting at home by myself and felt too tired and lazy to do something more productive. And the hawks had moved on.

* * *

I sat on a stool at the bar and watched the bartender, Nita, mix and serve drinks. This was playing with fire, and I knew it. There sat all that liquor, practically within grabbing distance, and I ordered a Coke and lime. There were four other people at the opposite end of the bar, all drinking liquor or something containing it.

Nita served my sad excuse for a drink. "So how about that deputy you work with?" she asked. "What's the story on him? I suppose he's married?"

"He's married."

She seemed disappointed. "Happily?"

"Yes, I would say so—definitely."

She contemplated that with a frown then brightened. "I bet he's really hung."

She walked off while I choked on a wayward swallow of soda.

Then she came back and leaned on the bar. "You haven't ever seen him, you know," she whispered, "naked?"

I nearly spit soda all over the bar. "No. I only work with him."

"You can tell me. I'll never say you did, I swear."

"No, I haven't seen him naked, Nita."

She waved her hand dismissively. "You wouldn't tell me anyway." She left to fill a waitress's order but returned in moments. "You'd assume the same thing, right?"

"Well, he's a large man."

She winked. "Uh-huh, so you do think about it."

* * *

"What do you think of Billy?" I asked when Nita had a moment to talk.

"He's cute, but young for me, though." She is thirty-five, which made her about ten or twelve years older than Billy, but I was guessing.

"Sexy body," she observed, "but I think he's gay."

My heart sank. "Why do you say that?"

"Well, he's cute—extra cute. Look at that hair, and he dresses well. He doesn't slobber on the women that come in here, and he's funny as hell. His eyes are dreamy. Have you noticed them? They're so blue."

I nod mutely.

"Last night, he stayed around after he got off work and had a few drinks. We got to talking about deep things. So, there's that. Add all these things up, and I'd have to say he's gay."

"Jeez, Nita, you don't think he could be an attractive, intelligent, funny straight guy with a bit of class?"

"Huh? You haven't dated in too long. There aren't any of those."

"That's a hopeless attitude. And I hope you're wrong."

She left to serve a beer. When she returned, she leaned in close. "There's one last thing I haven't mentioned."

"What's that?"

"Last night I tried hard to get him to go home with me. I dropped hints, batted my eyelashes, stuck out my chest, and pulled out all the stops. It was no go. So he has to be gay, or I'll go home tonight and shoot myself."

I laughed. "Don't do it, Nita. Maybe he's only shy. Maybe he has a girlfriend. There could be hundreds of reasons why he didn't let you take him home."

She leaned in still closer. "Give it up," she whispered. "He's gay. Gay, gay, gay, and I don't mean as in extra-happy."

I was contemplating that when Billy appeared. "Could I buy you another whatever, lovely Margarita-Not-Named-for-the-Drink?"

"Move on, Billy-Who-Isn't-Supposed-to-Hit-on-Customers," grumped Nita.

He ignored her. "Did you get my message?"

"Yes. I came to tell you to dress casually. Or dress up if you want. Either thing is appropriate."

"How are you going to dress?"

"I haven't been out in so long I don't know what to wear."

"I could come by if you want, and help you decide."

I knew that cinched it as far as the bet went, but I don't give up without a try. Before I could say anything, Billy said, "Oh, shit there's the manager. I'll be back."

"You didn't tell me you had a date with him," Nita said snippily.

"It's not a date the way you think. I'm taking him to the Rodriguez quinceañera because I think he'll be fun."

"I bet you get laid," she said with bitterness. "You're not too old for him."

"What I want is to dance with him."

"Yeah, right." She snickered and moved down the bar.

After a few minutes, Nita returned. "You know what?"

"What?"

"If you had any sense, you'd be screwing that hung deputy."

I needed a double shot of tequila. No salt, forget the lime, and triple that.

* * *

"Customers can be so annoying," Billy bellyached. "They expect a waiter to cater to their needs and bring them things."

"I can see why that would be irritating." I was again seated at a table by a window, but this time I could see the Rio Grande in the fading afternoon light, and the last bit of the U.S. before Mexico begins. I was forced to move from the bar because of Nita's cold resentment and liquor's bold proximity.

"What did you do today?" Billy asked.

"I rode in a helicopter."

"Shut up! You did not."

"Yes I did. We were searching for a man from Houston who's missing."

"Did you see any sign of him?"

"He seems to have disappeared off the face of the earth, like my other case."

"Are there two people missing?"

"One has been gone from home about thirty days and the other for thirty years."

Billy heaved a dramatic sigh. "Well, I guess that eliminates the possibility that they ran off together."

CHAPTER 9

On Friday, we planned to leave for Ojinaga at noon. There was no reason to look for night owls at an early hour since people who work all night are seldom up before late afternoon.

I left my house early for a run, jogged past Cimarron Mountain, and then down a bumpy dirt road to the post office. From there I crossed the highway and ran along the lane that winds back towards Indian Head. The rising sun slung various shades of red against its ruddy-brown stone, from barely-pink to deep crimson as the light took hold.

I started out with sweats over running shorts and a t-shirt, but soon had to remove them. The sun was bright and warm coming over the mountains, and the exertion made it seem warmer. I tied the sweatpants around my waist and kept going. By the time I returned, the sky was the same brilliant shade of blue as yesterday.

I ran along the shoulder of the highway to a convenience store and café to pick up a few things. The locals' table of oldish men with nothing better to do stared as if they had never seen running shorts, or a female.

Barney says they bug him about why a girl chooses to be a lawman. Yeah, why did I? On a 'how exasperating are they?' scale of zero to Wynne, they're an eight.

"Here's the little prizefighter now," was the first witty comment I heard.

I smiled and refrained from insulting retorts. I'm used to them in a resigned way.

"When's your next fight?" "I'd invite you to go out, but that didn't work out so well for Wynne." "If I tell you're gorgeous, will you break my nose?"

On it went. And these men wonder why I won't go out with them.

"You guys are so clever I wish I could stay all day and chat." Not. I wanted out.

Billy came from behind and saved me. "Excuse us gentlemen," he said with an elegant British accent, took my arm, and escorted me to my original destination, a bank of refrigerators at the rear of the store.

"I've gotta say I don't like sharing you, Ruby." He sounded like the Godfather. "I begged you not to take your love to town."

That doubled me over.

"Those ol' boys are too ancient for a sweet young thing like you."

"You're telling me! What are you doing here, Billy?"

"I'm offloading some cash. After a while, it starts to pile up." He took my hand. "You're a vision, you know that?"

"Well, I—"

"You can't blame them ol' boys for staring." Now he sounded as fake redneck as Wynne. Then he resorted to his regular voice. "I guess you know everyone here, and everyone knows you. Aren't you the sheriff of Dodge City?"

"Dodge City deputy," I corrected.

"Well, whatever. You're the law 'round these here parts, however you cut it," he announced and took up a gunslinger stance with his hands on imaginary pistols. Then he looked serious. "Do you run every day?"

"Most days. I love to run."

"Could we go together sometime?"

"Are you a runner, Billy?"

"No, I'm a wannabe at this point, but I'm a fast learner. I won't get in your way; I promise. I'll stay a worshipful distance behind and hope an occasional bead of your perspiration will hit me in the face as I drag myself along."

"Worship is not necessary. However, that perspiration thing was a nice touch. When would you want to start?"

"Why not now?" He shrugged. "I'm wearing sweats and running shoes." Then he looked me up and down appreciatively. "You're dressed for it I see, Babycakes." The man had more characters than Robin Williams.

"Let's go then."

I paid for orange juice and three yogurts and waited while he 'offloaded his cash' on apples and cottage cheese. Then Billy ran with me towards my house, which is about a mile and a half from the store. He wheezed and panted as we started up the last sloping road.

At that point, I took pity on him. "Let's walk. Walking is good, and it's important to cool down before you stop moving."

He hung on every word. When we reached my house, I showed him stretching exercises I do as a cool-down. He followed my instructions to the letter. At times, he strutted and threw his arms around like a drama queen; then he would admire my legs and take on the persona of Larry the Cable Guy at a strip club. Billy was a combination of feisty, show-off adult and shy, adoring child. I hoped he wasn't gay, but on the other hand, it was just as well.

We went inside and drank water, orange juice, and more water. I made egg omelets and toast with Billy whining the whole time that I was going to make him fat.

"If you run a lot you can eat a lot," I assured him. "If you don't want what I'm making, I have oatmeal, apples, strawberry yogurt, and bananas."

"You have gorgeous legs, Babycakes," he said with a thick New Jersey accent. "I'll eat whatever you're havin'."

* * *

I went from breakfast with Jersey Boy to visit my mom at her clinic. Doctores Fronterizos is a non-profit organization that provides free or low-cost medical care to people living along the border on both sides of the Rio Grande. It is staffed by nurses and physicians from all over the U.S. and Mexico who donate their time in two-week tours of duty. My mom is the director and the only doctor who works full-time.

She looked up from her desk and smiled when I walked in. She stood, hugged me, and gave me the once-over. "You look good," she concluded.

"Why do you sound so surprised?"

"Well, you're known to withhold key information from your parents."

I gave her the short version of my close encounter of the bone-headed kind.

"Well," she said, "I'm relieved to see you're unharmed, but watch your back. Wynne has been 'beaten up by a girl' to use his words. You shamed him in front of his cronies, and he might retaliate."

"I'm not afraid of him. He's a coward."

"True, but I think he's the type to pull something, don't you? I mean something devious and underhanded. Don't let him catch you alone."

"Okay, Mom, I won't. Please stop worrying, and could you tell Papi I'm fine?"

"We do worry about you sometimes. You're so hard-headed."

"I wonder where that comes from."

She grinned. "I believe the last time you gave somebody a shiner you were in fifth grade. It was that mean girl—what was her name?"

"Lilly."

"That's right, Lilly."

"She called Victoria a dyke. I didn't know what that was, but she made it sound like something terrible. I think I gave her a black eye twice, or more like four times."

"And you wonder why Ms. Jablonski doesn't like you." Ms. Jablonski is the school superintendent. And no, I didn't wonder.

I was saved from further scrutiny and well-meaning motherly advice by the arrival of a pregnant patient.

* * *

At the office, I took out the file of the Serena Bustamante investigation and set up the framed photo of a twenty-two-year-old smiling Serena next to it.

"Where are you?" I asked her, but she wasn't going to make it that easy.

I separated the search information from the rest of the file and set it aside. I re-read Sheriff Blanton's description of his cursory search of the Hampton property, feeling even more certain that he must have missed something important. Then I took out the interviews and went through them, thinking I could re-interview a few people by phone.

I separated them into piles by place of residence: Alpine in one pile, Terlingua Ranch Resort in another, the general Terlingua area in another and a pile of the people I knew had died. I read through interviews with the now-deceased, looking for anything. Serena's parents were in that group. They had been devastated by the loss of their youngest daughter and couldn't imagine that she had run off. She had never caused them problems. They insisted she wasn't seeing anyone besides Curly Hampton. Serena's aunts and uncles corroborated that. She was a joy, loved her family, and she loved Curly, and was thrilled to be carrying his baby.

"Everybody loved you," I said.

No comment from Serena. She knew there was someone who hadn't loved her. Or, someone who loved her had killed her by accident or in an act of passion.

I read through a doctor's report that confirmed the pregnancy and pronounced Serena a healthy female. In a separate statement, the doctor said he had known Serena practically from birth and that she was well-adjusted and happy. She never expressed discontent with her life or regrets about her pregnancy.

When I re-read the first report of Serena as a missing person, it reminded me that she drove a 1970 Chevrolet Camaro. Something about it bothered me. I shuffled through papers and found Sheriff Blanton's notes about the car. It was driven home from the arroyo by Joey Bustamante, which was a breach of protocol. It should have been kept by the sheriff's office until it could be examined for clues.

In his notes, the sheriff never mentioned a search of the car. That gave me an idea. I called Joey on his cell phone, expecting to leave a message, but after numerous rings he answered.

"May I ask you some questions about Serena's car?" I asked after we established that we were both fine.

"Sure."

"I'm reading through the reports, and it appears the vehicle was never searched by the sheriff's office. I wonder if you ever had a look through it. And secondly, what happened to it?"

"I meant to tell you this the other day, Margarita. I kept the car."

I could hardly believe it.

"You bet I looked through it," he continued. "I've lost track of the number of times I combed through that car."

"You're saying the '70 Camaro is in your possession?"

"Yes. I have it in my garage. I've kept it in cherry condition because at first it was my way of holding onto Serena. If I kept it for her, she'd come back. After ten years or so I began to realize she wasn't coming. Then I kept it as a shrine; I guess. I drive it now and then to keep it running, and it runs well. I've been offered a ton of money for her car, but I'll never sell it."

"May I examine it, Joey?"

"Claro que sí. ¡El Camaro es fantástico! You can even drive it if you want."

"I'd like that."

"When will you come?"

"I'm not sure. I'm working on something else right now but maybe next week. I'll call you."

"Come whenever you want."

"There's one more thing, Joey. I would like to meet your wife. I never got to meet her the other day."

"Right, I remember. She didn't come home until after you left. Well, you can do both things at once."

"I'd like to meet Sylvia's husband as well."

"He died a few years ago."

"Oh. I'm sorry. Well then, I'll call the first of next week and make arrangements to visit. Okay?"

"You name it."

I felt excited and not sure why. What could I hope to find in a car abandoned thirty years ago that wouldn't have been found already? Joey had said I could drive it. Maybe that was the source of my excitement, but not entirely. The car held a secret. I knew it.

I picked up the file again and read the interview with Serena's best friend, Samantha Arzate, now Samantha Harding. She had been distraught and almost incoherent at first. In subsequent interviews, Samantha told the sheriff, or sometimes a deputy, that Serena had confided in her about her affair with Curly Hampton from the beginning. She was "head over heels" with him and had sex for the first time, not something she took lightly. Samantha had met Curly long before Serena's family met him, but she was sworn to secrecy.

Samantha described him as "dreamy-looking and worldly." She was concerned that he was married, but it added to his mystique. Being young and idealistic, they were "sure everything would work out."

Interestingly, Samantha was the only person who spoke up for Curly and felt certain he was innocent. "He would never have killed Serena," she insisted to Sheriff Blanton on several occasions. I wondered if thirty years had changed that opinion, or if she had remembered something important during all that time.

I called the last number listed for her, when the investigation was re-opened twenty years ago. "I'm calling Samantha," I advised the noncommittal Serena.

A woman answered, and I identified myself. She admitted to being Samantha Harding but was incredulous, and seemed angry, that we were re-investigating the disappearance of her friend.

I studied Serena as I spoke. "I understand what a long shot this is and that it must bring up pain for you, but I need your help. I've been asked to figure out what happened to her and I'm serious about doing that.

"I'm twenty-five years old, not much older than Serena was when she vanished. I already feel a kinship with her and want to know the truth. My investigation may go nowhere, but what if I could put this case to bed? What if you and her family could know for sure and be relieved of wondering and supposing? "

In what was almost a whisper Samantha replied. "That would be nice for all of us that loved her, Deputy Ricos. She left a hole in our lives. We're in limbo because we can't mourn her death. We don't know if she's dead. Did she abandon us for some other life? Where is she? Whoever killed her, if someone killed her, robbed us of the chance to bury her and mourn her and get over the loss."

"I understand what you're saying, Mrs. Harding. I spoke with Joey and Sylvia, and their sadness is as real as ever. It's heartbreaking."

"I named my first child after Serena," Samantha said, "and I've always hoped that one day I would see her again; she would come walking up with an explanation of everything. It's silly. She's almost bound to be dead."

"So you agree with her family that she wouldn't have left her life behind?"

"She would never have left it, not willingly. At first, when she didn't come back, I made up various scenarios, but they were far-fetched."

"Like what?"

"Oh, maybe she'd been threatened by mafiosos who were going to kill her family if she didn't cooperate, and they kept her enslaved. It sounds ridiculous I know, but Serena had the type of beauty that caught peoples' attention. Sometimes beauty can be a curse.

"Another scenario was that she'd been sold as a sex slave. That one used to keep me up half the night. Remember that I was young, too, and frightened for Serena. Whoever killed her hurt many people and keeps on hurting us."

80

"That's the hurt I'm trying to end."

"You've taken on quite a challenge, Ms. Ricos."

"That's okay. I enjoy a challenge."

She laughed. "You must."

"I keep thinking that to be successful where everyone before has failed, I must discover something that was overlooked, some tidbit that leads to something crucial. That brings me to why I'm calling you."

"Yes? Why are you calling me?"

"Is it possible you've remembered something that may have seemed insignificant thirty years ago? You're older now and I thought your perspective might have changed, or some obscure memory may have floated forward."

"I do know what you mean. As a matter of fact, since you ask, some time ago I remembered that Serena told me she was being followed. This was before she ever knew Curly. Also, sometimes the phone would ring and someone would breathe at her, but usually nothing else. It was giving her the willies. Once, a man did speak to her and said some very filthy stuff. The next time, he was groaning and moaning and making other similar sounds. He breathed, 'oh baby, oh baby, oh baby' and another time he said, 'I'll come on your face.' Then the calls stopped. We wrote it off to an obscene caller, or one of our crazy friends messing around with her."

"Did you say anything to the sheriff about it?"

"No. By then, it was mostly forgotten. What I should've told the sheriff and didn't think was important at the time is that after Serena started seeing Curly, she thought she was followed again. It happened several times. One time she came home, and some of her underpants were on the bed. She knew she hadn't left them there.

"A while after that she realized that two of her sexiest pairs were missing. One day she came home from work and some lacy, sheer undies that Curly had given her were on the bed. The bed was rumpled, as if someone had been lying there, and the panties were—well, the panties had been ejaculated on."

"Did she ever report any of that?"

"She reported the last incident. The Alpine police came to investigate but didn't determine much. They acted as if the whole thing was her fault. It was not overt, just a definite undercurrent. Back then if you were pretty and sexy and wore underwear like that the police thought you were asking for trouble."

"I don't believe things have changed much."

"You're probably right."

"What happened to the underpants?"

"The officers took them in an evidence bag. They shoved each other and had a fine time with them. There was no DNA testing then so eventually they were returned to Serena, who threw them away. She told Curly they'd been ruined in the dryer and he bought her more, and that was the end of it."

"Why didn't you tell the sheriff about this?"

"I'm not sure. I guess it was mostly because of the way the police treated the other incident. The sheriff and his crew struck me as even more lecherous than the police. Also, I was in shock and couldn't think clearly about anything.

"It was believed Curly had killed Serena to protect his marriage and the status quo in general. That idea caught on like wildfire, and he was tried and convicted without the benefit of court. I guess I thought it was futile to bring up the underpants and be treated with such disdain. And, in a way, I felt it would be a stab in the back to Serena."

"In reading all the different statements," I said, "you were the only one who believed in Curly's innocence. Would you please comment on that?"

"I saw Serena and Curly together in a way others didn't. The way he'd look at her, it would tear your heart out. The man worshipped her. I was her best friend, and I was privy to the things he would do for her and to her."

"Did she ever indicate any fights or major disagreements?"

"No, and she would've told me about anything serious because she told me everything. I knew how he treated her, what he bought for her, how he made love to her. I was her confidante, and she was mine. I knew details that were embarrassing because they were so intimate. We'd been friends since first grade. We were young and innocent and had no secrets from each other. I've never had another friend like Serena." She sniffed, and I realized she'd begun to cry.

"I'm sorry to make you go through this again, but you've already told me things I couldn't have gotten anywhere else."

"You need to understand that I kept a lot to myself during the investigation because it was between Serena and me. I didn't see how it would help. No matter what I said, everyone thought Curly had killed her."

She blew her nose and continued. "When Serena told him she was pregnant, he cried with joy. He was so happy and proud. It was not an act. It couldn't have been."

"So your opinion of Curly's role in the disappearance hasn't changed?"

"I don't believe he had a role in it, except as a scapegoat. When Serena was barely twenty she met Curly, and they fell in love. Serena was a virgin. She always believed she would fall in love with someone special, and she was old-fashioned enough to want to wait for that someone."

Samantha paused as if in thought, then continued. "One day she told me she'd met her someone. It was still months before they had sex. Afterwards, she told me about it. Let's just say that a man who courts a woman the way he did, and then makes love to her like he made love to her would not be a killer, no matter what. No. He's no killer. I'm not sure of much in this life but of this, I'm damned sure."

I liked Samantha Harding and told Serena's photo that as I scribbled out some notes. What Samantha said carried significant weight with me. She was in a more intimate position than anyone else Serena had known, apart from Hampton. If she believed so passionately in his innocence, then so would I, for now.

CHAPTER 10

In Ojinaga, we found the address Darcy had given us, parked the Explorer, and walked up the blue-tiled path to the front door. The place looked like a country estate, not a home you'd expect to find near downtown Ojinaga. The house and a lush yard were surrounded by a tall stucco privacy fence. There were a few flowering plants, even though it was December.

A maid in a light blue dress with a starched, white apron came to the door. She looked concerned to see two people in uniform standing on the stoop.

"Buenas tardes, señora. ¿Esta Rudy Ramón en casa?" I greeted her and asked if Rudy was at home.

She returned my greeting, indicated he was, and invited us into a house with floors of gleaming Saltillo tile. The rooms were spacious and tastefully decorated, and with an abundance of plants. We were led into a glass-enclosed porch with doors leading to a small swimming pool. The room was full of white wicker furniture and so many green growing things it felt as if we had stepped into a jungle.

The maid invited us to make ourselves at home while she went to get Señor Rudy.

"I hope he won't be dressed in a string bikini," commented Barney in English when she walked away.

"I hope he is," I said to shut him up.

"Tell me again how you know this man."

"I know Franco Orozco, his lover. All I know about Rudy is his name, and that my friend met him in Chihuahua while he was there on business. They fell in love, and Rudy moved here to live with him."

After a few minutes, a man came bounding barefoot down the stairs with the exuberance of a child. He was dressed in short cut-off jeans and a pink bikini top stretched across a masculine but hairless chest. As he approached, he moved with feminine grace, and looked sculpted, like the statue of David, but darker-skinned. Even his feet were shapely and smooth, with toenails painted bright pink.

I glanced at Barney, but he wasn't looking at me.

Rudy's expression was questioning but friendly. "Yo soy Rudy Ramón," he announced and bowed theatrically.

I introduced us, and Barney shook his hand with his mouth open. Rudy regarded Barney in silence, taking in the size of him.

Then Rudy let out a long sigh. "I do have a weakness for a man in a uniform."

Brad Pitt only wishes he was as good-looking as Rudy.

"Please, sit," Rudy said, "and tell me why you're here. I can't be in trouble in Texas. I've never been there."

"Rudy, I'm a friend of Franco's."

I was about to say more, but he interrupted. "Is Franco in trouble?"

"No. I wonder if he's here, too."

"He's at his office. Why do you ask for Franco?"

"I want to say hello to him. We came to speak with you."

He began to squirm at that news.

"We're looking for a norteamericano who is missing," I continued. "He was last seen in Ojinaga. We know he was sent to you by Darcy McGill, from Terlingua. She wanted you to set him up with a date. Do you remember that?"

"Yes, yes, I do remember." He sat with dramatic crossing and re-crossing of his shapely legs, showing off for Barney, whose attention he had.

"I brought a photo of the man." I unfolded the fax and handed it to him.

Rudy nodded. "Yes, I know this one. He came to me, and you're right, he was looking for sex. But aren't we all?" He laughed and tapped Barney on the knee, grazing him with the tips of his fingers.

Barney laughed too, and seemed at ease with this unconventional man.

"I don't usually make these kinds of arrangements," Rudy said, "but it was a favor for Darcy. I called a dear friend who would treat him right. His name is—Wait a minute. Will he be in trouble?"

"No, nobody's in trouble, but we want to talk to him."

"Francisco is his name. I'll go phone him. I think they got on well, no?"

"I can't answer that because I'm not acquainted with the man. We're looking for him because he's been missing for two weeks."

Rudy had gotten up to leave but stopped and turned. "Maybe you're thinking he's still with Francisco? But no, that can't be."

"Why is that?"

"Because I've seen Francisco four or five times since then and he never mentioned anything. He would tell me if he was in love, or even in lust. It happens, you know?" He shrugged and strutted out.

Barney looked at me, deadpan. "Interesting fellow."

That cracked me up until the arrival of the maid. She brought a tray of limeade and just-baked pan dulce. She told us Señor Rudy would be a while. He was calling friends on our behalf. With that, she left us.

The aroma from the warm, sweet bread made my mouth water even though we had eaten lunch. Barney poured each of us a glass of limeade and sat back down.

"I could live like this," he said with a contented sigh.

"You should've married a rich attorney."

He gave me a withering look.

"I didn't say the attorney had to be a man, you chauvinist."

"Oh, true. Sorry, Pard." He didn't look sorry and took an oversized bite out of a piece of pan dulce. "Oh wow, this is good. It's still warm."

We chatted about various things while Barney ate more than our share of the treat, leaving a small piece for Rudy.

"He's watching his figure," assumed Barn. "Want to bet me?"

"I'm sure you're right, and I see you're not at all concerned with yours."

After twenty minutes, Rudy came back and apologized for his long absence. "I have spoken with many people. Quite a few saw the missing man with Francisco. All of them say he paid Frannie to spend two days with him. Frannie bragged about it to the others. It's just like him to get a good deal and rub it in everyone else's face; he's such a whore!"

We were riveted, and since we didn't ask questions, Rudy continued to entertain us. "My friend Armando says when the gringo left he claimed he was going to move to Baja. Armando says Frannie cried, and the man said he would send for him when he gets settled. That blasted Francisco, he cries for everything, especially to get his way with men who like him." Rudy crossed and re-crossed his legs in agitation. "And he's always falling in love."

Rudy sprang to his feet. "Please come with me a moment, Margarita," he said, surprising me. He turned to Barney. "Will you excuse us?" He started bounding back up the stairs but paused. "Well come on, chica," he prodded, "we shouldn't keep el grandote waiting." 'El grande' means 'the large one;' 'el grandote' is 'the *really* large one.'

"He speaks Spanish," I reminded Rudy on the way up.

"Oops! I thought when he laughed he was being polite. You know, the way gringos do when they don't understand."

I followed Rudy into a room so aggressively girly I felt intimidated. On a femininity scale of one to ten, I'm a six, maybe. Rudy is a fifteen. Pink was everywhere, and frilly, flowery things. Clothes, wigs, and sexy shoes were scattered all over. Rudy swept some lacy things from a chair and invited me to sit.

"This is my room," he said as if I wouldn't have guessed. I knew the second I entered that Franco had no part of it, and I wondered if he'd even been in it. "Our bedroom is down there." He waved his arm dismissively towards a room down the hall. "This is my special room."

"I see," I said. "Well, it's very—you." I picked up a sexy red shoe with a death-defying heel and examined it. Trying it on crossed my mind, but it wouldn't have fit and its owner was guarding it.

"I once worked as a drag queen in Chihuahua." He pointed out a wall of posters announcing various singing performances by 'Rene' Ramón, who appeared to be a drop-dead gorgeous woman.

Rudy perched on the end of a bed covered with slinky dresses, lingerie, and hats. He checked his perfectly-groomed nails. "I was kind of famous."

"Is that how you met Franco?"

"No, I met him at a coffee shop. I was wearing blue jeans and a t-shirt, with no wig and no make-up. We hit it off so well I forgot I wasn't dressed up." He sighed. "Franco likes my Rene Ramón look, but he prefers Rudy."

"Well, isn't that good? He's in love with the real you."

"Rene *is* the real me—well, mostly anyway. I play around in this room, but when Franco comes home I'm just plain Rudy."

There was not one thing about him that could be called plain.

"So why are we here in your room?"

"I felt nervous to ask this with that huge man watching. Tell me the truth. Is Frannie going to be in trouble?"

"No, not at all. We're following the trail of James Taggert, and it led us here."

"You wouldn't lie? Policía lie all the time."

"No. We're not here to make trouble for anybody. We don't have any jurisdiction in Mexico anyway."

"I guess I don't have much trust for policía," he said. "I'm afraid if Frannie sees you in those uniforms he'll run the other way."

"We'll change before we meet him."

Rudy sighed and checked his bikini top several times as if expecting his breasts to fall out. "Frannie will know where your man went if I can find him."

"So you don't know where he is?"

"He's working. I left a message for him to meet me at the Tecolote at seven-thirty. You and Grandote should meet us there."

"Will Frannie be free by then?"

"Yes, unless he falls in love."

* * *

"Well, what was that about?" Barney demanded to know the second we stepped off the stoop of Franco and Rudy's house.

"Oh, it was just girl talk."

"Did you try on clothes together?"

"No, but I sure like some of his shoes."

"For real, what was it about?"

"He wanted me to assure him that his friend Frannie wouldn't be in trouble. He's distrustful of police and was intimidated by you. He calls you Grandote."

"Yeah, like I never heard that before."

"He didn't mean it as an insult. In fact, I think he liked you, Grandote."

"Drop it, Ricos."

"I'm just sayin'. Who can resist a big man in a uniform?"

* * *

Back on the streets of Ojinaga, Barney spotted lingerie he liked in a shop window. He wouldn't go in because "the itty bitty women will stare at me."

"Why would you object to that?" I wondered.

"I don't like it." He handed me a wad of cash. "Buy two of whatever sexy thing you like, so I can give one to Jules."

I did that, and when I came out of the shop said, "Don't you think more women stared at you out here than the two sales clerks in the store?"

He ignored me.

We had brought a change of clothes because we assumed we would have to go to bars and were afraid no one would talk to us if we looked like the law of any country. We went to some public restrooms at a city park and changed our clothes. Both of us came out wearing jeans with cotton shirts, sweaters, and boots.

"Jeez," said Barney, "we look like twins."

I looked up at him. "Oh sure, the same way Arnold Schwarzenegger and Danny Devito are twins."

CHAPTER 11

Tecolote Nocturno is a motel advertised by a neon sign at the road, so it is easy to find. I wondered if the tourists staying there had a clue about the unmarked building behind the office.

When we arrived, two men holding hands walked together into a room at the far end of the complex.

Barney sucked in a deep breath and let it out slowly. "This is getting weird."

"You don't think it's been a bit weird already?"

"Yeah, I guess so."

Inside, the club was elegant. The room was paneled in dark wood and the bar gleamed. It was made of wood polished to such a high sheen it resembled glass. There were shelves of liquor and glassware behind the bar, on either side of a huge painting of two men embracing.

We sat at a table for four near the bar. There were few customers. Rudy had said that even though it was Friday night, it wouldn't be busy until at least eight o'clock. At nine a live band would play, and by ten it would be packed and stay that way until dawn.

A bartender came around the bar and sashayed towards us on high platform sandals. She wore a short, tight skirt and a lacy short-sleeved blouse. Her legs were sleek and shapely. She could have passed for a sexy woman, except the mellow voice of a man gave her away.

"What can I get for you?" she asked as she sized up Barney head to toe. Her vision automatically deleted me from the picture.

We ordered sodas, which seemed to disappointment her.

"I'd have taken you for a beer man," she flirted, moving closer and shifting her weight from foot to foot, thrusting one hip to the side, then the other.

Barney mumbled something about not being able to drink because of work. She gave a displeased huff and strutted her stuff back to the bar for the sodas.

"I thought she—he—was going to jump on me," Barney whispered. "She looks like a woman. She's the size of a woman, but sounds like a man. Did you think that was a woman? How's a person supposed to know?"

"I guess we shouldn't make assumptions."

"That's not playing fair," Barney complained.

To the right of the room was a raised stage with a dance floor in front. We were surrounded by paintings of same-sex couples in various stages of undress and different positions. They were not pornographic; every painting had a tender, high-classed quality. They depicted couples in love and were about caring and tenderness, and made me wish I had someone to hold me.

A flashy jukebox played a tune by Los Rieleros, perfect for dancing. Barney asked me to dance and I accepted, to his surprise. Our waitress left the sodas on the table, and threw a long, lustful look at my partner before she returned to the bar. There were a few other people on the dance floor, two pairs of men, one of women.

"Looks like we're the only heterosexual couple here," whispered Barney as we twirled around.

"Get a grip, Barn. We're not a couple."

"Well, we are heterosexual."

"Try to remember that we're working."

He craned his neck and peered around. "I hope nobody from Terlingua sees us. It won't take fifteen minutes for it to get back to Julia that we're having an affair."

"True, but she knows we're not."

"Couldn't we pretend to be a couple, for the sake of the bartender?"

"For your sake, you mean."

"She was coming on to me," he whined.

After a few more dances, a flurry of activity at the door signaled the arrival of Franco and Rudy. We went to greet them. Franco looked more handsome than I remembered. He was dressed in grey corduroy slacks, a grey turtleneck shirt and a red sweater. He looked like a model from an expensive male clothing catalog.

Rudy was dressed sedately for Rudy, in tailored black slacks and a loose-fitting white blousy top and high-heeled black leather boots. He wore no make-up, wig, hat, and no slinky anything that was visible. An elegant black suede coat was slung over one arm. Franco checked it for him at a room by the door.

Then Franco grabbed me and pulled me against him. "You look wonderful! It's so good to see you, Margarita!"

"Franco," I said when I could get my face off his neck, "you're better-looking than ever."

Rudy took a step towards me. "Keep away from my man," he warned in heavily-accented English, "and nobody gets hurt."

We laughed at that, and then I introduced Barney to Franco. He received hugs from both men.

"Um, um, que grandote," clucked Rudy. "I couldn't help but notice earlier what a large man you are." Without the heels, he would be about half Barney's height.

"Rudy, behave yourself," admonished Franco and pulled him close.

"Well, I was only stating the obvious," he fussed comically as his partner herded him towards our table.

Franco is polished and charming and is masculine in his mannerisms and speech. He put Barney at ease immediately.

Several waitresses had come on duty and one headed our way dressed much like the bartender. This one was a woman. I think. Rudy ordered Presidente with coke, and Franco ordered a Tecate with lime.

A couple of prissy men blew in and sashayed up to the bar in a flurry of giggles. Rudy mouthed to me that they were working girls.

I nodded in understanding. Then a man entered wearing a fluffy, faux fur coat and stiletto-heeled red leather boots, my kind of boots.

"Here's Frannie," said Rudy. He stood and motioned him to our table.

Frannie sparkled with an abundance of jewelry and a bright smile. A glittery temporary heart tattoo decorated one cheek. His short, platinum blond hair was cut in layers, some of which were neon pink and different shades of purple. I liked it! The sheriff would have a stroke if I wore my hair that way, not to mention my parents.

Franco pulled a chair out for him between Rudy and me. He introduced him to us as Francisco, not Frannie. Then Franco walked over to the bar and brought back a glass of white wine and set it down in front of his friend.

"Thanks, Darling," sighed Francisco. His perfect face and smooth skin made him look boyish and innocent. "What an afternoon!"

"Well, I'm sure our friends don't wish to hear the details of it," said Franco with a stop-it-right-now expression.

"Of course they don't. Even I don't wish to hear the details of it. But, alas, it's my life." He sighed, heavy on melodrama, sat back in the chair and wriggled out of his coat. Franco, ever the gentleman, helped him and then took it and checked it.

"My, my, my, the man you have," Francisco murmured to Rudy.

"Don't even think about it," threatened Rudy.

"I can't think about it, or I'll die of jealousy."

Barney coughed to suppress a laughing fit. I didn't dare catch his eye.

Franco returned to the table. "Francisco, my friends need your help." His look said *straighten up or else.*

"Oh! How so?" Francisco pretended to study his nails which were well-manicured, but not painted. He studied Barney from the corner of his eye while I tried to get a better look at his boots.

"Frannie, these are the people I left you the message about," explained Rudy.

"Well, the message said to meet you here at seven-thirty and I came as quickly as I could. I didn't know you needed my assistance." He looked around the table. "Of course I'll help if I can."

Franco nodded to me, so I said, "We're looking for a man who's missing."

"Well what makes you think I have him?" Frannie patted himself down comically. "I could have misplaced him, I guess. What does he look like?"

We laughed at his antics. Then I handed him the faxed photograph. "This may not be the way he looked when you saw him, but this is the only photo we have."

Before Frannie said a word, the look in his eyes softened. "Oh, I remember this one." He waved his hand in the air, his rings glinting. "He wore me out!"

"Francisco!" chastised Franco, "we do not want to hear the intimate details of your time with him. For once in your life could you cut the drama and just answer the questions?"

He began to pout. "Sure, I guess so. I let you be you, why can't you let me be me?"

Franco touched his arm. "I want you to be you," he soothed. "It's just that sometimes you're too you."

Francisco dropped his act and turned to me. He spoke in a serious tone, in English. "How can I help you ma'am?" The voice was masculine and firm.

"We're from Terlingua, Texas," I said. "We're deputies."

Francisco interrupted in Spanish. "I don't speak English, only what I've memorized from old westerns."

"Oh. Sorry."

"I know 'Saddle up, boys' and 'Don't shoot!' 'Which way did they go?' 'Hands up!' and a few things like that."

I spoke in a constrained voice, trying not to laugh. "We're deputies from Texas," I began again in Spanish. "A few days ago, Taggert was reported missing. He never returned home from a vacation trip to Big Bend National Park. We're trying to determine what happened to him, and if you could help us we'd appreciate it."

Francisco gazed at Barney. "You're a deputy sheriff?"

Barney nodded. "Yes, I am."

"You're bigger than John Wayne and your eyes," he sighed, "are very blue."

"Francisco," Franco tried to keep him on track.

He wasn't going to be deterred. "What happened to your uniform?"

"It's in the car," Barney said. "We thought we'd be too conspicuous if we wore our uniforms."

Francisco licked his lips and studied Barney. "It must be large."

My partner started to become flustered.

"Please help us, Francisco," I said, but I might as well have been at home.

He addressed Barney. "What do I get for helping you, guapo? Would you let me wear your uniform? I adore uniforms." His masculine voice was out the window.

Franco rolled his eyes and smiled. "Lo siento", he mouthed. I'm sorry. He seemed to be washing his hands of it.

I shrugged at Franco and smiled. I knew we would get the information we needed if we were patient.

"Did Jimmy mention where he was from or where he was going?" I tried again. Francisco frowned at the interruption.

"He said he was from Houston and that he was not going back there."

"What else did he say?"

Frannie was already off-track, again gazing at Barney.

"Please answer her question," Barney said, and only then did Frannie help.

"I had the impression—but it was just an impression—that he was in trouble. He didn't ever say, so who knows. He told me he was headed to Baja California." Frannie sighed. "I liked him. He was gentle and funny—and loving. He invited me to come with him, but I can't drop my life, pitiful as it is." He glanced towards Franco and saw that he was whispering something to Rudy and no longer paying attention.

"So he was bound for Baja," I said in an effort to keep him on course.

"Yes. He said he'd send for me when he got settled. I'm not holding my breath, but it would be wonderful. I think he said that so I wouldn't cry. I get so emotional sometimes."

"Hysterical, you mean," commented Rudy.

"Give me a break. Not everyone has your luck. Some of us still have to work for a living."

Rudy gave his friend an affectionate look. "Frannie is looking for true love."

"What's wrong with that?" Frannie asked Barney.

"Nothing," said Barney. "Everyone wants true love."

"And you, Grandote, you got it?"

"Yes, I do."

"Barney is married," I said pointedly.

"Aren't all the good ones?" he laughed and then gave me an exaggerated wink.

* * *

"I wonder if Julia would freak out if I brought her to that bar," Barney said on the way home.

"I doubt it, but it might freak her out to know how attractive you are to the gay blades."

He sighed as if his life was over. "I knew you would hold that over my head."

"I'm not holding it over you. I simply mentioned it in conversation."

"Well, it would be good if you didn't mention it in conversation to my wife."

"Why? You haven't done anything wrong. Is it your fault all the gay blades are crazy about you, Grandote?"

"Shut up, Ricos."

"It's okay, Barney. My lips are sealed. What happens when we're working is our business and nobody else's, unless we're required to tell the sheriff."

"Which we are not."

I agreed that we would keep the nitty-gritty details to ourselves, and he called Julia to tell her we were on the way back.

A few miles passed in silence.

"The fellows at the café told me they saw you buying stuff with a young, cute guy with a British accent. And you went running off with him. What's that about?"

"I knew those old gossips would say something to you."

"Oh, you know how they are. They think you're too hot to be a 'lawman.' On the other hand, you may be a lesbian because you carry a gun and know how to use it. Bottom line, they're terrified some stranger has beaten them to you."

"Well, let them think whatever they want since they're going to anyway. It's innocent. I ran into Billy."

"Your very own gay blade."

"That hasn't been proven yet."

"When are you planning to prove it?"

"I'm starting to panic about going anywhere with anybody, as a date, I mean. Do you think he thinks it's a date?"

"I don't know what he thinks."

"I thought it would be a friendly gesture to invite him, but I'm having second thoughts. What if he's not gay? I can't go out with anybody, Barney. I'm not ready."

"Maybe you should've thought of that before you invited him."

"Will you call him in the morning and tell him I'm ill? I have the flu. No, I need to have something more gruesome than that."

"I could tell him you have the clap."

"Very funny."

"Listen, Ricos, you should tell him the truth. He seems like the type of man who would understand. But if you go out with him, maybe you'd have fun. If he tries something you don't want to do, then tell him."

"You're right. It's that he's obsessed with my legs, which makes me think he's not gay, which makes me feel panicky."

"Well, Ricos, you do have exceptional legs."

"Thank you, but you're not helping."

"Maybe you should wear pants."

"Oh God, what would Kevin think?" Whenever Kevin came to mind, I didn't see how I could go out with someone else.

"Kevin would say you should move on."

"*You* say that. You don't know what Kevin would think. Anyhow, let's talk about something else."

"It's getting around that you whooped Wynne's ass. He's takin' a bunch of shit about gettin' beaten up by a girl."

"I didn't beat him up."

"Have you seen him?"

"No."

"He has a swollen, taped nose and two—count 'em—two shiners. His knee is wrapped, and he's hobbling on crutches. It's sort of hilarious—unless you're Wynne."

"My mom is afraid he'll retaliate."

"You can count on it. He's already pissed that a *girl* is working a job he thinks should be his. Now his buds are makin' fun of him. And pretty much everyone else in the community."

"What is the big deal? I'm a grown woman who knows self defense. I'm not some frail, pitiful, helpless little girl."

"Yeah, no shit." Three seconds later, he said, "Hey, I could introduce Billy to Wynne and take care of your date problem. Come to think of it, maybe I won't. Billy might be your last chance to snag a man."

"You're hilarious."

"It figures, Ricos. The only man in Terlingua not afraid of you is gay."

"Ya basta, hombre! Enough. The next shiner in Terlingua will be yours if you don't knock it off."

CHAPTER 12

I ran early Saturday morning with Billy slowing me down. It was entertaining, though. He limped back to my house, complaining in his exaggerated way that his leg and butt muscles were on fire.

"You're butt looks fine to me," I said brightly.

"I'm starting to hate you," he whimpered, but after dragging a few hundred more yards asked, "You think my butt is fine?"

"Listen, Billy, I told you to start at a slow pace. You should walk and run until you can go a mile without feeling like you're about to die."

"If I faint, will you catch me in your arms?"

So it went with Billy.

I went from running to the office, hoping to speak to a few of the people on my re-interview list. Some had been impossible to catch on weekdays. I knew the sheriff wouldn't approve of running clothes in the office, but surely he would appreciate my work ethic.

Talking to Curly Hampton was on my mind, but it was something I had to work up to. Serena sat on my desk, non-committal on calling Hampton and everything else I ran past her.

"You aren't much help," I said to her smiling face.

I forced myself to call Mrs. Jablonski, the superintendent of the school. She was on the *get it over with* list I had going in my head. She and I don't get along and haven't since I was in fifth grade. There were the black eyes on Lilly, who deserved worse than what

I gave her. Also, Jablonski allowed me to be bullied by one of my teachers, who used my slow comprehension of the multiplication tables to ridicule and shame me in front of the entire class. The dresses thing was part of it, too. She liked for girls to wear them and I didn't want to.

Dena Jablonski was interviewed by Sheriff Blanton on several occasions. She had served as an informal character witness for Christina Hampton. The sheriff took Mrs. Jablonski's word about things and never followed up. On the surface, his investigation seemed acceptable, but taken apart it wasn't complete, and interviews with Jablonski were a good example. He asked too many questions of some people and not enough of others.

When Mrs. Jablonski answered, I realized I had been holding my breath. I forced myself to relax. I was the one in charge now. After I identified myself, I explained the reason for my call.

"I'm sure I have nothing new to add to what has already been said," she informed me, her voice as frosty as the snowman.

"In thirty years, nothing has occurred to you that you didn't think of before?"

"Why are you bringing this up again? Haven't Curly and Christina suffered enough? You people drove them away from here."

"I wasn't even born thirty years ago," I said with attitude since I resented her 'you people' comment. "I'm not out to cause anyone pain, but I'm pursuing a new investigation at the request of Serena's family. They feel Sheriff Blanton didn't do as good a job as he might have."

"How do you mean?" She sounded offended.

"They believe he showed prejudice because of Serena's race."

"That's ludicrous. Serena was a slut, a home-wrecker. She had many men, and she lured Curly into her web of sex and lies. He was a good man and she ruined him. She asked for it."

"So it's Serena's fault she was killed?"

"You know what I mean. She brought it on herself. Any one of half a dozen men could have killed her. I always thought she ran off with one of them."

"I've read through your previous statements, and I have a few questions. Do you know the names of any of the men she was dating besides Curly?"

Jablonski had made the same claim to Sheriff Blanton twice, and he had never asked her for names. What was that about?

"Well, Roy Baker was one. Preston Gutierrez was another. Let's see. It's been so long it's hard to remember. One of those Mexicans building the dam, he was hot for her. Rumor was she enjoyed him on the side. I think his name was Rigo Mendez."

"That's three. You said there were half a dozen."

"Well, those are the ones I heard mentioned by name. There were others. Surely her brother could give you some names."

"On the contrary, her brother and sister say Curly was her only love."

"Well, they would, of course."

"Do you know where any of these men live now?" I asked.

"Roy lives in Lajitas. He's the restaurant manager. Preston works for the country club in Alpine as the greens keeper. I never heard what happened to Rigo Mendez. He might have returned to Mexico."

"Do you stay in touch with Christina Hampton?"

"I do, but now it's Christmas card exchanges," she said. "She goes by Christina Moore."

"Oh, she re-married?"

"No, she took back her maiden name."

"Sheriff Blanton asked you if you knew whether or not Christina was aware of what was going on between Curly and Serena. You replied that she suspected he was having an affair but didn't know with whom."

Jablonski huffed with impatience. It took me back to fifth grade. I was ruining yet another of her days, but now she couldn't do a thing about it. "Christina was suspicious because he spent more and more time in Alpine. When he came home, he was preoccupied and seldom touched her. A woman knows."

"Did she confront him?"

"She planned to, but Serena went missing before she had the chance."

"You stated that on the day Serena disappeared you and Christina were together all day, which gave her an alibi. You also said she was distraught because of her husband's philandering. Do you remember saying that?"

"Yes, of course I remember."

"And you stand by that statement?"

"What are you getting at?"

"According to Sheriff Blanton, when a phone call was made to Curly about the whereabouts of Serena, Christina Hampton was hysterical. She cried and screamed. She told the sheriff she never had a clue that Curly was cheating on her."

"That's ridiculous. She spoke to me about it several times. She even suspected it was his secretary."

"Don't you find it questionable that she lied to the investigator? I mean, why lie?"

"I'm sure I don't have any idea."

"People lie to cover up something."

"Christina had nothing to cover up!"

"What were you doing thirty years ago?"

Take that, you old bat.

Jablonski sucked in a breath. "Surely you don't suspect me?"

"Were you teaching or going to school or what?"

"I attended college in Alpine part-time. I wasn't teaching yet. I was taking classes and having babies."

"Aren't you younger than Christina?"

"What does that have to do with anything?"

"I was just asking a question. She was thirty-two when Serena disappeared, so you were about twenty-five?"

"That's right."

"I'm trying to picture things and people the way they were then. I appreciate your help. Will you please call me if you think of anything I should know?"

"You should tell Sheriff Duncan he's an old fool to reopen this case."

"It's not being reopened. It's still open because it was never closed out by Blanton. We're trying to do that now."

"Well, it's taking long enough."

When I hung up I let out a long breath. "What a bitch," I confided to Serena. She smiled as if she knew that.

I was excited. Look at all the information I got by asking a few questions. Jablonski named three men who had never been named before anywhere in the investigation. How could that be? Maybe Sheriff Blanton really had been prejudiced.

Why would a woman who spends an entire day with a close friend, distraught over her husband's unfaithfulness, later claim she knew nothing about his affair? To cover up the fact that she had killed the offending woman, maybe?

I made a few notes. As I gathered my sweats and prepared to leave, I lifted Serena's photo. "I have so many unanswered questions. You can chime in any time."

If she had said anything I'd have wet my pants, or worse.

* * *

At home, a scribbled message from Billy was taped to the door: *Margarita, I'm sorry, but no can dance. I want to go with you, but I'm in pain. Could we do something else instead? I will understand if you choose to go without me. Yours forevermore, Billy P.S. Please leave a message at the Ocotillo.*

I left word that I would meet him at the Ocotillo at eight o'clock unless he called to tell me something different. I couldn't believe how relieved I felt.

* * *

I ate a quick lunch at home, eager to find out about the men Mrs. Jablonski mentioned. It was hard to believe Serena had multiple sex partners, but it couldn't hurt to see what they said after thirty years. Mrs. Jablonski's story was so different from Samantha's that it begged investigation.

I started with Roy Baker since he was closest, seventeen miles away in Lajitas. I spoke with someone in the restaurant who informed me that he wouldn't be in until Monday morning. A quick look through the phone book gave me his home number.

A man answered on the third ring. "Roy Baker."

I explained the reason for my call.

"Yes, I remember Serena. I know that her whereabouts were never determined. It made me feel sad."

"Dena Jablonski told me that you and Serena had a sexual relationship."

He laughed. "That's not true, unless wishing it counts. I pursued that poor girl just like any horny young man would have, I guess. I was just a kid."

"Did you ever date her?"

"I took her to the movies and for sodas and to dances, very innocent stuff. We never had sex, if that's what you're asking. She was a sweet girl from a good family, a religious family, I think. That was my impression."

"Why would Mrs. Jablonski think you and Serena were lovers?"

He hesitated and then claimed not to know in a way that made me think he was holding something back.

"Could I meet with you in person? I won't take but a few minutes of your time."

"I'll be home all day. Come whenever you want. I live in the first rock house on the right on Sky View Mesa in Lajitas."

"I know where that is."

"I'll be expecting you."

Next I called Rigo Mendez, who was easy to find. His number was listed under 'Rigoberto Mendez' in the Alpine phone directory. A young person answered and went to get her father—grandfather?

I introduced myself and asked if he would prefer Spanish or English. He chose Spanish, but spoke good English, and we went back and forth between the two languages. At first he was timid, not sure why someone was calling from the Brewster County Sheriff's Office.

When I explained, he said, "Yes, yes, I remember Serena Bustamante. She was a lovely girl. I saw her a few times when the boss took me to Alpine to help him with property he had there. We stopped at his office, and she was working."

"Did Mr. Hampton say anything to you about her?"

"No, but I knew they were lovers. The way they looked at each other, their feelings were obvious. I remember thinking that if the boss's wife ever saw the way he looked at Serena, it would be the end of their marriage."

"You worked for Mr. Hampton as a foreman, didn't you?"

"Yes. I was only twenty-five, but I had more experience than the other workers and more time in the States. I spoke better English. Well, bad English, but I was still ahead of the others."

"Were you overseeing the building of the dam on Mr. Hampton's property?"

"Yes I was, among other things. I know there was talk about the dam. We knew Mr. Hampton didn't put a body in there. He never came around the work except to see that it was going his way. He would tell me what he wanted done and then leave me to do it. I know every inch of that dam and I swear there's no body in there."

"There's no way Mr. Hampton could've done it without your knowledge?"

"Well, of course anything is possible, but he would've had to do the work himself. And he'd have done it at night and that would've awakened us. You see, we slept in an outbuilding at the back of the property, and he couldn't have worked on the dam without us knowing. If we'd known he was working, we'd have gone to help him."

"And none of you could have helped him without the others being aware of it?"

"No, Ms. Ricos. We were undocumented laborers, and we had to stick together. Working illegally made us afraid to cause trouble or make the boss mad enough to call Border Patrol, or worse. I should tell you that William Hampton was a fair and decent man.

We were never afraid of him, and he was not the type to withhold our pay. He treated us well."

"What if he had asked you to help him hide a body?"

"We would have run away."

"The dam was submitted to an ultrasound about twenty years ago that revealed nothing," I said. "What I question most was the way the sheriff took your word for it. All he did was ask about it and walk away. I don't get it."

"That surprised us, too. We figured the sheriff would make us tear it apart and we would have to rebuild it. We thought he didn't question it because he believed Christina Hampton had killed Serena. And there is no way she could have torn down and rebuilt the dam by herself."

"So the workers thought it was Mrs. Hampton?"

"We thought she did it, but we knew the body was not in the dam. I never mentioned it, but I thought she had seen the way her husband looked at Serena. I always knew that would be the end of it."

"Do you know Dena Jablonski?"

"I don't think so."

"She was a friend of Christina Hampton's."

"I don't recall that name."

"She told me this morning that you had 'the hots' for Serena, to use her words, and Serena was seeing you on the side."

He hooted at that. "Excuse me for being blunt, Ms. Ricos, but yes, I had 'the hots' for her. But seeing her on the side? How would I have done that, even if Serena had agreed to it? I lived and worked on the Hampton property. If I left, it was with Mr. Hampton. He knew my whereabouts all the time. It would have been impossible to see his lover under his nose. Besides, I've never been a man to go after another man's woman."

"Mrs. Jablonski swears that Serena had various men behind Curly's back and one of them was you. She named you specifically."

"Why would a woman who doesn't know me say such a thing about me?"

"How would she even know your name?"

"She must have heard it from Mrs. Hampton."

* * *

It didn't appeal to me to drive to Lajitas twice, so I visited Roy Baker about an hour before I was supposed to meet Billy. A rotund man of medium height and with graying brown hair came to the door, and we introduced ourselves.

"Thank you for speaking with me on short notice," I said. "I prefer meeting face to face when possible."

"Please come in and have a seat. What's this about me being Serena's lover?"

"Your name was given as one of many men she was seeing."

"Are we still talking about Serena Bustamante?"

"Yes sir."

"She didn't date anybody in a serious way while I knew her. She did go out a lot, but there was no hanky-panky that I ever heard about."

"Do you know Dena Jablonski?"

"The superintendent of the school?"

I nodded. "She mentioned you as someone who had an affair with Serena."

He leaned towards me. "Listen, I was in college when Dena was, so we knew each other. Once we were at a dance in Alpine. I had brought Serena. She was lively and fun, not to mention being a knock-out. At one point, I talked her into going outside to sit in my car. I kissed her. Then I put my hand on her breast and whispered some lame thing or other." He pushed wire rimmed glasses back up his nose and looked around guiltily. "I'd prefer my kids didn't hear this."

"Would you like to go outside? We could sit in my car."

"It's okay, this was before I ever met their mother." He continued in a lower voice. "I looked up to see Dena standing at the window watching. I knew it looked wrong. Serena had her hand on mine, and it might have looked like she was encouraging me, but she was trying to push me away. I never corrected Dena's wrong impression. I was twenty and didn't care if everyone thought I was making it with Serena."

"What happened after Dena saw you?"

"Serena was angry and made me drive her home. I'm sure Dena thought we had gone somewhere more private. I never said either way. I let her think what she wanted."

"How old was Serena when that happened?"

"She was nineteen, I think. I was a year ahead of her in high school so yeah, she was nineteen at the time."

"Then she wasn't seeing Curly Hampton yet."

"She never went out with me again, so I never knew anything about her affair with Hampton until she went missing and it became news."

"What did you think when you heard she disappeared?"

"I thought whoever had gotten in her pants must have been somebody she cared about a great deal. That made the whole thing sadder. I felt jealous, too. Why couldn't I have been the one, you know?"

* * *

When Billy saw me walking towards his table, he stood and bowed low. "You look like ten million dollars," he said, even though he was dressed several notches above me on the fashion scale.

"Thank you, Billy." A compliment like that would do a job on any woman.

"What did you do today?" he asked as he pulled out the chair for me.

"I worked."

He rested his hand against his heart. "My little superhero," he sighed, "working on Saturday. It would be impossible not to love you."

"Crime never rests," I stated dramatically.

A waiter came, and I ordered a Coke with lime, a long way from what I wanted.

"Are you still looking for a woman who's been missing thirty years?"

"Yes, I am."

Billy was wide-eyed. "Do you, like, not ever give up?"

I laughed. "It's an old case I've been asked to reinvestigate."

"And do you always do what you're asked?"

"No, but I like to cooperate with the sheriff since he's my boss."

"You're not the only sheriff in Gotham City?"

"We were in Dodge City last time we spoke. And I told you, I'm a deputy."

"Okay, but who are you really? Who are you when people aren't looking? Tell me something secret about yourself and I'll tell you something about me."

I could smell his drink, bourbon on ice. It made my mouth water. The waiter set my Coke down and left. *Hey, you!* I was tempted to yell, *this is bullshit!*

"I'm an alcoholic," I blurted, "but that's not secret."

"Whoa—" Billy jumped back in the chair, causing it to screech. "I was thinking more along the lines of a secret hobby or better yet, something kinky, but okay, so you're an alcoholic. Should we leave?" He stood. "Oh no, I'm drinking in front of you."

"It's okay, Billy, sit down. I don't know why I said that."

"I asked for a secret, and you gave me one. We should get out of here."

"Wait, let's eat first. Then I'd like to show you something so beautiful you won't believe your eyes."

"Margarita," he said and dropped all his personas and feminine affectations. "You're the most beautiful thing in Terlingua."

"Thank you, Billy." I smiled at him. "I want to take you to a place. It's the most scenic piece of private land I know. I call it my bluff, but it doesn't belong to me."

"Who owns it?"

"I don't know."

"Is it hard to get there?"

"We'll have to take my ATV. The road is in terrible shape."

"No one ever goes there?"

"I've never seen anyone else there."

"So you're the law, and we're going to trespass."

I shrugged. I never considered it trespassing.

"I'm intrigued." He bowed his head. "May God forgive us our trespasses."

* * *

Billy and I, dressed like Eskimos, lay on sleeping bags admiring the sky. It was too cold for hanky-panky, not that there was going to be any.

"I should have brought you in the daylight so you can see the view," I said.

"You must be kidding. Look at this sky!" The stars were so bright they illuminated the top of my bluff.

"When you asked for a secret," I said from out of nowhere, "I should've told you I have a shoe thing."

Billy's head whipped around. "A shoe thing?" His hand moved to his heart. "Do you mean a fetish? Do you want to wear my shoes?"

I laughed. "No, I like them high-heeled and slutty."

He took my hand. "Ah, now that's what I'm talkin' about when I say secrets." He turned on his side to face me. "Who else knows about it?"

"Nobody and I'd like it to stay that way. My husband knew, but he took the secret to his grave. He used to buy me the sexiest shoes you ever saw."

"You still love him, don't you?"

"Yes, but how—I haven't said anything."

"Well, you still wear a wedding ring, for one thing. And you seem—" he searched for the right word, "unavailable." He sighed and squeezed my hand.

"I really loved him, Billy."

"I understand. You don't have to explain anything."

After a long time, he took my hand. "Do you want to know my secret?"

"Yes, of course."

"I would like to wear your clothes." He sat up, animated by the thought of it. "I don't mean in public or anything, just to—play with them, you know?"

"You're too big for my clothes."

"There's the hell of it." He sighed like it was the end of the world. It was comical and sad at the same time.

I sat up, too. "You can wear anything I have that fits you, Billy, but don't touch my shoes."

CHAPTER 13

On Monday, Barney and I unloaded the horses at the main gate of the Hampton place. They were frisky in the chilly morning air and curious about each other. My dad's horse, Indio, is a gelding, but he still shows interest in females. He kicked up his heels, ran around the horse trailer, jumped the stone fence, and circled the house. Then he galloped back to the fence and stood with his head draped over it, looking innocent.

I motioned for him to come, a hand signal my papi taught him when he was a yearling. He ignored me and tossed his head, showing off. Then he whinnied, made a tear around the yard, re-jumped the fence, and came to a halt beside the large bay mare and nudged her in the right flank. My hand signal meant nothing. Indio was like a kid with a new babysitter.

"Yeah, boy, you like Big Mama, don't you?" Barney crooned as he saddled the mare. Her name was not 'Big Mama,' but he called her that. She didn't seem to mind and observed us calmly with huge brown eyes. I held the bridle and stroked her while Barney got the saddle on. Indio nudged my arm as if to say, *Okay, I'm ready now.*

Saddling him was easy, thanks to Papi's training. If he started to fidget, all he ever said was *Whoa* and Indio would stand still for almost anything.

I slipped Serena's photograph into my saddlebag. I didn't know why I wanted her with me, but I did.

"You're getting weird, Ricos," was Barney's take on it.

When we mounted, we sat staring at the oddly-shaped house. *Did Serena ever come here?* I wondered, and doubted it. This was Christina's domain. Still, I felt nervous about what we would find and afraid we wouldn't find anything.

"Your call," said Barney, and indicated I should lead the way. I didn't have a clue.

We rode the perimeter of the six hundred and forty acres. I didn't know what we were looking for any more than Barney did. Anything that looked wrong. It had been thirty years, so even something wrong could look right by now. Anyway, I told Barn I needed to get a feel for the land, how it was laid out, and what it looked like. He nodded in understanding.

A fence of native stone, hand-built by the Hamptons' Mexican workers, encircled the five acres closest to the house. The rest of the land was enclosed with standard cattle fencing. Bougainvilleas had been planted along the stone wall on both sides of the house but no more than their skeletons remained. A native species of morning glory had used the long-dead stems and branches as a trellis. That must have been a sight in the late spring and early summer when they bloomed.

The Serena file contained a thirty-year-old photo of the house. It had been a colorful place, with roses in beds at the front. They were a velvety green color in the photo, but were not yet budding on the April day that Serena disappeared. Wildflowers had been blooming around the yard, and there were planters full of pansies, marigolds, petunias, and other flowers I couldn't name. Now the place was a sad jumble of weeds, brown from lack of rain and the cold of winter.

For a while, we rode towards the Christmas Mountains. They were resplendent in the clear morning air, standing against a deep blue, cloudless sky.

We came to the building Rigo Mendez had described, where the workers slept. It had fallen in on itself and was overgrown with the miniature vines. I dismounted and poked around but didn't see anything suspicious.

It was pleasant ambling along with Barney. He was not put off by periods of silence, but if I had wanted to talk he would have been willing.

At one point, the property line went to the top of a small clay hill where we could look down into the arroyo where Serena's Camaro was found. The exact spot was about a mile away, but it was the same arroyo. It gave me goose bumps.

We stared into it as if mesmerized. "Barney, what if Serena didn't drive her car here? What if someone brought it after they murdered her to make it appear that she had been meeting Curly? Why would he ask her to meet him near his house? He always went to Alpine. He almost never brought her to Terlingua, and if he had asked her to come, he wouldn't have met her near his home."

"I agree."

"So if Curly killed her, why bring her here to do it? That just makes him look guilty. All along he said he never saw Serena in Terlingua, that he visited her in Alpine, or he took her somewhere else. Sheriff Blanton was convinced he lured her to the spot where her Camaro was found. Wouldn't it have been easier to kill her somewhere else?"

"Well, yes, but in another locale there would be witnesses, or at least a better chance of being seen. Out here, nobody saw anything. And maybe he didn't intend to hurt her. It could've been a crime of passion."

"Yes, there's that." I continued to stare into the arroyo. "His wife was right there." I indicated the direction of the house. "He would never have met her here."

"It's not as if they were looking for that kind of trouble, or so we'd assume."

"It's hard to put a story together after thirty years have passed," I said. "Especially when we never knew any of the people involved. I hadn't even been born. It's hard for me to get my head around it."

We got moving again and soon came to the dam. I had dreaded it, had thought it would give me the creeps. In reality, it was just a thing, not even a large or intimidating thing. It had been collapsed in the center so that the water it was meant to collect could run free. Once, it was a small obstruction across a minor arroyo; now it wasn't even that.

I got down and sat on it while Indio wandered off in search of something green. I felt sure the dam held no dead bodies. Rigo Mendez's story rang true when he told it, and now I was certain of it.

We moved on until we came to the front of the house again.

"I guess we should go in," I said without much conviction. "I don't think it will tell us anything."

"It's up to you," said Barney. "We're here. It couldn't hurt to look around."

We checked out the house, wandering from one room to the next, looking in closets and cabinets. The place was devoid of life, except for spiders and mice. It was dusty and stuffy, a house that had been left behind thirty years ago. I wondered why the Hamptons had never sold it.

For all the money they had, the house was not pretentious. A spacious study was located next to the living room, an area that had clearly been Curly Hampton's domain. It still contained a masculine desk of dark wood and a black leather office chair. Bookcases that were crammed full lined one wall. Did Hampton still come here? Thick dust and cobwebs said he didn't. A file cabinet still sat in one corner. It had been emptied, but there it was.

On top of the desk sat a photograph. I rubbed the dust off so I could get a clearer look at it. Movie star-handsome Curly grinned. Scrawled across the bottom corner were these words: "I love you Serena, and always will, Your Curly."

Why would this photo be here? Wouldn't it have belonged to Serena? Had he never gotten a chance to give it to her? Why was it left here, and by whom? Every other room in the house was bare, but that one had been left as it must have been when the family lived here. Why? Did it matter?

I posed those questions to Barney, who gave them his consideration before answering. "I think those are things you should ask Hampton when you talk to him. My guess about the photo is he never had the chance to give it to Serena. Whether he killed her or not, seeing that photo must have broken his heart."

I perused the books but found nothing relating to murder if you didn't count the mysteries. We went back outside and sat on the steps. I stared off at the mountains, wondering where to go from there while Barney went to give the horses water.

Before he returned, Sheriff Duncan called with interesting news. "I got the information you asked about," he said.

"What did you find?"

"Dena Jablonski was enrolled at Sul Ross that semester. Not only that, but she was in class the day in question."

"You're sure?"

"Well, as sure as I can be with thirty-year-old information. That's what the records show. I asked for a copy, and they faxed them over a few minutes ago. Back then, attendance records were turned in by the professors at the end of every week. A careful record was kept because a certain number of days were required to pass a course. Dena Jablonski was present and accounted for. Not only that, but she presented some sort of report. There's a check by her name under that column."

"So then, she's lying," I said. "Christina Hampton couldn't have been with her all day if Jablonski was in class giving reports."

"That would be my guess. Sheriff Blanton didn't take a careful look at Christina Hampton because of Dena Jablonski's testimony. She gave Christina a strong alibi."

"Thank you, Sheriff. I'll take it from here."

"Are you at the Hampton property now?"

"Yes, sir."

"What have you found?"

"I think I was wrong to suspect there would be anything here. There's nothing here, and Sheriff? Forget the ultrasound. There's not a body in that dam."

"What makes you so sure?"

"It's a feeling, and it's mostly collapsed. I spoke with a man who was working on it. He pointed out that neither of the Hamptons could have messed with it without the workers knowing about it. Seeing the layout here, I understand the truth of what he was saying."

"Okay. We'll see where this goes. I'd bet money on that gut sense of yours. If you feel there's no body, then let's go with that, at least for now. We can always do it later if you change your mind."

"There's something else, Sheriff."

"What's that?"

"There are no longer any outbuildings, except for the old lean-to where the laborers slept. It has fallen down and is covered with vines. I get the sense that what I'm looking for is not here."

"Carry on then," said the sheriff.

Barney came back and sat with me. "I heard you talking, Ricos. I hope you weren't whining to Serena. She's never going to help you."

"It was Sheriff Ben. He did some research for me with the college. Mrs. Jablonski lied to protect Christina Hampton. She was in class the day she says Christina spent all day with her."

"Well that changes everything, doesn't it?"

"Christina Hampton is now my number one suspect. She had motive and opportunity and a trumped-up alibi. Sheriff Blanton never took a second look at her because of what Mrs. Jablonski told him."

"I think he and ol' Mrs. J. were lovers."

"Where do you get that?"

"Well, he believed everything she said without question."

"Do you believe everything Julia tells you without question?"

"Well, no, but I do trust her. I still say they were lovers."

"Oh, yuck, I can't think about her being his lover. That's nasty."

"Well she was young once, Ricos. Speaking of that, how did your date with Billy go? Did I win the bet or what?"

"It's none of your business."

"He's gay, isn't he? You can't admit my win."

"I took him to my favorite bluff."

"And?"

"We talked and watched the stars, and we held hands."

"There's the proof. Any other guy would have been all over you."

"What? He's classier than you, Barney. You should've seen how he dressed."

"He's gay. Of course he dresses."

I refused to say more about Billy.

"Ricos, you shouldn't go to that bluff anymore."

"Why not?"

"That land is owned by William and Christina Hampton."

"You're making that up to aggravate me."

"You're always so suspicious of me."

"I wonder why."

"I'm not lying to you. I know because Julia and I went there once. We knew we couldn't afford it, but we asked at the real estate office anyway. There're asking one million dollars for the one thousand acres. Did you know it was that large?"

"I know it's huge."

"You might want to consider the fact that the Hamptons own it."

My heart sank. I loved that bluff so much. It was my private get-away, above it all. It is carpeted with wildflowers in spring and blooming cacti in summer. It has some of the largest ocotillos I have ever seen. It overlooks all of Terlingua and its southern side borders national park land. The Chisos Mountains are in-your-face, and when you stand facing that direction, there is no civilization except a winding two-lane road that disappears into the rugged landscape. Maverick Mountain looms on one side, and from the other you can see into Mexico. It overlooks Rough Run Creek snaking through the desert towards the Rio Grande. Looking north, Cimarron Mountain stares back.

I discovered the bluff while running, and Kevin had never been there, which meant it didn't blow up in my face like other places.

"I'm sorry, Ricos. I didn't mean to ruin it for you."

"Yes you did."

"Neither of us could even afford the property taxes."

"That's true, but I would still love to buy it."

"Are we done here, you think?"

"I think so." I looked around. "What is it I'm missing, Barney?"

"Lunch?"

* * *

We returned Big Mama to Neal's corral and left him a note of thanks. Indio demanded to go with her and stomped in protest, rocking the trailer back and forth and creating a racket. I told him 'whoa' several times. Each time he stopped, stared at me, and started again. He knew I wasn't my father and took advantage of it.

Barney and I stopped at the Terlingua Ranch Lodge for lunch. The waitress was talkative and wondered what we were doing there. We weren't wearing our uniforms, but our jackets bore *SHERIFF'S OFFICE* in giant letters as well as our caps.

"We ain't having criminal-type problems here, are we?"

We assured her that we weren't; we had been riding. I didn't feel like going into the details of our day, and neither did Barney. He said nothing.

When she ambled off, he grumbled barely loud enough for me to hear. "Cut the chit-chat and just bring us the danged food."

I laughed. "What about Jimmy Taggert, Barney? Shouldn't we close that case? The sheriff won't want us to follow him to Baja, will he?"

"I forgot to tell you something. The mechanic looked over the Taggert car and said that it's sound."

"Well then, he purposefully left the car behind, for whatever reason."

"Sheriff says we're done unless he turns up locally. I think he's in Mexico and will never come back. I called Aunt Angela to break the news to her. She took it pretty well. She was glad to know we think he's still alive."

"Well, searching seems like a waste of time now. At least we got to meet those entertaining guys in Ojinaga."

Barney glared at me and then started laughing. "Yeah, there's a silver lining for you." He added more sugar to his iced tea. "What are you going to do about Mrs. Jablonski and her lies?"

"I'll confront her. I don't relish the thought, but I need to know what her excuse will be. She told me all this garbage about Serena being a slut and named men that were supposedly involved with her."

"Were they named in the original investigation?"

"No. It's strange. Mrs. Jablonski made the same comments to Sheriff Blanton, but he didn't ask for names."

"He was sleeping with her, Ricos."

"So you say. I think he was so sure Curly killed Serena that he made only a feeble attempt to find any other suspects."

"Will you be able to find the men Mrs. Jablonski named?"

"I've already followed up on two of them." I told Barney what I had learned.

"So Dena Jablonski invented the relationships with other men?"

"It appears that way."

"That further incriminates Christina Hampton."

"Yes, I'd say it does."

"Or Mrs. Jablonski killed her, maybe?"

"She'd look good strapped to a gurney with the warden looking on."

"You'd better find a body or get a full confession."

"I'd like to visit her on Death Row."

"You're cold, Ricos."

"When a person is on Death Row, they need visitors. I could take some of the school kids with me."

"You're hopeless."

On the way out of the lodge, we removed the Missing Person flyer from the bulletin board. None of those people would see Jimmy unless they went to Baja and started hanging out with gay men.

* * *

Before we headed back to the office, I asked Barney if he'd mind if we stopped at the bentonite mine. There were two men employed there that worked on the dam, and I thought I should hear their stories. I would feel better about ignoring the dam.

We stopped at the mine office, and I inquired about Frederico Orozco and Timoteo Villa. The secretary said they were working together in an arroyo about a mile away.

We found them moving rocks around with front-end loaders. I got out of the vehicle and motioned for them to stop. They cut the motors and jumped down, looking more puzzled than anything.

I started to introduce myself when Sr. Orozco said in Spanish, "Aren't you Miguel Ricos' daughter, Margarita?"

"Yes, I am." When you grow up in a place, people know you even when you don't know them.

After they inquired about the health of my parents, I told them I was working on the Serena Bustamante case which seemed to surprise them. We sat on some boulders, and I explained that I had been investigating at the old Hampton place.

"I'm here to inquire about the dam you were building," I said. "When the sheriff investigated, he didn't suspect the dam, yet everyone in Terlingua thought Serena was buried in it."

"Oh, no, that would've been impossible," insisted Frederico.

"We would have known about a body in there," added Timoteo.

"But what if you helped him hide it?"

"That's what everyone was thinking, wasn't it? We were just a bunch of wetbacks that would do anything for an American dollar. Well, it wasn't that way. If Señor Hampton had said he killed a woman, we would have left."

Timoteo said, "We lived there, not far from the dam, and we'd have known if Sr. Hampton was fooling around with it. And we never helped him hide a corpse, either. You should ask your father about it. He was there."

"I'll ask him," I said, playing it cool, as if they hadn't just shocked the breath out of me. I had no idea my papi ever worked for William Hampton.

"I'm sure you both remember Rigo Mendez," I continued when I found my voice.

"Sure, he was our foreman."

"His name was mentioned as someone who had an affair with Serena."

The men laughed at that. "Are you kidding? She was the boss's woman, hombre. There wasn't one of us that stupid and definitely not Rigo," said Frederico.

"He told us about her, but we never saw her," said Timoteo. "He swore the boss had this pretty Mexican girl he was seeing in Alpine. We spent hours talking about women. We were young, and there were no eligible females anywhere near us."

"We talked about Serena, sure," agreed Frederico. "We talked about all women. The stuff about Serena was make-believe, based on things Rigo told us." As each one spoke the other nodded in agreement.

"So you're sure Rigo never saw her behind the boss's back?"

They lost it then. They were still looking at each other and laughing and cutting up when Barney and I pulled away from the arroyo.

CHAPTER 14

At the office, I showered and changed into my uniform. Barney sat behind his desk, still wearing riding clothes. He was about to head for the shower when two guys in dark, ill-fitting suits came through the door asking about the Taggert investigation.

My first impression was that this was a joke.

"I'm Deputy Ricos," I said in an attempt to take over so Barney could go ahead and get cleaned up. "How are you involved with the Taggert case?"

Barney stood rooted to the floor. The men introduced themselves as Harold Spasky and Clint Underwood from the FBI. They flashed identification so quickly it was impossible to see it. We didn't need to see it to know it was fake.

Barney shook hands and invited them to sit. He and I exchanged a glance. Maybe this case was going to get interesting again.

"What can we do for you?" Barney asked politely.

"It has come to our attention that youse have been conducting an investigation into the disappearance of James Taggert," stated the one calling himself Harold Spasky. "Mr. Taggert is wanted on drug trafficking charges." I swear he said *youse*. He sounded like a low-ranking hood from *The Sopranos*.

"We just completed our investigation of his disappearance," I said. "We don't know about any drug charges."

"We were closing the case," added Barney. "There's nothing else we can do."

"This has been an undercover operation for a number of months," said the one claiming to be Clint Underwood. "We were about to nab Taggert, but he disappeared. One of his co-workers informed us of his trip to Big Bend National Park. At that point, we decided to wait for his return. But he didn't, see? We spoke to his co-workers again, and they said he vacationing at Terlin—this place here. That's the last they ever heard from him."

"He's now late by more than three weeks. That gives us reason to believe he's on the run," said Spasky. "What did youse turn up?"

Barney studied the two men before answering. I thought he was considering whether or not to tell them anything, or else he was trying not to laugh.

"We found his car and camp, but he was long gone. The car runs fine, so that wasn't the reason for leaving it. Following a lead, we traced his movements to Ojinaga, in Mexico. Witnesses there said he spent two or three days and then moved on, saying he had gone to Baja California to live."

The two men looked at each other. They were so not FBI that Barney and I were on the verge of hysterical laughter. I was dying to ask them where they got the suits.

"So youse are sure he's not hiding out around here?" Spasky asked.

"We're sure he's not here," said Barney with a tightly controlled voice. "We're a small community, and we notice strangers."

"He coulda changed his appearance," suggested Underwood.

"Why would he bother? Nobody here knows him anyway."

"So's in case the law'd come looking for him," said Underwood with exaggerated patience, as if we were the idiots in the room, "which it has."

"Right," said Barney, and leaned back in his chair, relaxed, as if he'd bought the performance. "As best we can tell, there are no strangers hanging around that look like James Taggert or any version of him. We do have tourists here, but they come and go. We don't pay much attention unless they cause trouble."

"If we do spot somebody that looks like Taggert, how can we get in touch with you?" I asked.

"Call the FBI and leave a message."

"Don't you have a card?"

Neither man could produce one.

"Alrighty then," said Barney. He stood. We didn't dare look at each other. "Pleasure meeting you gentlemen," he said. "Good luck."

"Likewise," said Spasky. "Youse have a good day."

Underwood was already at the door.

We watched them get into an old, blue beater sedan, and then we laughed until we hurt. Tears rolled down our faces. I had to sit and try to recover my breath. We were still laughing when Barney headed for the shower ten minutes later. When he came out, we took one look at each other and started again.

"Call the FBI and leave a message," he howled.

* * *

When I recovered, I called Sheriff Ben and told him about the want-to-be FBI characters. He got a laugh out of it, too.

"Keep your ears to the ground in case they cause trouble," he said. "I suspect it's a last-ditch effort by some hoodlums to collect a debt or something like that."

We thought so, too. I promised the sheriff we would be vigilant until we were sure they had gone. After that, I asked if I could fly to Jackson Hole to interview William Hampton. From there I would drive to Cody to interview Hampton's former wife.

He balked. "Is that really necessary?" The sheriff is budget-minded, and we were talking about a thirty-year-old case. But it was his idea to solve it.

"I think it is, or I wouldn't ask. Former Sheriff Blanton's investigation implicated Curly Hampton. I think it might have been his wife. If you expect me to close this case I must talk to them, and I can catch them both on one trip."

"What about using the telephone?"

"Aren't you the sheriff who taught me that interviews are best accomplished in person so a suspect's reactions can be observed?"

What could he say? He caved. "Okay, make the arrangements, but coordinate your calendar with Barney before you plan anything. And use caution. Odds are that Hampton is a killer. Please remember that."

"Yes sir. I will."

"You can't jump to conclusions because he's tall, handsome, and charming."

"Give me a little credit, Sheriff."

He laughed but advised me to remember his words.

When I asked Barney about it, he said for me to proceed as needed, but he added, "You know he's a big, hairy mountain man living in the backwoods of Wyoming. He kills whatever he eats and picks his teeth with the bones. His chest is so hairy small rodents live there. If I were the sheriff, I'd forbid you to go."

"If you were the sheriff, I would look for another job."

I turned, walked back into my office, sat, and stared at my hill. The colors of winter—various shades of brown, gold, and yellow—had taken over, but some of the trees are slow to give up their leaves, so bits of green remained in the vista. The catclaw acacia had thrown its leaves to the ground at the first hint of drought. The plants on my hill are gutsy, and they do what they must to survive; I could say the same about the people in my community.

My attention moved to the photograph of Serena. Then I called the last known number for William Hampton. It made me feel queasy. I would either be talking to a cold-blooded murderer or an innocent man whose life was ruined by Serena's disappearance. Either way, my stomach was doomed.

On the third ring, the phone was answered by a man who said he wasn't William Hampton, but if I would identify myself, he would get him for me. I had a moment of hesitation then told him my name, and that I was calling from the Brewster County Sheriff's Office. At first I thought Hampton was not going to come to the phone, and who would blame him.

After a long wait, a deep voice said, "This is William Hampton. Please pardon the delay. I was about to go for a ride and was saddling up when Brian called me to the phone." His voice was pleasant, and he seemed friendly.

"I'm sorry to disturb you. I've been assigned the task of re-investigating the disappearance of Serena Bustamante. Naturally, you'd be crucial to that."

He paused a long time. "Naturally," he finally said. "How may I be of help to you?" I had expected anger or hostility, maybe sad-ness. He seemed resigned.

"I want to visit you, sir. I promise not to take up much of your time. I need to clarify some points and get your opinion on a few things."

"And this couldn't be done by phone or e-mail?"

"No sir. I'd prefer not. In person will be preferable if you don't mind."

He gave something like a laugh. "I can't tell if that's good or bad."

"I can't tell either, but it's the way I investigate. I have to get a feel for the person I'm interviewing, and that's difficult by phone and even harder by e-mail."

"Okay. When will you come?"

"Would Wednesday work for you?"

He laughed. "You don't waste any time, do you?"

"I'm trying not to. Thirty years have passed already. I don't have time to waste."

"I think I'm going to like you," he said.

"I'll fly into Jackson Hole and rent a car. I imagine I could be at your home by two or two-thirty that afternoon. I'll call you back after I make all the arrangements and let you know the exact time."

"I can pick you up from the airport if you'd like. My ranch is about thirty minutes from there."

"Thank you, but I'll rent a car. After I speak with you, I'll be driving to Cody for another interview."

"I see. Well, have it your way, then. You could stay here if you like. I have a guest house. You'd have total privacy, of course, no strings attached. You're coming too late to drive away at night. Sometimes the roads are icy."

"Thank you, I'll plan on doing that if it wouldn't be too much trouble." *And if you aren't picking your teeth with the bones of woodland creatures.*

"It would be no trouble at all, Ms. Ricos. If I'm not here when you call back, leave a message with my personal assistant, Brian. You'd better bring warm clothes. Winter in Wyoming is a different ballgame from winter in Terlingua."

After I hung up, I studied Serena as if she were about to divulge something. She probably wanted to tell me that Hampton was a fine-looking, educated man living in luxury on a multi-million dollar ranch, not a hairy cave-dweller.

Before I lost courage, I called the former Mrs. Hampton. She answered on the third ring. Her manner was cool when I told her who I was and the purpose of my call.

"I don't have anything new to say," she claimed. She was a breath away from groaning into the phone. "Can't you do the interview by telephone? I can't face all those questions again."

"I wish I could spare you, but you're crucial to the investigation." I gave her my spiel about preferring face-to-face meetings over telephone calls, which was true. But I also promised not to make her re-hash every detail, which might not have been.

"Come on," she said, "and get it over with. When will you be here? It's very cold in Wyoming, you know."

"I'd like to speak with you on Thursday or Friday. I'll have to call you with my plans after I make the airline reservations. Is it okay if I call in the morning?"

"Yes. I'll be here."

I sat back in my chair and breathed a sigh of relief. So far, so good; at least they weren't hostile.

"Serena," I whispered, "want to go to Wyoming? I could use the moral support."

"I heard that!" Barney yelled.

I got up and moved into his office. "Why am I letting this become personal? It's like Serena is my friend and I'm charged with avenging her death."

"When she speaks to you, I'll start to worry," he said in a kind way. "How did those people react to your calls?"

"They weren't hostile, but they tried to scare me away with the Wyoming cold."

"They don't know who they're dealing with, Batgirl."

"I wish you wouldn't call me that. It seems like you're making fun of me."

"Well, I'm not. Believe it or not, it's a compliment. Besides, I would never make fun of you. It would look bad if a *girl* gave me a black eye."

To change the subject I asked, "Will those 'FBI' fellows cause problems for us?"

"It's hard to say what they'll do. I wonder if they think we bought that act."

"I don't see what they could accomplish here, unless they wanted to look around for themselves. If they think we bought their act, then maybe they believe we're too clueless to recognize Jimmy Taggert if he sat down with us and held up his missing person flyer."

"Youse got that right," said Barney.

* * *

"Mrs. Jablonski," I practically barked, "you lied in your statement to Sheriff Blanton and then you lied to me. I'm asking you once more to tell me about the day of Serena's disappearance and I would like the truth this time."

"How dare you! And why are you bothering me with this again?"

"I have information from college records that places you at classes all day. In fact, you gave some type of project report that's noted on the attendance sheet."

Long pause. "That's impossible. There must be some mistake."

"No mistake," I said, waiting with my fingers drumming the desk.

"Well, I suppose I could have gotten it wrong."

"Mrs. Jablonski, thirty years ago you lied to Sheriff Blanton when you told him you had spent the day with Christina Hampton. Tell me why."

She hesitated, but finally said, "Christina and I were best friends. I was afraid the investigation would turn to her right away. You see, she had more motive than Curly. He was a cheating dog, but he would never murder anyone."

"You thought Christina murdered Serena?"

"I thought so, yes. She was the one with everything to lose. She must have hated Serena. Women will do what they feel they have to in order to keep their lives from falling apart, especially when there is a fortune involved. I feared for my friend, so I told Sheriff Blanton what I did so he would look somewhere else."

"In other words, you protected a probable murderer. You obstructed justice." If I had been in her presence, I think I would've kicked out her teeth. Some interviews are best done by phone after all.

"I didn't mean any harm. I was trying to protect my friend. We were both young. In retrospect, I guess it was the wrong thing to do."

Ya think?

"What can I do about it now?" she asked, with attitude.

"You gave me the names of three men you said were having sex with Serena at the same time she disappeared. I've spoken with two of those men, and it seems obvious that what you told me was more lies."

"Everybody knew she was a tramp."

"Everybody says just the opposite. She was a virgin until she met Curly—"

"You can believe that if you want," she interrupted, "but I wasn't born yesterday. Virgins don't run around screwing older men and breaking up marriages."

"Have you considered the possibility of love, Mrs. Jablonski? It seems to me that Serena and Curly fell in love. Neither of them planned it, but it happened, the way love tends to. I know it's an old-fashioned idea, but this *was* thirty years ago."

"I'm telling you it wasn't that way. That tramp had designs on the money. She thought she could get her hands on it by offering up her shapely body. It would have worked, too, if she hadn't gotten what she deserved."

"She didn't deserve to die, no matter what she did," I said. "I'll tell you this, Mrs. Jablonski. If I prove it was Christina that killed Serena, I'll make sure you serve time for obstruction of justice in a capital murder case."

"I hardly think—"

I hung up in frustration. Who cared what she thought?

* * *

Preston Gutierrez happened to be in his office when I called. He was not the greens keeper at the Alpine Golf Club, as Mrs. Jablonski said. He was the general manager.

I explained the reason for my call.

"You've been given wrong information," he said. "I never had anything to do with Serena romantically. I did know her, of course. I was friends with her brother, Joey. We're still good friends. I was ten years older than his baby sister. To try to date her would have interfered in my friendship with Joey. Besides, he and I have been friends since before Serena was born. She was like my baby sister, too. Have you talked to Joey?"

"Yes I have, but not about you."

"Ask him if you want. He knows I would never have touched her in that way. For one thing, by the time she was fifteen, I was happily married. Still am."

I thanked him and hung up. What I had was another dead-end lie, courtesy of the same bitch.

* * *

Miguel Ricos had never been interviewed during the Serena investigation as far as I could tell, and I shouldn't be the one to do it. A daughter interviewing her papi as a possible witness to a murder is—it's not done. I went to see him anyway. For one thing, it was dinnertime, and he would be making something tasty. If I discovered he knew things that were crucial to my case, I could ask Barney to do a formal interview with him.

"I'm about to eat tacos," Papi said with a grin when he opened his door to me.

Oh, yeah.

"How do you always know?" he teased, his dark eyes full of humor.

"The smell draws me from miles away, Papi."

After the hugging and "¿que paso?" conversation, he said, "People say you beat up that cabrón, Wynne." My papi doesn't waste much time on small talk.

"He asked for it."

"That's what I figured."

"I should have walked away."

"He must have brought out the Comanche in you."

I laughed. "Yes, that must be it."

Papi maintains that since the Comanche were always raiding and plundering in Mexico, many Mexicans have at least some Comanche blood. Whenever I had a fit of temper as a child, he used to say it was "the Comanche coming out."

"Do you want some help making the tacos, Papi?"

"No, Mija, I only need to make a few more. Sit at the table and talk to me."

Tacos, the way he prepares them, are created from scratch. First the corn tortillas have to be made from masa, and then the ground meat-based stuffing. That mixture is pressed into the tortillas, and they are fried together. You have to watch what you're doing, or the tortilla shells will harden with too small an opening for sticking in the shredded cabbage or lettuce, and slices of tomato.

I sighed. "I'm supposed to help people, not hurt them."

"Yes, but you can't let people run all over you, either."

"Every time he sees me, he makes comments about the 'girl deputy', as if a man would be better—as if *he* would be better at it just because he's a man."

"God help us all if Wynne ever becomes a deputy."

"Sheriff Ben would never hire him."

My dad put a plate with eight tacos on it in front of me. I have never eaten that many at one time, but his serving size never changes.

"Eight, Papi?"

He set a bowl of fresh salsa on the table and sat next to me. "You look hungry."

"I am, but eight is too many."

"Do the best you can and I'll eat what you can't."

We munched tacos, and the room was quiet for a while, except for crunching sounds and spoons hitting the salsa bowl.

"This tastes so good," I said with a full mouth.

He winked at me but kept eating. After dinner, I offered to do the clean-up but instead, we did it together. We talked about my mother. Had I seen her? Was she okay? They were the usual questions. My parents are divorced, but sometimes I wonder if they forget that.

Then I switched subjects without preamble. "Did you ever work for William Hampton?"

Papi looked surprised. "What makes you ask that?"

I explained that I was working on the Serena Bustamante case, but no more than that.

He remembered the incident well but had his own questions. One of them was, "Why are you working on a case older than you?"

"The sheriff asked me to figure it out."

"He knows how smart and dedicated you are."

"Thank you, Papi, but it's because Serena was a young Mexican-American, and so am I. I can't tell you more than that because it's a still-open case."

Papi is hilarious. He said, "Well. Next thing you know, they'll put you on the case of César Chavez. Nobody knows who murdered him, either."

"But there's no proof he was murdered."

"That's what they always say."

"What about William Hampton, Papi?"

"I worked for him a few months, building the stone fence around his house."

"It's beautiful. I had no idea you built that."

"You know my fence?"

"Yes, Papi. I was just there."

"Why?"

"Barney and I went to look for clues."

"There won't be anything there," he said.

"Yes, we figured that out."

"If Hampton killed her, he would never have buried her anywhere on his property. He was too smart for that."

"Did you ever work on the dam?"

"No, but I knew the guys who did. We lived together."

"And?"

"They weren't murderers if that's what you're wondering. Our only crime was being in the U.S. illegally, but that wasn't such a serious offense back then."

"Did you ever meet Serena?"

"No. I heard talk of her, but I didn't know if it was true—or care."

"What was your impression of William Hampton?"

"I can only judge him by how he treated his workers."

"Which was how?"

"He was good to us. We always had plenty to eat, and he would bring us fresh fruit and vegetables, in addition to the usual beans, rice, and makings for tortillas. I had worked for other men who treated Mexicans worse than they did their animals."

"Papi, why have you never told me about that?"

"Why do you need to know?"

"I'm your daughter, for one thing."

"When I was a young man I did desperate things to make a better life for myself. No need for you to know all that. I never hurt anyone or stole anything, but I endured terrible working conditions, bad situations, and bosses who had no more morals than a mule's behind."

"Didn't it ever occur to you that I might like to hear your stories?"

"Mija, those stories are for another time."

"Okay, but I'm not going to forget, Papi. You know how I am."

He laughed. "Yes, you're like me."

"Tell me more about Hampton."

"Sometimes on Friday he brought us beer. And he'd hang out with us a bit after work when he had time. It was strange behavior for a rich white man, especially back in those days."

"You must have been a mere child, Papi."

He laughed. "I was twenty when I worked for him."

"What did you think when people said Hampton had killed his girlfriend?"

"I thought they were wrong. The guys and I believed Señora Hampton was the culprit but in truth, we didn't know much about either one of them. They lived in a different world. I felt lucky to be working for a man who paid us on payday and wasn't the type to call Border Patrol when he didn't need us any longer—or shoot us, which was just as common."

Papi rarely spoke of his early life in this country, but when he did it made me sad.

CHAPTER 15

Icy dark and a billion stars greeted me when I stepped outside my house at six-thirty the next morning to go for a long run. A frosty sliver of moon glowed from a distant mountaintop, hooked there like a Christmas ornament. I stood still to admire it and give my eyes a chance to adjust. Pre-dawn is an amazing time to run, and there is usually enough starlight or moonlight to pull it off once the eyes adjust.

When I took off, I tried to keep my head on my life's big picture, and when that failed, the sky. But nagging details bugged me, such as why should I apologize? Wynne should apologize to me. And why is it so hard for my papi to talk about his early years in the United States? Would I ever have the guts to go on a date again? Was I flying off to interview a cold-blooded murderer? Which Hampton did it, or had they collaborated? Would they hurt me in Wyoming? If I took up bull riding, would that get me a little respect around here?

By the time I left for Wynne's, the moon had been unhooked from the craggy peak, and our planet had once again turned its face to the sun. I had convinced myself that I should be the bigger person and apologize to the bubba. I had damaged him, after all. My job is to serve the public, not hurt them, cavemen included.

Wynne Raymore lives in a wood home someone started before he was born. Strange that no one in the sequence of occupiers had finished it. The walls on one side are commercial-grade black plastic nailed on thin strips of wood attached to the house. Instead of completing the job, the plastic is replaced when it becomes brittle from long exposure to weather. Considering the intensity of our sun, it seems like constantly replacing the plastic would be more expensive and time-consuming than finishing the walls. But I was not there to criticize. My goal was to make an apology and head off future difficulties.

Wynne came to the door, after making me wait five minutes, but he carried a double barrel shotgun and was dressed head to toe in camouflage. I'm sure I would have laughed if it hadn't been such a surprise. I was armed, but my department-issue Beretta was holstered with the safety on. It would be impossible to make a quick draw and win. Crap!

My adversary grimaced with pain, and one pants leg had been cut up the front to accommodate his swollen and bandaged knee, but he wasn't using crutches.

"I'm done fuckin' with you," he said. It was so nasal it was hilarious; at the same time he made me furious. I reminded myself not to buy in to his baggage. Say sorry and get out.

I took a calming breath. "Please don't shoot me, Wynne. I'm here to apologize."

"The hell you are! You came to gloat."

"No. I came to apologize. That's the truth."

He propped a torn screen door open with his booted foot so he could see me better, but didn't invite me in. There was still the matter of the shotgun pointed at me. "Let's hear it then," he growled.

"I'm truly sorry for hurting you. I lost my temper, and I'm ashamed of myself."

"Did that stupid sheriff make you come here?"

"No. I came because I wanted to. Would you put the weapon away and let me speak with you adult to adult?"

He thought about it. "I suppose you'll want to come in."

"Well, it is cold standing out here."

He lowered the shotgun. "Okay, come in, but don't try anything. The place is a mess since I don't get around too good now."

"I understand." I guessed his place was always a mess, but I kept the thought to myself and stepped inside.

Wynne hobbled around, knocking papers and food wrappers off the sofa. "Sit," he commanded. A heavy, gray, long-haired cat appeared from somewhere and jumped into my lap to purr in my face.

"Fluffy, get down from there," Wynne ordered, but Fluffy gave him a look of disdain and stayed put. Having a well-cared-for kitty named Fluffy earned Wynne a few points in my book.

"What is it you have to say?"

"Why does the sight of me make you so angry? Please be frank. It's just you and me here if we don't count Fluffy."

First he hemmed and hawed and picked at his clothing. I bit back wisecracks until he spoke. "It makes me pissed off when a woman gets a man's job."

"Law enforcement is no longer considered a man's job. It hasn't been since forever. The other thing is that I am qualified for the job."

"That doesn't matter."

"But it does."

"That old man hired you so he could get in your pants. Everybody knows that."

"Sheriff Duncan hired me because I beat out the other applicants in test scores and shooting accuracy. He liked the way I handled the interview and my reasons for wanting to work in Terlingua."

"Bully for you."

"There were men and women who applied. I acknowledge that you think women can't do law enforcement work, but I'm not going to quit because you want me to. At some point, you have to accept that women can do jobs that, in the dark ages, were claimed by men."

"Women didn't do them for a reason."

"Yes, because women were discriminated against."

"God, you make me sick with that bullshit."

"Look Wynne. You live here, and I live here. We're never going to agree, and that's all right. Leave me alone and I'll leave you alone."

"That's not what I want."

"What do you want? And I need a serious answer, not 'I want to put my hands up your skirt,' or any other bullshit."

"But what if that's what I want?"

"If that's true, you sure go about it all wrong."

"Well, I already know you don't like white men; that's obvious."

"That's ridiculous. I don't care about the color of a man's skin."

He was determined to push my buttons. "If your father's Mexican and your mother's white, doesn't that make you a half-breed?"

I tried to stay calm and pretend I didn't have buttons. "I didn't come to here to fight with you about who I am."

"I would like to see you be less high and mighty. Most of the time, you don't even see me. You won't give any local guy a chance 'cause you think you're too good for the likes of us."

"That's not true, Wynne. My husband died a year and a half ago. I'm not ready to replace him. My heart feels not just broken but gone. I've been withdrawn because of emotional pain, not because I believe I'm better than anyone else. Sometimes, when I think of what I lost, I can barely get out of bed."

"That's sad." His tone was mocking, and he had dismissed my honest response. It made me feel foolish—and fightin' angry.

He shifted around so that the shotgun was aimed at me again. "I don't believe a word of it."

"Well, I guess I'll be going, Wynne." I stood. "You're determined not to work this out, so there's nothing else to say."

"Not so fast. Sit down." He motioned towards the sofa with the shotgun. "Let's talk about this. You're sayin' you'll go out with me someday?"

"You have no respect for women, Wynne. Why would I go out with you?"

"But I like women."

"I'm overdue at work. I came to say I'm sorry I hurt you and I said it. I know you aren't trying to hold me here against my will."

He looked sheepish. "That's true. It's not loaded." He let the weapon clatter to the floor beside his chair. Fluffy gave a squeaky cry of surprise and fled the room.

You wouldn't believe the relief I felt.

Wynne limped after me. "Come back sometime when you can stay longer."

Not even if he was the last breathing man on the planet.

"I'll see you, Wynne."

"I hope you get your heart back."

"Thanks."

Then Wynne offered me his hand and I took it. "Margarita, I'm sorry I said I didn't believe you. I guess you musta loved that ol' bull rider of yours in a big way."

"Yes, I did." *To the next galaxy and back.*

* * *

After Wynne, I needed time off, but I went to see another character on a different subject. He had been interviewed during the original investigation into Serena's disappearance, and of course he had an opinion because he's Mr. Opinion, Jeff Smith. Jeff was old when I was a child, so imagine him now. Yeah, forget it. He was on the *get it over with* list right below Mrs. Jablonski.

He wasn't at home, and his neighbor said he was pontificating at The Porch. That should have been my first guess since he was there more than not there.

When I pulled up, Jeff was yammering and flinging his arms, making a point I was glad not to hear. I didn't recognize the people he was entertaining; maybe they were tourists. If so, what were the chances they would ever return?

"Hey, Margarita!" Jeff called. "Folks, meet one of our local crime fighters, Deputy Ricos. She's the pretty one of the bunch." Well, at least he didn't say I was the 'girl deputy.'

We greeted each other, and it turned out they were visiting from Houston and love the area and had been in the park. I never get tired of hearing other peoples' take on the land I adore. My arrival gave them an excuse to move on, so they hustled.

Jeff patted the bench. "Sit with me a while. You haven't done that in too long."

It made me feel guilty for dreading a visit with him so much. Jeff is a landmark in a way. He's been here ever since I've known the place, just like The Porch. He wears his gray hair long and in a ponytail. He's smoked so many unfiltered cigarettes for so long his fingertips are golden-brown. Smoking and whiskey gave him a raspy voice. Maybe whiskey has nothing to do with the voice but he does drink. Copiously.

He gave me a sideways hug. "What brings you this way?" He smelled of strong tobacco, Old Spice and whiskey, and it wasn't unpleasant exactly; it was just Jeff.

"I was looking for you, Jeff."

"No kidding?" A pause, and then a guilty look. "What have I done?"

"Nothing, I hope. Let's talk about the Serena Bustamante case."

"The what?"

"Thirty years ago a young woman from Alpine disappeared from an arroyo on Terlingua Ranch. Do you remember that?"

"Oh, yes, I do remember. That ol' rich sonofabitch killed that poor girl."

"That was never proven."

"Well, some things you just know."

"The law doesn't work like that, Jeff. I'm trying to find out the truth."

"But that case is older than you!"

"True, but it's still open, and the sheriff wants me to close it."

Jeff laughed. "Has he asked you to find Jimmy Hoffa, too?"

He was as hilarious as Papi. I got the joke, but to tell the truth, I didn't have a clue who Jimmy Hoffa was except to know he's missing, and people have looked for him a long time.

"If I find Serena," I said, "I might be assigned to Jimmy Hoffa next."

That got a big laugh out of Jeff, but the slim chance of finding either one of them hit me between the eyes.

"There're too many places out there to stash a body," Jeff said, indicating the vast landscape with a sweep of his arm.

148

"Yeah, I know."

"How will you get proof of anything thirty years after the fact?" he asked. "Even if you find a body, there won't be any forensics to go on."

"I know that, too."

"Can you get a dead person's DNA from a skeleton that old?"

"Yes, most likely."

"That's amazing."

"I'm re-interviewing people who were questioned during the original investigation, and you're one of them. Were you acquainted with either of the Hamptons or Serena?"

"I knew both Hamptons by sight, but that was it. They were too good for us poor people. I figure Hampton offed her, put the body in a crate, and paid to have her shipped away from here and buried somewhere. Rich people always get away with murder. If I had done it, I'd be in prison, or dead by injection."

"Your theory doesn't help me, Jeff. I know everyone believed Hampton did it, but I need a fact. Do you know anything that can be proved?"

"Hampton killing her is the one thing that makes sense. He had his fun with a lovely young thing and then she was in his way. You be careful who you get involved with, Margarita. Don't go for somebody just because he's rich and good-looking."

One problem with growing up in a small place is that everyone old enough to be your parent thinks they are.

"I won't, Jeff."

"You went for that handsome teacher before, Kevin the bull rider."

"Yes, but he wasn't rich. He had many things about him that were more important to me than his looks."

Jeff nudged me. "His looks didn't insult you though, right?"

I laughed. "No, he was very handsome." *And I would give everything I have in this world to see him again.*

I was about to cry, so I went back to my reason for being there. "I need to know if you ever saw anything suspicious, or heard anything. Do you know anyone I should interview? I need something to sink my teeth into."

"Well sugar, I could buy you some lunch."

* * *

Investigation-wise, it was a crummy day.

In other news, the hawks were out in number showing off. Jeff went to lunch after I declined his sweet offer. I stayed on the porch a while to watch the air show.

My friend Ron came to get something at the store and sat with me a while. He is an archaeologist who works in Big Bend National Park. We watched a hawk strike with deadly speed and then rise with the grace of a prima ballerina.

"Hawks are my favorite," he said. "I can't count the times I sit and vicariously soar with the ones that fly through my space."

I opened my mouth but couldn't think of a thing to add.

* * *

Back at the office, I called a few more longtime Terlingua residents, but it was more of the same and a whole lot of yada, yada. Jeff had covered what the locals thought about the Serena disappearance and in particular, Curly Hampton. He was a rich white man with a taste for young Hispanics, and he was guilty as sin. Maybe everything they said was true, but I needed facts, ma'am, just the facts.

There were more people on my list, but they would have to wait until I came home from Wyoming. I couldn't stand to hear another non-fact-based opinion and went home to pack.

CHAPTER 16

As the jet circled for a landing, I was struck by the beauty of the serrated mountains below. Their chiseled profile dominated the landscape, even from above. These were the great peaks of the Teton Mountains. I could see the glacial spars, the gray color of the exposed rock, and the lush forests below that. The mountains tower more than a mile above Jackson Hole Valley. Grand Teton National Park is south of Yellowstone National Park and not far north of Jackson Hole, Wyoming.

In a rented Jeep Cherokee, I drove away from the bustle of the airport and soon found myself in wide open country with trees on one side. A broad meadow gleamed on the other, and behind that, a thick, dark forest. The Grand Tetons loomed to my left, magnificent as a snow-covered backdrop.

If Terlingua was brown in winter, Wyoming took it a step further. Everything appeared to be dead or sleeping, except for stands of evergreens. Even the lowest hills were covered in snow, and the meadows appeared to be buried in it.

I pulled into a deserted picnic area and called Barney to tell him that I made it. "You wouldn't believe this scenery, and it's freezing here. Is everything okay there?"

"Fine, but I feel like you've been gone for days already."

"Have you heard anything more from the FBI?"

"Not a peep. They didn't even ask around."

"We did their work for them."

"It seems that way, Ricos."

"I never met Jimmy," I said, "but I hope those hoods don't find him."

"Me, too, and I wish we hadn't told them he went to Baja."

"Well, it won't be easy for them to find him there. Baja is far more populated than Terlingua, and the Mexican authorities aren't going to buy their feeble FBI act."

"I hope that's true. Have you met your mountain man yet? Jeez, Ricos, he might drag you off into a cave, and you'll never be seen again."

"That might be okay—depending."

"He's old. You've already forgotten that, haven't you? And he's covered in fur. Why else would somebody be called Curly?"

"If he's old, then I oughtta be able to take him in a one-on-one."

"True. Have him call Wynne."

I ignored that. "I had better get this car moving so the heater will work. I can't even feel my toes, Barney."

"Good luck," he said, "Youse better watch your backside."

"I'm armed."

"So is he, probably."

I called William Hampton to tell him I was fifteen or twenty minutes away from his spread, the Pinto Canyon Ranch. He was in the barn checking on horses, but Brian promised to give him my message right away.

The detailed directions Hampton had given me made finding the ranch easy. The views along the unpaved road to the house were a wonder. It was lined with aspens, now leafless, but still splendid. Ahead I saw the sprawling house, a giant barn, and several outbuildings. Patches of snow were everywhere, and behind everything were the Grand Tetons, keeping silent watch.

When I pulled up to the house, a tall man approached walking fast. He was dressed in riding boots, jeans, a wool plaid shirt and a red insulated vest. A bright red wool cap was pulled down onto his head, but even from a distance I could see the curling mop of black hair sticking out around the edges. His hands were gloved, but he removed the right-hand one to shake.

"I'm William Hampton." He clasped my cold hand in his warm one. "Welcome to Wyoming."

"Thank you, Mr. Hampton. I'm Margarita Ricos."

"Please call me Curly. I hardly know to answer to anything else."

He stood much taller than I and was regal, like the mountains behind him. And he was still disarmingly handsome.

"It's so scenic here I'm speechless," I said.

He laughed. "Yes, it is, but come on inside where it's warm. I'll have someone get your bags in a moment. Did you have any trouble finding the ranch?"

"Your directions were easy to follow, but I nearly ran off the road in several places gawking at the views."

We went into the house, where a younger man stepped towards us when the door opened. Curly introduced him as Brian, his personal assistant. He shook my hand and was cordial but aloof. He took my coat, scarf, and wool cap and put them into a closet in the hallway. Brian was bald, with a chiseled face. He looked like a bodyguard-type who did serious working out. While I sized up his build, I noticed he was checking out mine.

"We'll be in here, Brian, if you need me," Curly said. He indicated closed double doors.

"I'll be in the office, sir."

When Curly opened up the room, my first thought was, *I could live in here.* It reminded me of the type of great room you see in photos of hunting lodges, although thankfully there were no dead animals on the walls. In place of the usual trophies were enormous, awe-inspiring photographs and paintings of the Pinto Canyon Ranch, the Tetons, and of Wyoming in general.

A towering balsam fir filled one corner and was decorated with twinkling white lights and glittering ornaments. It made the room smell like a forest.

Dark knotty pine paneled the walls and the floors were gleaming hardwood. A large stone fireplace was filled to capacity with a blazing stack of logs. On the mantel were fresh evergreen boughs adorned with red velvet ribbon. They were festive and their fragrance added to the illusion of being in the woods.

"The tree came from my forest," Curly said when he saw me gaping at it.

I was speechless. Two trees grew in my yard; this man had his own forest.

Colorful wool rugs of a Native American design were scattered everywhere. In spite of its size, the room felt cozy and inviting. To one side was a grouping of expensive-looking red leather furniture, a couch, easy chairs, and artfully crafted side tables. Towards the center of the room was another collection of couches, love seats, and overstuffed chairs in beige-colored leather.

A desk of dark wood sat on the far side of the room, with a black leather desk chair that had room for two to sit. The wall behind it was lined with enclosed glass bookshelves from floor to ceiling, packed with books. The effect was dazzling to me, being a lover of leather, heavy wooden desks, overstuffed chairs, and walls and walls of books.

Below the windows were polished benches. The oversized panes of glass provided a stunning view of the Grand Tetons on one side of the room. On the red leather end, the windows looked out at a barn and corral, a deep conifer forest, and relatively small snow-covered mountains behind that. Evergreen boughs with huge red velvet bows and pairs of golden bells hung above the windows.

I realized Curly was watching me check out his room, and I wondered if my mouth had been hanging open.

"I thought we'd sit over here." He indicated the red leather section. "It can get too hot close to the fire."

When I didn't move, he said, "You're welcome to look around first. You like my room, I can tell." He seemed proud without being haughty.

"I think it's the most fantastic room I've ever seen."

I checked it out since he had invited me to. I grazed the beige couch with the tips of my fingers. The leather was as soft as baby's skin. Behind me, Curly shut the double doors and moved towards his desk. I followed like a newly-rescued puppy.

He picked up a wall phone and punched a button. "Andrea, would you bring coffee?" He paused and addressed me. "Is coffee okay with you? Would you prefer something else?"

"Coffee is fine. I like cream and sugar, if it's not too much trouble."

"With cream and sugar on the side please, Andrea, and some of those cookies you just made. Thanks."

The first thing to catch my attention on the desk was a photo of Curly and Serena. He had his arms around her, and they looked like a movie stars smiling at the camera. She was dressed in a form-fitting blue jacket that had probably stopped hearts. Curly looked like a man without a care. And he was a hunk.

His face was lined now, though not unpleasantly, and a bit of silver streaked his jet-black hair around the temples. It made him look more distinguished than old. At the same time, his unruly curls made him boyish. Curly Hampton was a far cry from the hairy, illiterate mountain man Barney had warned me against.

In another photo, an attractive woman, older than Serena, sat high in a saddle with the Tetons in the background. It had been taken on the Pinto Canyon Ranch. There were also pictures of two small boys, older boys at various ages, and adult men. At every stage, they looked alike and resembled Curly. The attractive woman was in several other photos, and one taken with Curly, his arm around her protectively.

"Those are my sons," said Curly from behind me in a voice full of pride. "And the woman with me there is Madeline. She saved me from the pits of despair and is the best friend I ever had." His voice softened when he said, "And of course you know Serena. I have never forgotten her."

I nodded numbly, my eyes full of tears.

"Let's have a seat," Curly said, "and you can get what you came here for."

The truth is I thought I already had it, the most important thing anyway: this man did not kill Serena Bustamante.

I followed Curly, and with a gallant gesture he indicated a red leather chair. I sank into it. He sat across from me, but not far. I liked that he was unafraid to be close, to be scrutinized by me. It was another indication of his innocence. Yes, I jumped to that conclusion in spite of having been trained to be suspicious and watchful, and to always reserve judgment. It wasn't that I had forgotten Sheriff Ben's warning about tall, handsome, charming men, either, but my boss was in Texas, and I was on my own.

Curly removed his riding boots, stretched his wool-socked feet, and wiggled his toes. "Ah, that's better." He smiled. "So what is it you came all this way for, Deputy Ricos?"

I took a deep breath. "I came to get your story in your words, to see who you are, and to try to understand things from your perspective. I'd like to record our conversation if that's okay with you. It's more for my reference than anything."

"Sure, I don't mind."

I started my small digital recorder. "Do you have any idea what happened to Serena?"

"You don't assume I killed her?"

"No," I said, "I don't think you did."

"Well then, you would be one of very few."

"That's okay. I'm used to standing away from the crowd. It gives me room to breathe."

He studied me before he spoke. "You're very young. You weren't even born thirty years ago. How can you know what I might've done?"

"Did you kill her?"

"No," he said softly and teared up. "I would never have hurt Serena."

"It's true I'm young, but that gives me a fresh perspective. I'm looking back on something that happened five years before I was born. I'm trying to look at it in a new way. My boss, Sheriff Duncan, assigned me to this case because he has faith that I can solve it. He knows I'll give it my best."

"I didn't mean to insult your professionalism or your abilities, Ms. Ricos. I don't hold your youth against you, believe me. You're refreshing in many ways."

"Please call me Margarita," I said. "For you to be clear about what I'm doing, let me say that I've read and re-read all the investigation notes and every interview. I know exactly where they searched. I've read Serena's private thoughts, things she wrote to you and about you. I've read things you wrote to her that were not meant for anyone else's eyes. I interviewed Serena's brother and sister and called her best friend, Samantha. I talked to Christina's friend Dena Jablonski. I explored your land and house in Terlingua, and I spoke with several men who were reportedly having affairs with Serena at the same time you were."

"What I had with Serena was much more than an affair."

"Yes sir, I know."

A gray-haired woman in a red apron came in with a tray of coffee fixings and a plate of oatmeal cookies. She set them on the table beside Curly. She said nothing, but he grinned at her and said, "Thank you, Andrea."

She smiled pleasantly and left the room.

"Please help yourself, Margarita." Curly poured two steaming mugs of coffee. "Who told you Serena had numerous affairs?"

"It was Dena Jablonski. I made her give me names, and I spoke with the men. Their stories differ substantially from hers, and I believe them. You don't have to defend Serena's honor. I already feel the truth of her."

"One thing I know no matter what," he said, "is that Serena loved me and only me. Other men lusted after her, I knew that. She was gorgeous and seemed unaware of it. Those men never gave me a moment's worry. I knew her heart."

I put cream and sugar in the coffee and tasted it using the spoon. "Oh, this is delicious."

"Andrea makes the best coffee," he said, "and countless other things too. I'd weigh three hundred pounds if I didn't ride and jog and work out."

"Yeah, me too."

He laughed. "At least you have youth on your side. Every day is a minefield of temptations around here. Andrea spoils me terribly. By the way, will you stay for dinner? I intended to mention it when I invited you to use the guest house."

"I would love to." The promise of dinner didn't stop me from eating cookies. They were the melt-in-your-mouth kind and still warm.

"Are you ready to hear my story?"

"Please."

"When I met Serena I was looking for a secretary for my Alpine office. I wanted an office there because it was hard to work with the boys around. I didn't want to be a dad that yelled at them all the time to be quiet. I needed a place to go to be serious and do my job. I also needed UPS, FedEx and other things, like an office supply store. Truthfully, I needed some space from Christina, too. I won't say I had stopped loving her, but we had grown apart."

He flexed his feet again and sipped coffee. "I didn't see a need for someone full time, but I needed a person I could trust with sensitive business matters, and I was willing to pay well. When Serena came in to interview, she seemed too young. She was dressed professionally and was well-spoken, so I gave her a chance. I asked her quite a few questions and was impressed with the sincere way she answered them. She didn't pretend she knew everything and said she was willing to learn new things.

"I can't tell you her beauty didn't give me pause. It did. But I was married with two sons, and it was my desire to keep my family together. I admired Serena the way men admire beautiful women. I didn't hire her so I could take advantage of her."

He paused to drink coffee and eat another cookie before continuing. "Serena was a fast learner. She was careful with my records, and was a perfectionist when typing anything for me. She was fun to work with and always cheerful. I began to look forward to seeing her. I started taking her to lunch when I was in Alpine, and she enjoyed that. I spared no expense. It was fun to have someone to spend money on who appreciated it.

"Once, she reached across the table and touched my hand. It was an innocent gesture on her part, but I felt as if I was on fire. It was like the first time a girl ever touched me. It was then I realized I had fallen in love with her."

Curly took an audible breath and stared at the fire so long I wasn't sure he would continue. I was determined to let him tell the story in his own way. By the time he spoke, his voice startled me.

"I took Serena to that upscale restaurant in Marathon for dinner and afterward, we danced. Being near her was intoxicating. It was difficult to contain my desire for her, but I knew she was no tramp. Too, I realized while holding her close, it wasn't just her body I wanted. I wanted to capture her heart. She already had mine." He leaned his head against the chair and closed his eyes.

"She showed her innocence in so many ways. She was barely twenty, so fresh and beautiful. I suspected she was a virgin, so I moved slowly and courted her in what is now considered an old-fashioned way. We dined, danced, talked until late, went to movies and concerts.

"One night, I was bringing her home from a dance and she suggested we look at the stars. She said she knew a good spot for it, on a hill away from the lights of the town. We went there and talked about the sky, our hopes and dreams, and then she kissed me. She leaned over and kissed me with a passion that took my breath away."

Curly opened his eyes, but he was looking at the ceiling. "Then we kissed some more. She took my hand and brushed it against her lips. I thought I would die from the wanting. 'I think we've fallen in love,' she said. I told her that I'd been in love with her for a long time. She asked if I would take her back to her apartment and make love to her."

My heart was pounding so hard I was afraid he could hear it.

"I felt I had just begun to live, Margarita. My life until that point had been empty. I have never loved anyone with such abandon. I tried not to think of Christina, or of losing my boys. I knew if I told Christina the truth, she would take them. I also knew I had to tell her. I could no longer make love to her because I couldn't be unfaithful to the love of my life. I never loved Christina like I loved Serena, not even close."

He sat up straight, took out a handkerchief, and wiped his eyes and blew his nose before continuing. "I know that what we did was wrong, but don't blame Serena. She was so young and innocent. Blame me, not her."

"I'm looking for the truth of what happened to her, not a way to place blame on either of you."

I asked to use the bathroom, and when I returned, Curly was putting on his riding boots. "Do you like horses? We could get in a quick ride before it gets dark if you like."

I love horses, and I needed a break from the intensity of his sad love story. We put on our jackets and walked together to a guest house a short distance away.

"Brian put your suitcase in your room," Curly said. "After you change, come to the barn. I'll get the horses ready. You'd better dress in warm clothes." He put his hand on my shoulder, and I looked up at him. "Thank you, Margarita." His voice broke. "I think Serena has sent me an angel."

He walked away before I could respond.

CHAPTER 17

The guest house was meant to be shared by many, with rooms on either side of a long hallway. It had a spacious living room, similar to the one we had left. Next to that, a door to one room stood open. I saw my suitcase on a stand at the end of the bed and went in.

The room was paneled, and the floors were hardwood, like the main house. A double bed was piled high with blankets and quilts. The motif was Tex-Mex, and an oil painting of a desert-mountain scene of the Terlingua area hung on the wall.

Lying on the bed was a bouquet of greenery with red berries. It looked like Christmas and smelled divine. A handwritten note read: *I hope you enjoy the Terlingua Room, Ms. Ricos. I picked these berries for you. Welcome to Wyoming and the Pinto Canyon Ranch, Brian.*

I changed my clothes and put on more layers than I ever wore at home: long underwear, flannel-lined jeans, a long-sleeved t-shirt, another shirt over that, and a wool shirt on top. My good leather boots would have to work as riding boots since they were all I had. I stuffed my multi-layered self into a fleece-lined jacket and felt like the Goodyear blimp. Next, I wrapped a wool scarf around my neck, added wool gloves and a cap, and hurried out to find Curly in the barn.

Brian was helping him saddle two horses. Since he was talking business with Curly, I nosed around. The barn was clean and smelled of hay, grain, and leather. I found a mare and colt in a stall towards the rear and stopped to speak to them. The mare came to me to be petted, but the baby stayed back, suspicious.

Curly appeared at my side. "Ready?"

Brian held a massive paint mare by the halter and spoke softly to her. His breath and hers looked like smoke mingling in the cold air.

"Thank you for the berry bouquet, Brian. It's lovely and made me feel welcome here."

If Curly hadn't been watching us with such amusement, I would have said more.

Brian blushed. "You're welcome." He held up his hand and boosted me into the saddle.

"Thanks," I said again. He nodded, his face expressionless, but his eyes were full of smile. Then he turned and headed back to the house.

"He's a man of few words," commented Curly.

"He seems to hold multiple jobs around here."

Curly nodded. "He's a wrangler. He's my personal assistant and provides security. He gives one hell of a massage, and he can fix anything. He's good company once you get him talking. He's shy at first, but then, you better watch out."

"Does he live here?"

"Yes. He has a suite at the other end of the guest house. He works ten days and then is off for four."

"What about Andrea?"

"She has rooms at the back of the main house. She lives here, too, during the week, and has most weekends off. You could say we're a family."

We ambled down a dirt road towards a copse of evergreens. The snaggletoothed Grand Tetons loomed to our left, covered with snow and ice. Their color was battleship grey wherever they weren't white. They were a breathtaking sight that wouldn't let my eyes rest.

"The national park boundary is past the fence you see in the distance there," said Curly, pointing to it.

After we rode a short way, he asked, "What do you think of the Pinto Canyon Ranch?"

"It's stunning."

"I love it here. Those mountains tower about seven-thousand feet above Jackson Hole Valley. The tallest peak is Grand Teton and is over thirteen thousand feet high."

"Do you ever climb? The tourist pamphlets claim these mountains are more accessible than they look."

"I used to climb when I was younger," he said. "When I was a kid I spent most of my summers in these mountains."

"Was this your family's ranch?"

"No, we lived north of here, in Cody. But my brothers and I spent many days exploring in the national park."

"I've never climbed mountains so high. Does it take long?"

"In normal weather you can get to the summit in two days. The first day is spent working your way up to Garnet Canyon, to the rocky saddle between the Grand and Middle Teton. We'd spend the night at around twelve thousand feet. Even as a boy, I could never get enough of that star-studded sky." Curly's eyes sparkled as he spoke of the mountains he loves.

"We would get up before dawn and start pushing towards the summit. The steep inclines and sheer rock faces never bothered us. It was breathtaking. We'd go until we ran out of rock to climb. Then, we'd sit and marvel at the view before returning to the valley floor. The minute we were down, we would want to go back up again." He laughed at the memory. "The extreme terrain was an endless challenge to young boys. We loved to invent hair-raising ways to gain and lose elevation."

Curly stopped his horse and grabbed the bridle of mine, halting her in her tracks. "Look," he whispered. A short distance ahead was a small herd of elk. "They're often down there by the lake. It's frozen everywhere except where Brian and I break up the ice near the edge every day."

We noticed dark storm clouds gathering over the mountains. They had come up suddenly, like they do where I live.

"We'll get snow tonight," Curly said. "Come on, I want to show you something."

We rode on past the lake. The elk backed up into the trees as we neared, but came out again as soon as we passed. After about another half mile, we rounded a bend, and there stood an exquisite canyon.

"This is Pinto Canyon," said Curly. He again stopped his horse and mine. "A herd of wild paints lives here. They have the run of the ranch, but they like the canyon better than anywhere, and during the winters it gives them shelter."

"You have wild horses?" I couldn't have been more astounded.

"Would you like to see them?"

"Oh yes, I'd love to."

"Come on then. It'll get dark soon with those storm clouds moving in."

I followed him into the narrow canyon. It soon widened for a quarter-mile or so, and then narrowed again. Near the end was a small pool of unfrozen water. I stared at it in confusion.

Curly laughed. "It's fed by a hot spring. It never freezes over, even in the worst weather. This treasure makes my ranch a winter haven for wildlife. I get deer, elk, moose, bald eagles, coyotes, raccoons, and occasionally bighorn sheep, and of course the pintos."

Outside of the canyon, in a meadow, frolicked the horses. Curly turned when he saw me looking. "Aren't they something?"

I nodded but had no words.

We watched them run around with their thick manes flying behind them. Feral horses were the epitome of the Wild West, strong and unfettered, servants to no one. The wind changed direction and they caught our scent. They stopped and stared with curiosity, ears perked.

"I brought Serena here once," said Curly so softly it was difficult to understand him. "She loved the paints as much as the mountains and forests. We spent a week here running as untamed and free of worry as these horses."

He seemed to be in his own world, and I wondered if he had gone back in time thirty years to be with his love. I felt a missing-Kevin pang and longed to hear his voice. He would be astonished by the pintos, my horse-loving cowboy.

As we observed the horses observing us, it began to snow big, wet flakes. They landed on my mount's eyelashes and mane, and on me.

We were silent until Curly pulled his horse close. "May I ask you something?"

"Sure."

His eyes held mine. "What makes you think I didn't kill Serena?"

I wasn't expecting the question, but I answered it easily. "I have several reasons. For one thing, it's too simple an answer. The arroyo scene is too pat. Another thing is that I've read your private thoughts, the personal things you wrote to Serena." My face got hot remembering those things. "For a man to go from what you wrote to premeditated murder could only be explained by insanity. You don't strike me as being insane."

He laughed.

"It was also in the way you said, 'I've never forgotten her'. Those words came from your heart, and I heard the truth of them."

Curly fought back tears, which made my heart hurt.

"As if to reinforce what I already believe, you bring me to see these magnificent horses." I stared down at the saddle horn and tried to get my emotions under control. "You're no murderer," I said softly.

He reached out and lifted my face so he could look directly into my eyes. "You're right, Margarita. I could never murder anyone."

* * *

Pinto Canyon was darker when we headed back through. The snow began to fall harder. By the time we reached the elk herd, it poured down, obscuring the scenery.

Curly pulled alongside me. "Margarita, those people in Terlingua—they hated me. Most of them didn't know me, but I was wealthy and that was enough. They tried and convicted me in the bars and around their bonfire socials and on that Porch. That godforsaken Porch ought to be burned down. Those people yap endlessly about things they don't know and none of them ever heard of innocent until proven guilty."

"I'm sorry, Curly. I wish I could say it was different now. Terlingua is a fantastic place but some of the people—well, they thrive on gossip and bad news. I've been the brunt of it too."

"Because of your job?"

"Yes, it's that and my unconventional friends."

"The world is full of stupid people." He chuckled but seemed bitter for the first time. I thought his comment was true—and sad.

"I don't mean to trash everyone there," he said. "There are some good people in Terlingua, but you understand my frustration."

"I do. How do you know The Porch? I can't imagine you hung out there."

"No, I didn't." He hesitated a minute before he spoke. "I hired a private investigator," he admitted. "I was hesitant to tell you that."

"Why, Curly?"

"I don't like talking about it, but I suppose I should tell you everything, even it makes me look guilty."

"How does that make you look guilty?"

"The detective never came up with any likely suspect but me. He mixed in with the locals to find out that everyone thought I'd killed her because she got in my way, and a few variations on that theme. You should've heard their theories and scenarios. It bordered on the ridiculous."

"I can imagine."

"Some of them thought Christina and I kept to ourselves because we had such dark perversions. We lured young women, abused them, and murdered them. They were so sure. They spoke like their theories were fact and one ol' boy on the Porch said we had lured his sister, and she narrowly escaped. Surely you don't want me to repeat that mess?"

"No, not unless you think there's a clue in there somewhere."

"No. Those people were clueless, literally."

"What happened with the investigator?"

"His determination was that Serena had been murdered, but he couldn't say by whom. Fingers were pointed at me, but there was nothing factual to go on. He ended up going back to Dallas. I spent a ridiculous amount of money but got nowhere. His take on it was that her murderer would not be found unless someone came forward."

"So he was about as useless as the sheriff."

"Yes, and he took some information from the sheriff at face value. I think he thought I had done it, too, and was paying him to find her in order to make myself look innocent. I guess he figured I had money to burn." Curly gestured towards the Tetons. "Look up there. Can you imagine what this storm is like for them?"

The mountains were personal to Curly, and I liked him even more for that. The ones at home were personal to me, too. His were surrounded with dark clouds that moved fast. Not much of them was visible.

"It's nice to have money," Curly continued, "but I would've given every dime I have to get Serena back. People say money is power, and that's true to a point, but what good did money do me? I lost the only thing that mattered, and all the money in the world couldn't make up for it."

I understood that and didn't think I needed to say so. We watched the snow fall harder and harder. Curly wore a cap, but his dark curls stuck out from it in every direction, capturing snowflakes. It was beautiful.

"Do you have a dream, Margarita?"

I nodded. "Yes."

"Can you share it with me?"

"My dream is to write."

"Novels?"

"Well anything, but yes, novels would be my first choice."

"Are you writing?"

"All the time, but mostly it's in my head. I try to get my thoughts on paper as often as possible. I have a novel going now, but no time to write."

"I think it's important to have a dream."

"What is your dream?" I asked.

"You'll laugh."

"Why would I laugh?"

"Painting is my dream. I'm trying to paint the pintos, and the mountains."

"Why would that make me laugh?"

"Well, I guess it wouldn't unless you saw my paintings." He laughed and then got serious. "I used to paint, Margarita. I used to paint all the time. I quit after Serena disappeared and didn't try to start again until Madeline brought life back into me."

"May I see your paintings?"

"No. No way. Not until I improve two hundred percent."

"Are you painting regularly?"

"No."

"In order to improve, you'll have to paint, you know."

"Yes, I know."

Meanwhile, it was snowing! I wanted to shout with joy, run around in it, and catch the delicate flakes in my mouth and eyelashes. I finally understood all that fuss about a winter wonderland.

Curly had a mischievous grin on his face. "Can you gallop?"

"Sure."

"I'll beat you to the barn," he challenged, and we took off.

What a thrill that short ride was. Wet snow blew in my eyes, the powerful animal moved smoothly beneath me, and cold air smacked at my face. I felt as free and untamed as the pintos back at the canyon.

CHAPTER 18

Curly beat me to the barn, but barely. We arrived laughing and gasping, our breaths pluming in the frigid air. From out of nowhere appeared Brian, dressed in so many heavy layers his head looked too small for his body. A blue wool cap was snugged down to protect his bald head. He lifted me down from the saddle as if I weighed nothing, and then helped Curly dismount. We didn't need help, but we didn't refuse it, either.

"I'll get the horses dried off and put away, Boss," Brian said.

We thanked him, and Curly walked me to my quarters. He clicked on an electric heater then glanced around to be sure everything was as it should be.

"This'll help get rid of the damp chill," he said, "but the bathroom will be cold."

"If the water's hot, I'll be fine."

"The water is hot, and there are plenty of thick towels you can wrap up in. Would you like to shower in the main house? It's warmer there."

"I'll be fine, but thank you. Thank you for everything. What an incredible day!" I hugged him with glee. He seemed startled at first but returned the hug.

"Come on to the house when you're ready. Do you like wine? I have some good red wine. Or do you prefer white, or beer?"

I swallowed hard. "I don't drink, but thank you. I'd like some water or hot tea."

"Come and get it when it suits," he said. "I'm going to shower, and if you get to the house before I'm finished, make yourself at home." With that, he stepped out into a blowing curtain of white.

* * *

When I returned to the bedroom after a steamy shower, it was warmer. I dressed in grey wool slacks, a red silk shirt, and a dark grey cashmere pullover sweater, and short black dress boots. While rummaging through my suitcase, I saw Serena's photo and took it out.

"He's something, Serena. He even has wild horses."

It was hard to tell what she thought about my visit, but I knew she had loved Curly Hampton and been loved by him. No wonder she smiled.

I wasn't sure what to do with the heater, so I changed the setting to low and left it running. I placed the photo back into the suitcase, wiggled into the warm jacket, and stepped outside. At first I was lost. Then I spotted the glow from the main house and ran, bent against the wind. The cold seemed to cut canyons into my face.

After stomping my feet on the mat, I entered. Another mat had been set inside the door to catch extra snow. Andrea hurried to take my jacket. Curly stood behind her, toweling his heavy mop of curls.

"I forgot to ask what kind of tea you'd like," he said. "Man, you look nice."

"You look very nice yourself."

He wore tan wool slacks with a green pullover that brought out the green in his hazel eyes. Moccasins protected his feet. When he removed the towel, his hair was black and shiny with no sign of

170

gray. It was so unruly he could have been one of his young sons, except for his size.

He threw the towel over his shoulder. "Green tea? Mint? Peppermint? Spice?"

"That's too many choices. Any of those would work. Surprise me."

"I'll make you a mug of peppermint tea," Andrea said.

"That would be perfect. Thank you."

Curly opened the door to the living room and ushered me in. "Wait here. Make yourself comfortable. Take off those boots if you want and stick your feet near the fire." He left but came back. "Margarita, will it bother you if I drink a beer?"

"No, please do. Make yourself at home, Curly."

He laughed and disappeared.

While he was gone I took off the boots and leaned back against a loveseat and put my feet on a hassock by the fire. I was drifting into sleep when Curly came back with a beer and a mug of tea with a candy cane in it.

He sat in an easy chair and put his feet next to mine. "This is the good life." He clinked his bottle of Heineken against my mug of tea and winked.

"This is great," I said. "I wish I could spend the winter in a place like this."

"I wish you could, too, but they might miss you at home."

"Will I be able to leave tomorrow?"

"It depends on how much snow we get. That Jeep is four-wheel drive, isn't it?"

"Yes, it is."

"Well, we'll have to see in the morning. Don't count on going anywhere early. Snowplows will clear the highways, but it usually takes until noon or so. I think we can get you out to the main road. After that, it'll depend on the road crews."

I could think of worse places to be trapped.

"Curly, will you continue your story? I don't like to ask you to do it, but it's my job. I'll have a few questions but after that, I won't bother you."

He looked at me a long while before he spoke. "Do you think you'll ever find out what happened to Serena?"

"I can't answer that."

"But you're going to try?"

"Yes, that's why I'm here. Now I know you didn't kill Serena, but I'm not sure how I'll find out who did. So I can't imagine where this will go."

Curly hesitated and drank a sip or two before he continued his story. "I took Serena to Europe after the Christmas holidays. I told Christina I needed time to think, to be alone, but I didn't mention Europe. She knew by then that it was over between us, but I think she was afraid to bring it to a head, so she kept playing the game.

"I promised Serena I would get a divorce when we returned from Europe. I felt pressure to get on with it. It's a hard thing to do, to break another person's heart and disrupt a family. I hated myself for what my family would go through. But when I was with Serena all I could do was love her. Everything else paled when I was with her."

Curly studied the beer. "I went to see my attorney and told him the whole story, more or less. I explained that I wanted to be fair to Christina, to set her up for life, and in return, I wanted to be able to see my sons.

"Then I went home and told Christina I wanted a divorce. She was hysterical and accused me of sleeping around, of sleeping with whores. She even said I'd been seen there with whores, 'there' being Terlingua. All I could say was I'd never been with a whore, which was true. And until I met Serena, I was a faithful husband."

He drank a few more swallows of the beer. "I never told her anything about Serena," he said. "I knew it would make things worse for Christina to know the truth about her, that she was young and so attractive, and that we were so much in love. Christina didn't ask, either. She didn't honestly want to know."

Curly stood. "This is a two or three-beer story. Do you need anything?"

"No, thanks."

When he returned, he continued. "It wasn't long after I asked for the divorce that Serena went missing. All hell broke loose then."

He paused so long I prodded him. "Please tell me about it."

"I called Serena's brother because she didn't come in for work on Monday morning. I had phoned her home over the weekend and got a message saying she would be away until Sunday. The week before, I told her I wouldn't be up until Tuesday, so I thought she'd gone off with a friend. After I spoke with Joey, I called Samantha. She didn't know anything, either. I began to worry because it was so unlike Serena not to call in if she was sick or had problems. And the fact that she had not spoken with Samantha concerned me."

He sighed at the memory. "I called Joey again and we talked each other into waiting until Tuesday. He went by her apartment Tuesday morning and then went to look for the sheriff. When the sheriff came knocking on my door, I knew something was wrong. He walked with me a few yards from the house and asked if I'd been seeing Serena Bustamante on the side. It sounded so filthy the way he said it, but I admitted it. He asked me to come with him, said her car had been found in an arroyo near my house."

Curly took a long drink of beer. "So we went to the arroyo, and there was her blue Camaro. Everything about the scene looked wrong to me. I had never asked Serena to meet me anywhere in her car. I usually picked her up in Alpine. I had ridden in her Camaro a few times and had even driven it. Her fingerprints and mine were all over it, and no one else's. I couldn't explain it.

"When the sheriff looked in the overnight bag and saw the way it was packed with that see-through stuff, he gave me a look that said he knew it was me who lured her. Joey tried to attack me. I've never felt so alone or so terrified. My wife hated me. My sons had been sent to her mother's while we fought and argued. My love was missing, and everyone thought I knew something. I knew nothing. Remember that whoever had Serena also had my unborn child." His voice broke, and he set the beer on the floor and put his head in his hands.

I tried to think of something comforting to say, but words failed me. I felt useless. "I'm so sorry, Curly."

He lifted his head. "It's like it happened yesterday. It's been thirty years, and I feel the pain the same. It's not like I sit around crying every day. I enjoy my life now, but talking about it brings it back so vividly."

"I'm sorry, but there are things you know that nobody else can tell me."

"Please don't apologize for doing your job," he said as he wiped tears from his face with the back of his hand. "You'd be doing me a huge favor if you could find out what happened to Serena."

"Maybe we should take a break."

"Please ask your questions," he said, but his eyes looked haunted. "When we go to dinner we'll talk about something else."

"Dena Jablonski told Sheriff Blanton that Christina had been with her all day on the day Serena disappeared. She also told me that Christina knew all about you and Serena, and was planning to confront you about it. She said Serena was a tramp and when I pressed her to, she named a few men. I contacted them, and they were blown away by the accusations. One had dated Serena a few times when she was nineteen. He said he tried hard to make out with her but got nowhere. Another of the accused is Joey's age and is a good friend of his. He always thought of Serena as a younger sister. He and Joey were ten when she was born. He said by the time she was fifteen, he was happily married and still is."

"Dena Jablonski is a lying, meddling bitch."

"Right, so the third man she named was Rigo Mendez, your foreman at the time."

Curly shook his head emphatically. "No way."

"He now lives in Alpine. He remembers Serena and speaks of her with awe and respect. He was about her age when he worked for you, and he thought she was lovely, but he says he saw that the two of you belonged to each other."

"He was a good man," Curly said. "I knew he was attracted to Serena. He was young and lonely for female company. But he was a man of honor."

I nodded in agreement. "He also said he was sure you had not stashed a body in the dam. In fact, he never believed you would harm Serena. He explained to me that he and the workers would have heard you—or anyone else—messing with the dam at night.

He also stated that had you asked him to help bury a body, he and the guys would've run away first."

Curly laughed softly at that.

"Since everything Jablonski told me was a lie, I checked out her whereabouts on the day she says she was with Christina all day. She was in class in Alpine."

"Are you sure about that?"

"Positive. Why would she lie about something this important? I called her back and told her I had discovered the truth. She admits that she thought Christina killed Serena. She felt sorry for her and wanted to draw the investigation away from her. She said Serena got what she deserved, and Christina was a good woman who had been wronged."

"My God."

"So my question to you is this. Could Christina have killed Serena? Do you know where she was that day? Could she have lured Serena to the arroyo, or moved her car there after the fact in order to implicate you?"

"I always thought it was weird that Serena's car was so close to my house. She would never have come there looking for me. I knew I hadn't lured her, but nobody believed me. I was so distraught I didn't even try to explain it in my own mind. One of my friends suggested she had planned to confront Christina, but that would have been out of character. Serena trusted I was divorcing Christina, and she would never have wanted to embarrass me or herself.

"On the day Serena's car was found I had been riding. It was a glorious day. Wildflowers were blooming everywhere, and the temperature was perfect. I couldn't stay in the house any longer, so I rode my horse way up into the mountains and didn't come back until nightfall. So to answer your question, I can't provide an alibi for Christina, nor can she provide one for me."

"I want to ask you about something else. Joey says when you saw the overnight case you said, 'she could have been meeting anybody', and of course it had that revealing lingerie in it. That infuriated him because he thinks you were saying that she was cheating on you. He knows in his heart she would never have done that."

"I wasn't functioning," Curly said. "I don't remember most of what I said or did. If I said that, then I must have meant to suggest she was meeting a friend. I don't know what I meant, but I never would've accused Serena of cheating. I was being assaulted with questions—questions which indicated people thought I had hurt her." He shuddered. "I couldn't bear it. I was in an untenable situation, and God knows what I might've said."

"I have two theories, Curly."

"Well, I sure would like to hear them."

"One is that Christina killed her. Because Serena had left a message that she'd be away for the weekend, I think she lured her. I can't explain how. Serena had to think she was meeting you. If Christina called her as herself, asking to meet with her, Serena might've gone, but she wouldn't have taken an overnight bag.

"Maybe Christina had a male call for her and he pretended to be you, but what male? He would have to be a stranger who would never hear about the disappearance or a person with no qualms who would never talk. I'm not sure; it sounds weak."

"What's your other theory?"

"A man lured her, posing as you. Maybe someone who had stalked her, who knew she was in love with you, and who knew where you lived. This would've been a man fixated on Serena, who wanted her for himself and in frustration, killed her."

"But who?"

"That's what I'm trying to find out."

We were silent while the wind moaned and battered the house. It seemed like a bad omen.

"I spoke with Samantha Harding," I said. "She was Samantha Arzate when you knew her."

"I know her as Samantha Harding, too. We've kept up with each other. She's the one person who believed with all her heart in my innocence."

"That's because she was Serena's best friend, a person she could confide in. Serena told her intimate details about you and her. They were together since the first grade and were true friends. She knew, for instance, that Serena was a virgin when she met you and that you had courted her, not rushing her."

I took out my small notebook and read from it: 'Well, let's just say any man who courts a woman the way he did and then makes love to her like he made love to her would not be a killer, no matter what. No. He is no killer. I'm not sure of much in this life, but of this I am damned sure.' End of quote."

More than thirty years after the fact, Curly was flaming red.

"In our conversation, she mentioned a few things which alarmed me. Were you aware that before Serena became involved with you, she was followed several times?"

"No. She never mentioned it."

"Samantha says she was, and she also received obscene phone calls." I described the calls to Curly, quoting Samantha.

He paled. "How awful."

"Then, after she met you, she was followed again."

"She never told me any of this."

"She came home once and her underpants were on the bed. She was sure she hadn't left them there. A while after that she realized two of her sexiest pairs were missing. Then, an even more disturbing thing happened. Evidently you had given her some super-sexy, lacy panties."

"I gave her many things like that."

"She came home one day, and they were on her bed. Her bed was rumpled, and someone had ejaculated on the panties. It was then that she called the police."

Curly's eyes were wide. "Why wouldn't she have told me?"

"It's because of the attitude of the police. They treated her like she was guilty of something sordid. It's the mentality that 'if you wear panties like this, what can you expect?' It's ridiculous, but not uncommon among lawmen. It's the same treatment a pretty rape victim gets. If you're good-looking or sexy, you must have asked for it. The police took the underwear in an evidence bag, had their fun, and brought them back to Serena. She threw them away and told you that she had accidentally ruined them in the dryer."

"I remember something like that."

"The reaction of the police is the reason Samantha didn't tell the sheriff about it when he interviewed her. She felt she'd be subjecting Serena to ridicule and scorn again. She couldn't bear to see that happen. So she kept this secret until I dragged it out of her a few days ago."

"This could be important."

"Yes. Following a woman, breaking into her house to steal her underwear, using her bed, it's stalking. To answer your question, my second theory is that the person who stalked her killed her, a man who lured her to Terlingua by posing as you."

"My God, I never had any clue about this."

"Curly, can you think of anybody who could have wanted to harm her? Do you remember someone yelling at her, or looking at her in an odd or creepy way? You know what I mean."

"Men always looked at her. She was ravishing. Even when I was with her men would ogle her, click their tongues, or whistle. I took the attitude that they could eat their hearts out. I paid them little attention, and she paid them none. While I was at her side, no one ever touched her or approached her or did anything out of turn. But there were the hungry looks, men undressing her with their eyes, that kind of thing."

Andrea knocked and called us to dinner.

"I hardly feel like eating now," Curly said.

"I don't either, but we have to remember that whatever happened was thirty years ago. She can no longer be hurt by anybody."

"Some small comfort," he said bitterly.

* * *

For all our protesting, we did eat. Andrea served us in a cozy nook with a warm fire, to one side of the kitchen. Christmas was all over that room, too.

"This house has a dining room," Curly said, "but I seldom use it unless I'm entertaining a group. When this place was originally built, I pictured it as a dude ranch. I discovered I don't like dudes, so I enjoy it myself. Everything about it is too large, but it sits on land I adore, so I have stayed. My sons visit with their families, and I do have friends. I'm a recluse, to tell the truth."

Andrea first served red wine and a salad made with all types of greens and a tasty dressing she made to go with it.

Curly removed the wine from my place. "What would you like to drink?"

"Water would be fine, thanks."

He brought a goblet with ice water while Andrea served freshly-baked bread and real butter. I was in love with her the minute I smelled the bread. Then she served grilled steaks that were perfect, along with creamy mashed potatoes and buttered asparagus.

Curly and I talked about his sons and their unwavering faith in him. They weren't told the truth of the move from their home in Terlingua until they were old enough to understand. Christina agreed to let Curly help raise them. They needed him, she realized, and he loved them dearly. They helped him get over what he called his 'old life' and kept him focused on the future.

"I taught them to climb in the mountains," he said, "and to fish, ride horses, to snow ski, and ice skate. My boys named the pintos and watched them so much they could distinguish their personalities. They even tried to name the elk, often getting the names confused. When frustrated, they called all of them 'Rudolph.'"

Curly was good company. He seemed a contented man now, except for when certain nosy deputies came around to open old wounds. He was a man comfortable in his own skin. People called him a murderer, liar, and a cheat, and his community drove him away. Serena's family had accused him and wouldn't consider another scenario, or listen to his side. He prevailed through all of it because he knew who he was and his conscience was clear.

Andrea cleared the dishes while we talked and then brought out decorated Christmas cookies for desert.

"This is what I mean," Curly said with a grin and bit a Christmas tree in half.

We were about to return to the living room when Curly received a call on his cell phone. I could tell it was private, so I motioned that I was going back to the front of the house. In the hallway, I almost ran into Andrea.

"That was the best meal I ever ate," I said and gave her a bear hug.

She beamed. "I'm not sure who you are, but I'm so glad you came to visit Mr. Curly. I haven't heard him laugh so much in a long time. You're good for him."

"Oh no, I'm not," I blurted.

She touched my cheek. "I think you are."

I cupped my hands and put my face against a window in the great room, but all I could see was white. The wind blew snow in swirls against the house, and gusts pounded and rattled the windows, demanding to be let in. I couldn't imagine what the weather must be like at the highest elevations. It was serious below.

I didn't hear Brian's soft approach, so I jumped when he spoke. "Do you like it here, Margarita?"

"Oh, yes. It's unbelievably gorgeous."

"You might be snowed in here a few days." He sounded hopeful.

"That would be okay, Brian. I love it here."

"Would you go with me tomorrow on a snowmobile to check the herd of pintos? We'll take hay to them."

"I'd like that," I said with enthusiasm that made him blush. He moved closer.

"Sorry, Margarita," Curly said from behind, which startled us. "Forgive my rudeness. I had to take that call."

"No problem. Brian was entertaining me."

Brian stared at his feet.

"Brian was *talking* to you?"

"Hush, Boss, please don't start."

"Brian is the strong, silent type," Curly teased. "If you have him talking, that's good."

Brian was as red as the Christmas ribbons.

"We're going to feed the pintos tomorrow," I said, excited about it.

"Is that so?" Curly leaned back in the chair and enjoyed Brian's discomfort, but it was more affectionate than unkind. "Do tell."

"I'll see you tomorrow, Margarita," Brian said.

"Are you leaving?" I was surprised and disappointed.

"I'm going to look for another job," he grumbled.

"I bet you won't," Curly called after him, "at least not until the deputy leaves."

Brian shut the door hard on his way out.

Curly rose and tended the fire until it roared. "Poor Brian, I love to give him a hard time."

"Yeah, I saw that."

"I'm sorry if I interrupted a moment."

"I wouldn't call it a moment, but he was talking to me."

"He's a fine man. He's not good with women—or any strangers."

"You don't have to sell him to me, Curly. I can see he's sweet—and attractive."

"You noticed? Okay, I talk too much, and Brian doesn't talk enough."

Curly resettled himself into the chair, holding a glass of wine. I tried not to dwell on it. "Are you in love with someone, Margarita?"

I started not to tell him, but didn't think it would be right since I knew such personal things about him. "Yes, but my husband died about eighteen months ago. I loved him with all my heart, and I still love him."

"Oh, I'm so sorry. I saw your ring and assumed—" His voice trailed away.

"I wear my ring because I'm not ready to stop."

"I understand. You don't need to explain."

The fire crackled and fell in on itself, sending sparks flying and popping.

"I'm in love with someone," Curly said. "Madeline Richmond came into my life about five years ago. She's the beautiful woman in the photograph you saw earlier. She came here to buy a horse I advertised for sale. She was so lovely and poised. And oh, the way she laughed. I was captivated. We talked about horses and riding, and discovered we had a mutual love of climbing, the Tetons, and everything Wyoming. She sat up on the corral fence and charmed the socks off me.

"I'd had girlfriends through the years, but they meant nothing to me. My heart was stone cold. In one afternoon, Madeline warmed it. It was like she held it in her hands and brought it back to life." He drank a bit of wine and was quiet.

We watched the fire crackle and spark.

"This is none of my business," Curly said, "but do you not drink for religious reasons or is it something else?"

"After Kevin died I started drinking because it dulled the pain and then I couldn't stop. It took a while to get it under control. Maybe I could have a drink now and then, but I'm afraid to try. What if I can't stop?"

"You're doing the wise thing."

"I lost friends and the trust of nearly everyone. I was about to lose my job. Every morning I thought *no more*, but I was powerless to quit. I would mean to have just one, but then I would have another and another. Now that I've stopped hurting myself, I don't want to start again. I would rather feel things, even if it's painful."

Curly nodded thoughtfully, finished the wine, and set the glass down. He got up to add a few logs to the fire and poked it until it was blazing again.

"I want to tell you something, Margarita. I don't take just anyone to see the pintos. I have to feel a bond first, and I don't bond with hardly anybody anymore. Then, I have to feel they'll appreciate them for what they are. If I don't feel that, I don't ever mention the horses. Can you understand that?"

I nod solemnly, so proud he had taken me to see them.

"I took Madeline to the horses the same afternoon we met. When I told her that I wanted to show her something special, she could have feared me, but the trust was already there between us, as if we knew each other well.

"Of course she was astounded by the pintos. We watched them for several hours, talking about things in our lives. And we laughed and laughed. I felt like a part of me had come back from wherever it had been. At some point in the late afternoon, she leaned over and kissed me. The kiss was soft and sweet. She thanked me for bringing her to see the horses as if she understood how I was with them."

He stood. "I'm going to get brandy. I hope you don't mind."

"No, I don't."

He walked to a cabinet and took out a snifter and a cut crystal decanter that glinted in the firelight.

"I invited Madeline for dinner," he continued. "Andrea was off, so she had to endure my cooking. We didn't eat much anyway. We were flirting and drinking wine and kissing. I couldn't get enough of her kisses. She stayed that night and by morning, I was alive again in a way I hadn't been since before that awful day in the arroyo."

He swirled the amber liquid, then sipped it. "I tell you all this to say that I should marry Madeline. She saved me from a fate worse than death. I've started to ask her many times, but the words won't leave my lips. I'm not ready. I know it sounds stupid, but what if Serena comes back? Consciously I know she can't, but somewhere deep in me is the hope that she's not dead; she might return. I can't marry and unconditionally give myself to another woman until I know what happened to Serena."

"She isn't going to come back, Curly. I'm finally accepting that Kevin won't be back, either. It's the hardest thing I've ever done."

"Yes it is, but I assume you know what happened to Kevin."

"Yes. It must be even worse not to know."

"It eats me alive—or did. I thank God every day for giving me a second chance at love." He studied my face. "Please find out what happened to Serena."

"I'll do everything I can, Curly."

"Is that a promise?"

"Yes. It's a promise." I felt a terrible weight add itself to the Joey-Sylvia load I already carried.

CHAPTER 19

Curly and I stayed up late visiting as if we were old friends. Then he insisted on walking me to my room, but it was more like we skidded there. The ice would have been treacherous enough without the wind trying to knock us down, but we held on to each other for support and made it without mishap.

Curly checked around the room like he had done before. He turned the electric heater to its highest setting and pulled the heavy curtains across the window in an effort to keep the cold out, but he didn't seem satisfied.

"I'm re-thinking this. I should've put you in a room in the main house. I didn't know you when I offered to let you stay here, and I didn't want you to think I was a nasty old man. Also, I thought this room would give you more privacy. Now I'm thinking it'll give you pneumonia."

I laughed. "This room is fine."

"I can move your suitcase in a few minutes if you don't mind going back out into the storm."

"I just want to crawl under those covers and pass out. I'm exhausted."

"All right, but call me if you change your mind."

"I'm fine. Now go so I can go to bed."

As soon as he left I stripped off my clothes, but decided it would be warmer to sleep in my thermal underwear. I was nervous to turn out the light but when I did, a nightlight glowed near the door. Also, the light switch emitted a dim light, making it easy to find in the dark. Curly had thought of everything.

I lay on my back, buried under layers of blankets and quilts, and stared at the ceiling, waiting for the bed to warm or to fall asleep, whichever came first. The wind rushed at the windows with such fury it made the double-panes rattle. I was used to furious windstorms, but this one was driving a level of cold I had never felt before. To get my head off the storm, I wondered about shy Brian at the other end of the house until I fell asleep.

A screaming, howling racket awakened me. The heater had quit, and without its comforting hum, the room was deadly still and cold as a tomb. Crashing came from the forest behind the building, as if a giant beast was demolishing it. It was branches breaking, I realized, or the wind ripping trees up by the roots and tossing them away. I gripped the blankets to my thudding chest and waited, wondering if the windows would hold.

When I heard footsteps thudding down the hall, I couldn't breathe. My pistol was in the suitcase, but I was too afraid to get out of bed. I watch too many horror movies for my own good.

Then the front door of the guest house slammed open and the yowling wind was more deafening and terrifying than before. Loud banging, then screeching as metal was sheared from metal. Then I heard what I thought was male voices yelling, but I couldn't make out even one word. The wind ripped the sound away the second it hit the air.

A loud knock on my door made me jump, and I heard "Margarita!" I hurried, tripped over my boots, and flung open the door. Curly and Brian burst in, along with a blast of bone-freezing air.

"The wind ripped the front door away," advised Brian in his take-it-in-stride way. His face glowed in the light from the battery-powered lantern he gripped in one hand.

"I've brought some warm clothes for you," said Curly. "The power is out and it's going to get cold fast."

I thought it already had.

"We've come to take you to the main house, where we can at least have a fire," explained Curly as he handed me a snowsuit, a pair of heavy gloves, and snow boots. "These things are Madeline's. She's taller than you, and her feet are larger than yours, but we have to make these things work."

The snowsuit had a plush lining that felt wonderful. Curly zipped it and pulled the hood over my head. "If you'll sit, I'll help you get the boots on. These are Maddy's ski boots and they're tricky until you get the hang of them. I stuck socks in the toes. They'll be awkward, but you won't have to go far in them."

Brian held the light high and watched wordlessly.

Curly touched my shoulder. "Now listen. There is zero visibility. Before Brian and I went to bed, we rigged a rope from the main house to the guest house, and another to the barn. It's very important to hold onto the rope no matter what, understand? If you should lose it, you won't be able to see or hear anything. You'll be lost to us in an instant."

My hair practically stood on end at the thought of being lost in such a cold place. "I understand," I said, although I didn't, not yet.

"Have you ever been in a hurricane-force blizzard?" inquired Brian gently.

"No."

"Then, with all due respect, you can't understand what this will be like," he said with more urgency. "When we exit this building there will be a rope to your left, by the door frame. There's give to it, like a bungee cord. I'll exit first and when I grab the rope, I'll move a few inches, then I'll make sure you have it before I proceed. Curly will come behind you. You check to be sure he has a grip on the rope. Don't let go of it, no matter what happens. We might lose each other but don't lose the rope."

"The ground is slick with ice," added Curly. "The wind will hit us with such force it will knock you off your feet if you aren't careful. Should that happen, keep holding the rope. There's enough give in it so it will go down with you. Just get back up and keep moving."

"We'll stick close," said Brian. "If we're separated, follow the rope. It will take you to the house. Whatever you do, do not go back."

Curly adjusted the hood of my suit and fastened various pieces of Velcro until my face was almost hidden. Then he and Brian did the same with their suits. Curly unplugged the heater and closed and locked the door of the Terlingua Room.

In the hall, the wind was fierce and snow was already piled against the wall. A white nightmare raged where there should have been a door. I tried to calm myself by concentrating on breathing and walking in boots that didn't fit without tripping.

Brian took a brave step over the threshold. "Here goes." He grabbed something I couldn't see and disappeared.

"Now you," said Curly behind me. "Think heavy. You weigh a ton. Now go." He hustled me through the doorway. "See you at the house."

The suit was cumbersome. It felt like walking in a cocoon, but it kept me warm. The boots were the worst problem. Every step I took was a near-fall, before I even got out the door.

With Curly's encouragement, I entered the blizzard. I had never seen anything like it. I would've had more visibility at the bottom of a coal mine with my eyes taped shut. And it would have been less terrifying.

I took a few steps forward, gripping the rope, and ran smack into Brian who was waiting for me. He reached out, felt that I had the rope, squeezed my hand, and moved on.

I reached back for Curly's hand but didn't find him. I longed to tell Brian, but it was useless to scream, even though he was close. I saw nothing but felt Curly's presence. I trusted and kept going because Brian continued. It would be devastating to lose him, too. The roar of the wind was fearsome, as if it was trying to blow the Grand Tetons to Texas. Panic mounted in spite of my best efforts.

The first time I stumbled I lost Brian and felt deserted, like the sole survivor on a frozen Earth. I concentrated on moving one foot and then the other, keeping them low and sliding in a shuffle. For a second I thought I spotted the bright blue of Brian's snowsuit, but it must have been my imagination. A swirling wall of white had erased everything.

It was tortuously slow but I continued. After an indeterminable amount of time, I reached the door. Brian pulled me inside and hugged me. The hall was lit with lanterns and candles that caused his face to glow. He turned to pull Curly in but didn't let me go until they had to shut the door. It took both of them to do it. Once it was closed we laughed and hugged each other again and again. We had survived! The hallway was so crazy with light it seemed warm even if it wasn't. I felt like dancing salsa and the thought made me laugh.

Andrea appeared out of nowhere as if she had teleported. She hugged us and helped us shed the bulky suits. She handed me a thick flannel bathrobe, along with a pair of fur-lined moccasins that were too large but were soft and warm. She and Brian hung our suits in the closet over a rubber mat.

Curly tousled his already tousled hair. "Come and sit by the fire." He turned to Brian and Andrea. "You guys, too. I'll get blankets."

"I'll do a storm check around the house," Brian announced.

"Who wants hot chocolate?" Andrea asked, and three hands flew up. "I've already made it on the camp stove. In a minute I'll bring it in."

"I'll help you with the blankets," I volunteered to Curly.

He picked up a lantern and motioned for me to follow. We went down the rest of the hallway and through a door to another wing. The first bedroom on our stop was an interesting mix of young boy things and grown boy things.

"This is Bill's room," said Curly. "He's my oldest son."

"Is he William Hampton, too?"

"Yes, he's William Hampton the third."

We took all the blankets from the closet and the pillows from the bed. Then we went to another room belonging to Jeremy, Curly's youngest son, and did the same thing. Loaded, we headed back.

"Where is your room?" I asked.

Curly looked around at me. "It's on the opposite side of the house in a small wing where there's the master bedroom, a bathroom and walk-in closet, and a weight room." He grinned. "I like my privacy."

"I don't mean to pry," I said, "but I love your house."

"I'll give you a tour later when the lights come back on. I don't feel right taking you to my bedroom in the dark."

* * *

We chose our spots and set up makeshift beds around the room. There was plenty of space for it, but none of us wanted to sleep. Although the fire roared and did its best, the room was still chilled. An icy wind howled and raged and forced itself inside.

"Don't worry," said Curly, "This house is built for these storms."

"I'm not worried, except about the horses."

"They're safe in the barn," said Brian.

"I think she meant the wild ones," Curly correctly guessed. "They'll be huddled together in the canyon. It provides protection from the worst wind. I suspect one reason their bloodline has survived so long is the solid protection of that canyon. Once the storm passes and we can dig our way out, we'll take them hay."

"We've got that covered, Boss," Brian reminded him.

"Oh, that's right." Curly closed his mouth, opened it to say more, then didn't. I was thankful he let it go.

A thunderous crashing sound came from the rear of the house.

"Trees," said Curly. "It's said the reason God gave Wyoming an abundance of trees is so extras could be spared for the wind. These storms are why there is not one planted close to the house."

Curly got up to make sure nothing had been flung through a window or smashed through the roof.

In his absence, Brian asked, "Are you married, Margarita? Curly says you are."

"That was before I explained that I'm a widow."

"Oh, I'm sorry. I was thinking—" He stopped abruptly when Curly returned, and put his attention on poking the fire.

"We've dodged another bullet," Curly said, then looked back and forth between us, suspicious he had missed something.

Andrea fell asleep on the couch and snored softly. Curly covered her with blankets. "She works too hard," he whispered, "but try and stop her. She's like the Wyoming wind."

We talked about the ranch, living in Wyoming, and about the state's sometimes extreme weather. Curly and I told Brian about the violent thunderstorms of the Big Bend country.

"I used to think the wind there was terrifying," I said, "but I had that wrong."

One by one we fell asleep. At some point during the night the power was restored, but we took no notice of it. The heating system in a closet near the kitchen came back to life and began moving warm air through the house, but none of us heard it. The keening and screeching wind prevailed, yet still I managed to sleep. When dawn arrived no one knew because snow had piled in drifts against the windows. For us, it was still dark as night.

* * *

The first thing I noticed on waking was the absence of wind. That racket had been replaced by an eerie silence. I sat straight up wondering what was wrong. At the same time, the others began to stir.

"It's over," said Curly. "Now we dig out."

"Not until you've had some breakfast," said Andrea from the doorway, where she stood holding a tray of coffee and mugs.

Brian had a grin on his face. "You're a real doll, Andrea!"

"Yeah," I said, "I'd like to take you home with me."

"Everybody back away from my Andrea," said Curly with mock anger.

Then Brian began teasing her. "I should marry you Andrea, but I had hoped to snag an older woman."

Brian couldn't be more than thirty and Andrea was at least sixty. She walked off in a playful huff. Curly winked at me from across the room.

Brian stoked the fire until it roared again. We drank coffee in silence until he spoke.

"Have you heard from Madeline?" he asked his boss.

"She called last night to say she was snowed in at Denver. I guess this is one huge mother of a storm."

"Maybe she can get back today once the runways are cleared," said Brian. "I'll go see if any door can be opened."

"Good luck," said Curly. "We're snowed in, I'm sure." He called after the retreating Brian, "Don't go hassling Andrea in the kitchen." Then he turned to me. "It's better not to anger the cook."

I laughed and agreed. "Does Madeline live here too?"

"She has her own house in town. You wouldn't know it to look at the walk-in closet. It holds as many of her clothes as it does mine. That's where I've been getting things for you."

"That worked out well for me."

"Madeline is an independent woman, to say the least. She travels because of her work. When she's here, we go back and forth between our houses. Mine gets used more because of Andrea's cooking and my fireplaces."

After a few minutes he added, "She'll live here when we marry."

I said nothing. My heart sank, remembering the promise I made the day before. Why had I promised?

Brian returned to tell us all the doors were blocked. "The good news," he said, "is that Andrea is making waffles."

We sat together in the cozy room by the kitchen, drinking orange juice from crystal goblets, and devouring waffles. Andrea kept our mugs full of coffee as she popped up and down to be sure we had everything we needed.

After breakfast, Curly took me to his bedroom to find something of Madeline's to wear. His room was as boldly masculine as his office area in the great room. A king-sized bed was covered by a tartan plaid quilt and there were three or four huge red pillows at the head of the bed. Above it hung a giant painting of Pinto Canyon and the herd of horses which gave the canyon its name.

"I had that commissioned by a famous western artist," he said with pride.

Another wall displayed a striking painting of a Big Bend scene by a locally-known Terlingua artist. A stone fireplace and a brushed corduroy conversation pit grouped around it looked inviting. And there were more bookcases.

I perused books while Curly went to a dresser. "Let me show you something, Margarita."

From a dark wooden box he lifted half of a gold locket. The side he held was engraved 'Serena.' She was wearing the other part in the photo I carried.

"She gave me this for Christmas before we left for Europe. Serena wore the half with my name. It was her intention to unite the two sides when we could be together as husband and wife. That won't happen now, but I'd still love to have the other half."

I didn't know what to say. What were the chances anyone would find it? He looked sad, as if he had read my mind.

Curly showed me the closet, where Madeline's influence was conspicuous.

"Pick anything you like, but make it something warm."

"I'll help you guys dig us out," I said.

"In that case, these would be good." He handed me insulated coveralls, a long-sleeved t-shirt, and a quilted work shirt. He searched among the shoes and came up with a pair of warm-looking work boots.

He looked panicked. "What about underwear?"

"I'll make do with my long johns until I can get to my own underwear," I said. "As long as it's this week," I added with a laugh. "Thank you, Curly. There are plenty of choices."

"Well, make yourself at home. I'm going to grab a few things and change my clothes. It won't take five minutes. I'll shut this door so you can have privacy. Come on to the front door when you're ready."

"Could I use your phone to check in with the sheriff?"

He grinned and tossed it to me.

CHAPTER 20

Brian and Curly were hard at work at the wide-open front door shoveling snow into two buckets. They took turns dumping it into a tub in a hallway bathroom. I offered to dump or shovel, and they seemed glad for help. On the plus side, we stayed warm, sweating in fact.

Curly leaned against the door frame to catch his breath. "You know, I bought a snow-blower for this. Where do you suppose it is?"

"The barn?" I guessed because I had seen tools hanging on a wall there.

"Yep. It's doing us a lot of good out there."

"It's not my fault," claimed Brian. He was breathing hard from the strenuous work.

"Did I say it was?"

"Well I'm the one that was using it."

"Well, then? Should we blame the horses?"

"I thought you'd be proud of me for hanging it with the other tools."

"Well now I wish you'd left it here for me to trip over."

"There's just no pleasing you, is there Boss?"

Curly grinned. It was evident there were no hard feelings between them.

It wasn't long before we broke through the drift blocking the front door. Brian stepped out first.

"Margarita, you've got to see this!" He held out his hand. I took it and we slogged through the wet snow on the porch.

Although there was no sun, the world was bright white, a marvel of ice and snow. Brian drew me across the porch, but the going was slow. Once we got out from under the roof, he pointed to the Tetons. Even though parts of them were still shrouded by remnants of storm clouds, we could see that fresh powder had been dumped on them. They gleamed and seemed taller, as if by standing up to the storm, they had grown in stature.

"My gorgeous girls made it through just fine," said Curly from behind us. "Did you ever see anything more fantastic than my girls, Margarita?"

I could honestly say I hadn't. The snowy forest below them was a wonder, too. Everything was achingly beautiful.

"Let's see if we can get that snow-blowing contraption from the barn," Curly said to Brian.

We had to move a five-foot drift to get to the door. It was serious work, harder than digging out of the house. Finally, we were able to get the door open enough to squeeze through one by one.

The animals seemed glad to see us. They snorted and stomped with impatience as Brian brought fresh hay and grain to each stall. He spoke softly to them as he tended to his chores.

Curly took his snow-blower from its place on the wall. "We don't need this now that we dug our way to it."

"There's the guest house," I reminded him. "That will be a mess."

It wasn't as bad as I pictured. We shoveled snow instead of melting it so that we didn't flood the place. The work took nearly an hour but in the end, doing it that way made the clean-up easier. A bit of mopping and it was finished. I was able to get into my room and saw that all was safe there.

Curly returned the mop and bucket to the hall closet and pronounced the job finished, except for getting a new door.

"Who knows?" he said. "Maybe we'll find the old one once the snow melts."

"It could be anywhere by now," said Brian.

We walked back to the barn.

Brian sidled up to me. "Do you still want to go with me to feed the pintos?"

"You know I do!"

"Have you ever been on a snowmobile?"

"Are you kidding? I live in the desert."

He laughed at that.

"I'll go too," announced Curly.

"What for?" blurted Brian, who should've known better.

"Won't you need a chaperone?"

Brian groaned. His face was red from the cold but it went a shade or two redder. He pulled a sleek machine with two seats around to where the hay was stacked. Then he and Curly loaded a bale onto the second seat and strapped it down.

Brian stood beside it, waiting. "Well? Get on, Boss."

"Where will we put Margarita?"

"Get on if you're going."

"Oh," said Curly, as if he had just figured it out, "you're taking her on the other one." Then he hopped on and drove into the yard with a big grin on his face.

Brian brought a second machine around to where Curly waited.

"You're going to have to hang on to Brian," Curly said. "Just grab him around the waist. I know you'll hate that."

I ignored him, got on, pulled a wool hat and muffler tight, and then put my arms around Brian. Curly watched every move.

"Let's go!" I said.

We rocketed past a surprised Curly.

"See ya, old man," Brian called.

Curly picked up speed and we raced to stay ahead of him, but stopped near the frozen lake to admire the crystalline landscape. There was no sign of the timid elk. Curly sped ahead of us and Brian took off with a sudden jerk, trying to catch him.

When we reached Pinto Canyon both men slowed their machines to a crawl. It was amazing to glide when yesterday the horses had picked their way over stones and around puddles of slushy snow.

We unloaded the bale together at the far end of the canyon, where the pintos were seen yesterday. The snowy field was covered with hoof prints, but there were no horses in sight.

"Where do you suppose they are?" I asked.

"They've gone farther down the valley," said Brian. "Want to go see?"

I was remounted before he was.

We took off with Curly dogging us. Before long we saw the pintos running and kicking up their hind legs. Their joy was contagious. Brian slowed the snowmobile to a crawl, and then stopped it.

Curly pulled up next to us. "Isn't that a sight?"

We watched them in awed silence until Brian suggested, "Let's bring another bale from the barn."

"Good idea, but leave Margarita here."

"She's coming with me."

"I need to talk to her, Brian. It's important, and the reason she came. You can take her through the woods later. She'd like that."

Brian relented since he had no choice.

"He's not happy," said Curly.

I was tempted to say *duh*. For a time I had forgotten I was there to work.

"I need to let Christina know I've been delayed," I said.

"I'm sure she knows that. But here, call her." He handed me his cell phone.

"Well, I don't know the number offhand."

"Allow me," he said, and took it back.

"Wait, let's talk first."

"I'm listening."

"Joey said Sheriff Blanton told him when Christina heard the news of your affair she was hysterical and claimed she hadn't known. That doesn't fit with what you said about her having already figured out that you were in love with someone else. And Dena Jablonski says she knew. Nor is it consistent with the fact that you had told Serena you filed for divorce. That incident made Joey feel you had lied to Serena all along and had no intention of getting a divorce. Do you see how easily he went from that thought to the idea that you had done away with her because she became a threat to your family life?"

Curly's face was full of pain. "It's true that Christina was hysterical, but I don't recall her saying the things Blanton said she did. She never said she didn't know I was seeing someone else. She did know."

His eyes were on the pintos, but I don't think he saw them. "She got upset when Blanton showed her a photo of Serena. And Blanton's attitude unnerved her. He seemed anxious for her to see how young and good-looking Serena was, how sexy. He rubbed it in, in other words."

"Yesterday you never said what you thought about my first theory. Do you believe your ex-wife is capable of murder?"

He tried to laugh. "Doesn't everybody think their ex-wife is capable of murder?"

"I only care what you think about her."

"I think she's capable of it. Do I think she lured Serena in that cold, premeditated way? No, I don't believe that. Christina might have killed her in a rage, but she would never have planned a murder. That's not Christina. I would bet my fortune on it."

"Thank you. That's what I wanted to know. What about Dena Jablonski?"

"My opinion is she's a bitchy gossip who lies, but she's no murderer, either. Whoever lured Serena planned it. What would they say to Serena to make her think she was talking to me? And what would they say to her when she saw it wasn't me? How would they subdue her? Where would they stash her body without being seen? Do you see what I mean?"

"Yes."

"Your theory number two is the only one that works." He continued to stare at the horses. "A cold-blooded killer took my love from me. It was not a crime of passion but a carefully planned execution. I wonder if they did it to kill her or to kill me."

His comment gave me a chill. "Curly, if you suspect someone, please tell me. I need to hear even the craziest theories because right now I've got nothing."

"Yesterday, when you told me about the underpants incident, you mentioned the policemen and it made me think. It reminded me of something that happened before I knew Serena. Our house was broken into when we were away and I called 9-1-1. They sent Sheriff Blanton to talk to us. His unspoken attitude was that if we were so wealthy, we were asking to be robbed, as if it was our fault. He didn't do anything but file a report that was meaningless. Glass was broken out of a window, but he took no fingerprints. Instead he was surly and arrogant."

"What did you do?"

"I spoke with a friend who worked for the Sheriff's Office in Cody and he said I should file a formal complaint with the county judge and I did. That caused quite a stir. I had stepped on Blanton's toes. Some time passed, and one day out of the blue he called me and apologized. He said his wife was dying of cancer and he had acted out of line."

"Did his wife die of cancer?"

"I think so. Anyway, all was forgiven. I felt bad for him and told him so. Then, shortly after that I bought some land through my company and it happened to border land owned by the sheriff. He had put up a fence six feet into my property. It was not a big deal to me and I would've let it go because the property I bought was over three thousand acres. I had what I wanted and didn't care about the fence. He got so ugly with me when I only asked him about it that I pressed the point. He had to move the fence. He called me a 'fucking rich bastard.'

"After that, but unconnected as far as I knew, Christina received a pornographic magazine in the mail. I still don't know that it's connected."

"It doesn't matter. Please tell me what happened."

"It was accompanied by a typed letter that read, 'See page 37. I will come on your face.' It wasn't signed. Page thirty-seven was a—a—come shot on a woman's face. Pardon the crudeness. When you told me about Serena's unknown caller, the two things connected in my brain."

"Did Christina receive any other mail?"

"Yes, more came, and it was equally offensive. But then she received a pair of lacy panties in the mail. She brought them to me and said it looked like somebody had used them to masturbate. I was afraid for her because it had escalated."

"What did you do?"

"I called the Sheriff's Office and asked to speak with a deputy. I was trying to avoid the rude sheriff. I told the deputy the story and he said he'd get back to me about what to do. Within fifteen minutes he called back and said the sheriff wanted to see me in Alpine with the evidence because there was a sexual predator was on the loose."

"Did you go?"

"Christina and I went up together the same day and the sheriff acted—strange."

"Strange, how?"

"He concentrated on how Christina felt about it. Was she insulted? Horrified? Had she seen pornography before? He was lewd. She was put out with him. He seemed to be making fun of her in some subtle, hard-to-explain way.

"When we were ready to walk out, he said in that damn redneck drawl of his, 'You're a mighty pretty woman, Mrs. Hampton. Looks like you turned somebody on real hard.' Let me tell you that was not a comforting observation. Again, he took no fingerprints and did nothing. But the weirdness stopped."

Curly shifted on the seat and continued. "Several years passed, and then I was involved with Serena. Once we were talking about men and how they sometimes made her feel. She said there had been an older man who tried to date her and wouldn't take no for an answer. She indicated he held a position of power and respect in the community. She was about to tell me his name when our attention was turned to something else. We never picked up the thread of that conversation again. It didn't seem important since it was something from the past. Now I wonder if the powerful, respected person was Sheriff Blanton."

I felt chilled to my soul. "It would explain a few things, like why he paid no attention to Christina as a suspect and why he passed by the dam."

"He knew there was no body in there. But there's one more thing."

"Please go on."

"The day the sheriff saw the overnight bag with that red wisp of a thing, the look on his face was lecherous. The expression was fleeting, and afterward he turned to me with a murderous look. That's the look everybody saw. It was the murderous glare that made Joey attack me and condemned me as a killer. But I saw the other look first."

Holy crap, the sheriff!

Whoa.

"The whole community thought I had killed Serena and hid her body in the new dam. Yet the sheriff never checked."

My mind raced. "I'm sure I can locate him, but without a body I still have nothing unless he confesses." I was thinking out loud. "He's lived with his crime for thirty years. What would make him confess now?"

"I guess you'll have to get creative," Curly said, turning in the seat to look at me. "Somewhere down there is a pile of beautiful bones."

* * *

Sitting by the fire again, I removed the jacket, gloves, hat, and scarf and I sat with the top of the coveralls folded down to my waist. I called Christina to explain that I would see her tomorrow. She understood about the storm.

Curly and I were drinking coffee and waiting for Brian. He seemed pensive and unusually quiet. When his cell phone rang it startled both of us. He fumbled to answer it. "William Hampton." He smiled. "Hi Honey! Oh, I'm so glad." A pause. "Yes, it's cleared here, too." Another pause while she spoke. "Not too bad. It could've been worse." A longer pause. "I think Brian went to check on your house. He was going up to the highway but he's still not back."

He listened to her, but was looking at me. "Yes, she's still here. She was hoping to meet you, too, but she's leaving in the morning. Okay. I love you, too, and miss you so much."

He flipped his phone shut. "Madeline."

"Curly, what does Madeline think about Serena?"

"How do you mean?"

"She must know what she meant to you and the painful legacy she left behind."

"Madeline has heard the story, or most of it, anyway. It makes her sad. She knows how it made me feel to be blamed for murdering the woman I loved along with my child. She has helped me move on. Frankly, when Madeline is around I seldom think of Serena. It's like she was with me in a different lifetime. It's when I'm by myself that I let my thoughts go back to Serena, and then only sometimes.

"The pintos make me think of her, and a few other things. I feel like I'm cheating on Madeline. At the same time I feel I'm cheating on Serena when I'm with Madeline." He took a long drink of coffee. "You're probably thinking what a fucked up individual I am."

"I wasn't thinking that at all. I was thinking what a good man you are. What a true heart you have. I would like to have a man like you."

"Thank you Margarita. I hope we can remain friends."

"I would like that very much."

"Could a friend give you some advice?"

"Sure."

"Don't be afraid to love again. I know it takes courage. But love is the one thing in the world worth being courageous about."

"I'm not afraid as much as loyal. I want to love someone else, but I feel like I'm cheating on Kevin."

"I understand that. What was I saying a second ago? I guess we need to know that the people who loved us would want us to move on and love again."

"I haven't convinced myself of that yet."

"Brian thinks you hung the moon, I guess you know."

"No he doesn't."

"Oh yes he does. He very much does."

"He had planned to take me through the woods, but he left to check on Madeline's house without saying a word, and I don't see him, do you?"

"He wants to take you, but he's shy. He's sitting up there in Madeline's empty house knocking his head against the wall."

"I doubt that. He probably has a girlfriend."

Curly laughed and got up to tend the fire.

* * *

The next morning, Brian helped me get my suitcase to the Jeep. "I hope you can come back sometime, Margarita. I really like you."

"I like you, too, Brian. You take care, okay? Keep your head covered and all."

He laughed. "You really brighten up a place."

"I think that's the nicest thing anyone ever said to me."

"Mr. Hampton thinks so, too."

"He does?"

"Yes, he told me." He stared at his feet. "I wish you didn't have to go so soon."

"I live in Texas," I pointed out. Brilliant.

I gave him a quick hug of good-bye and he walked away.

Curly strode up as Brian left. "Thank you for everything, Margarita." He extended his hand. "I hope you'll come back sometime."

"I would love to do that."

"I'll take you hiking in the mountains."

"Oh, that would be almost as awesome as the horses!"

"Are you going to put the paints in your novel?"

"I intend to put all of it Curly."

"Even the part about Brian?"

I grinned. "Yes, especially Brian."

"You'll be in touch, then?"

"Soon," I said. Then I hugged him and he hugged me back, pressing me close to his heart.

I got into the Jeep, but Curly stood with his hand on the door so I couldn't shut it. "What will I do about Brian?"

"What do you mean?"

"You've broken his heart."

"You're crazy!"

"Oh yes, he's a lovesick puppy." Curly laughed and stepped away.

Then I put the vehicle into four-wheel drive and began backing out.

I put the window down. "Curly, don't forget to paint. When I come back I want to see your work. I mean it."

"And I look forward to reading your novels."

I smiled and nodded. Then I slowly pulled away from the Pinto Canyon Ranch. It hurt my heart to leave.

CHAPTER 21

Cody is about one hundred and sixty-eight miles from Jackson Hole and the Pinto Canyon Ranch. The highway had been plowed, but hurry was not on my mind. I took time to watch the unreal, pinch-me-now beauty of the countryside. After sixty miles, I pulled into a rest stop and called Barney at the office.

"I thought you were never going to call me, Ricos. I didn't know if you'd been killed and consumed, or if you married that curly-haired mountain man."

I laughed. "You should see him. He's quite good-looking."

"You fell for some ol' *grandpa?*" Barney was incredulous.

"I didn't fall for him, but I know a handsome man when I see one. He's one of those ageless types. He'll still be a knockout when he's eighty, I bet."

"You fell for him."

"Maybe I did, a little. It's a long story I might, or prob'ly won't, tell you later."

"You know you're gonna beg me to listen to every sordid detail. Did you get what you went there for?"

"Definitely."

"What did you think of Hampton? Assuming you did something besides gawk at him."

"To make it short, I think he loved Serena with all he had. For sure he didn't kill her. We put together some information that strongly implicates someone else. I'll tell you all about it when I see you."

"Sheriff said you got snowed in."

"Yeah, we had an incredible storm night before last, a blizzard. You should see how drop-dead gorgeous this place is."

"Yeah, I've always heard that about Wyoming. Anything else going on?"

"Brian, Curly's personal assistant, fell for me."

"I guess you'll be unbearable now."

"You can count on it."

* * *

Christina Moore was different from the way I pictured her. She was an attractive woman with silver hair that was cut stylishly short. She wore small diamond studs in her ears. Her face was a bit freckled, and like Curly, the years had been kind to her. Well, that's wrong. I mean to say that the years didn't show. There had been nothing kind about them.

"I thought we could sit in here," she said. She led me to a sunny, glassed-in room that overlooked rolling hills of white. Sunlight gleamed like shards of diamonds and dazzled the eyes.

When we settled she said, "Before you say anything, Deputy Ricos, I have to say it's painful for me to go back to the time when my grand life was taken away."

"I know, and I'm sorry. But who else can tell me what you can?"

She thought about it and must have decided to let me off the hook. "I know you saw Curly. How was he?"

"He seems happy, overall. My coming was painful for him, too. I don't like causing people pain, but I take my job seriously. I'm supposed to find out what happened to Serena Bustamante."

"And you think you will?"

"I hope so. I'm doing everything I know to do, which is why I'm here."

"At first, I hated Curly so much for what he did and couldn't deal with it. I distracted myself with our sons, and tried to get my life together. It was easy to tell myself Curly was a monster, that he had killed her. I became aware that it was a ridiculous belief to have. Curly couldn't kill anyone, especially someone he loved so much. The thing I had to face was that he wasn't having some sordid affair. He loved the woman. And he had stopped loving me."

"I'm sure that was awful."

"It was painful beyond anything you can imagine."

"I'll try to make this brief and go on my way. I have a few questions I'd like to ask, and I would appreciate it if you'd let me record our conversation."

"Why record it?"

"So I can refer to it later. Otherwise, I have to take notes and that limits my ability to converse with you in a natural way."

"I suppose it'll be okay. I don't have anything new to say anyway."

"I spoke with Dena Jablonski. She was your best friend, wasn't she?"

"Yes, she was the best friend I had in Terlingua."

"How did you come to know her?"

"I met her in a bar. I know that sounds wrong, but let me explain. Curly was good about taking the boys and letting me have time for myself. The problem was, there wasn't much to do in Terlingua back then. I'd go shopping, such as it was. Eat out. Sometimes I would go into the national park and sit on a bench and read. Small boys don't allow time for much reading."

We laughed and then she asked if I'd like something to drink. I declined her offer and she continued. "One day I went into a tiny hole-in-the-wall bar on Highway 118 called Camel's Hump or something like that. It's long gone from there now. I ordered a glass of white wine and the surly, unkept bartender informed me it was either beer or beer. I was beginning to think I had made a mistake in stopping.

"Then, a female voice from behind me said, 'The Miller's good and cold.' There was Dena, a college student at the time, sitting at a table behind me. I smiled at her and ordered a Miller. She invited me to sit with her, which I did. We had fun laughing and talking. She said she was waiting for her husband to get off work and that he worked on a local ranch. We were friends from that time on."

"Dena lied during her interview with Sheriff Blanton, and told him you spent the day with her the day Serena disappeared."

"Yes, I know. She thought I murdered her. I had figured out by then that Curly was in love with someone else—or at least he no longer loved me. Dena told me he was dating a Mexican slut named Serena. According to Dena, she was after his money. Dena had a mouthful of heated things to say. In fairness to her, she was my friend and was trying to defend me."

"Because of her lies," I said, "the sheriff passed over you as a possible suspect. I mean no offense, Ms. Moore, but you would've been my first suspect after Curly. I would have checked you out at length."

"I guess I can understand that, me being the thrown-away wife."

"Most murders of husbands' lovers are crimes of passion, done in the heat of the moment. For you to murder Serena would have fit, except it was premeditated. That rules out crime of passion. I think someone lured Serena to the arroyo. That took cunning and planning."

"Yes. I always thought that, too."

"Dena's lie took me down a wrong path. I suspected you, but I no longer think you had anything to do with Serena's murder."

"I had never even seen her!" she cried.

"I believe that. You were as much a victim as Serena. You, Curly, and Serena were all victims of the same person."

"Yes," she said softly with tears in her eyes.

"Did Dena ever mention the name of Serena's other lovers?"

"Yes, she named a few. I thought at the time she was trying to cheer me up. I think she thought if she could make me believe Curly was straying, chasing a skirt, I would feel better."

She sighed. "Dena didn't know Curly like I did. I could say many things about him, but he was never a skirt-chaser. He's a serious, deep man. Women came on to him all the time. I'm sure you noticed he's quite handsome."

"Yes, he is."

"He is also very, very wealthy. He was a rich before I ever met him. Girls were always flinging themselves at him. It was sickening. He thought so, too, I know. After we were married it continued, but he seemed oblivious. You could ask any of his friends."

"I believe you."

"Dena tried to make me feel better but it didn't help. I already knew the truth of Curly. I had lost him and I was bereft."

"Do you remember any names?"

"No, I paid no attention to her. As she told me what a slut Serena was, I knew she wasn't. She told me Serena was after his money and I knew she wasn't. She said Serena was having sex with other men. She was not doing any such thing. The names Dena threw at me were fictitious, or based on men she knew, but they meant nothing to me, except for one." It was unconscious, but I held my breath until she said the name. "Sheriff Houston Blanton."

"She told you Serena was having an affair with Sheriff Blanton?"

"Well, Dena didn't put it that tactfully. She said, 'That hussy is screwing Houston Blanton's brains out.' I'd had a few creepy run-ins with Blanton and I pressed Dena about what she meant. Even before Serena disappeared, I feared for Curly. Blanton hated him. We suspected Blanton had sent me some pornography."

"Curly told me about it."

"Then you already know."

"Yes. It's hard to believe Serena would've given him the time of day."

"She didn't. Dena admitted that Sheriff Blanton only wished Serena was screwing him. It seems he had a real 'thing' for her."

"Serena was seventeen years younger than Blanton. It doesn't seem like he would have known her."

"Dena said Blanton saw Serena at a dance where he was providing security. He followed her outside and made a rather crude pass at her. Serena blew him off and some friends of hers came up, and they all went off together. After that night, Blanton began to follow her. He stayed in the background, showing up wherever she was. He made it look innocent since he was the sheriff, after all. He could be at dances, rodeos, restaurants, and most public gatherings. He was all over that town. Dena said he even followed Serena and would look in her windows at night."

I was covered in goose bumps. "How would Dena know all this?"

"You should ask her. I never did."

It's a wonder I didn't tear out the door, dialing old Jablonski as I ran. It was hard to sit still. "Is there anything else relevant you remember from that time?"

"Yes, there are two things. When Sheriff Blanton interviewed me, I was a wreck. Curly was the primary suspect and wasn't allowed to be with me for the questioning. I remember that as Blanton began to interview me, he was looking at my breasts. He was so nasty. He'd lick his lips and then smile this sick smile. It was like he was interviewing my body, not me. I was terrified he would touch me. I felt so alone and vulnerable."

"Did you ever tell anyone about this?"

"No. How could I? I was estranged from Curly, my protector and confidante. He was suspected of murder, for heaven's sake. We seldom spoke."

"What was the other thing?"

"What other thing?"

"You said there were two things."

"Oh, yes. The other thing was about the underwear. Curly told you about the underpants sent through the mail?"

I nodded and she continued. "Dena told me Houston Blanton had a collection of girls' underpants he kept in a secret place. She said he used them, whatever that meant. Judging by the ones mailed to me, I could guess how they were used. I asked her how in the hell he got girls' underpants in the first place. She said, 'He breaks into their bedrooms, of course,' as if that was a normal thing for a man to do."

Oh, Mrs. Jablonski, what other dirty little secrets do you keep? And how do you know the ones you do?

"I have one more question. I explored the land and home where you used to live. The house is empty, except for Curly's office."

"Curly came back to Wyoming before I did. He told me to sell the place, keep it—he didn't care what I did with it. The kids were with my parents back here in Cody, so I was alone there. I gave all the furniture away except for the stuff in Curly's office. I couldn't bear to part with it. It was so Curly. I still loved him, you see. I would sit at his desk, close my eyes, and go back to a time when he loved me. I know that sounds pathetic, but that's how it was."

"I understand." She was speaking to a woman who had smelled, held, and even slept with the bloody clothes her dead husband was wearing when he died. I knew all about 'pathetic.'

"One day," Christina continued, "I opened a cabinet he kept locked so the boys wouldn't get into it. I don't know what made me do it. I found a padded envelope inside with a photo of Curly. He was so damned handsome it hurt. At the bottom he had scrawled his undying love to Serena. I cried for hours. I've never known such pain. I knew he loved her, but to see it written…" Christina put her head in her hands.

After the former Mrs. Hampton composed herself, she said, "When I left the house for good, I meant to put the photo back in the envelope and give it to Curly. When I started to replace it, a note fell out. It was from Serena's brother, Joey, and it read, 'This was found on the front seat of the Camaro. Blanton had it when I arrived at the scene. I demanded he give it to me, but I think you should have it.'

"I decided to leave the photo on his desk. It wasn't going to do anybody any good anywhere else. If Serena is found, perhaps it should be buried with her."

CHAPTER 22

How I made it back to Jackson Hole without wrecking the Jeep, I can't say. I was a mess, crying and sobbing the whole way. My head and heart were reeling. I felt as if I had been there, felt their loss, and knew their pain. I had seen into their hearts. By the time I reached the city, my eyes were puffy, my nose was running, and my cheeks were blotchy. I stopped at a gas station restroom and splashed cold water on my face.

"Get a grip," I told my pitiful reflection, but I couldn't do it yet.

My return flight to Texas was scheduled to leave at nine the next morning, so I was forced to get a hotel. When I passed the turn-off to Pinto Canyon Ranch, I longed to stop and see my friends again.

I had caused enough pain for one trip. Instead of turning, I went on.

* * *

I sat on the queen-sized bed in my room, waiting for room service. Out the window I could see the Grand Tetons, an imposing sight from everywhere, the way the Chisos Mountains are where I live.

I decided to call Dena Jablonski. She had some explaining to do. The problem was I had hung up on her the last time. She might not talk to me without a court order, but with what I now knew, I would have no trouble getting one.

When she answered, I didn't hesitate. "Mrs. Jablonski, I'm calling from Wyoming."

"You hung up on me." She sounded more insulted than angry.

"I apologize for that. I was upset."

"Don't hang up on me again, young lady."

"Today I spoke with Christina Moore, and she told me some interesting things."

"Do you still think she killed Serena Bustamante?"

"No, I don't believe she did."

"Well, that's a relief."

"I need to ask you about some things she said."

"Okay. Ask, but if you insult me, I'll be the one to hang up."

"Fair enough. When you told Christina about Serena's affairs, you mentioned that Sheriff Blanton had eyes for her. You said he had followed her and even looked into her house at night. Is that true?"

"Yes, it is. He had quite a thing for her."

"She also said you were aware of an underwear collection he kept."

"That's true."

"You said he broke into girls' homes and stole their underpants. Is that right?"

"Yes. Yes, that's what I told her. She wasn't supposed to speak to anyone about it. She promised me."

"Was it the truth?"

"Oh, yes, it was true all right."

"With all due respect, Mrs. Jablonski, how would you know something so personal about Sheriff Blanton?"

"Houston Blanton is my older brother."

I nearly choked. "Mrs. Jablonski, why did your brother collect underpants of young women he didn't know?"

"Oh, he knew them, or thought he did. At times, he spoke to them. He followed and observed them. Of course, it wasn't to harm them or anything like that. He just had an insatiable lust for young Mexican women."

My head practically exploded.

"Did he approach them?" I asked in a voice much smaller than I would have liked.

"Sometimes, but they turned him down. He never raped them or harmed them in any way, if that's what you're getting at. He was harmless, really. And he swears he's stopped doing that."

My first reaction was to scream and keep screaming until the world made sense. Instead, I swallowed hard and spoke calmly. "Was your brother married?"

"Yes, he was. I know what you're thinking. Certainly he had sex with his wife. This other thing was a different craving. It was something he was driven to do most of his life. His wife died of cancer, and then he seemed to get worse."

"He was a stalker," I said, more to myself than to Jablonski. "Sheriff Blanton stalked Serena Bustamante."

"Now you just wait a minute," she said, anger flaring. "He might've looked at her more than he should have, but he wasn't stalking her."

"What would you call it?"

"He was obsessed with her. She was built, you know. He used to say she was a cock-tease, and he'd laugh about it because he thought one day it would get her into trouble. He sure was right about that."

My blood had turned to ice. Room service came and went. I scribbled my name on the bill without looking at it. I took a long drink of tea but didn't taste it.

"Yes, I guess he was right." I decided to back off before Mrs. Jablonski got a clue and alerted her brother that I was onto him. "Did you tell anyone besides Christina about his secrets?"

"No, it was embarrassing. Houston and I are close, even though we're fourteen years apart. So I know things about him that no one else does."

"Was there a reason you told Christina?"

"I guess I got on the subject because I had told her Serena was having sex with Sheriff Blanton. I said it because I wanted her to understand that her husband would come back to her after he saw the truth of what Serena was."

"And what was the truth of her, Mrs. Jablonski?"

"She was a beautiful woman, that part is true. But she was a cheap whore who wanted to have sex with everything that moved. She was a wanton home-wrecker."

"Did you know her?"

"Not in a personal sense, no."

"Then how do you know anything about who Serena was?"

"My brother told me about her."

* * *

I sat on the edge of the bed, stunned to immobility. The sun was down, and the snow was a soft pink color. I should've been standing by the window to admire it. My food was surely cold. After too much thinking, I went into the bathroom and threw up.

After that, I lay on the bed and willed myself to think of the horses at Pinto Canyon. I thought they should be named after famous characters in literature, but Boo Radley popped into my mind, which made me feel worse.

I needed to keep my head off the cold truth of Serena's demise, but that did not work. Something with alcohol would help, but what if I couldn't stop? What if I got too drunk to go home? What if? What if?

My eyes wandered to the smiling photo of Serena on the bedside table, then my head went to the way the snow had fallen on Curly's remarkable black curls.

Every thought led me back to Serena.

"You never knew, did you?" I asked her photo, "Until it was too late."

After I cried a while, I felt better and called Curly.

"I was thinking of you," he said, which put me at ease. "I was looking at the pintos and waiting on Madeline. She'll be here about eight o'clock."

"I saw Christina."

"How is she?"

"She seems fine. I like her, and she was honest with me, I think. I agree with you that she could never have killed Serena."

"Did you ask her?"

"I wasn't as blunt as 'did you kill her?' but she told me in the things she said. She's innocent, I'm sure. I found out more about Dena Jablonski and Sheriff Blanton."

"Oh?"

"Houston Blanton is Dena Jablonski's older brother."

Curly didn't say anything. For a moment, I thought we had lost the connection, but I realized he was crying. When he spoke his voice was choked with tears. "He killed her, didn't he?"

"Yes, Curly, I think he did."

An even longer time passed before he spoke. "So that sick pervert pretended to conduct a murder investigation. He searched for a woman he knew was already dead. He had all those good people out there looking for her, including me and Joey, when he knew where she was. The sonofabitch hounded me unmercifully." A sob escaped him.

"Curly, I'll see that he is brought to justice; I swear it."

"What good does that do now, Margarita? He's had thirty years of freedom, and I've had thirty years of hell."

"Well, now it's your turn for freedom and his turn for hell. Your freedom will be very, very sweet, and his hell will be very, very—hellish."

He laughed at that, and it seemed to lift the cloud of despair.

"You're a wonder," Curly said. "I wish you were here so I could hug you tight."

"That's the second nicest thing I've heard since I've been in Wyoming."

"What was the first?"

"That I brighten up a place."

"Brian! What a blabbermouth he is!"

"I would never call Brian a blabbermouth."

Curly laughed. "I'm glad he told you because it's true. You brightened things here, and I'm grateful to you for that—and for everything."

* * *

I picked at the cold food, thinking I should eat, but I didn't feel hungry. Then I took a shower and went to bed. I planned to cry myself to sleep, to wallow in self-pity, torture myself with thoughts of Curly and Serena and their lost love, and my own, but it didn't work like that. I fell asleep and slept the whole night.

Before my alarm went off the next morning, I had a dream of Serena. She was trying to tell me something, but I couldn't understand. She tried and tried. Then, as I was slipping back to consciousness, I heard her say, "Thank you."

Maybe Serena was going to talk to me after all, in the only way she could, through dreams.

CHAPTER 23

When the plane landed at the El Paso Airport, it felt surreal to be back in Texas after only a few hours of flying. The frigid wonder of Wyoming and the dry, much warmer desert-mountain country I love seemed millions of miles apart. As I pulled away from the airport, I was nearly blinded by the bright Texas sunshine.

Once the traffic became sparse on I-10 coming out of El Paso, I called Sheriff Ben at home and asked if he was busy.

"No," he said, "I'm watching a college basketball game."

He is a sports addict, I know, but when I said, "I have unbelievable news about the Serena case," the die-hard lawman in him took the bait.

I told him everything, starting with my perceptions of Curly and then the ranch, the wild pintos, the haunting beauty of Wyoming, and the incredible blizzard I had witnessed. Then I related the information I got from Curly about the former sheriff's peculiar behavior and explained how I put that together with what Christina told me. I explained what Mrs. Jablonski said about Serena and how one thing led to another until I discovered that Houston Blanton is her brother. I revealed the awful things I knew about Blanton including the nastiest parts. I was relieved not to have to sit face to face with the sheriff and talk about masturbating with underpants.

"I feel sure he killed Serena," I said, "and why. The trick will be to prove it."

"It'll be difficult without a body unless you can make him confess. Do you have any ideas?"

"I'd hoped you could help me think of something brilliant."

"Let me sit with it a while."

An idea nagged me. "Sheriff, if Blanton stalked and killed Serena, he might have done it before, or since. Using his position of power he could have gotten away with a lot."

"You're absolutely right. I'll go into the office after a while and see what I find in open cases. I'm not aware of any, but I'll check."

"Do you know where Blanton lives now?"

"He retired to Balmorhea about three years ago, I believe."

"Do you know him, Sheriff?"

"Not really, no. I saw him a few times at Texas Association of Sheriffs meetings. He greeted me once and said he had once held my job. I didn't think anything about it, or him."

"First, I need to visit him."

"That's fine, but you can't go alone." It was the putting-his-foot-down voice.

"But I need to, Sheriff Ben."

"The man is a cold-blooded murderer of young Hispanic women, or at least one young woman. You'll take Barney or else I'll go with you."

"Please, Sheriff, I have to go alone if I'm going to find out anything useful. He'll know I come as a deputy assigned to close the case. I'll ask for his help and he'll appear to give it. He won't have any idea that we're on to him. Don't forget that I'll have my weapon."

"I'm thinking of your safety. Barney is going with you, so get used to the idea. Don't be such a hot shot."

"I'm not a hot shot! And if it was Barney, you wouldn't try to stop him."

"He is not a young Hispanic woman. And besides, I would send backup with Barney. One day you're going to realize that I'm not trying to protect you because you're a female, Margarita. I'm trying to protect you because you're a deputy, and I'm responsible for your safety. You're a good deputy, and it would be a tragedy if some pervert killed you, though you're so hard headed you make me tear at my hair."

I laughed at that. Arguing with the sheriff is like arguing with my papi. It's aggravating to everyone involved, and he always wins.

"I still think it will go better if I go unaccompanied."

"Next thing you know, he'll be stalking you and stealing your underwear."

"That would be a serious mistake on his part."

"But he won't know that, Margarita. He's killed and gotten away with it, maybe more than once. He'll be bold by now."

"I'm younger and faster. And I have the law on my side—the real law."

"He's older, yes, but he's also cunning and dangerous."

"He's sixty-nine!"

"You're standing on my toes now."

Dang, I hate the taste of my foot.

"Sorry. But you're not sixty-nine, and even if you were, you don't look old and you sure don't seem old to me and—"

"Hush now. You're just digging in deeper."

* * *

I was in the home stretch on Highway 118, amid the majestic mountains of South County. Sunset's colors were history and even the twilight was fading fast. I flew past the Terlingua Ranch Resort's main road, then past the Longhorn Motel, and came to a steep, winding part of the drive that requires slower speed to negotiate safely. If I hadn't braked at the right moment, I might not have spotted the accident.

One vehicle, a boxy, seen-better-days-looking thing, lay on its side in a deep ditch, and something (a body?) was crumpled beside it. I radioed the dispatcher to send the medics even before I had come to a complete stop. Then I grabbed blankets and a first-aid kit from the rear of the Explorer and ran with my heart in it. Darkness had settled, and my flashlight's beam seemed pathetically inadequate. I was on top of the scene before I recognized Wynne Rayburn's ancient green Chevy Blazer with the cut-off roof.

There was so much blood.

At first I thought Wynne was dead, but as I felt for a pulse he grimaced and tried to move. Blood spurted from a gash on his forehead and joined a dark pool already collecting in the dirt. He moaned with the effort and fell back.

I wasn't sure if he could hear, or understand if he did, but I spoke to him and squeezed his cool, limp hand. "Please don't try to move, Wynne. The medics are on the way. I'll do all I can for you until they get here."

One puffy eye struggled open at the sound of my voice. His disappointment was bitter. "Oh, it's you." That was groaned, but he still managed a derisive tone, as if he resented me for stopping to help.

"It's you" was the last intelligible thing he said for a while. He began to mutter and make no sense, and his breathing was rapid and shallow; he was going into shock. I set the flashlight in the dirt because there was no way I could hold it and do the things I had to do. It did its best to keep the vast black night from swallowing us.

Every time Wynne's heart beat, blood gushed from the contusion on his head. The bandage my mom had placed on his broken nose was now red instead of white. That, plus two sinister-looking shiners, a broken arm, and bleeding from too many places to count made him a grim sight.

The first step in the treatment of shock is to stop bleeding, but before I tackled that, I dragged a rock from a few feet over and put his feet up on it. Then I covered him with blankets and addressed the worst cut, the one on his head. I pulled on gloves for his protection as well as mine and held the laceration together with my fingers. I couldn't see another way to keep it closed, and besides, that worked.

I have first-aid training and was raised by a doctor, but I felt seriously under-qualified for the tasks at hand. I needed to be doing five or six things at once. There was no ambulance siren yet, and panic was creeping in.

Then Wynne stopped breathing.

"Wynne! Can you hear me? Wake up! Wynne? Wynne!"

If there's one thing about first-aid I know well, it's CPR. Every two years I'm required to renew certification for my job, but Mom trained me to do it when I was a child and made me prove what I knew over and over through my growing-up years. She used to say that I would save a friend's life one day. Ironic, isn't it?

"Wynne! Stay with me, Wynne."

I need more hands! I'm all by myself! With a dead man! In an arroyo in the dark! It's so cold! I was shivering, sweaty, gasping, and fully into panic mode when my patient took a labored breath and began breathing on his own again.

"That's good, Wynne. You hang in with me. The ambulance is coming."

Is it? Why are they taking so long? How much time has passed?

"Keep breathing, Wynne. You're going to be all right."

"Dying," he grunted.

"No, you're not going to die. The ambulance is coming. You don't want to die here with me, in a dark ditch. Think about all the millions of reasons to live."

Wynne appeared to be unconscious again, but I kept talking to him. "I wish you could open your eyes and see tonight's gala presentation, sponsored by the stars. The sky looks bloated, as if it will cave in with the weight of them."

No response from Wynne, but he continued to breathe. Dead men don't breathe; mentally, I repeated that like a mantra.

As I squeezed the edges of that wound together for what seemed like hours and monitored my patient's scary, faltering respiration, and tried not to scream, I described the constellations with incredible calm. It was more for my sake than his. I know too few by name, so I was sure I identified some that can't be seen from this hemisphere. I doubted Wynne would call me on it. Some were straight out of my imagination for entertainment's sake. If you look up long enough, you see all kinds of surprising things.

While we waited, I leaked the truth about the Grand Tetons—their magnificence—and the terror and wonder of experiencing my first blizzard. I chattered as if we were old friends from way back, and forgot I was speaking to a man who insulted me for sport, and had challenged me to a duel. Curly, Brian, and Andrea became William, John, and Greta in my tale, for the sake of their privacy and that of my case. I related the enchantment of the wild pintos, the bone-freezing cold, and Pinto Canyon. And snow. I told him about snow.

The siren! It sounded eerily faint at first, and then deafening as it neared. In the absolute silence of that dark ditch it was creepy, but also a relief. Soon my friend Mitch and another medic, Galveston, were scrambling towards us—with light. One carried a camping lantern, the other a jumbo flashlight.

"Hey, Margarita," Mitch said and touched the base of my neck in greeting. Then he turned to Galveston. "Put on some gloves, and take over for her, please." Those were sweet words to my ears.

"He stopped breathing," I nearly sobbed. The fear of bursting into tears kept me from saying more.

"And you gave him CPR?"

I nodded.

"Are you hurt, Rita?"

I took a shaky breath. "No, it's his blood, not mine. I think his arm is broken—"

"I wonder if he went through the windshield," Galveston said.

"I think he flipped in this thing without a seatbelt to keep him in," was Mitch's take on it, and that's what it looked like to me, too. It would be easier to understand the scene in daylight, and after some rest.

I helped Mitch carry the stretcher. Galveston hurried along beside us, holding the wound closed until we got Wynne inside the ambulance where they could go to work on him.

"What took you so long, Mitch?" I asked as we eased the stretcher into place.

He gave me an exasperated look. "You're kidding, right?" He glanced at his watch. "It was twenty-five minutes from the call! That's not bad considering the curving road and the distance."

"That was the longest twenty-five minutes of my life."

"We would've teleported, but it's hard to bring the ambulance that way."

I laughed and gave him a relieved, heartfelt hug.

* * *

A long shower and a call to the hospital in Alpine made me feel better. Wynne was in surgery, but his condition was listed as stable.

Billy called to say he had made spaghetti with meatballs, salad, and garlic bread as a welcome back. He invited himself to come over with the dinner, and mentioned trying on my clothes as if that wasn't reason number one for the visit. Any dinner I didn't have to make sounded perfect, so I told him to come on.

"I've missed you so much," he said with feeling as we were clearing the table after eating.

"I missed you, too."

"I missed you more."

"Go ahead and check out my closet, Billy. You don't have to say you missed me or cook dinner. That was thoughtful, though."

"You stay here, and I'll surprise you."

Doubtless.

I was finishing up the last of the dishes when he came into the kitchen wearing a short red skirt that was super-short on him. It had an elastic waist he was putting to the test. With it, he wore a denim vest so small it caused his shoulders to hunch. The two sides wouldn't even consider meeting in front. He was also wearing my make-up, not that I used it much. His lips were bright red to match the skirt. Without make-up or with it, he was a beauty.

"I can't wear your blouses or dresses," he said in a pout, "or much of anything. You have a closetful of the fabulous things. And oh my goodness! Your shoes are to die for."

"I told you."

"I so wish I could wear them."

"You know there are companies that make sexy shoes for men, right?"

"Right, but they're expensive and I'm broke."

"What size shoe do you wear?"

"Eleven."

"I can look at the resale shop if you want. Maybe there are some women with large feet in Terlingua."

"Well," he said, "there are women with large everything else."

I laughed. "True. Give me a few days. I'm working on something critical now."

"What could be more critical than sexy shoes?"

"A man who stalks and murders young women."

"Oh, no." His hand flew to his heart. "Is there someone like that here?"

"He's not here, no, but he was. Look, I can't talk about it."

"Oh! My God! He killed your missing woman from thirty years ago!"

"Yes, I think so."

Billy stood and paced, throwing his arms around. "You're so smart! How did you figure it out? Did the man in Wyoming tell you? Was it the man in Wyoming? Did that bastard hurt you?"

"Billy, calm down. Nobody hurt me. The man in Wyoming knew more than he thought he knew. That's all I can tell you right now. I'm going after a perverted killer, and I don't want him to know I'm coming."

"Oh! You're so brave!" He came and put his arms around me. "You're just a teensy thing. I can't even wear your clothes. I could just eat you up!" He kissed me on the neck. "You smell nice, too."

I pulled away. "Billy, please."

"When I'm with you, I wish I wasn't gay." He looked surprised. "Oh God, I said it. It popped out. I just came out to you."

"I'm not terribly shocked, Billy."

"Will you still love me and take me to special places?"

"Of course I will."

We moved into the living room. Billy sat on the sofa, and I sat in an easy chair across from it.

"Billy, if you're going to wear my skirts you need to learn how to sit, and underwear would help. What I'm seeing isn't usually seen wearing skirts."

He snapped his legs together. "Sorry."

"I don't mind looking, but if you're going to wear my clothes you should act a lot more ladylike."

"Right, I'll remember that." He perused a magazine upside down, and then peered over it. "When you first met me you wanted me, didn't you?"

"I was interested."

"Damn. I thought I had that right. Have your feelings changed?"

"Not really, but you just came out to me."

"For you, Babycakes, I could be all man and then some."

"Billy, you're wearing my make-up and clothes. Your lips are redder than mine. I don't think that'll work."

"I could shower and meet you naked in fifteen minutes."

"Thank you, but I'm just getting back on the horse, so to speak. And I don't want to be second best to what you truly want, you know?"

"Yeah, besides, you probably don't want to have sex with a man who's obsessing about a way to wear your shoes."

CHAPTER 24

The following morning, Barney started on me the second I walked in the door. "The talk this morning says you saved Wynne Raymore's sorry ass. First you whoop him, and then you save his life. People are confused."

"You've got to stop hanging out in that café."

"Did you save his life or not?"

"You shouldn't say I saved him, but I did the best I could."

"Mitch says you did. He thinks he would've bled to death if you hadn't known what to do. Wynne is now listed in satisfactory condition."

"That's good."

"Don't you think it's ironic that of all the people to come along it happened to be you, his archenemy?"

"Yes, I get it." I didn't know if the lesson in that was for him or for me, and I disappeared into my office to think about it.

Barney followed. He stood in the doorway, dwarfing the space. "I hope you aren't planning to sit in here and stare at that hill."

My boots were already on the desk. "Do you have something more important for me to do?"

"Aren't you going to tell me what you found out in Wyoming?"

I related more than he ever wanted to know about the Serena Bustamante case. He was shocked.

"So Sheriff Ben is going to let you go see Old Man Blanton?"

"You'd better be careful about that 'old man' stuff. I made him angry yesterday by saying I'm younger and faster than Blanton. He's sixty-nine, for goodness sake. Sheriff Ben said I was stepping on his toes.'"

"Ouch."

"Yeah, he's getting touchy in his old age."

We had a laugh about our sheriff.

"Old men are like that."

"And he called me a hot shot."

"You are a hot shot sometimes, Batgirl."

"What? You, too? I'm totally into solving my case. Why does that make me a hot shot?"

Barney sat on the edge of my desk and studied me. "It's because you never want help, and you think you're surrounded by some sort of indestructible shield."

"That's so unfair. I know I'm not indestructible. It's all about the man vs. woman thing isn't it? Men think they know everything. They think they have to protect the poor little women. You guys make me sick." I stood and stormed around.

His expression was so self-satisfied it made me furious. "Go back to your office," I ordered.

"So now I'm just one of 'you guys'? That's the best you can do, 'you guys?'"

"It's the best I can do right now. Give me a second."

"Think about it. What if it was me going in alone to see a murderer who preyed on men? You would kill to go with me."

"Nobody preys on big ol' lugs." I plopped down and folded my arms across my chest. We glared at each other.

"Okay," I relented after a long silence. "I know where you're coming from. And I appreciate it, too. If I go and he freaks me out, I won't go back without you."

"What if he attacks the first time he sees you?"

"That's not his M.O. at all."

"Well, it doesn't matter because I'm going with you. You can whine and sob, but I'm going. The sheriff already called me and said I was."

I went back to glaring at him.

"How old are you, Ricos?"

"You already know I'm twenty-five."

"Are you a woman?"

"Yes. You know that, too."

"And are you Latina or what?"

"I'm an American, same as you—a *Chicana.*" I flexed my arms.

He laughed. "Okay, so you're a young and lovely Chicana. That will not escape Blanton, believe me. When you walk in his door, that old pervert will be checking out your boobs and wondering about your panties."

"Like you don't?"

"Oh, that was a low blow, Ricos."

I shrugged.

"I'm not old, either," Barney said.

"And that makes it okay?"

"Well, sure. Besides, I'm not fixated on underwear."

Sheriff Duncan called and turned my head back to serious things. "I have information for you, Margarita, but first I want to say how proud I am that you saved a man's life last night."

"Thank you, sir. I'm glad I happened by when I did."

"That was fortuitous for Wynne."

"Yes sir."

"Had he been drinking?"

"No, I don't think so. It looked like he lost control coming down the Alpine side of Luna Vista Hill. Barney and I will go check the scene later."

"Very well. I hope he'll change his tune about my worthless female deputy."

"I doubt it, Sheriff."

"He doesn't have to change it if he'll just not sing it at the top of his lungs."

"Right, that suits me, too."

"I told you I would check records and I did," Sheriff Ben said. "I went back in the files, and there are two open cases that were put to bed without being solved or marked as still open. Both happened while Blanton was sheriff. One was five years after Serena, the other twelve, both with the same M.O. as Serena."

"Oh, no."

"There's more. I checked with the Alpine Police Department, and they have scores of reports of women being followed, houses being broken into, underpants being stolen and used. Scores." He let out a long breath. "None of these cases are recent, and all of them are within sixteen years of the Serena incident."

"So it was during the time when Blanton was sheriff?"

"Yes. Not one incident since then."

"Was there ever a rape reported?"

"No. It appears rape was not a part of it. Blanton followed the women, well, you know the M.O. He never varied from it except that he murdered some of them. Why did he murder some and not others?"

"My theory is that his obsession was worse with the ones who were in love with someone else."

"Why do you think that?"

"It's a hunch. I think Serena was murdered because she and Curly were in love and he hated Curly. If he couldn't have her, Curly wasn't going to have her, either."

"You might have something there," the sheriff said. "Sixteen years after Serena's disappearance Blanton got a job as sheriff in a small town outside of Dallas. They also have many reports of women being followed in the same manner. Ditto their police department, and the Dallas P. D. There's one missing person, and it fits the M.O. I'm faxing you the names and address of possible victims and the names of the people I've spoken to in the various departments."

"Thank you, sir."

"I know this is bad, but there's more, and it's worse. Last year a seventeen-year-old girl went missing from Balmorhea. Her family reported that she'd been followed, their home had been broken into and underpants left on the bed. About a year before she disappeared, someone started following her. When the family would leave the house for any length of time, there would be the gift of the soiled underpants on the young woman's bed. They were also mailed to her, and it was always her underwear. The parents got so scared and upset they were thinking of moving. They didn't do it fast enough to save their daughter."

I seriously wanted to throw up. "How long did you say Blanton has been retired in Balmorhea?"

"Three years."

"Are there any other instances of stalking?" I asked.

"None there, but now it has begun in Fort Davis, which is thirty-odd miles from where Blanton lives. We have to stop him. He's following younger and even more vulnerable women than before."

"This gets worse and worse."

"Yeah, it's hard to get my head around the way this man abused his position."

"He's careful. In spite of his perversion and weirdness, he is one careful son-of-a-bitch." I never curse around the sheriff or much at all. I had started to slip.

I used the fax the sheriff sent to make a timeline of the disappearances. Serena was the first missing woman as far as I could tell. Blanton worked as a deputy in Brewster County for fourteen years before becoming the sheriff. He started when he was twenty-two and was elected sheriff at age thirty-six. He was thirty-nine at the time of Serena's disappearance.

What was he doing during that time? Old Jablonski talked like he always had a fetish for underwear and following young women. Perhaps he was not yet acting on it so regularly. It was hard to figure out a person so warped.

Barney suggested that he had been acting on his perversions during that time, but not fixating on one woman as much as he did in later years.

"Maybe he'd follow someone home, look in her window, but not break in," Barney said. "Or if he did break in and steal panties he didn't break in again. He was being more careful and was less obsessed. The chances of following a woman once or twice and not being caught are high if you're careful about it." Then he was quick to add, "Not that I've ever done it."

I was deep in thought and barely acknowledged him.

"Blanton could look in the window a few times, and she'd never be aware of it," he continued. "Maybe he made more phone calls and got his jollies that way. There was no caller I.D. back then. Most women would write off the calls to pranksters unless they had other things to put with it, like the underwear stuff."

"Even though he was still a young man when he became the sheriff," I said, "he had started to lust after women fifteen to twenty years younger. And his wife was ill. And he had the powerful position. All those things may have escalated his sickness."

"He became less careful," commented Barney.

"Yes, and sometimes it was as if he didn't care if someone figured it out. Like the way he acted with Christina Hampton. That was lurid. He was starting to play on the edge more."

"The riskier the behavior," said Barney, "the bigger the thrill."

"You talk like someone who knows."

* * *

I made a list of the missing women, and it looked like this:

5 years after Serena, Gloria Abelard, 21, (Brewster County Sheriff's Office)

12 years after Serena, Victoria Ricardo, 20, (Brewster County Sheriff's Office)

18 years after Serena, Estella Rodriguez, 19, (Dallas County Sheriff's Office)

29 years after Serena, Pamela Amador, 17, (Reeves County Sheriff's Office)

During the years in-between there were more reports of stalking, peeping, breaking-and-entering and other demented behavior than I would ever be able to read. There were at least five possible murder victims, including Serena.

I had uncovered a madman.

CHAPTER 25

Barney volunteered to go with me to Alpine to check out Serena's Camaro. He was more interested in the car than my reason for looking it over, but I was glad to have someone along. I had looked forward to driving it, but now I dreaded seeing it.

After I introduced Joey and Barney, we followed Joey to a garage at the rear of his house. Before he opened the door, he stopped and turned around. "Are you making any progress in the case? Didn't you go to Wyoming to question Curly Hampton?"

"Yes, but the only thing I can say is that neither Curly nor Christina killed Serena in my opinion."

He looked shocked. "How can you be sure?"

"Because now I know who did."

He looked as if he had been struck across the face. "Oh Dios mio, who was it?"

"Joey, I'll tell you everything as soon as I can."

"Why can't you tell me now?"

"First we have to catch him. He's still stalking young women and sometimes he murders them."

"I—I need to sit down." The color had drained from Joey's face. Barney helped him to a bench and sat beside him.

"We'll get him, Señor Bustamante," my partner assured him.

Joey stared at his hands. "Then you think she's dead?"

"Yes, Joey, I'm sure she is," I said. "I'm so sorry."

"I guess I always knew she was, but I couldn't face it. I kept hoping she would come back somehow." He looked up at me. "You will stop him, won't you?"

"Yes, we will." *Just let me slip into my cape and fire up the Batmobile.*

Joey rose and with Barney's help, opened the garage. There sat the car I felt as if I already knew. It looked like it had just rolled off the showroom floor.

"She bought it used," Joey said, "but it only has 16,500 miles on it now. I've kept it like new. I drive it enough to keep it running like it's supposed to."

A vanity license plate read 'Serena 22'. The color was Marina Blue according to Joey. Back in the day, it was cool. Way cool. Now these cars are known as muscle cars, still way cool.

I knew it would affect me to see it, but I was unprepared for how strong the feeling would be. It was almost like being with Serena.

"It has a 396 big block V-8," Joey said, but it wasn't registering. "It has dual electric fans, a turbo 400 transmission, Hurst ratchet shifter, power front disc brakes, front and rear spoilers, and power steering."

The car was awesome. A tiny spark of enthusiasm for driving it swelled in me.

"Please get in." Joey opened the driver side door. "Go ahead and start it."

I sat in the racing seat a minute, checking out the interior. When I turned the key, the powerful motor came to life with a roar. The car trembled. My enthusiasm grew. Maybe it wouldn't be a bad thing to drive it.

"Vroom, vroom," teased Barney and hopped in beside me.

"Listen," said Joey as he leaned in the window, "drive it as much as you want. You can keep it overnight if you need to—or longer. It just sits here going to waste. Kids like you could have some fun in it."

* * *

We roared through town showing off like teenagers. The power of the car was sensual, alive. At stop lights I revved the motor, delighting in the sound and feel of it. I took it out Highway 118 North and sped up. Soon we were doing 100 mph and climbing. Flying was more like it. This was *so* my kind of car!

I stopped at a pullout and asked Barney if he wanted to drive. Of course he did. We switched seats while the motor rumbled impatiently.

Barney gunned it. "Where to, Pard?"

"Let's go to Fort Davis." It was twenty miles from where we sat, and there were some good stretches of highway where we could fly. Barney pulled back onto the highway and jammed the accelerator to the floor. I was thrown back against the seat; it was great!

"Man, this baby is slick as a 1950s hairstyle," was his opinion.

I laughed and agreed. "I was born to drive a car like this."

Barney glanced over and grinned; he looked sixteen. He took all the curves and hills too fast while I encouraged him to go faster. When we got to a flat stretch of highway he opened her up, and we laughed and whooped, worse than teenagers. As we approached Ft. Davis he slowed the tiniest bit.

"We're the law," Barney declared when I suggested he cool it through town.

"God help the citizens."

He slowed as we entered the town limits, but tore past the courthouse, still well above the speed limit.

"We should drive the scenic loop," he suggested.

The loop circles the Davis Mountains and is impressive, but there are few places to speed because of the curving highway.

"What we should do," I said, "is drive to Balmorhea and take a look to see how things are set up. Besides, there is some open highway between here and there."

Barney considered. "Okay, but we're only checking it out. No more than that. No hero stuff."

"No hero stuff," I agreed. "But wouldn't this make a seriously fine Batmobile?"

* * *

"Scrunch down in the seat," Barney bossed as we approached the lake. "Here, wear my hat." He shoved it at me. "It'd be better if Blanton didn't see us checking him out before we go to him for help on the case he screwed."

"This won't fit me, Grandote, and what about you? If I wear your hat, then you don't have one."

He raised an eyebrow at me and yanked it back.

I slipped way down in the seat, but that didn't do anything for my galloping heart. "I should've brought my mask and cape," I grouched.

"No hero stuff." He looked over at me. "I thought we agreed to that."

We passed the marina and a public parking lot, then a picnic area. There were few others out, even though it wasn't very cold.

"I don't want to see him Barney," I blurted. "I feel sick."

"We're going to drive by his place if we can find it, nothing more."

We crept past the houses and house trailers on Lake Road West. For a while, I closed my eyes and willed myself to be calm.

"We've passed it," said Barney. "I didn't notice it until I saw the metal sign that announces 'H. Blanton' by the driveway. I'll go up here a way and turn around."

"Our license plate is 'Serena 22'. What if he sees us in her car? We didn't think about that." I had jumped from trying to be calm to the hand-wringing stage.

"If he sees anything, which I doubt, he'll see us go by on the road. He won't be able to see the tags."

"But it's her car!"

Barney was calm and reasonable. I was his opposite. The monster had killed Serena and let Curly be blamed. I took it damned personally no matter what I learned in the law enforcement academy.

Barney drove to a promontory over the lake, a paved area with covered picnic tables. "Get out," he ordered. "Let's talk."

"What if he sees us?" I didn't like the panicky sound in my voice, but I was powerless to get rid of it. "We're dressed in our uniforms and we have Serena's car. We stand out, Barney."

My partner said nothing at first. He sat at the closest table, one that faced the lake, and I sat down across from him.

"You seem a tad worked up," he observed.

"You noticed."

"I wonder how it's going to be when we come here and have to go into his house. How will it go when you have to sit down with him and tell him that you need help with a case from thirty years ago? He sabotaged that case, and he knows it, and what if he thinks we know it, too?"

"I can play it cool."

"Ricos, you don't seem cool. No offense but we're only driving around, and you're pale and sweating."

"We shouldn't have come; I'm not prepared yet."

"It was your idea."

"I'm okay." I looked over my shoulder in an attempt to see the house, but it wasn't visible from where we were.

"All I'm sayin' is you gotta get a grip before we go see him."

"I know. I'm trying to."

"Aren't you the deputy who told Sheriff Ben you should come alone?"

"Yes, yes, just shut up. I still think I would get more from him that way."

"If he has any idea you're on to something, then going to that house could be the last thing you ever do. Think about that."

"Don't be so melodramatic."

Barney watched the lake. There was one lone sailboat tacking back and forth in a gentle breeze. "Should we talk to the family of the missing girl while we're here?" he asked after a while.

"No, I don't want to talk to them. I can't take any more heartbreak right now."

"Now you're being melodramatic."

"Oh, you think so? Well, you go and listen to how it is for someone you love to disappear off the face of the earth. Think about some perv snatching your daughter."

241

Barney looked stricken. His daughter was two, but I could see he understood the horror of that, and I felt guilty.

"I'm sorry, Barney. That was mean. It's not your fault I'm in this mess."

"Ricos, what was that thing about not taking our jobs personally? Do you recall anything about that?"

"I know, Barney, I know. I've gone against everything I was taught. I couldn't have gotten myself more involved. It's wrong, but there it is." I took out my cell phone and stared at it. "I guess I should call them first, huh?"

* * *

The parents of Pamela Amador seemed not only willing but eager to talk about their daughter's case.

"You're welcome to come to the house any time," Señora Amador said.

Barney offered to accompany me on the visit, and I accepted. Our problem was the car. What if former sheriff Blanton drove by and saw it sitting at the home of his last victim? When we got to the Amador house, we saw the solution. They lived near the highway on a dirt road that went back about four city blocks to farmland. We drove to a small clump of mesquite and tamarisk brush, parked the Camaro there, and walked back to the house. When we looked behind us, we couldn't see the car.

We introduced ourselves and were invited into a small, neat living room. The Amadors, Gregorio and Julia, were in their early forties and were friendly. Julia brought us iced tea and beamed at Barney when he said his wife was also named Julia. Their English was heavily accented, but good.

Before we got started, Señora Amador showed me a photo of Pamela, who was beautiful. "Please keep it, Deputy Ricos. Maybe it will help you find her," she said. It broke my heart. I set it in my lap, unable to tell her no.

I began to explain that I was working on another missing person case involving a young woman. I did not say that my case was thirty years old, or that there was more than one other missing person.

The two held hands and watched me intently.

"Please don't mention our investigation for now. That could jeopardize it."

They nodded in agreement, but I never trust people not to talk. Because of that, I would give them nothing to talk about.

"It would be helpful if you could tell me about the events leading up to Pamela's disappearance. Any detail you remember might be pertinent."

Señora Amador began. "May we speak Spanish?" I nodded, and she continued. "It began about eighteen months ago. Pamela attended a dance at the Legion Hall. It was for all the young people here and was well-chaperoned, so we allowed her to go. At some point, she went around back to the bathroom and when she came out, a man was leaning against the building near the ladies' room. His presence startled her. She jumped when he said, 'Good evening' but he seemed friendly at first. She was walking back to the dance, and he followed. He said, 'You're a fine-looking young lady. I hope you aren't giving yourself to any of those boys.' The tone of it scared her."

"What did she say?"

"She said nothing and then he said, 'Hey—I'm talking to you, young lady.' She said something like, 'What I do is not your business.' He said, 'Yeah, I can see how you would think that.'

"Pamela said he kept watching the kids dance and talk. They were coming in and out of the building as kids do. Every time she looked his way his eyes were on her with what she called a 'sick pervert' stare."

"Did he speak to her again?"

Señor Amador answered. "No, but he winked at her several times. She came home about midnight and went to bed. She thought she heard her cat at the window, so she opened the curtains and saw a man. She screamed and I came running. If there was a man there, he was already gone."

"What happened next?"

"I think the next thing was when she walked down the road a few blocks to her friend Jenny's house. She stayed too long and was afraid I would be mad. So instead of calling me for a ride, she walked home alone. When she got here, she told me she thought someone had followed her."

Gregorio Amador paused and cleared his throat. "The next thing was a call. Julia answered the phone and a man asked for Pamela. She asked who was calling, and he said he was her teacher and gave a made-up name. 'Is she in trouble?' asked Julia, and he said no, that she was a fine girl.

"When Pamela came to the phone he moaned and groaned and said, 'I want to come on your face.' She thought it was the man from the dance.

"Another time he called and asked if she was having sex with the boys, not 'a boy' but 'the boys.' Then our house was broken into. We weren't sure of it, but both of us would have sworn we locked the door when we left. We always do. We couldn't see anything missing, so we let it go and didn't report it."

"Did you ever report anything to anyone?"

"Not until it was too late," said Julia in a sob. "She received some underpants in the mail, and they were hers. I was furious with her at first. How could someone get hold of her panties, you know? Then I looked at them and, well, they were all stuck together and—and—it looked like a man had—had—used them and I remembered when the house had been open." She began to cry. Her husband tried to comfort her.

"Do you still have those underpants?"

"Dios mio, no! I threw them away."

"Was Pamela dating anyone in particular?"

"Yes, she had a boyfriend," said Sr. Amador. "They were serious even though we kept telling her that she would have time for seriousness when she was older. Julia feared she was having sex with him and tried to speak to her about it, but she said she didn't want to talk about her personal life."

"Why did you think she was having sex, Señora Amador?"

"Oh, it was little things. She wouldn't talk to me anymore. And she was anxious to wash her own clothes all of a sudden. It was a strong suspicion more than anything. I never found out for sure."

"What happened on the day Pamela disappeared?"

Now they were both crying. I hate my job sometimes.

Sr. Amador said, "She walked to Jenny's house and never got there, but we didn't know it until she didn't come home. It got dark, and we waited a while. Then I called Jenny's mom, and they hadn't seen her. She never made it to Jenny's, and we never saw her again." At that point, he broke down.

"I'm so sorry," I said. What else was there to say?

"At first they suspected her boyfriend," said his wife through tears, "but he'd been working at the time. He's employed at a gas station near the Interstate. They decided he didn't have anything to do with it. I think it was that filthy man who kept contacting her and wouldn't leave her alone."

"I think so, too."

"Do you know who he is?"

"I suspect someone."

"Why haven't you arrested him?"

"I need proof before I do that. What is her boyfriend's name?"

"Tom Cartwright. He's a good boy, the serious, hardworking kind. We like him, but we didn't want her to be so involved with him at such a young age."

I gave them my card, and they promised to call if they thought of anything else that might help.

Barney and I walked back to the car in the dark.

"I see what you mean," he said. "How could you not take that personally?"

"I'm carrying another photo of an innocent young woman Blanton murdered. I wish I could go kill him. To hell with due process, fair trials, and all that slow wheels-of-justice-legal-crap. I think he should be hung by his balls until dead."

It was unbelievable, but there was no argument from my partner.

CHAPTER 26

We decided it couldn't hurt to see if Tom Cartwright was working. Besides, we needed gas. Barney filled the tank while I went inside to check.

"Are you Tom Cartwright?" I asked a young, blond man behind the register.

He took in my uniform and swallowed hard. "Yes, I am."

"I'm Brewster County Deputy Margarita Ricos. I'm investigating the disappearance of several young women from this area." He looked so panicked I added, "You're not under suspicion. I understand you've already been investigated."

"Yes, ma'am, I was. I was here working when Pammie disappeared." He swallowed hard. "I would never have hurt her."

"I'm sure that's true, Tom. I'd like to ask a few questions. We have a lead, but we need some crucial information from you. I realize you can't talk here, but we could meet somewhere later?"

"I get off in ten minutes if my replacement comes in. There's a rest area about five miles up on I-10. Could we meet there? I don't want people to see me talking to cops again, no offense."

"I understand. We'll meet you there. My partner and I are driving the Camaro," I pointed to where Barney was filling it, "so don't look for an official vehicle."

On the way to the rest stop, Barney turned on the heat and the vent fan started making a weird whistling sound. He shut it off and it was quiet. When he turned it back on it started making noise again.

"I wonder what that's about," he said. "It sounds like there's a piece of paper in there. I'll check it when we get somewhere with light."

Tom arrived soon after we did. He was so nervous I felt sorry for him. I introduced Barney and assured him again that we wouldn't keep him long.

"Tom, I'm investigating several disappearances similar to Pamela's. I've been trying to find a pattern, and I have one I think. Whoever took her first observes his victim and then follows her. After a while he looks in her windows, and then breaks into her house and steals her underpants."

"I know all about that gross stuff."

"Yes, well, the thing is, sometimes he only looks. What I mean to say is he kills some of his victims, but not all of them. I'm trying to figure out why. What makes him kill some and not all, you know?"

Tom watched me with huge eyes.

"Here's my theory. The prettiest women are the ones he takes a special interest in. If they're with someone else, he gets angry. Do you understand what I'm saying? If he can't have them, he doesn't want anyone else to have them either."

"I think I understand. Pammie was the prettiest girl at school, and she was sweet and kind, too."

"So I need to know if you and Pammie were having sex and if it is even remotely possible this man knew it. I know this is personal, and I apologize, but it's crucial to my investigation. I need to know the truth."

Tom studied his hands as he spoke. "Yes, we did have sex. We didn't have a chance to do it a bunch, but we did it every chance we had."

"Is there any way this man could have known?"

"Yes, there was a man that knew."

"Please tell me what you can."

"Pammie's dad agreed to let me take her to a dance in my truck. A man was hanging around there in the shadows. Pammie thought he was a guy she'd seen before, at a dance she went to before we started dating. We sat on a bench outside and started to kiss, and he was watching. At first I didn't care, but then I thought it was kinda sick, so we left. We went up by the lake to this deserted place where kids go to make out and stuff." He stopped, examined his hands, checked his watch, and then his hands again.

"Please go on, Tom."

"We were making out and talking. Then pretty soon we were making out and not talking. Finally we—er—did it, and a man was spying on us. He was standing at the window watching."

"What happened? Did he say anything?"

"No, he ran off when he saw me looking back at him."

"Was it the same man who saw you kissing at the dance?"

"Well, I couldn't tell for sure, but I think it was. What other weirdo would do that?"

"I appreciate your honesty, Tom. You've helped a lot."

"Were the other women having sex too?"

"Yes, that's my theory."

"He saw us again," Tom volunteered.

"You mean he saw you making love?"

"Yes, two other times. It was like he followed us around. One time Pammie was babysitting and I knew we shouldn't, but I came by to see her. We were doing it on the floor in the living room and I happened to look up afterward. A man stood in the kitchen window watching. I couldn't believe it." Tom paused and looked away.

"Another time we were at my house in my room. We were supposed to study, but we got to kissing, and one thing led to another. After we did it, I heard a cough and when I checked, a man was walking away from my window."

"Could you see who it was?"

"No, but he looked like an old man."

* * *

We roared back from the Interstate, past the gas station where Tom worked, back through the town of Balmorhea, past the Amadors' house, then the Balmorhea State Park entrance, and by the time we reached the flat, open road on the other side of the town, the speedometer was at 110 mph.

Barney patted the dash. "This baby flat out moves!"

"I don't like to pee in your Cheerios, Grandote, but sometimes there's livestock on these roads at night."

Barney slowed and brought it down to 95 and then 85. "That better, Grandma?"

"I'm talking about huge cows and horses."

He took his foot off the accelerator. "What's the speed limit here anyway?"

"I think it's seventy, but on the curves coming up it's thirty."

He pressed on the accelerator again instead of slowing down.

"It's thirty for a reason, Barney. 'Deputy I-Swear-I-Will-Uphold-the-Law.'"

"You're one to talk."

"I like to speed, but not in the mountains with livestock on the road."

Before we reached the curves, he slowed abruptly. "You satisfied?"

"I'm too young to die, and I have so many things to do first." That thought brought me back to the bones.

* * *

While we waited in Ft. Davis for an order of hamburgers, Barney checked out the whiny noise in the heater fan. To get to it, he had to remove the dashboard and to do that, he needed a screwdriver. He borrowed one from a guy in the burger place who came out to help. When they got the dash taken apart, Barney pulled out a piece of yellowed, half-chewed paper.

He held it out to me. "Here's the problem. It looks like it's been in there forever, doesn't it?"

I unfolded it and read a note printed in black ink. "Serena, please come to T. It's urgent, my love, or I wouldn't ask. Meet me at BS as always. With all my love, Curly"

Holy crap! I could be holding the note that had lured Serena to her death. I assumed T was Terlingua but what was BS?

We talked about it all the way back to Alpine. I drove because Barney hates to eat and drive and he couldn't, not while devouring two double bacon burgers with an order of fries, and a coke.

"What are you thinking, Ricos?" he asked between bites.

"That you eat like a pig."

He patted his massive chest. "This fine machine needs fueling often, like this car. I was talking about the note I found, you smart-ass."

"It proves my theory that Serena was lured to Terlingua by someone posing as Curly. What could BS stand for?"

"Other than bullshit, I can't imagine. What if it turns out to be Curly's writing?"

"Then I'll resign. If I'm that bad a judge of character I shouldn't be working in law enforcement."

"Wouldn't she have recognized her lover's writing?"

"Not necessarily," I said. "This note was printed. Curly signs his name in a straightforward way, so it wouldn't be hard to copy."

"I hope it's not his writing."

"I'm telling you it isn't."

"I still say you fell for him."

"He's innocent, Barney."

"So you did fall for him."

I wanted to smack him. "I'm saying he's an innocent man."

"You fell for some old guy in *Wyoming*?"

"Well, I like him. Anyway, this isn't about my feelings for Curly."

"Oh my God, now you have *feelings*. Is it because he's so manly and has that black, curly hair? Oh, it's the money! You like all that money."

"Will you knock it off? As usual, you don't have a clue."

"He made moony eyes at you and did a long song and dance about his innocence. You could be setting yourself up for a hard fall."

"Don't think so."

"Let's see what Joey says about the note. Then I would like to hear how a hairy old man from Wyoming got to you."

I sighed and thought about how cool it would be to own Serena's car.

* * *

"Well, it looks like Curly's signature," said Joey, "but I can't be certain. You know, this piece of paper has been in there rattling around all this time. When I would take the car out, I would sometimes hear it if I turned on the heat, but then it would stop. I'd always forget to check it until the next time."

"Joey, what do you think 'BS' stands for?"

"I don't have any idea."

I read that part of the note to him again, "Meet me at BS as always."

"I can't imagine what it would mean."

"I understood Serena almost never went to Terlingua. Curly came to Alpine, and he'd either be with her here or take her somewhere else. So what is this 'as always'?"

"It could be about Curly's BS," said Barney.

"Curly didn't kill Serena," I said heatedly, a hair away from stomping my foot, or better yet, his.

"Ricos, you're forgetting the second rule of the lawman's code."

"What's that, pray tell?"

"Always keep an open mind."

"Then what's the first rule?"

"Never, ever let your work get personal."

"Yeah, well, I guess I'm going to break every rule there is."

* * *

It was painful leaving the Camaro. Joey invited us to enjoy it a while longer, but we figured the longer we drove it, the harder it would be to give up. There was no point in getting attached because he said he would never sell it.

Before we left Joey's, I had the opportunity to meet his wife. I had intended to see if her thoughts on Serena matched what Joey and Sylvia told me. That didn't seem so important now. Still, to stay true to my investigation, I asked her to give me her impressions of Serena.

Claudia Bustamante said that she, too, had loved Serena and missed her. She hoped I would find out what happened to her. She also believed Serena would never have run away. After I took her statement, we left for home.

"You broke rule number three, also," Barney pointed out.

"Which is?"

"Don't break peoples' noses."

"That is not an explicit rule."

"Oh, I'm sure it is, but it may not be stated in those words."

"Please stop talking so I can think."

"Why don't you call Curly and ask him about his BS?" Barney suggested.

"It's after ten o'clock."

"Not where he is. It's eight or nine there."

He was right. I took out my cell phone and punched the only number I had for Curly, his home. After a few rings, a machine answered. I left a brief message asking Curly to return my call when he had a chance. About fifteen minutes passed, and my phone rang.

"Margarita, this is Brian. I got your message. Are you heading back?"

"Not soon, I'm sorry to say. I need to talk to Curly."

"He and Madeline have gone to Maui for a week."

"Wow. Was that a plan when I was there?"

"No, it came up after the storm. Curly got tired of the cold, so he left for somewhere warm. He does that."

"Well, could you tell him I called, and I would appreciate it if he'd return my call when it's convenient?"

"Sure. I'll do that."

"Aren't you working late?

"Oh, I'm not working. I'm taking care of the house while Curly is gone."

"Hey—did you ever find the door to the guest house?"

"Yeah, we found it on the other side of the highway, about three miles away."

"That's hard to believe. It was one heavy door."

"Yeah, but that was some wicked wind."

"That's the truth. Well, you take care, Brian."

"Sure. Listen." He cleared his throat. "You come back up here as soon as you can, okay?" Cleared his throat again, "I—uh—Curly said he told you how I was—uh—how I feel about you."

"Yes, he did. I'm complimented, Brian." I glanced over at Barney. "Listen, I can't talk to you right now."

"I think you're beautiful and—and I saw the way you ride—and the way you care about people."

"Thank you, Brian. I'm working, and my partner is here."

Barney was making gestures and carrying on like it was junior high study hall.

"Just say yes or no, could I come visit you sometime?" Brian persisted.

"Let's talk about that later. I'll call you tomorrow."

"Okay, I hope you do."

"I will, Brian. Good night."

I shut my phone, and Barney started. "Oh, Brian, I'm working. Just because I gave you those hot kisses didn't mean I was serious," he said in a falsetto.

"Shut up, Barney. There was no kissing. He's my friend."

"I think he's more than a friend."

"He's not. He was cute, though. And he's built."

"Ricos, did you fall in love with every man in Wyoming?"

"No, but I noticed them, that's all. I haven't noticed men in a long time, and it felt good. I enjoyed being with them." I sighed. "You had to be there to understand the magic. Well, I'm glad you weren't there, actually."

"So you've been cheating on Billy."

"I didn't cheat on anybody."

"What if Curly didn't have a girlfriend?"

"I don't know. "

"Oh, Lord."

"He does have a girlfriend. He's going to marry her."

"But if he—"

"Stop with the 'ifs,'" I interrupted. "I can't tell you 'what if.' And it doesn't concern you."

"I was just wondering."

I stayed quiet, but Barney was determined to annoy me. "Speaking of Billy, do you concede the bet?"

"Yes, I concede."

"Want to know what I think?"

"No, but you'll tell me anyway."

"I think you need a man."

"Well duh, good idea, but I'd like to be picky if you don't mind too much."

"You need a man that's not gay, for one thing."

"Gee, Barney, thank you for that. You saved me the struggle of trying to reason it out for myself."

"You're such a smart-ass." He sighed. "I'm only trying to help."

"If you really want to help, figure out what BS means."

CHAPTER 27

The next morning, I went for a long run in hopes of getting rid of my frustration. On top of everything else, Barney and I planned to interview a depraved killer, and I dreaded it. I also had a severe case of muscle car withdrawal. And I hadn't called Brian.

When I returned home, Billy was rocking on my porch, irritated that I hadn't waited for him.

"I'm sorry, Billy, but I had to go without you. I have a lot to do today. I would've called, but you don't have a phone."

"That's okay." He was in pout mode. "I can't keep up with you anyway."

"Cheer up, Billy. You could go by yourself, at your own pace."

He brightened. "You could make it up to me by wearing those brown suede shoes with the open toes, the super-high ones. They must make your legs—"

"I know the ones."

"Oh, be still my heart." He had his hand there, of course.

"I can't play dress-up today, Billy. What is it with you and my legs?"

Naturally, he couldn't give me a straightforward answer. As he explained, or tried to, he moved around theatrically and gave his hands a workout. Boiled down, he said when he observed my legs he felt he might not be "all that gay."

* * *

On the road to Balmorhea, I began to lay out my case to Barney. "I want you to listen and consider what I have to say before you get how you get, okay?"

"You're planning something stupid, that much is clear."

"Please let me talk without a bunch of snide comments. What we're doing is serious. As far as I know, I've never been in the same room with a twisted freak like Blanton and it makes me sick."

"I hope you don't throw up."

"I do, too." I waited a beat. "I have a plan, and I want you to hear it."

He raised his eyebrows.

"Please try to be open-minded for once."

"Well now you're insulting me."

"And forget Sheriff Ben for a minute."

"Oh, that's easy. He's our boss, but go ahead," he said. "Knock yourself out."

"I believe if you go in with me Blanton will know we're onto him. And you have a—a—" I sought the right word, "*presence* that can't be ignored. If I go in alone, he'll see me as a little Hispanic slut."

"His favorite kind."

"Let me speak, please. He'll be less wary with me because he's killed others like me and gotten away with it. He'll condescend and appear to want to help me. It'll give me a chance to observe him. You could wait outside where he won't see you. If I need you, I won't hesitate to call you in."

"Call me how, Ricos?"

"I was thinking to leave my cell phone on in my pocket. You would be able to hear everything. If I become silent, come in. If I say your name, bust in ready to kill."

"I'm thinking of all the ways that could go wrong."

"Think of all the ways it could go right."

"To start with, Sheriff Ben will take my badge."

"He won't know," I pointed out.

"How will I explain that you've been strangled with your own underpants?"

"Have some faith in me. Besides, that isn't his M.O. He isn't going to reach out and kill me first thing. Where's the fun in that?"

"You don't know what he's like now. You said he was getting worse. He might get a load of you and think *oh, goodie, a succulent one.*"

I laughed. "That sounds more like you having a fantasy."

"Yeah, well."

We argued, and he came up with every 'what-if' there was, but in the end my big ol' partner saw the light.

"I'll give you twenty minutes," he said, "on the condition that I can hear you speaking. And providing he doesn't say anything that makes my blood run cold. Is that understood?"

"Yes! You won't regret it, Barney. We're going to get him weeks ahead of following the sheriff's slow plan."

"If the sheriff hears about this I'm going to say you drugged me."

"Fine, I'll never tell him. He expects me to solve this case, and I'm about to. If I do it, he'll be so happy he won't need the details."

"You wish, Ricos. You better get a damned good story ready in case."

"I'll think of something."

"Keep in mind that I have a family. We have babies, and Julia can't work right now. My family depends on me."

"Please, I'll cry if you don't hush. I'm trying to mentally prepare myself for meeting a cold-blooded murder."

"The Pervert from Hell, you mean."

"Yes, the Pervert from Hell."

Before long we passed the marina and then the house, scoping it.

"Okay," Barney said, "I see a way. Let me out and you take the Explorer. I'll wait till you go in, then I'll run to his garage and wait there. You better keep the conversation going because if there's a lull I'm coming in. Got it?"

"Yes. You won't be sorry about this, Barney."

"Huh." He got out. His last words were a whiny plea. "Think of my lil' babies, Ricos."

I checked my weapon for the hundredth time and went to do it.

* * *

A tall man came to the door. I didn't expect him to be so tall. I pictured a short, hairy, hunched-over creature covered in warts, like a troll. Blanton was plain with a wrinkled face but didn't look hideous. He shook my hand and seemed full of friendly as he invited me in.

"I think," he said, peering at me over bifocals, "that we should sit at the table over here. There's good light and room to lay your things out." He referred to the dining room table which sat by a window overlooking the lake. "This is the best view of the lake, too. I find it inspiring when I have difficult work to do." He drawled exactly the way Joey described it. It was humorous—and scary as hell.

How could a warped deviate sound so normal?

"What a peaceful view," I said, remembering that I needed to speak to keep Barney out.

The house was neat and appeared to be clean. It was decorated more for function than for style, but it wasn't the filthy, bone-littered den I had dreaded—except the clean, inviting view of the lake seemed out of place.

I set the file down and took the seat he offered.

"Would you like coffee or tea?" A mug of strong-smelling coffee was sitting on the table.

"No thank you, I brought a bottle of water. I've had enough coffee for one day." No way could I drink anything he touched.

"Well, I'm ready when you are." It was good that Barney couldn't see his predator eyes rake me up and down. Aye, Dios! It turns out Wynne isn't as awful as I thought. Blanton took lechery to a level Wynne would never reach; I hoped.

Blanton saw that I noticed his practically drooling inspection of my body and tried to cover it up with talk. "You seem young for a deputy, but I started young, too."

"I'm old enough."

"Maybe you seem too young because I'm so old. Where would you want me to start? I intend to help you all I can."

He made light of it when I asked to record our conversation, but he didn't give his permission. "You'll make fun of my accent with the othah deputies," he drawled.

"But taking notes will slow me down and take more of your time."

"I'm sure you have bettah things to do than spend all day with an old man, pretty as you are." It sounded like *pretty as you ahh* and made my skin crawl. He still didn't give the permission I needed to record him.

With shaky hands, I opened the notebook. "If you could please make a statement about the case," I began, "just your impressions."

"Sure, okay. Joey Bustamante came to see me one morning and told me his sister had gone missing. He said she'd been seeing Curly Hampton, which I already knew. I drove down to Terlingua Ranch to see ol' Curly, and I came to the arroyo where Ms. Bustamante's car had been left."

"How did you know to go there?"

"Well, I didn't, but I was on my way to see Hampton and passed the car. I knew it was hers from her brother's description. I stopped to see what was going on. I figured she had come to visit Hampton." He licked his lips.

I touched my gun.

"She wasn't in the car," he continued in his maddeningly slow way. At this rate I would be here past Christmas.

"I went on to the house," he continued. "I called Curly out and asked him about her. He claimed not to know anything, said he hadn't planned to meet her that weekend. But there was her car near his house. I figured he was lyin', and I watched everything he did."

Blanton paused. My weapon was still there. He drank coffee. Still there. "So we went down to where the car was. He was still claimin' not to know why she was there. She went there to get fucked, of course. Those Mexican girls can't get enough of it."

Whoa.

"So we looked in this overnight bag, and it was packed for a weekend of sex. It had the skimpiest lil' red thing I've ever seen, and those underpants. There were silky pink ones and the white see-through kind, also black lace. They had no substance at all. I wonder if you know the kind I mean, Deputy Ricos?"

I pictured Barney slamming through the door, and the image was comforting. "Yes, I know the kind."

"I looked over at Curly because I could see he'd invited her down for sex and got rid of her afterward. He had a lovely wife, and I'm sure he never intended to leave her for that slut."

He attempted to get control of himself. "I apologize, Deputy Ricos. It was so sordid, the whole thing, and talking about it brings it back so vividly."

"Go ahead, sir. I'm not offended." I shifted in the chair so that the leather of the holster rubbed my thigh. It reminded me that I was armed, and was a comfort in a small way.

"There isn't much more to tell. We searched and searched for that girl. I spoke with a trainload of people as you can see from the reports. Nobody knew much, and Curly never admitted his guilt. After a few months, he moved to Wyoming. I couldn't keep him without a body."

"I understand. And you always thought it was Curly and never suspected anyone else?"

"It was Curly. He was the one balling her, wasn't he? Excuse my crudeness, Deputy Ricos, but I can't be delicate about something so twisted."

Yeah, I totally get that.

"I've since thought about this case and wonder if I got it wrong. Maybe Serena took off and works as a prostitute now. She could be anywhere. Curly was just an ignorant white boy to that horny Mexican. They can't ever get enough. That's why so many of them become whores and the like."

Was he insulting me to my face or did he not even see me?

"White boys aren't enough for those nymphos," he continued. "They got to have it constantly."

I cleared profanities from my throat. "A dam was being built on the Hampton property. It seemed like a good place to stash a body, so I was interested to see that you didn't seem to think so."

"Oh, I thought so at first. But it was too obvious. And those boys working for Hampton would've known about it. They lived there and slept there and everything. They'd have known." He stretched and moved around in the chair.

I was primed to run.

"Of course, that one guy," he continued, "Rico or Rigo, something like that, the foreman, he was ballin' her, too. He wouldn't have let Curly get away with hiding her body there."

"How did you know about the foreman and Serena?"

"I saw the three of them together sometimes in Alpine, and it was obvious. He was sticking it to her whenever Hampton turned his back, I imagine."

"I have another question. You interviewed Dena Jablonski who said Christina Hampton had been with her the day of the disappearance. Do you remember that?"

"Sure."

"Why were you so quick to accept Mrs. Jablonski's alibi for her best friend?"

He leaned back in his chair and looked me up and down again in that slow, creepy way of his. "I believed her because she's my sistah."

"Oh, I wasn't aware of that. That explains it."

Like Hell.

"I'm older than Dena, and many people don't know about our relationship. Dena would nevah lie to me. Her word is as good as gold to me as mine is to her."

"I want to find the body, Mr. Blanton. I disagree with your theory that Serena ran away. Do you have any idea where to look?"

"I'm sure if I could tell you that I would've found the body myself and played the important hero." He leaned back again to casually peruse my breasts. It was hard not to place my arms across them.

"It's been thirty years," I said. "Maybe you've thought of a place you overlooked before?"

Our eyes met, and my stomach slammed up against my liver.

"I can think of thousands of places I nevah looked. You know that country, Ms. Ricos. That woman's body will nevah be found."

Then he reached to adjust himself the way men do. That did it for me. I gathered the file and tape recorder without a word and touched the cell phone like a talisman. I still had to make it out of the house.

"Leaving so soon?"

"Yes, I have to go."

"What if I treated you to lunch? There's a good Mexican restaurant near here. Aren't you hungry?"

I didn't think I would ever eat again. "No sir. Thank you so much, but it's time to be on my way." I stood to emphasize that I was leaving.

"Is there much crime in Terlingua these days?"

"Not much. We manage to stay busy, though."

"One of these mornings I'll come down there and take you to lunch."

"Thank you for your help, sir." I shook his hand, but had to force myself.

"Anytime, honey. You call me whenever I can help with anything."

I hurried out to the Explorer, trying not to break into a dead run. Barney was already seated in it. I could feel Blanton's eyes on me. When I crawled up into the passenger seat, he was still lechering from the door. I don't think he ever noticed Barney.

Neither of us spoke until we had passed the marina.

"Holy hell," said my partner, and he let out a long breath, "wasn't that a load of fun?"

"Aren't you glad you didn't have to look at him?"

"I couldn't have done it without hurting him. My hat is off to you, Batgirl."

"What did you make of that?"

"He's a sick old freak. It must've been hard for you to sit still while he talked about balling Mexican sluts. I half-expected you to kill him, and for the record, I would never testify against you."

"Thanks. However repulsive you think he is, triple that if you're in the same room with him."

"No doubt."

"No matter how warped and crude and full of crap he is, I have no evidence. I can't bring him in because he makes my skin crawl. I need solid proof, one body at least. As nuts as he is I don't see him confessing, do you?"

"Heck, no. He's a pervert with a problem with young Mexican women, but he isn't stupid. Look how long he got away with this shit."

"Yeah, so long that now he thinks he's invincible."

"Well that's 'cause he doesn't know Super-Deputy Ricos is on his trail."

I sighed. "I miss the Camaro."

"I do, too."

"It would've made a perfect Batmobile."

He laughed. "Exactly what a Batgirl needs."

I waited a few beats and then blurted, "I need to drink."

"Count me in."

"You know we're going to have to lie to Sheriff Ben's face, right?" In the next breath I said, "Let's go to a bar."

"I can't lie to the sheriff and take you to a bar on the same day."

My cell phone rang, and a familiar voice greeted me when I answered. "Margarita!" Curly boomed. He sounded so happy. "Brian says you're looking for me."

"Hey, Curly! Thank you for calling. I want to ask you a question, but I hate to ruin your trip with Madeline."

"Ask me anything you want. I'm in Maui and Madeline is good therapy. No matter what it is, I can take it if she's with me."

"Yesterday my partner and I drove Serena's Camaro. We drove it like it was meant to be driven."

He laughed. "It's some car, isn't it?"

"Yes, it's fantastic. But listen, the fan was making a funny noise so we took the dash apart and found a piece of paper stuck in there. I think it's the note that was used to lure Serena to Terlingua. I'd like to read it to you."

"Okay," he said in a small voice.

I read it, and then he asked me to read it two more times.

He said, "Of course I never wrote that note."

"I didn't think you did, but I have a question. I assume T is Terlingua, but what is BS?"

Curly drew in a breath and let it out slowly. "It's Buena Suerte, a place we used to go. I should've told you about it, Margarita. I hesitated to speak of it because it meant so much to me, the time I spent there with her. It was our secret place."

"But you told me Serena never drove to Terlingua."

"She drove down once, and if she'd read the note carefully, she would've seen the mistake in it. It says, 'Meet me at BS as always.' She met me there one time. Every other time I went for her. Nobody could find us there, and time stood still. It was as if we were the only people alive. She must have seen the 'BS as always' part and went without hesitation."

"Well, this makes sense then."

"Do you know what this means, Margarita?"

"It means you were followed."

"Yes, that bastard followed us there. He knew about it." Curly sucked in a breath. "Oh, God, that's where Serena is."

A shiver ran up and down my spine. It was true. The sicko would have killed her in the place she probably loved more than anywhere else in the world. Then he took her car back to the arroyo and let Curly take the blame.

"Where is Buena Suerte? Is it a ranch?"

"It's a former cinnabar mining village in the mountains near Lajitas. It's eight miles from the resort, but it might as well be on the moon as remote as it feels. Wind and birds are the only sounds, and there are no lights at all. It's part of Big Bend Ranch State Park now, but when we were there it was private land. I had permission from the owners to visit it whenever I wanted. Sometimes I would take horses before I went to pick up Serena. It always delighted her to have them waiting. We rode all over those mountains."

I didn't know what else to say. My heart hurt to think that Houston Blanton was the last face Serena had seen.

"Now you can find her, Margarita," Curly enthused. "Now you know where to look."

My stress level shot off the chart.

Before we disconnected, I asked Curly about the using his bluff.

When I described it, he said, "You're talking about my land next to the park."

"Yes. I'd buy it from you if I could. Since I can't, I'd appreciate your permission to keep visiting it."

"Well, of course. Go there all you want. I love that land."

"I love it, too. I found it one day when I was running."

"Maybe you'll write a bestseller on my bluff," he said happily. "Feel free to go there anytime you wish. Think about me once in a while, okay?"

"I will. Thank you, Curly."

* * *

We didn't stop in Alpine. If I had to lie to the sheriff, I didn't want to look at his face while I did it. Barney agreed.

Once we were back in the office, he said, "You call him. This is your case."

I sat with the phone in my hand.

"Go on," encouraged Barney.

"Sheriff Ben, this is Margarita. We saw Houston Blanton." Not a lie.

"How did it go?"

"It went fine, but he's a revolting piece of work." Also not a lie.

"Well, we expected that, didn't we? Aren't you glad you took Barney along?"

"Yes sir." Still not lying.

"Tell me everything."

I did. As I had with my parents, I left out the things that would make him twist off. I lied by omission, which, when I do it, is not really lying.

Barney was incredulous that we'd gotten away with it, although we knew it might be temporary.

"I'll tell him the truth one day," I claimed.

"Which day? I'll plan to be out of the country."

"I'll tell him the day we put Blanton behind bars. It will impress the old guy so much he won't care that I bent his direct order a bit."

"Ha! You make me feel kinda sorry for the sheriff. Nobody can manage you."

"Remember that."

CHAPTER 28

That evening I called Brian and told him the truth; I found him attractive, but I still missed my husband. I wasn't ready for another man in my life. I didn't want him to visit me, not yet. I put him off kindly but indefinitely.

He took it like the tough guy he is, but he said the strangest thing. "You're even left-handed. That is so, so sexy." I had never heard that one before.

* * *

The next morning I took a ride to Buena Suerte. I went alone except for lovely, silent Serena on the seat beside me. Barney offered to go, but I declined. I felt I had to see it first, to get over the pain of it before anyone saw what a tearful mess her case had made of me.

I took Serena for moral support and her smiling outlook. Okay, I believed she might lead me to her bones.

In order to get the combination to the gate, I stopped at the State Park office in the Barton Warnock Environmental Education

Center. They wrote down the numbers and gave me a printed sheet about the danger of the area's still-unclosed mines. It included a bit of history about Buena Suerte, which is Spanish for 'Good Luck.'

For wages of three pesos, or less than thirty cents a day, the miners dug shafts up to three hundred feet deep. They also built the tipple, or tall wood frame, that is still astride Buena Suerte's main shaft. That was where they tipped the carts of cinnabar ore, which was refined into mercury.

Reading on: "the area around Buena Suerte is riddled with excavations of ten to twenty feet deep, due to the miners digging for ore, finding none, and moving on. A thin crust of earth covers some of the holes, and a rotting wood ladder descends into the main shaft to invite the foolish to take a closer look."

I would not be going into any mine shafts.

I read on with interest: "Nearby is the Whitroy Mine, now part of the Big Bend Ranch State Park but closed to the public because of twenty-five to thirty mine openings and pits. A makeshift barrier, not substantial at all, protects trespassers from falling into the main shaft, which miners cored through solid rock.

"These mines are among the last to be covered. As part of the state's effort to make the area safer for tourists, a closure process by the Railroad Commission of Texas was begun in 1984. More than five hundred mines have been closed, at a cost of about one point one million dollars."

I stopped at the first gate, jumped out, and put the numbers into the lock. I drove through, got out again, and locked the gate behind me. The dirt road twisted behind Lajitas Mesa, a mountain with a huge hunk of bare stone at the top. It is sometimes referred to as Lajitas Peak and provides a back-drop for the town of Lajitas. I don't know if the mesa gave the town its name or if it was the other way around. Regardless, the appeal of the area was undeniable. For one thing, there were no other humans. It was clear why Curly and Serena had loved it.

I passed through a small arroyo, cut the motor, and got out to look around. Even though I had come barely a mile from the highway, the quiet was absolute except for birdsong. The land was rich in native grasses and various cacti, along with creosote and other low-growing bushes like mesquite.

I got back in the Explorer and moved on. For a while, I was in a short, colorful canyon between rocky hills. Then I went up and over several rises. The road wound around humps and bumps and followed an arroyo. I gradually came closer to a sheer rock face and the mountains that stood behind the abandoned settlement.

My first glimpse of ruins was the Whitroy Mine, which still had tall wood towers and various mining equipment, long unused and rusting away. It was a picturesque sight, the massive machinery standing silent against the rugged cliffs.

To my right I saw Buena Suerte. It was hard to believe that at the turn of the century, the place was home to hundreds of miners, primarily Mexicans, who lived in the sandstone barracks ahead. Once so alive, the buildings now sat quietly melting back into the desert-mountain landscape.

The closing of the mines began in Terlingua after a young boy at a chili cook-off hiked to an open mine and began swinging on the overhead timbers. He plunged to his death when the rotting wood gave way.

It occurred to me that I had been to Buena Suerte before, as a child, when my uncle's outfitting company brought back roads tours. The tourists ate it up, both the scenery and the lore. My uncle, or whoever the guide was, would tell about the mining days, and the village came to life.

Once, I spent the night there when my family was invited to attend the company's campout Christmas party. The bonfire impressed me more than anything. Wondrously terrifying, its flames danced and hissed and shot high into the sky. "Nobody ever lets kids make fires like this," I whined to anyone who would listen. A "campfire" of this magnitude was entertainment enough for me, but everyone else sat around the blaze singing, telling stories, and admiring the wonders of the night sky.

From the guides, I heard about the intensity of mining cinnabar. The miners could stay in the shafts no more than twenty minutes at a time, and the only men who would go down were Mexican. The temperatures often reached one hundred and forty degrees due to the thermal water vapor. I felt proud to come from such hardy, determined people. The miners were history now, as were my young pyromaniac days, and Buena Suerte was eerily still.

I pulled into the dirt driveway which ended at the old general store/post office building. I climbed down and unlocked the gate. In front of it was the fire circle we used long ago. I walked over and sat for a while on a heavy wooden bench made from lumber hauled out of a shaft. As I looked around at the beauty of the area, I realized I was remembering back sixteen or seventeen years. If she was there, Serena had been there for thirty. She would have been there during the time when Winter Texans visited, combing for rocks and crystals. Why did no one ever run across Serena or any sign of her? That was probably because she was at the bottom of a mine shaft. The idea sickened me.

She was there the night of the Christmas party, but none of us even knew she was missing. We had never heard of her.

I walked into the store building. The mammoth table made from mine timbers was still in place, along with equally heavy benches. I snooped around inside, searching for some sign from my childhood, but found nothing.

CHAPTER 29

It was nearly Christmas, yet the weather had gotten so warm we didn't need jackets during the day, only at night. It was nothing compared to the layers of clothes I had worn in Wyoming, what seemed like a lifetime ago.

I needed to take a closer look at Buena Suerte, but going alone to look for a corpse was a grim prospect. Well, after thirty years there would be nothing but bones. Barney would go if I asked him, but he thought I was obsessed and had no patience with me. He said it made him crazy to hear me speak to Serena's photo, and sometimes to Pamela's. It wasn't as if I expected them to answer. It was my way of connecting to them, making them real. But I had made them too real.

When I mentioned to Billy that I was going, he begged to go. "We'll rough it my sweet little Candy Cane."

He had begun referring to me as 'Candy Cane' in deference to upcoming Christmas holiday. It was irritating, and I told him it sounded like a stripper's name, but he liked it. It's not worth trying to stop Billy.

"We'll sleep on the ground," he said excitedly, "and I'll cook hunks of meat over an open fire, like a macho caveman."

"Oh yeah, I can see that now, Martha Stewart."

When I admitted my macabre reason for going, he clapped his hands together as if delighted. "Oh! You've invited me to a date with the dead! How charming!" When it came to being a smart-ass, Barney had nothing on Billy.

We went the weekend before Christmas and took two horses Sheriff Ben rented from a local outfitter. I planned to sleep in the back seat of the Explorer, Billy farther back in the vehicle's storage area. Even without tents, it seemed like we hauled tons of gear for camping and cooking, along with food and bedding.

We left early on Saturday morning and had the horses saddled and our camp set up by noon. I suggested we pack a lunch and check out an area I referred to as the 'Horseshoe Valley' because of its shape. It was a flat, open area surrounded by cliffs on three sides. The fourth side was open, facing Buena Suerte.

We let our horses plod along as we talked about our work. Billy made me laugh with his outlandish descriptions of restaurant customers. I tried to say something comical about my job, but nothing about it seemed funny.

Billy entertained me non-stop until we broke for lunch. We chose a spot by a spring near some stately, now-leafless cottonwoods, and ate in the shade of a cliff. I didn't mention it, but the area seemed wrong for bones hunting. Serena and Curly rode there maybe, but she was not there.

After lunch, we galloped back to camp with Billy screaming the whole way. "I don't know how to gallop! I'll fall! You're killing me!"

We nosed through the various buildings, but if Serena had been in one of those, someone would've stumbled across her long ago.

While Billy sat in the sun, I wandered among a few of the mine shafts. Some of them had been filled in with dirt or cement, the work done within the last ten years by a local contractor. If Serena's bones were in any of them I would never find them, nor would anyone else.

I came to a shaft covered with a heavy grate that was chained down. I leaned over it and peered down to get a feel for its depth. I dropped a rock through the grate and waited to hear it land, but I never heard a sound.

I knew from reading the state park material that some of the shafts were three hundred feet deep. The deeper ones that had been sealed were covered with grates so bats could go in and out. There are fourteen species of bats in Big Bend. Some of the shafts are connected to caves in the cliff, and the bats fly in and out both ways but weren't there then. They winter to the south, in Mexico, where I should have been.

I wandered back to Billy. He was basking in the sun, wearing cut-offs so short I should've been looking. Instead, I sat on a bench at the fire circle and put my face in my hands.

"What's the matter, my little superhero?"

"Even if she's here, there are still thousands of places to look. Curly said, 'now you can find her', like it'll be easy. He expects so much of me. Everybody always expects so much of me."

"Pity party much?" He squinted at me over his incredibly girly sunglasses. "You're going to make me cry. Seriously."

"You're going to burn up if you don't use sunscreen. Seriously."

"Oh no, you don't, Candy Cane. You're not going to rain on my parade."

"Shouldn't you be out killing something for dinner, Caveman?"

* * *

We brought steaks and potatoes to cook on a grill because killing something was out of the question for either of us, and against State Park regulations. Billy built a campfire in the fire ring while I prepared dinner. Then he moved the Explorer away from the smoke and close to a building that once served as a schoolhouse. He set up his bed and came back to check the fire.

"That's the bedroom area," he said. "If you get cold you can sleep with me."

"How thoughtful, Billy, but I would never go near that schoolhouse."

"What's wrong with it?"

"It's haunted."

He looked back as if he expected it to be chasing him. "Who says?"

"Well, many people. They say the ghost of an old Mexican man wanders at night. A guide who worked for my uncle saw him twice. Once he was looking in a window and saw the ghost glide across the room. Another time, two guides went in and saw him sitting at an old desk. They swore it was true."

"Now you tell me."

"One time a guide told me a story. I don't know how correct it is because they're known for making stuff up."

"You mean they lie."

"It's more like telling tall tales."

"The same way you lie."

"Are you going to let me tell the story?"

He shrugged, and I continued. "He was in a sleeping bag in the doorway of the school house. It was cold, so he was half in but the sky was awesome so he was half out. He felt his bed being pulled slowly out the door. He cried out, thinking it was some of the other guides messing with him, but there was no one there."

"You're pulling my leg."

"I'm repeating what I heard. He thought he had imagined it, so he tried to go back to sleep and it happened again. After that, he moved into the main building with the rest of us."

Without a word, Billy moved the Explorer back to where it had been.

After dinner, we admired the stars and talked about space travel and other things we wanted to do. Then we got on the subject of ghosts.

"What if Serena came to you as a ghost?" Billy asked.

"I would ask her where she left her bones."

* * *

The next morning I took the horse called 'Rambo' and wandered off to the Whitroy Mine by myself to poke around the scattered equipment. I took a few photos with my digital camera.

When I headed back, I heard Billy calling to me but didn't see him.

"Where are you, Billy?"

"I'm over here by the mesquite thicket."

Rambo and I came up beside him. "What are you doing?"

"I was wandering around, and something caught my eye."

I jumped down. "What's that?"

"Check it out. It looks like women's underpants, or pieces of them, stuck on thorns. See what you think." He stepped back.

The underpants had weathered, but not for thirty years. They were more recent than that. Still, it was too coincidental to ignore.

"And over here," said Billy, pointing at the ground. "Look at these shafts. They have steps. Not that I would go down them."

I walked over and stood beside him. There were two shafts fairly close together, both covered haphazardly by weathered boards. A heavy-looking metal ladder went down into one of them.

"Help me take these boards off, Billy. Be careful not to get close to the hole."

"Don't worry about that."

"Let's set them over here."

I looked into the darkness and felt chilled, but at the same time, I was sweaty. Was there a faint odor of rotting flesh—or was it my imagination? Or was it just a deep place that had been too long without fresh air?

"Billy, would you go to the Explorer and get the black case I keep in the back? I think you moved it to the front seat when you made up your bed."

"Sure." He took off in that direction.

I dropped a rock into the dark to gauge the depth. I heard it hit with a distant thud—maybe three hundred feet deep—maybe not that far.

I examined the ladder; it looked sturdy but rusted. It was attached to a piece of rebar that was set into a cement platform.

In the other shaft, the ladder was broken off. What was left of it started at least fifty feet from the top.

Billy ran back with the evidence collection kit. I took out gloves and put them on. "I need those underpants, Billy."

"Oh, yuck."

"Yeah, you don't want to try this at home, people." I carefully picked the trashed panties from the thorns, trying not to damage them further, and put them into an evidence bag.

Billy watched wordlessly.

"I hope there's DNA," I said.

"Like what?"

"Semen would be best."

"But those are women's underpants—unless your perp is a cross-dresser." He looked confused and then went crazy. "Oh my, are you looking for a man who wears women's underwear? But they're too small for a man."

"Billy, please stay calm. The man doesn't wear them, but he does use them."

"Uses them how?"

"Can you stay quiet about this?"

"Of course I can."

"It's important, Billy. I don't have him in custody yet."

"Why not if you know who he is?"

"I need proof."

"Oh. What does he do with their underwear?" He had both hands on his heart. "The suspense is about to kill me."

"First he steals the underpants. Then he masturbates with them and mails them back or breaks in and leaves them on their beds."

"Oh, gross. That's sick."

"He's a charmer."

"And you think he killed Serena?"

"I think so. I can't rest 'til I catch him, Billy."

"What a pervert. I sure couldn't do your job. You have to do such nasty things."

"I need to call Sheriff Duncan, and I can only do that if I get up high enough to use my cell phone. I'm going to ride up on the ridge. Want to come?"

"Naw, I'll stay here and read and try to forget that pervert. You go ahead."

Billy went to retrieve his book. I remounted Rambo and rode to the top of the ridge that overlooks Buena Suerte and the Whitroy Mine. Instead of the sheriff, I called my partner.

When he answered I said, "I've found something."

"Whatcha got?"

"Underpants or what's left of them. They were in a mesquite bush near two mine shafts. I think there's a body in one of those shafts, Barney."

Long pause. "That's not good."

"Would you call the railroad commission or whoever is filling in these mines, and see if they'll send somebody to look down there?"

"The commission is only in charge of covering them, I think, but I'll call and see what they say."

"Thanks, Barn. Maybe you should call the sheriff, too. He might be able to get things moving."

"I'm on it. Should I call you back?"

"Yes, as soon as you can. I won't get your call unless I'm high, so if I miss you leave me a message."

"So you and Billy are out at BS getting high?"

"You know that's not what I meant," I snapped.

"Are you touchy much, Pard?"

"Yes, I'm too touchy, too weepy, too everything. Name it. You can't imagine how eerie and upsetting this is."

"Do you want me to come there?"

"No, that's not necessary, but thanks for asking. It'll be more help if you make the calls. Please. I'm going back to camp, but I'll call back."

"Got it."

I rode back to where Billy was seated in the sun still reading, but now wearing purple underwear and nada más.

I plopped onto the fire ring bench, also in the sun. "Man, I would kill for a beer," I practically wailed.

"Well I don't have one, so back off, Candy."

After a thirty-minute wait, I remounted and headed back to the ridge. I checked my phone, but since Barney hadn't left a message I ambled around looking at things and seeing nothing.

Ten minutes later Barney called. "Can you hear me, Ricos?"

"Yes, what did you find out?"

"It's Sunday, so there's nobody at the Railroad Commission."

"Crap! I forgot it was Sunday."

"I called the Sheriff and he says he knows who to call about those old mines. The problem is he can't do it until Monday."

"Okay, Barney. Thanks."

"Do you think there's semen?"

"Maybe, but that underwear had been there a long time. A body would be more likely to have something usable."

"Not a body that's been there thirty years."

"Oh no, those underpants hadn't been there that long. I'm thinking a more recent body, like Pamela Amador or Estelle Rodriguez."

He sighed. "Oh, man."

"I don't think I can go down there, Barney."

"Good God! I can't believe you're even thinking about it."

"If there's a body, I need it. And I think there is one."

"If there is a body down there, Ricos, let someone else bring it up."

CHAPTER 30

On Monday morning I paced the office, waiting for the sheriff to call. I went from the visitors chair at Barney's desk to my desk, to the overstuffed chair by my window, and then back to Barney's desk. I crashed heavily onto the chair again.

"Will you stay put, Ricos? You're making me nervous. Why don't you enjoy a cup of coffee and relax?"

"If I drink coffee I'll bounce off the walls."

"You're doing that now," he observed.

At ten o'clock, my cell phone rang, causing me to jump as if stung.

After the usual pleasantries, Curly said, "Listen, Margarita, I want to say something for your ears only. No one else can know about it yet."

"You got it." I was standing in my office, staring out the window at the distant Chisos Mountains. Granted, the Tetons are fabulous, but the Chisos have my heart.

"I'm in negotiations with Texas Parks and Wildlife to buy Buena Suerte. The deal includes a trade of land I own to the west of there. It borders other state park lands, and they want it. They don't want Buena Suerte as much because of the liabilities and the high cost of removing them."

He hesitated. "I should've told you this before. I was having a hard time with the memories. If I own Buena Suerte, it will be the second-best thing to burying Serena. Do you understand?"

"Yes. I think I do."

"I'll make sure all the holes are filled in or covered so nobody gets hurt there. The place will be a private memorial for Serena. I don't care what it costs; I have the money to do it."

"I like the idea."

"What I mean to tell you," he continued, "is that I was wrong to ask you to find her bones. I've thought about it, and I don't see how that's going to happen. If she's at Buena Suerte, which I believe she is, there must be thousands of places to look. I can't ask you to do that." His voice was full of emotion. "Besides, she's most likely in a shaft, and there are hundreds of them. Some have already been bulldozed in."

"I've thought about that, too," I said.

"There's something else. Last night I asked Madeline to marry me, and she accepted."

"Oh Curly, that's wonderful!"

"We'll be married Christmas Eve at Pinto Canyon Ranch. After you left, I spent some time at the canyon watching the pintos and thinking. I've been given a second chance. How many men get two chances at great love? I'm taking it, Margarita."

"I'm so happy for you, Curly."

"I'll do what I can for Serena and will honor her final resting place. I'll always love her and carry her in my heart, but I'm letting her go. Thirty years have passed. I'm taking myself off the hook, and I'm taking you off, too. I'll never hold you to the promise you made, and I was wrong to ask you to make it."

I let out a huge breath, unaware I had been holding it. "Thank you, Curly. After I close out this case, I'll let her go, too."

When I hung up, I felt one hundred pounds lighter.

While I was talking to Curly, Sheriff Ben had called. Nobody would do anything until the New Year. Some of the state offices were already closing since Christmas was less than a week away. He had called everywhere but was getting nowhere. Each person he spoke with warned against going into a mine shaft without the proper equipment and training. The old mines were unstable, and some contained stores of unexploded dynamite or other dangerous things. He was sorry, but there was nothing else he could do until after the holidays.

The bottom line was that finding ancient underpants hanging in a mesquite did not mean there would be a dead body in one of the nearby shafts. I was the only one who believed the two things were connected.

Barney explained it to me as I got more and more upset.

I went back to my office to stare at the Chisos and think about it before I returned to Barney. It didn't take long.

"Okay. I'm going." I didn't give myself time to think about the reality of doing it. I knew it had to be done, period.

"Are you completely out of your mind? Do you have a death wish?"

"There's a ladder, Barney. All you have to do is wait at the top to be sure nothing happens to me."

"Oh, so now I'm going with you?"

"Who else is there? Surely you don't want me to take prone-to-hysteria Billy? Our sheriff is too old. If something happens to me, he won't be able to help."

"Ricos, the sheriff will never let you go. And you had better quit referring to him as too old."

"I'm not going to mention it to him, and neither are you."

"You can't tell me what to do."

"When did you make that rule?"

He stared at me. "This can't wait until after Christmas? We don't even know if anything is down there. You could get killed for nothing."

"No, it can't wait. What if it's Pamela Amador? Should her parents have to spend another Christmas not knowing what happened to her? Does that seem right to you?"

"But to find out at Christmas—"

"It's worse not to know," I insisted. "I only weigh one hundred and twenty pounds, Barney. That won't bring the rock crashing down. If it does, at least my parents will know where I'm buried."

"That's not funny, Ricos."

I hadn't meant it to be.

In the end, Barney went. He has a big heart to go with the rest of his big self. Hope is a compelling force, and we were filled with it.

We took four hundred feet of climbing rope borrowed from the Search and Rescue team in Big Bend National Park. I thought of asking them to come with us, and then decided I'd see what we were dealing with first. It would be up to the sheriff to call in the proper personnel. The terror of what I was about to do hadn't hit me.

We gathered two bright, battery-powered lanterns and a few other supplies and hit the road. I felt guilty for not telling my parents, but I hated to freak them out over what was most likely nothing.

I confided in Billy, who became hysterical, but promised not to mention anything to my parents or anyone else unless something happened.

"It's no big deal, Billy," I consoled. "I'm just going down in a hole to see what's there and coming right back up."

"If it's no big deal, then why aren't you telling your parents?"

* * *

My partner and I stood at the mouth of the first shaft. Neither one of us moved or spoke. I was too terrified. Since Billy and I had removed the boards, the odor of rotting flesh had dissipated, but I still felt the same conviction about a body being down there.

"It sure is dark." Barney sounded seven instead of thirty. He took an audible breath and puffed it out in a whoosh. "Are you ready for this?"

"I'm going—unless you want to."

"Those steps won't hold me," he said. He stared down into the dark hole. "I think I'll be of more use up here, getting you back up."

"I agree. Let's do it before I lose my nerve."

First we lowered a battery-powered lantern on a hook. It hit the ground at about three hundred and ten feet. Barney wiggled the hook around until it was free of the lantern and brought it up. Then he left another. I peered down to comfort myself with the light, but it was as if the darkness had sucked it away.

"The dark ate it," I said.

"You'll see the light again when you get closer, Ricos," Barney said, attempting to reassure me. "Now it's your turn—if you still want to go."

He secured the rope around me by winding it through a climbing vest, also borrowed from the park. He jerked on it several times to be sure it would hold. One end of the rope was attached to the Explorer. The thick rope was my insurance that if the ladder gave way I wouldn't plunge to my death.

Barney nodded once, and I moved to the ladder. Then I was on the first rung.

"You don't have to be a hero, Batgirl. It's a long way down. Come straight back up at any time or tug the rope and I'll pull you up."

I started down, gripping the ladder so hard my hands began to throb. I tried to relax. It was down and back, nada más.

At first I didn't look below. I watched the sky and concentrated on descending and staying calm. *The walls are hard-packed dirt; I'm not afraid of dirt. It's a hole in the desert floor; I love the desert; this is nothing.*

After I'd gone more or less seventy-five feet, I stopped and peered down. The light was back. I saw bones and could barely get a breath.

"Bones!" I yelled, and continued climbing down.

At one hundred feet, the ladder ended. I hung there, holding onto the sides and staring down. That old, stale air, faint smell of rotting flesh was back.

"No more steps," I yelled. "Let me down slowly."

He lowered me with precision, as if he'd done it hundreds of times. The hardest part for me was letting go and hanging suspended above a corpse, even if it was only bones. My feet hit the floor at last. I was standing by the bones of a human.

The skeleton looked old, but it hadn't been there thirty years. For one thing, there were still some clothes, although it was hard to tell what they were. They lay in filthy tatters around the bones. The skeleton was so fallen apart I couldn't tell if it was male or female, but I expected it to be a young woman. Leather sandals of the type women wear surrounded feet that no longer filled them. They lay askew. The sandals were the only hint as to the sex of the skeleton.

I removed the larger flashlight from the vest and clicked it on. As I did, I went over the missing women in my head. There was Gloria Abelard, who disappeared five years after Serena, and Victoria Ricardo who came twelve years later, and Estella Rodriguez who disappeared eighteen years after that, twelve years ago. Most recent was Pamela Amador whose body would be newer-looking and would probably still stink.

I ran the flashlight around but didn't touch anything. I observed the position of the body and the bullet hole in the front of the skull. Then I saw something near the hand and examined it with the light. It was a bracelet of linked hearts, so tarnished it was black. I felt sure I had found one of the missing women, but I didn't know which one.

I gathered the lanterns and clipped them to my vest. Then I yanked on the rope. Barney began to pull me back up.

Once I reached the ladder I yelled, "The bones belong to a woman who's been dead for years." I kept climbing until Barney lifted me out.

"Did you find Serena?"

"No, it's another one. She was shot in the head. There's no flesh left, and what clothes are left are rotting rags. Feminine sandals and a bracelet of linked hearts are the only way I can guess she's female."

We sat down near the edge of the shaft, and Barney went up on the ridge to call the sheriff and explain what we had discovered and what we suspected. It took guts for him to make that call. Without doubt, the sheriff would be livid.

To his credit, Sheriff Ben wasted no time on questions or anger. He said he was on his way, and would make arrangements for a forensic pathologist and crew to evacuate the bones. He was already familiar with Buena Suerte's location. Barney didn't mention the second shaft or that I was about to descend it.

He lowered the lanterns again. They stopped at two hundred and ninety-five feet. I took a deep breath, nodded, and he began to lower me. I rappelled down the wall, going slowly. Down and down. I watched the circle of blue above me and Barney's concerned expression, and tried not to think past that.

As I got closer to the bottom, I looked below. A human was lying there. And the odor was worse. This shaft was where the rotting-flesh smell was coming from.

I looked up and saw Barney lying at the edge of the hole watching me.

"It's a body," I yelled, and my voice echoed eerily. I wanted to scream.

"Come on back." He gave the rope a hard tug.

"Don't do that! Give me a minute. Keep going." One sentence echoed on top of another, but he understood.

I was curious to see the details, so I kept going down.

Before I reached the bottom, I knew it was Pamela. Her body was in the last stages of decay, so far gone that the stench was no longer strong. There was almost no flesh left on her bones. Insects and other small creatures had done their part in hastening the decomposition of the body. She was a horror.

A recognizable Pamela was gone, but for a second I saw her as she was in the photo I carried. She'd been a vibrant, happy young woman with her whole life ahead of her. She was dressed in blue jeans and a t-shirt. Both were decaying but were still identifiable. Around her neck was a faded bandana covered with tiny hearts. Tennis shoes and socks covered whatever was left of her feet.

Pamela had been shot in the forehead, same as the first one. I felt heartsick and stomach sick. I got as far as I could from the body and vomited.

Barney panicked and began yelling. "Get back up here right now! I'm bringing you up." He was freaked out, and he wasn't even there. I gave the rope a hard tug, and he began to hoist me.

I glanced back once and saw the panties. What looked like a nearly rotted-through pair of women's underpants was crumpled and discarded beside the corpse. The thought occurred to go back for them, but I was trembling uncontrollably.

Barney reached down and grabbed my arms near the elbows and lifted me out. I fell against him, shaking. He put his arms around me and held me tightly.

When I pulled away from him, I collapsed under the mesquite bush where Billy found the first pair of underpants.

"It's Pamela." I choked on the words.

He sat next to me. "Are you sure?"

"She's wearing the clothes described in the missing person posters. He shot her in the head and threw her away."

"Damn."

"I should have gotten the panties."

"What panties?"

"The panties he threw in beside her."

Barney grimaced and looked ill. "Was she dressed?"

"Completely dressed."

"Then maybe he didn't rape her."

"Raping is not his M.O."

"So she was shot?"

"Yes, it appears he shot her and dumped her body in there so she would never be found. Serena is probably in a shaft, too, but which one?"

I ran up on the ridge to call Billy to tell him the highlights, leaving out gruesome details. I asked him not to tell my parents. I would do it later. The worst was over. Well no, it wasn't; Pamela's parents had to be informed.

"Who'll tell the Amadors?" I asked Barney.

"Who knows what the sheriff will say, but I think we should do it. They already know us. It'll be easier on them to know you found her, as you said you would. If some deputy goes who doesn't know the case or care about it, it would be wrong."

I thought so, too, but I didn't want to do it.

* * *

Sheriff Ben stood at the shaft as rigid as the Tin Man. Impossible to tell what he thought. "You went down there, Margarita?"

"Yes sir, that's how we know she's there."

He said nothing, but I would've sensed his anger from Europe.

"It's my fault," I blurted since it was. "I didn't think it should wait. I believed that finding the underpants would mean a body was down there. I know you didn't agree that one thing meant the other, but you weren't here, sir. I thought her parents had the right to know what happened to their daughter as soon as we could tell them. It's so awful not to know. This will be painful, but it's better than not knowing." I spoke fast so he couldn't. "I promised them I would find her, and I intended to keep my promise. It's almost Christmas," I practically sobbed.

When I stopped speaking, the sheriff opened his mouth to begin and I cringed. "Sometimes I feel like an old man watching the action from the sidelines. I don't like the way you two leave me out of the loop."

Barney glanced at me. One of us should have responded, but what would we say? We couldn't argue, and it seemed wrong to agree.

"I can't fault your reasons for doing what you've done, Margarita. I'm in awe of your courage. I can't imagine how you went down there."

"I had to go, Sheriff."

"I suppose you know I would've forbidden it."

"Yes sir. I know."

Mentally I prepared for the axe to drop. It would be unlike our sheriff to curse me into the ground, yet I halfway expected it. Instead, he turned and sat at the edge of the mesquite thicket. We hesitated. Barney jerked his head slightly towards the sheriff and then sat next to him. Standing solo felt wrong, so I sat down, too.

I went over the names of the missing women and their ages. I explained that I thought the older bones belonged to Victoria Ricardo who disappeared twelve years after Serena. She was twenty at the time.

"You talk like you knew each one," Sheriff Ben said.

"I feel like I did. I've stared at their names so much I know their ages, where they lived and when they disappeared. I know who reported them missing and what each one was wearing."

He was about to speak to that when we heard the van. "Here's the team," he said. A white Ford van pulled up. "They were on their way back to Midland from El Paso when they received my call."

Three men from the Department of Public Safety got out and walked towards us. The sheriff said the oldest of the group was Dr. Charley Fletcher, a forensics expert with the Texas Rangers. He had come to oversee the removal of the bodies so that as much evidence as possible would be preserved.

I stepped up to Dr. Fletcher and introduced myself.

"Are you the woman who went down there?"

"Yes. I thought if a body was there it would get peoples' attention, and somebody would have to come and take care of it."

"You sure do know how to ruin a guy's Christmas," he said. It was crime scene humor and wasn't unkind, but it upset me.

"I'm sorry to ruin your Christmas," I snapped, "but at least you'll celebrate another one. Pamela will never have that chance." I turned away, near tears.

He hurried after me. "Deputy Ricos? I didn't mean to offend you."

I didn't turn around. "It's okay. I'm feeling touchy and frazzled right now."

Barney and a member of the crew eased the three men into the mine the same way he had lowered me. Then Barney, Sheriff Ben, and I watched from above as they started to work, first taking photos of the scene.

It was slow, maddening work, or at least it was maddening watching. The team began bagging various items. The bones would be last. I watched almost breathlessly as the underpants went into a bag.

After a while, I asked Sheriff Ben if Barney and I could be the ones to talk to Gregorio and Julia Amador. It seemed the right thing.

"I wouldn't have it any other way, Margarita. After that, I want you and Barney to arrest Houston Blanton for murder. That should feel pretty good to you."

He walked to his vehicle, pulled out a manila envelope, and handed it to me. "There's a search warrant in here. You don't need it once you arrest him, but you have it anyway. Please find something."

After two hours, the body bag was closed and hoisted up. I helped Barney pull it out of the hell hole, but it weighed almost nothing.

The men prepared to enter the first shaft, the one with the older bones.

CHAPTER 31

Not much was said on the way to Balmorhea. Barney drove and I stressed. It was hard to imagine what to say. How do you tell parents their beloved child was shot in the head and discarded like a piece of trash?

We decided I should go in without him since I did all the talking last time, and it was me who promised to find their daughter.

When we were about ten minutes away, I called and spoke to Señora Amador. "I have information about Pamela. May I visit in a few minutes?" It was hard to keep the quiver out of my voice. I suspected she knew what it was I had to say.

I stood with Pamela's parents in the foyer of their home, passing my hat from hand to hand, so nervous that I was afraid of throwing up. Never had I done anything more difficult. I explained that I had found their daughter's body in a mine shaft in an abandoned cinnabar mining town near Big Bend National Park. When I said she had been found dead, a sob escaped her parents. I helped them to chairs and sat with them.

"But why?" asked Señor Amador. "Why?"

I couldn't answer that, but I told them Pamela was shot in the head once and dumped fully clothed. I hoped that would give them some comfort. I promised I'd give more details as I could.

"Can we see her?" Pamela's mother asked.

"You shouldn't see her, Señora Amador. You'll want to remember her as she was the last time you saw her, not how she is now."

I had seen her, and she no longer resembled anything they would recognize. I hoped to spare them that sight.

"You will get the man who did this?" Sr. Amador looked at me with the most sad, plaintive look I had ever seen.

"Yes. I will get him."

* * *

Barney was waiting for me and started the Explorer the moment he saw me step out. I flung myself into the passenger seat.

"Now comes something that will feel good, Ricos," he said in an attempt to cheer me.

Yes, it should have. We were going to arrest Houston Blanton. But arresting him seemed way too good for him. I wanted him to suffer. A lot. For years and years. Thirty would be a good start.

"Barney, please take the lead because I'd rather shoot him than look at him. I don't see how I can make a proper arrest right now."

My partner agreed without arguing.

Blanton opened the door wearing pajamas and a robe. He was surprised to see two uniformed deputies standing there.

"We have a warrant for your arrest," Barney said. He had his hand resting on his weapon.

Blanton took a step back. "Do you now?" he drawled. "Did I forget to pay a traffic ticket or somethin'?"

He was amused until Barney spoke again. "You're under arrest for the murder of Pamela Amador." My partner proceeded to recite the Miranda rights.

Blanton smirked. "Young man, you can't arrest me for murder without a body. No body, no murder far as the law's concerned."

"Earlier today Deputy Ricos found Pamela Amador's body."

The former sheriff, the Pervert from Hell, said nothing.

Barney cuffed Blanton's wrists together and then put leg iron cuffs around his ankles. He sat him in a chair at the table where I had interviewed him and attached the leg irons to the table. Restraining his hands would have been enough, but Barney was sending a message. I hoped the old deviant understood it.

"You sit tight," my partner said then nodded to me. "Let's do it."

We pulled on gloves.

"You can't search this place without a propah warrant," said Blanton. "There's nothin' here anyway."

We didn't speak which angered him. We went into the bedroom first and began peering in closets and opening drawers. Barney got on his knees and searched under the bed. There was nothing there but storage boxes of extra blankets. We searched every room, every closet, and opened every drawer, box, and bag. When that turned up zilch, we moved outside to the one-car garage.

The first thing Barney did was shine his flashlight into Blanton's truck. On the seat sat a manila envelope that was bulky and mis-shaped with whatever was crammed into it.

Barney yanked open the door, lifted it out, and held up blue nylon underpants. What appeared to be semen glistened in the beam of the flashlight. The envelope was addressed to Elsa Moreno in Fort Davis.

"I think we have enough," said Barney. "The sheriff can send a crew tomorrow if he disagrees. We're through here."

His call was a good one. We were past exhausted.

Barney went to the Explorer, removed an extra-large evidence bag, put the entire envelope inside, and sealed it. We headed into the house for Blanton.

He looked up as we came in. "You can look all you want, but there's nothing to link me to any wrongdoing."

"Then I don't guess that's your semen on the underpants in your truck," Barney said as he unlocked the ankle restraints.

Blanton paled. Then he noticed me. "You can forget about me treatin' you to lunch now."

Yeah, I hate to miss that.

Barney helped Blanton to his feet, practically lifting him from the chair. I watched as he guided him towards the door. One wrong move and I would shoot out his knees. It was disappointing when he went so docilely.

* * *

It was nearing dawn when I got home. My house had never seemed so desolate. I was inconsolable and couldn't stop crying. After a long shower, I crawled into bed and buried my face in my pillow, longing for it to be Kevin.

CHAPTER 32

I awakened late to the aroma and distant sizzle of bacon frying. For a confused moment I thought Kevin had returned. Then I realized it was Billy.

My arms and hands were sore from the tense climbing, but other than that I was numb. For a while, I didn't move and stared at the ceiling. I had no desire to go to work. What I mean is I wanted a different job.

Billy sang Christmas carols in the kitchen, loud and with feeling, the way he does everything. It got me out of bed.

I dressed in blue jeans and a soft, red, long-sleeved t-shirt. When I came into the kitchen, Billy smiled. He looked preppie with tailored grey wool slacks and a darker grey shirt with a Christmas-red vest. And a Santa Claus hat. "I thought you could use some company, Candy Cane. I'm making you breakfast."

"Nice hat, Santa."

My eyes were red and swollen from crying. Billy noticed but didn't get hysterical. He gave me a long, heart-felt hug that I badly needed. I almost started crying again.

"How did you know to come, Billy?"

"Are you kidding? After what you did yesterday? So sit. Talk to me. I'll serve you some breakfast. Want orange juice?"

"Yes, please. What's in those boxes?"

"Christmas is waiting in those boxes! You don't have any decorations up, and it's almost here."

"Haven't you read *How the Grinch Stole Christmas?* Christmas doesn't come in packages, boxes, or bags."

"Yeah, yeah, of course I've read it. Maybe Christmas doesn't come from a store, maybe Christmas, my little superhero, means a little bit more," chanted Billy, rewriting, or at least misquoting, Dr. Seuss.

"So what are you, then, the spirit of Christmas Present?"

"I'll have you know I'm the Christmas Fairy." He started to go into one of his crazy routines but took a deep breath and held back. Instead, he served eggs, bacon, toast, and fried potatoes. "Want to go Christmas shopping?" he asked.

"Sure, but I have to talk to the sheriff first."

"Barney called earlier, but he said not to wake you."

I picked up my phone.

"Please eat first," Billy said when he saw what I was doing. "All the superheroes eat breakfast."

"How do you know? I've never seen them eat."

"Don't be difficult." He served two plates and sat down next to me. "Do you want to talk about it?"

"No, I'd like to not think about it for a while. This is good, Billy. It's exactly what I needed. Thank you."

"Eat up. Today we're going to get in the Christmas mood if it kills us. Don we now our gay apparel," he said and flung his hands in the air, "and all of that."

* * *

Barney was about to burst by the time I called him. "Talk about a merry Christmas! You won't believe this, Ricos!"

"Let's hear it."

"While we were still sleeping, Sheriff Ben sent two of our fellow deputies to Blanton's house because he realized the state we were in when we searched, and he thought there would be more evidence. I wonder how he knew that."

"He knew because he's spent forty years doing this, Barney. Why do you think his hair is all-white? Good thinking is why he's the boss."

"Yeah, he's pretty sharp for an old guy."

We had another laugh at Sheriff Ben's expense.

"A deputy from Reeves County met them there," Barney continued. Balmorhea is in Reeves County. "They found a key to a safe deposit box at West Texas National Bank in Alpine."

"Where? We didn't find a key."

"True, but we were drop dead exhausted as I recall."

"What was in the box?"

Barney had to tell it his way. "So our deputies went back to Alpine and in less than an hour they had the judge's signature on a search warrant for the bank box. At that point the sheriff joined them."

"What was in the box, Barney?"

"Many important things, Batgirl, like the photos taken from windows, looking into bedrooms or wherever. One was a close-up shot of Pamela Amador and Tom Cartwright going at it on the living room floor. There were photos of Curly and Serena dancing, kissing, and hugging—no floor shots, though."

"Barney, tell me what else. Quit dragging it out."

"They found a notebook the sheriff thinks matches the paper used for the note Blanton sent Serena. It held pages of practiced writing. He wrote 'Curly' until he could sign Curly's name believably, well enough that Serena fell for it.

"Sheriff said to tell you that it appears Blanton was more obsessed with Serena than anyone else. It must've sent him over the edge and pushed him to his first murder. There were more pictures of her and more of her things than with the others. He stole a book of poetry Curly gave her, and a scarf that belonged to her. He labeled it, Ricos, in his own hand. He stole and kept many of her things."

"That's proof." My spirits rose slightly.

"I haven't told you the best part. In that deposit box they found a key to another one at a different bank. They got another warrant."

"What did they find? Just tell me, please."

"Women's underpants, my impatient partner, underpants. They found a box full of them. They were in plastic bags, catalogued by name and the date they'd been taken, all in Blanton's handwriting."

"So even without DNA evidence, we have him."

"You did it, Ricos! By the way, there will be no bail for the twisted freak. His attorney pressed for it and even called the judge at home, using Christmas to sell it."

"Why not? Christmas is used to sell everything else."

"My point is that the judge didn't buy it. Sheriff Ben went to see him and told him the highlights. That was all it took. There won't be no stinkin' bail."

"Were there underpants from the missing women, too?"

"You bet. He kept souvenirs from all his panty raids. He thought he could never be caught I guess."

"Do you mind if I don't come in today?"

"Hell, no, you've earned yourself a day off—a month off as far as I'm concerned. Are you okay?"

"Not really."

"If you want to talk, you know where to find me. I hoped you'd give me some ideas about what to get Julia. I was planning to buy her some sexy clothing, but that's more for me than for her."

I laughed. "Sexy stuff works, or you could give her a day at the spa in Alpine where they wrap you up in mud and stand on your back and all. It's expensive, but she'd probably love it."

"Jeez. You have to pay for that?"

CHAPTER 33

The next day, Sheriff Ben came bearing a fruit basket for Barney and flowers for me. It was a generous gesture since I'm the deputy that makes him tear at his hair. Barney called to say he was at the office, so I went in. He told us to close until the day after Christmas, which gave us extra time off unless an emergency arose.

The best gift was the findings from the medical examiner's office. The older bones did indeed belong to Victoria Ricardo. She had lain there for approximately eighteen years. The apparent cause of death was a gunshot wound to the head. There was no longer saliva, semen, or any other bodily fluid to link Houston Blanton to her death. What linked him was his M.O., the underpants he stole, marked as hers, and kept in a bank box. And then there was the matter of the body of Pamela Amador, discarded next door, seventeen years later.

Pamela's temporary resting place told a clearer story. After shooting her in the head and pushing her into the shaft, Blanton had discarded her semen-stained underpants the same way he had thrown away her body. Ironically, he had covered the shaft to keep out the curious. Those boards had protected the evidence from rain and sun, preserving a tiny sample of dried but usable seminal fluid. DNA testing would prove that Houston Blanton was the source. Even without that, there were the voyeur photos of the young woman and her catalogued underwear.

The tattered panties I removed from the mesquite bush had been exposed to the weather too long to lift anything usable from them. But as Sheriff Duncan pointed out, they had done their job by alerting me to the presence of the corpses. I had Billy to thank for that. I might never have seen them.

After the sheriff left, Barney said, "You seem down."

"I am. I'm not staying in law enforcement after this case is closed."

"What are you saying?"

"That I'm quitting. I'm not cut out for it."

"You're perfect for it! What are you thinking? Look at what you've done with this impossible case! You weren't even born when Serena disappeared, and you solved the damn case." He leaned back in his chair until it hit the wall. It always startled him to find the wall was still there. "Don't make any hasty decisions. You're experiencing post-traumatic stress disorder or something."

"Everything has become personal, and it's eating me up. I'm not supposed to take my work home, and yet my work follows me wherever I go."

"Listen, Ricos, without people like you in law enforcement, things really would be hopeless. It's your taking it personally that makes you so good at what you do." He held up his hands. "Okay. I'm not going to say more. Maybe you'll feel better after Christmas."

"Maybe," I said but doubted it.

"Listen, I got you something. I think it will be meaningful, especially in light of what you just said. I hope so anyway." He handed me a gaily wrapped package.

"May I open it now?"

"Please do."

Barney's gift was a plaque that read: "When I despair, I remember that all through history, the ways of truth and love have always won. There have been tyrants and murderers and, for a time, they can seem invincible, but in the end they always fall. Think of it. Always." ~ Mahatma Gandhi

My eyes filled with tears.

Barney came around the desk and hugged me. "You're going to be all right, Ricos. You need some time off and serious rest." He punched me gently on the arm. "Some good sex wouldn't hurt, either."

I laughed. "Thank you Barney. This is so thoughtful. I have something for you, too. I made it myself and hope you like it."

I went to my office and brought a gift from the closet. He held it up. It was a framed caricature of him in full uniform, but with a Superman-style cape. He was stopping traffic with one over-sized hand. The front of the shirt read 'ROADBLOCK' instead of 'Superman.' I could tell he liked it.

"Who knew you could draw like this?"

"I wish I was better at it. I could've made it more detailed and perfect."

"You couldn't have made it more perfect. I love it."

"So," he said. "The sheriff says we can take off. What are we doing here?"

"I'm gone. Merry Christmas!"

* * *

My gift to Billy was the sexiest pair of size eleven slut-pumps ever made. They came from a company specializing in footwear for drag queens. He was speechless, and then clapped his hands together gleefully, like a child. Then he burst into tears.

"Don't cry, Billy. I know they'll fit. Why don't you try them on?"

When he continued to cry, I moved close and put my arms around him.

"I'm not who you think," he sobbed.

"I know who you are."

"No, I mean I lied. You think you know me, but you don't."

"You're Jimmy Taggert," I said softly. "I don't care, Billy. Your name doesn't matter to me."

He began to sob.

"Tell me about it if you want. If you don't, that's okay, too."

He leaned his head against my chest a while before he spoke again.

"I went to a bar after work two years ago, and this older man approached me. I knew he wanted to have sex." Billy took a shuddering breath. "To make a long story short, I went home with him. He was good to me and became my only boyfriend. He set me up in an apartment and bought me nice things.

"Then one day he asked me to deliver a package to a man called Bud. I didn't know 'til I got there, but the address was a seedy building in the warehouse district. Bud was a tobacco-spitting hoodlum with a pocked face and teeth missing. He looked me over and said, 'so you're Eddie's whore.' It was so demeaning and ugly."

Billy sniffed indignantly at the memory. "I told Eddie how his friend Bud had made me feel. He laughed and said, 'Well what would you call it?' Until that day I thought he cared about me.

"A few days later he asked me to deliver something else to the same nasty man, and I refused. Eddie beat me, and it was so vicious I couldn't go to work for two days. Then he said I would do whatever fucking thing he told me, or he'd kill me."

Billy wiped away tears with one hand. "So I did what he wanted. I carried more packages to different places. Sometimes it was drugs. Sometimes it was money, or important papers. I knew I should get away from Eddie, but he said he would kill me if I left him, and I couldn't see a way out. I finally told him I wouldn't do it anymore. I couldn't be his whore or his drug runner. He slapped me across the mouth and said never to use the word 'drugs' again in his company. Then he beat me again, and that time I was in the hospital for three days."

"Oh, Billy."

He laid his head against my chest again, and I held him.

"Then I thought of disappearing," he continued. "I had the idea to make him think I had come here and gotten killed in an accident. I know it's weak, but I was scared and desperate. I wanted him to believe I'd died so he would have no reason to look for me."

"Did Eddie come here?" I asked, thinking of the 'FBI' jokers.

Billy sat up and wiped his eyes. "No, it was some goons that work for him. They came here to kill Jimmy Taggert. They didn't know I had already killed him."

"You changed yourself drastically."

"Yeah, well, it wasn't hard. In Houston I let my hair get raggedy and grew a beard and wore glasses I didn't need. If I looked ugly, maybe Eddie would throw me out for a more attractive whore. I cut my hair before I came back from Ojinaga and bleached it and ditched the glasses."

"Are your eyes really blue?"

"Yeah, these eyes are mine. The brown ones are contacts."

"What made you decide to disappear to Mexico?"

"I was afraid if my body wasn't found they'd keep looking for me. I love it here and couldn't make myself leave. So I pretended to go to Baja to live. Then I came back to Terlingua as a newcomer and to be myself but with a different look. I even quit smoking. I thought it would work."

"Billy, it did work."

"But you figured it out."

"I'm observant. It's my job to pay attention to details. And the missing person flyer stated you had a tattoo on your left butt cheek. One day when you were trying on my clothes and dropping your pants, I saw it."

"Do you like my little flying dragon?"

"Well, I like your little butt."

He laugh-sobbed.

"Are you wanted by the law anywhere?" I asked.

"No. It never went that far. Nobody but Eddie wants me. I hope he's given up looking for me by now."

"Do you know how much effort we put into finding you? I could get mad if I thought about it. And the Sheriff's Office and Texas DPS were involved in the search. Your disappearance cost the taxpayers a bundle. Barney and I even went to Ojinaga looking for you. Of course, that part was fun."

"I'm sorry, but I couldn't stop you, could I?"

"I guess not."

"What are you going to do about Jimmy Taggert?" Billy asked.

I smiled. "Jimmy who? If you don't mention him, I'll never bring him up again."

He smiled back. "So you won't tell?"

"What's to tell? If you aren't wanted by the law there's nothing to tell."

"I know I should have told you before, but I was afraid. Who knew I would become friends with such a kick-ass crime-fighter?"

"Billy, there's something you don't know." He watched me expectantly. "There are others in Terlingua whose identities have been changed for one reason or another."

"Like witness protection?"

"More like self-preservation. I suspect some of them are running from the law."

"Really?"

"Oh yes. Some might have stories similar to yours. Or they're hiding from child support, or bad debts, or crazy ex-spouses. We might even have a murderer hiding here. Nobody cares as long as that person isn't a detriment to the community. Do you understand what I'm saying?"

Billy's eyes were huge. "Murderers live here?"

"No, I don't know that. I'm just saying that in Terlingua, people can be whoever they want to be. My mom says that a Texas governor came through Terlingua one time on his way into the national park. He stopped at the store and introduced himself to all the people hanging out there. When he claimed to be the governor, one old character said, 'Once you come south past that cattle guard at Bee Mountain, you can be whoever you want to be.' Of course there's no longer a cattle guard, but the point is still true."

"Yeah, I understand."

"If you're a good person who did a bad thing in your past, nobody here cares, as long as you're living here as the good person. If you start doing bad things, I'll have to kick your ass. It's as simple as that."

Billy laughed.

"So a man named Jimmy Taggert passed through on his way to Mexico. What's it to me? You should let your Aunt Angela know, though. She cares about you."

"I already called her. She'll be visiting me soon, but she has to call me Billy."

"Good, so much for Taggert."

"I didn't like him much."

"Well then, it's a good thing he's gone."

Billy smiled a sad smile, sniffed, and then brightened. "I wouldn't mind being the governor." A second later he said, "I guess I should try on my sexy new shoes."

CHAPTER 34

New Year's Day dawned clear and cold, and when the sun popped over the Chisos, spilling its light on everything, I knew I had a perfect day to do what I had planned. I would leave Serena's smiling photo at Buena Suerte. There was no logical reason for that, but logic had nothing to do with it. A ritualistic goodbye would make me feel better. I hoped. It would be a closure for me, one I seemed to need badly.

I wandered around the abandoned mining village looking for the right place. No matter where I put the photo, time would change and remove it. Still, I hesitated to set it somewhere. It wasn't the setting it down; it was the leaving it.

I couldn't understand why I felt such a sense of failure when I had solved the case. Houston Blanton would never hurt another woman. A teenager in Fort Davis had only lost her blue underpants. Sheriff Ben said I had insured his re-election, and he was effusive about it, not like him. Why couldn't I be satisfied? It didn't feel like a victory because I never found Serena. I was holding on, and I never even knew her. I had to let her go.

Serena's bones were at Buena Suerte, on land that would soon belong to Curly, so she could rest in true peace. She had been loved and still was. That should have been good enough, but it wasn't. I burned to know *where*.

"This is it, Serena," I said. "There's nothing I can do for you. I wish I had known you. In a way, I guess I did."

Of course, she smiled her heartfelt smile.

I wandered around the buildings holding the photograph close to my heart. All of them seemed wrong as a place to leave it. I ran up a rutted path to the ridge where I had ridden on Rambo. My thought was to set her down by the edge. The view was stunning. The photo would be ruined by the weather but so what? She's gone, I told myself; she's been gone longer than you have lived.

Still I held on. No place seemed right. Maybe any place would do.

I ran back down and sat on the ground to rest and gather my thoughts. I was at the bottom of a hill topped by a rugged outcropping of rock.

Set her down and get on with your life.

There was movement above me and dirt and pebbles showered down. I looked up to see a small creature scurrying around the opening of a cave in the side of the hill. A mesquite bush had grown down from above and hung over the entrance, nearly obscuring it. The view from there would encompass all of Buena Suerte and the layered ranges of mountains in the distance. A cave seemed a secret sort of place, and I liked the idea of that, although Serena wouldn't care either way.

Climbing to the cave was a hard scramble up, and holding a framed photograph made it worse. I pushed away the thorny mesquite and was surprised to see that the cave was deep and had crystals embedded in the walls.

I left the photo near the entrance and went back to the Explorer for a flashlight. My idea was to take a few crystals and leave some scattered around the photograph as a tribute to Serena.

I hurried back up and switched on the light. When I shone it along the walls, hundreds of crystals sparkled. I crawled farther into the cave to inspect the ones scattered over the floor. Soon I was able to stand upright. I continued running the light around until something caught the beam in the rear of the cave.

When I moved towards it, I saw the bones. They were stark white against the dark floor. Without another thought I knew I had found the beautiful bones.

A diamond ring still encircled a finger bone that was no longer attached to the hand. Curly had given it to Serena as a promise of marriage. There were no clothes or even signs of them, and the bones had been scattered, but not far.

I poked around and found a half-locket I recognized. With a stick I examined it, lifted it, and put it in my pocket. There were other things to link the bones to Serena, not the least of which would be DNA. Even thirty-year-old bones and teeth store our unique DNA. I would send the locket to Curly and bypass proper channels. He had already waited thirty years for its return.

I sat down with the bones and felt peace for the first time since the case was assigned to me. "I found you, Serena." My voice sounded hollow in the back of the cave.

After a while, I moved back to the entrance and sat next to the photo, letting my feet hang over the edge. "You led me here, didn't you, Serena? I always believed you would."

She said nothing. But she was smiling.

* * *

Time passed and still I sat dangling my feet, thinking.

At last I called Barney at home; he answered on the second ring.

"Happy New Year, Barney."

"Happy New year to you too, Ricos."

"I found Serena."

"You did? Where?"

"In a cave at Buena Suerte," I said, "a cave with crystals."

"I can hardly believe it. Does the sheriff know yet?"

"No. It's New Year's Day and I hate to interrupt his holiday."

"Have you called Curly?"

"I'm working up to that. I'll tell the sheriff in the morning—and Joey and Sylvia and Samantha."

"I don't see any problem with that. Those bones have been there for thirty years. I don't see how another day will make a difference."

"I'm going to sit here a while and think about things."

"Call if you want me to come. Just say the word."

"I will, Barney. Thank you."

Sunlight was chasing shadows across the distant Mexican mountains that go on and on into the west. The sky was a cloudless, clean, crisp blue. The sun was warm on my skin. Birds flitted and chattered with what sounded like joy. A cool breeze made a soft whooshing sound and flirted with my hair. It's a fine thing to be alive, I decided, even in such an imperfect world.

* * *

I was still sitting at the mouth of the cave when I gathered the courage to call Curly.

"Happy New Year, Curly! This is Margarita."

"Happy New Year to you, Margarita! You found her, didn't you?"

"Yes I did, but how could you know?"

"I was alone with the pintos this morning. The thought came, *Margarita has found the bones.* I knew you would I guess."

"I had quit looking for them. I came here to leave her photograph, to say good-bye to her in my own way."

"Sometimes when we quit looking so hard for something is when we find it," he said softly. "Thank you, Margarita. I can never thank you enough for all you've done."

"You're very welcome, Curly. You don't have to thank me. I was doing my job."

I didn't mention that I had the locket. My plan was to send it to him with a letter saying what knowing him and hearing his story had meant to me.

"I've been painting," he said. "I'm not good yet, but it feels wonderful. It feels like freedom."

I stayed a while longer, thinking about my job, and about the words of Gandhi. Maybe there was reason to hope. I scrambled down from the cave and ran as hard as I could. I never looked back.

CHAPTER 35

One mild afternoon in late January, I went for a long run and then collapsed into a rocker on my porch to observe the setting of the sun. Our scenery is knock-your-socks-off anyway, but at that time of day it's transformed into a landscape that is barely believable. The enchantment lasts minutes and then things begin to disappear as darkness descends.

But have patience. The show's not over; here come the stars. Sometimes they reveal themselves one-by-one, and then abruptly there will be billions. The darker the night, the more stars. The brighter the moon, the fewer stars but then you get a different kind of magic. There's no such thing as a bad night in Big Bend.

During the post sunset lull, I went inside to eat, put on warmer clothes, and then resumed rocking. I can't think well indoors, and I needed to think. That turned out to be a 'nice try,' because the dispatcher called to say someone had reported a vehicle off the highway with a body lying near it. He had alerted Terlingua Fire and Rescue to send the ambulance. A creepy sense of déjà-vu came over me. At least the accident was closer, not exactly like before.

I didn't bother to dress in my uniform, but I did grab my Sheriff's Office jacket and my Beretta because I never know exactly what is going on until I get to a scene. I drove pedal-to-the-metal, lights and siren.

An old truck was pulled to the shoulder, and a body lay next to it, but as I ran towards it a man sat up partway and said, "What the hell?" It was Wynne Raymore.

"What happened, Wynne?"

"What do you mean 'what happened?' Can't a man look at the stars without the diddly-blasted law showin' up to harass him?"

"Sure, but someone reported a body lying by the road."

"Well, it's not like I'm lying *in* the road."

"Whoever called thought you were injured."

I radioed the medics not to come since there was not a problem. They were so close we heard the siren, but then it receded, and the night was silent again.

Wynne patted the ground next to him. "Come sit. I've been meaning to talk to you about that night you saved my life."

I didn't move. "What about it?"

"You did a fine job—better than that. I guess you're a better deputy than I had figured." I think it pained him to admit it, but he manned up.

"Thank you, Wynne. I'm glad you're alive."

"Really?"

"Yes, of course."

He chuckled. "Who knew you were such an entertaining person?"

"How's that?"

"I could hear you, you know. I heard everything you said, but I couldn't respond. If I hadn't been in so much pain, I woulda been laughing my ass off."

"What did I do that was funny?"

"You told me all about some imaginary trip you took to Wyoming, and how you got snowed in by the storm of the century, and met this bald guy that was built and he sort of fell for you, but you still love Kevin so that went nowhere, and the rancher you visited was real handsome and had a Christmas tree from his own forest. A herd of elk stood by a frozen lake and wild horses lived in a canyon with a hot spring. And you described snow every which way, like I had never seen it or even heard of it."

"Well I—" I had no idea what to say.

316

"Then you named the constellations, with about half of them right. Some of the ones you claimed to be seeing can only be seen in the southern hemisphere, such as Betelgeuse and Hercules. It was hilarious. So I thought you made up that stuff about Wyoming, too, but I couldn't reason out why."

I sat down next to him. "I was talking to hear myself talk because I was terrified."

"Octanis is the South Pole star by the way, not visible here."

"I thought you were dying, and I was alone in the dark with a fatally injured man. I named whatever I recalled from wherever. Who knew you were listening?"

"I thought to tell you how you weren't fooling anybody, but it was all I could do to breathe. Thank you for saving my life."

"You're welcome. How are you feeling now?"

"They took the cast off my arm yesterday. I feel terrific!" He flexed his arm. "Want me to prove it to you?"

"That won't be necessary. I'll take your word for it."

"You're afraid of me, aren't you?"

"I don't want to fight anymore, Wynne."

"I don't want to, either."

"Good."

"Since you whomped my ass people laugh at me. I hope you don't mind if I call off the duel. I'm pretty sure you would kill me."

"I had no intention of ever having a duel with you. I'm positive 'no dueling' is one of the sheriff's hard and fast rules."

"I know I made a total ass of myself."

"We could let that go and start over."

He took that literally. "Hello," he said, "I'm Wynne Raymore."

I took the hand he offered. "I'm Margarita Ricos."

"I guess you have a shitload of radical feminazi ideas."

"It's not radical to ask to be treated equally. I thought we were starting over."

"I'm trying to get to know my new friend."

"Give it a rest."

"Please don't hit me."

"Don't start with your bullshit then."

"In truth I like you, Margarita, a lot." Wynne's eyes cut to the sky. "Now that we know each other, I wish you would show me the constellation you call 'Willie Nelson and His Guitar.'"

"Oh, that one's easy."

"I don't see it. I think it's another of your bald-faced tales."

"Pay attention, Wynne, and follow my arm. I'll point to it."

I then proved, sort of, that Willie is up there. With a bit of imagination, you can see practically anything.

CHAPTER 36

On a fine, spring-like day in late February, Serena's ashes were laid to rest at Buena Suerte. Curly, Joey and his wife Claudia, Sylvia, Serena's best friend Samantha and her daughter Serena, Barney, and I were gathered there. Madeline had not come. She thought Curly should have privacy to bury his first great love, and then come home to his second, free to love her without hesitation.

Joey and Sylvia wanted to place a grave marker somewhere on the property, a place where they could leave flowers or sit and remember their sister. Therefore, a small gravesite had been dug at the bottom of the hill with the cave that had protected her bones for so long. Into it was placed the urn and various items from each of the people who loved her. Curly surprised me by dropping in the locket. Now it was whole, with one side bright and shiny, and the other dark and discolored.

"She should have it," he said when he saw me watching.

I thought about putting in the photo I carried around for so long. In the end, I left it where it was. With Christina's blessing, I brought the smiling photo of Curly from the old Hampton residence and set it beside the other things.

After the short ceremony, Curly hugged me tightly and handed me a large envelope. "Don't bother looking at this now. It's something I want you to have to remember me by. Consider it my way of thanking you for everything."

"Thank you, Curly." It felt like it a photograph or a small painting.

After I hugged everybody and received more thank-yous and praise, they left together. It was good to see Joey and Curly talking again.

I walked with Barney over to the benches by the fire ring and sat to enjoy the peace and beauty of the day.

"I'm glad that's over," I said, "but it's comforting to know Serena's been laid to rest by her loved ones."

"You even amazed the sheriff, Ricos."

"Why would he be amazed? He told me to solve the case."

"I know, but maybe he didn't think you would."

"So what was it then, busy work?"

"Don't you think the sheriff knows you better than that? He would never give you busy work."

"I hope not."

"I was wondering what you decided. Are you going to keep on with the superhero line of work or are you going to retire your mask and cape?"

"I can't quit. Since I lost the bet, I owe you four weekends, remember?

"I wasn't going to hold you to that."

"I thought about moving to the beach. I'd buy a big 4-wheel drive truck and make my living pulling tourists out of sand. But I think I'll stay on a while."

"I didn't even know that pulling-people-out-of-sand thing was an option," he said. "I'll need to rethink my life plans. I wonder if Julia would go for that."

* * *

Later that day, I was dressing for a run when I remembered the envelope Curly had handed me and opened it. It wasn't a photograph of him or a painting as I had assumed. I wanted one of Curly's paintings as a remembrance, but this was far better, something I would never forget. I was stunned.

I was holding a deed to the million dollar bluff!

This note was attached:

"Dear Margarita,

I will never be back to live in Terlingua. I think you should have your own bluff. Such a fine piece of property belongs with someone who loves it. Giving this to you is about the only thing Christina and I have agreed on in thirty years.

I made arrangements to pay the property taxes for five years. After that, you're on your own. Write your books! Your fortune waits.

With love and gratitude,

Curly"

I read his words over and over. Then I set the envelope on the desk, bolted out the front door, and ran towards my bluff.

ABOUT THE AUTHOR

Elizabeth A. (Beth) Garcia has lived for more than thirty years in the Big Bend country of far west Texas. She has hiked, rafted, explored, and earned a living in this wild desert-mountain land near the Rio Grande, on the border of the United States and Mexico. It was experiencing the deep canyons, creosote-covered *bajadas*, and stark, jagged mountains, along with the wide-open spaces and dark, starry nights that eventually brought her to writing. Now she can't quit!

The Beautiful Bones is her second published novel, and the second of many Deputy Ricos tales. Each one stands alone so they can be read in any order. *One Bloody Shirt at a Time* was the first of this series. For a listing of where to find it, see below.

Beth lives with her cat, Bubs, who watches intently from his sovereign space on the desk next to her computer—when he isn't napping or critiquing her work. Beth is working on the next Deputy Ricos novel, as well as three others that are unrelated to the Deputy Ricos series. Bubs must be kept busy, or he gets in trouble.

Visit www.deputyricos.com or email the author: deputyricos@yahoo.com

On Facebook: www.facebook.com/ElizabethAGarciaAuthor

Made in the USA
Columbia, SC
01 March 2018